MYSTERY ON THE MENU

Nicole Kimberling

MYSTERY ON THE MENU

Nicole Kimberling

Mystery on the Menu
By Nicole Kimberling

Published by One Block Empire (an imprint of Blind Eye Books)
315 Prospect Street #5393, Bellingham WA 98227
www.blindeyebooks.com

Edited by Josh Lanyon and Zita Porter
Copyedit by Dianne Thies
Cover Art by Amber Whitney of Unicorn Empire
Book Design by Dawn Kimberling
Ebook design by Michael DeLuca

"Entrée to Murder," first published in *Footsteps in the Dark: An M/M Mystery Romance Anthology*, Vellichor Books, 2019

print ISBN: 978-1-956422-03-0
ebook ISBN: 978-956422-04-7
Printed in the United States of America.

Table of Contents

Entrée to Murder
7

Recipe for Trouble
123

Homicide and Hospitality
261

Acknowledgments
408

About the Author
409

ENTRÉE TO MURDER

Chapter One

When I saw the crumpled tower of waxed corrugated boxes filled with sweating tomatoes and limp romaine slumped on the back stair at eleven a.m., I knew it would be another rough lunch service at the Eelgrass Bistro.

Doubtless, if I were to go around to the front of the building, I would find Evelyn, my favorite octogenarian, peering through the window, wondering what fate had befallen my business partner, Samantha, that would cause her to fail to open our restaurant.

That's the problem with being unreliable around older people—they're at a time in life when any failure to appear means the absentee is most likely deceased. Or if not actually dead, the no-show could be lying somewhere injured and alone.

I needed to get in there to make sure Evelyn didn't do anything rash. Already once this month she'd dialed 911 after she'd spied Sam slumped over in the kitchen. In reality, Sam had just spent the night partying and then fallen asleep on a sack of potatoes in the back.

I sidled past the abandoned produce order to let myself in the back door of the Eelgrass Bistro, only to find it had been unlocked all night. Again.

Perfect.

With the lights off, the restaurant became a long tunnel leading from the service entry where I stood to the ornate doors and large windows up front.

Our restaurant sat mid-block in a row of Victorian brick buildings in the historic heart of downtown Orca's Slough, a six-block town on Camas Island in the middle of Puget Sound. The building's sandstone facade formed an almost perfect square: twenty feet high and twenty feet wide and stretched back nearly one hundred feet from sidewalk to alley—though the turn-of-the-century basement stretched much farther underground.

I squinted through the gloom of the kitchen and dining room to see Evelyn pressing her cupped hands against the plate-glass window to peer inside. Despite being in her mid-eighties, her loose-fitting jeans and sweatshirt lent her the look of a spindly kid. Her shock of short gray hair bristled atop her head like a raccoon skin cap. I hurried through the kitchen, flipped on the lights, and waved at her. I made it a big, theatrical, flagging-down-a-passing-ship motion so that she could see me through the haze of the cataracts she regularly claimed kept her from reading various CLOSED signs and KEEP OUT postings around town.

She waved back and went to stand in front of the door, waiting, like a cranky old cat, to be let inside and fed.

As I sidestepped the concrete stairs leading into the basement, my eyes adjusted to the gloom.

The Eelgrass was a wreck. Floors unswept, the steel prep tables in the kitchen strewn with debris. Dank, fetid water stood in the three-compartment sink. Empty, unwashed beer glasses on every surface. Party detritus.

I wondered if Sam had left any money in the till or if that too had fallen victim to poor impulse control.

I took a breath.

Getting angry would do me no good. First, there was no one here to be angry with, and second, mentally raging at Sam would only force a confrontation that would end in tears. Her remorseful tears. And I had no defense against that kind of emotional blackmail.

I could do nothing but give myself up to the ridiculousness of this day and try to enjoy it like some kind of tragicomedy I was watching from afar.

How much longer could my pride take it? I didn't know. For as long as I could turn my anger at her inward to fester as shame for consenting to enter this business venture at all? Six months, perhaps? Assuming I had enough nostalgia to sustain me.

Sam and I hadn't always been this way. Years ago I had adored her freewheeling spirit and sincerity. Back then, I and my then-boyfriend had hung out with her and her then-husband. Together we'd manned a high-end hipster restaurant in Seattle and spent three boozy years feeling impressed with ourselves and the newness of being adults.

But that had been before her husband started having his ongoing series of affairs and all of Sam's enthusiasm had devolved into personal makeovers and increasingly potent bouts of self-medication. My own private life had mirrored Sam's, with my boyfriend declaring that he needed the support of a less opinionated lover to truly feel appreciated. By that time, the restaurant started losing money, and my paychecks began to bounce like pinballs ricocheting off every possible overdraft fee imaginable.

So when Sam announced that she'd inherited a restaurant space from a distant cousin, I agreed to pull up stakes, empty what was left of my bank account, and venture into a partnership with her far from Seattle.

Well, not that far. Twenty-five miles and a ferry ride. But still: I'd left town. That was the important thing.

We'd been determined to put the bad times behind us.

Now the dining room at the Eelgrass looked like old times: the tables and chairs stood huddled together in one corner as though ordered to stand aside to make floor space for an impromptu after-hours dance party, which is most likely exactly what had happened.

Probably half the people in the local restaurant industry had been here getting loaded last night.

I walked behind the bar, hoping to find nothing alarming, and stopped dead in my tracks.

Lying prone and snoring on the floor was the seventeen-year-old dishwasher, Lionel.

He was half-Black and half-Korean and had yet to decide if he wanted to talk like a cartoon character or a member of NWA. Most of the time he just sounded like a dork. But he was a smart dork and a quick learner.

I nudged Lionel with my toe. "Time to wake up, kid."

Lionel lifted his face to squint at me. His cheek was marked with a hexagonal impression from the rubber fatigue mat he'd spent the night on. He had a slim build—more or less a replica of his Asian mother's. His skin was the color of dark mahogany. The combination ensured that no member of either race ever immediately recognized him as one of their own, which had caused Lionel to develop the bad habit of making gratuitously racist comments that, when challenged, allowed him to clarify his identity.

"Quit kicking me, chief," he mumbled.

"Quit sleeping on the job, and I will," I said. "Now get up and open the door. Evelyn wants her breakfast."

"Why can't you let her in?"

"'Cause I told you to. Why the hell are you sleeping here anyway?"

"Sam said I could sleep here since I had to open in four hours." He pushed himself up to all fours, then rose, hunched and wobbly as if this was his first-ever attempt at walking on two feet.

"You all were here till six a.m.?"

Lionel nodded.

"If you're going to puke, do it in the trash can. Not the sink," I advised.

"Jeez, chief, I'm sick—not an idiot."

It's weird how if someone calls you something enough, you can start acting like it's true. I suppose that's the magic of terms like champ or Dad. Once Lionel started calling me chief, I started feeling invested in his professional development. I began teaching him what I knew about being a cook. It also triggered in me a steady trickle of unsolicited guidance that made me sound and feel way older than thirty-one.

"You want to play with the grown-ups, you've got to get up and work like one," I said. Then, glancing at his hangdog expression, I added, "If you make yourself useful to me, I'll fix you an omelette."

"Okay." Lionel dragged himself to the front door, flipped the lock, and turned the sign to OPEN. Evelyn walked in immediately, heading toward her usual seat at the end of the bar.

I managed to find a towel and wipe down her place before she got onto the sleek steel barstool. She took her *Wall Street Journal* out of a plastic grocery bag and laid it out next to her place.

"I'm sorry to be opening late," I said. "Sam had an emergency."

"What was Lionel doing on the floor back there?" Evelyn asked.

"He was looking for something," I ad-libbed.

"He looks like he's drunk."

"I wouldn't know anything about that." I met her watery blue eyes. I knew she didn't believe me, but I wasn't prepared to admit to knowledge of any of the county statutes concerning alcohol that had been broken the previous night. "Anyway, coffee isn't brewing yet, but can I get you an espresso?"

Evelyn wrinkled her nose. "I don't need anything fancy."

"It'll take twenty minutes for the coffee pour-thru to heat up."

"I can wait." Evelyn unfurled her paper and put on her reading glasses.

"The espresso would be on the house," I said.

"I said"—she paused meaningfully and skewered me with a look—"that I can wait."

Behind her, I saw Lionel roll his eyes as he arranged the tables and chairs into their usual order.

"So what would you like for breakfast today?" I asked Evelyn. "One egg and one piece of toast?"

The Eelgrass didn't serve breakfast, but that didn't stop Evelyn from ordering it anyway.

"One piece of bacon today too. Crispy." She spoke without glancing up.

"Splurging on the cholesterol count, huh? Is it your birthday?"

"People my age don't celebrate birthdays anymore," Evelyn informed me. "I just feel like eating bacon."

"Can I tempt you into a slice of tomato? I can brûlée some sugar onto it." As far as I knew, Evelyn rarely ate any sort of vegetable except asparagus.

"I suppose." I saw a hint of a smile at the corner of her mouth. "So long as you don't charge me an arm and a leg for it."

Behind me, the coffeepot began to gurgle. I found some clean flatware for Evelyn and was just setting it down when I heard a colossal bang from the basement.

"What the hell—"

"Sounds like a pressure cooker exploding." Evelyn had worked in the restaurant industry for nearly fifty years and had apparently endured every possible form of catastrophe. "That happened once at a place I worked in New Orleans. Blew a hole right through the roof."

"I better check it out." I headed into the kitchen. To my surprise, Lionel followed me and cut me off right as I reached the concrete steps leading into the musty underground.

"I can go down there for you." His eyes darted from side to side, showing incipient panic. "Probably some junk way in the back just fell over."

It wasn't impossible that a cache of abandoned rubbish had collapsed somewhere in the basement. The space was cavernous and poorly lit. Dug in the mid-eighteen hundreds, it had once been a part of a much larger network that catacombed the entire downtown. Supposedly, gold miners and bootleggers had left a variety of mementos behind in the numerous tunnels beneath the city—though moldering rat traps and empty oilcans made up the bulk of what I'd encountered.

"Why don't you want me down here?" I took the steps down two at a time, ducking as I entered the low space. Something wasn't right about the air. A new tang seeped into the normally musty smell.

"It's nothing really bad—"

"Why does it smell like putrid garlic?"

I peered down into the darkness. A single bare bulb illuminated a few feet—enough for me to make out the five shelves of dry storage we used for Eelgrass. But beyond that, the light faded away. I knew from experience that after another ten feet, the poured concrete of the floor gave way to fine, silty dirt.

"You know how I was talking about how I wanted to reconnect with my Korean roots?" Lionel came hot on my heels, practically running into my back.

"Yes." I vaguely recollected that Lionel's grandmother had refused to teach him to cook because "his wife would take care of that for him," while his busy single mother possessed neither the time nor the inclination. While Lionel worked up the courage to tell me the rest of his story, I took a quick inventory of the dry goods on the shelves. Aside from a can of garbanzo beans standing among the canned tomatoes, all appeared in order.

"I decided to teach myself how to make traditional pickles," Lionel confessed. "And Dorian said the basement would be the perfect place to ferment them, so long as I didn't mess with any of the stuff he stashed down there."

The kind of "stuff" our sleazy, drug-dealing bartender Dorian might be hiding in my business alarmed me far more than any pickle Lionel could concoct or even the threat of a tunnel-collapse in the basement.

Just outside the circle of light, close to the edge of the concrete, a small red light blinked. And it seemed to me that the darkness around the blinking light was denser and more solid than the deep gloom surrounding it.

"And you think that noise was pickles?" I asked.

What was that blinking light anyway? I took a step closer. The pungent smell of garlic, fish, and fermentation gone foul did seem to be coming from the far wall.

"I think my kimchee blew up. I'll clean it up, I swear."

That would explain the bang and the stink. Fermentation in the wrong hands could produce all the wrong gasses and literally weaponize cabbage. That still didn't explain the blinking light, nor the dark shape behind it.

Sam kept a flashlight down here, but the batteries had run down around New Year. I pulled out my phone and approached by the harsh blue-white light of the flashlight app.

Lionel continued, "I used the space at the back of the cellar to mature my first batch. But I don't know. . . Maybe it got too warm?"

"Possibly." I knelt down. The blinking light turned out to be the message alert on an old slider-style cell phone. It lay in the dirt next to a hand. The hand emerged from the sleeve of a white-and-red hoodie that clothed the body of a man.

"What are you looking—" Lionel stopped speaking and froze.

I'm not sure what makes it so obvious at only a glance that a person is dead. There's the flat, unblinking eye, sure. But also the blood streaking from multiple stab wounds helps fix the idea that the man one is eyeballing has shuffled off this mortal coil.

For a second, I could not move or even breathe. Everything stopped, including my ability to feel—like someone flipped a giant toggle switch shutting down all nonessential functions.

Was this shock?

It occurred to me then that the hoodie wasn't red and white at all—just white and stained with red—and that it belonged to my least favorite employee: Dorian Gamble.

And the knife still jutting from his back belonged to me.

Chapter Two

Orca's Slough boasted a sheriff and two deputies, all named Mackenzie. The deputy who arrived at the Eelgrass was a fit young bison known as Big Mac. Evelyn said he'd been given the nickname because he held the record for the biggest baby ever born on the island. Even among the Mackenzie clan (widely rumored to be half Bigfoot) Big Mac's brutal muscularity stood out. He had thighs like tree trunks (which he displayed year-round in shorts) and biceps big as grapefruits.

I worked out when I had the free time, but compared to Big Mac I felt scrawny and sallow. My blond hair probably looked stringy and unkempt; it was hard to care about manscaping while witnessing my business fall apart.

I was pleased to note that I was just slightly taller than him.

And, I suspected, a whole lot smarter. Big Mac spoke in a slow, quiet way that gave the impression he might have repeated third grade a couple of times.

He ate dinner at the Eelgrass every Wednesday, always ordering the special, no matter what. He had dark hair, heavy brows, and the kind of perma-stubble that indicated his capacity to grow a prize-winning beard if only the sheriff's department had allowed it.

During the tourist season, he often manned the police kiosk at the ferry terminal and, as far as I could tell, spent most of his on-duty hours giving driving directions to the island's three hot-springs resorts.

After he had a look at Dorian, he returned to the dining room and joined me at the bar. Lionel sat at a table in the corner, slumped over and mumbling into his phone, most likely to his mother, who worked as a nurse at the local medical center.

Evelyn had been exiled to the sidewalk but continued to lurk, monitoring the interactions inside with a fierce, stricken expression.

Big Mac seemed to make a point of learning the name of every single person living in Orca's Slough, so it didn't surprise me when he remembered mine.

"So, Mr. Allison, quite the smell down there."

"That's the kimchee, I think." At least I hoped so.

"And that was what made you look in the basement?" He glanced at his notebook, probably checking to make sure I'd kept my story straight.

"No, we heard a bang, which we think was the crock exploding," I said.

"Mr. Allison, can you tell me when was the last time you saw Mr. Gamble alive?"

"Just Drew is fine," I said.

"Okay, Drew, when did you last see Mr. Gamble?"

"I worked with him the day before yesterday—Wednesday. You would have seen him."

Big Mac nodded and looked slowly up from his cop notebook. What color were his eyes anyway? Blue? Green? It was hard to tell.

"You know, that steamer-clam special was so good. Where did you get the idea for it?"

"It's a classic dish. Moules marinière," I spluttered.

"But you made it original." Big Mac spoke as if savoring the clams once more in his memory. "Don't suppose you can tell me how, though. Secret recipe."

"Actually, legally I'm required to disclose all the ingredients in anything I serve. And I have to have all the processes vetted by the health department, so it's only the proportions of a recipe that could ever be secret."

"That I did not know," Big Mac said.

"I think the whole secret-recipe thing is an advertising ploy."

"Oh, I don't know. Evelyn out there has kept the recipes for her preserves secret since she won her first ribbon at the fair. And she's been the Camas County Pickle Queen for as long as anybody can remember."

Despite the grim circumstances, the words pickle queen brought a smirk to my face. So sue me. I'm juvenile.

Big Mac smiled back—an action that dramatically improved the quality of his face. "So what's the secret to your clams, then?"

"Lemongrass-infused vodka," I said.

"See, I didn't even know that existed."

"It's house-made here by Dorian. He's very oriented toward signature cocktails. Or he was..."

"Did you speak with Mr. Gamble or see him between Wednesday and now?" Big Mac asked.

The swift return to the subject of murder startled me. How easily this cop had lulled me into complacency with his soft, complimentary voice.

"Dorian and I haven't really been on speaking terms for a while."

"Why is that?" Big Mac asked.

"I didn't think he was a good influence on Sam."

"Really? How so?"

Some lingering vestige of loyalty prevented me from

mentioning that Dorian's alternative revenue stream was generated through sales of cocaine, largely to other members of the restaurant industry, so I just said, "He encouraged her to make poor financial decisions."

"Such as?"

Big Mac held my gaze for a long moment, and I fought not to look away before he did.

"Ordering too much of expensive ingredients he wanted for his infusions. A lot ended up going bad before he got around to making anything. And half of what he did make was pretentious and terrible. Nobody is going to pay eighteen dollars to drink salmon-infused vodka. Nobody."

Big Mac nodded.

"So to recap your previous statement, only Mr. Fogle was in the building when you arrived, and he was unconscious."

It took me a minute to register who he was talking about. "You mean Lionel? Yes."

"And can you think of any reason why Lionel—or anyone—would feel like they needed to kill Mr. Gamble?"

"I haven't heard of anyone specifically out to get him. Especially not Lionel. He was always asking Dorian for advice about women."

"I've heard that Mr. Gamble was quite the ladies' man and that he could be insistent."

I almost asked where he'd heard that, but Evelyn had frequently made her opinion of Dorian's womanizing known.

"I've never known him to be the kind of person you'd have to use lethal force to escape, if that's what you mean," I said, offended on Dorian's behalf. Then again, now that the kernel of doubt had been sown, I began to wonder.

It wasn't like Dorian led a blameless life in any respect. Had he tried to force himself on some girl at the party, and she or her boyfriend had decided to take him out?

It didn't seem his style, though. He dealt coke, and he was smarmy, but a lot of women seemed to find him attractive and charming. On a couple of occasions I'd even overheard him complain about so many female clients pulling him into their beds that he was "shooting dust." Clearly, he wasn't hurting for action.

"Do you know what Mr. Gamble was doing here last night?"

"I don't know, but obviously, there was a party."

"You didn't attend?"

"No, I wasn't invited." Saying that somehow stung even after discovering a body. "I was at my apartment all night."

"Were you with anyone?" Big Mac had an expression on his face that told me he already had his own theory on my relationship status, probably based on my argumentative personality.

"No one. I live alone."

Big Mac made a special note of this. I watched him underline the word alone.

"And besides you and your business partner, who has a key to the building?"

"I have no idea," I said, shrugging.

"What about Lionel?"

We both turned our attention to the dishwasher. Lionel looked up in wide-eyed alarm. I hoped that Big Mac hadn't immediately decided that Lionel was guilty because he'd been passed out in the same building. Or because he was Black.

"No. Lionel doesn't have a key, and he didn't do this."

"You know that for a fact?"

"Listen." I lowered my voice. "Lionel's the kind of kid who can't bring himself to lie about setting up a secret pickle crock. And even if he did somehow get caught up in something like this, he would have called me and his mom right away to ask what to do with the body."

Only after I'd spoken did I realize I shouldn't have even made the joke. Big Mac's lips moved, but I cut him off. "Plus, Lionel didn't have any blood on him, which. . . he would have."

"And he didn't have a key." Big Mac paused to write something in his notebook. Belatedly I recalled that this had started with who had keys to the restaurant.

Sam and I.

"Who did or didn't have a key wouldn't matter," I said, "because the back door was unlocked when I arrived this morning."

Big Mac's smile faded, and he paused, seeming reluctant to continue before saying, "What can you tell me about the knife found in Mr. Gamble's body?"

"It's mine." There was no point in denying it. That would just make me look guilty. "But I don't know how it got downstairs. I keep it in my knife case, and I keep that locked in the office when I'm not here."

Big Mac made another note in his book, then asked, "Would you mind if I had a look at your hands?"

I did mind, but I silently held them out anyway, palms down. Big Mac reached out and caught hold of my fingers in a professional manner, firm yet gentle, like a doctor might. He took some time scrutinizing them, as if memorizing every scar, before turning them palms up.

"What's this here?" he pointed to a mark on my wrist.

"A grease burn." I squirmed a little, embarrassed to still be getting amateur injuries at my age.

Big Mac held my hands for about thirty seconds longer, then released me.

"I think that's all for now. Here's my card. Text me anytime." He stood and turned toward Lionel.

The thought of Lionel being interrogated scared me. I could easily picture him getting frustrated and saying something like, "Fine, okay, I did it. Will you just shut up now?"

as if he were arguing about dirty laundry with his mom. But Big Mac only said that they would wait till Lionel's mother arrived to have their conversation.

I relaxed enough to take a paper cup of coffee out to Evelyn in lieu of breakfast.

As I stepped outside the front door, the ambulance (Orca's Slough only had one) was just pulling up.

Evelyn stopped eyeballing the interior proceedings long enough to ask, "Dorian…is he really dead?"

In a town so small, all locals knew each other. And I vaguely recalled a waitress remarking that Dorian and Evelyn were related.

"Yeah," I replied, at a loss.

We stood together watching the medics. Evelyn sniffed and then took a swig of her coffee. The town's second deputy Mackenzie arrived: a sleepy, doughier version of Big Mac.

Clerks and patrons from the surrounding businesses gathered outside, staring at the scene. Two trim middle-aged women from the yoga studio across the street edged toward the restaurant. Then they caught sight of Troy Lindgren as he scowled from the doorway of his high-end sportswear shop.

Fit and fortyish, Troy was Sam's only non-deceased cousin and the owner of the beautifully restored historic building that abutted Eelgrass Bistro. Local fishermen called him a rich snob, but he exemplified the conservative taste that many yacht-owning tourists appreciated. I had never seen him without cuff links and a tie.

I missed most of what passed between the three of them, except the mention of Sam's name. Troy shook his head.

"Probably just another grease fire," he told them, then offered me a tight, forced smile before retreating into his shop.

"Prick," Evelyn muttered. She glanced to me. "Where is Samantha, anyway? She wasn't down there too?"

"No!" Just the suggestion rattled me. Frustrated as I was, I would never have wanted to see her like that. "She's probably just passed out somewhere. I'm going to try and find her."

Pacing the sidewalk, I tried Sam's number and got no reply.

The slanting autumn sun shone down on the fallen maple leaves that carpeted the sidewalk. I kicked at them, stirring them up as I went. The numb fog of shock began to wear thin enough that I started to feel. Not horror over seeing Dorian dead—that remained a void in my consciousness, still too terrible to be experienced—but worry about Sam's safety.

Her various social-media feeds showed no activity after she'd put up a bleary-eyed selfie captioned: "happy after a night with good friends" at four a.m. In the photo, she wore a silver spaghetti-strap tank top and a lot of red lipstick. She'd dyed her hair again and now sported a black bob with a bright-red streak. In the background I could see Lionel and Sam's plump, pink-haired friend Danielle trying to push their way into the frame.

So now I knew at least one other person who had been present, but a text to Danielle yielded no response either.

I sat down on the sky-blue powder-coat sidewalk bench across the street from the Eelgrass and stared hard at my phone. It had 213 contacts in it. I started going down the list, texting everyone I knew to see if anybody could tell me Sam's location.

Sixteen people replied with more or less the same story—they had been at the party but left before it was over.

Time passed. The sheriff arrived, spoke with the doughy deputy through the window of his police car, and then drove away. More onlookers gathered to gawk at the spectacle.

"Andrew, where is Samantha?" I glanced up to see Troy frowning down at me. "They're saying there's a dead body in her basement. Dorian Gamble."

"I don't know if I can talk about it," I replied. "You'll have to ask Big Mac."

Troy gave me a quizzical once-over.

"You look terrible," he said.

"Well, I'm having kind of a challenging day, Troy."

He didn't seem to know what to say to that and so made a little show of adjusting his jacket. At last he said, "I don't know who's going to eat there now."

Like I didn't have enough to worry about.

"You'll probably have to sell up," he continued.

I felt sure Troy would have gone on to give me some lowball offer, but thankfully the doughy deputy Mackenzie called Troy over. Muttering his disbelief that any of this terrible mess could have anything to do with him, Troy left me.

Time to get provocative.

I texted Sam: *I found Dorian's dead body in the cellar about an hour ago.*

Within ten minutes the woman herself sat down on the bench next to me.

She smelled like men's soap, wore an oversize blue hoodie that didn't belong to her, and sported dark sunglasses despite the autumn day's gloom. Behind her stood a burly, handsome surfer-looking guy. Maybe Sam's pickup from the night before? He looked kind of young for her, but I had enough to worry about at this moment without also bothering to card Sam's one-night stand.

Leaning close to me, Sam whispered, "Is this for real?"

"Yes," I said. "For extra real."

Sam stared at me in total shock, mouth agape, color draining from her already pasty cheeks. Her lip quivered as she whispered, "What happened? Did he OD?"

Sam's date shrugged like he thought the question was addressed to him.

I shook my head, and seeing tears forming in her eyes, the icy grip of shock receded. My throat tightened. Dorian hadn't always been the best person, but we'd all worked together for nearly two years. It hadn't all been bad times.

"He was stabbed." I could barely voice my response.

"Oh Jesus." Sam threw her arms around me in a tight hug.

Out of reflex, I returned her embrace. This attracted the attention of Evelyn, who leaned in through the door of Eelgrass and called something to Big Mac.

Sam's date just stood there with his hands in his pockets, looking bored. Then he asked, "Are you guys all right?"

"Look, we're obviously not all right," I snapped. "Who are you anyway?"

"That's Alfred." Sam dragged the back of her hand across her nose. "He's Danielle's brother."

I took a moment to process this, recollecting Danielle's jokes about her dorky kid brother and his recent high-school graduation. "You hooked up with Danielle's little brother?"

"Don't judge me," Sam mumbled.

"Never mind. Listen," I said. "The cops want to speak with you."

As if on cue, Big Mac emerged from the front door of the Eelgrass Bistro and jogged across the street calling, "Ms. Eider?"

"That's me." Sam pushed herself up to her feet and went to meet him.

I found myself sitting awkwardly alone with Alfred.

"It's crazy that Dorian is dead," Alfred finally said. "We were just partying together last night. I mean, we could have been still drinking when he was lying down there." Alfred's expression turned bleak and sick.

It occurred to me then that I didn't have to sit waiting for the cops to tell me what happened at the party. I could ask this guy and know. Or at least know his version.

"Why do you think he was down there bleeding when you were all still drinking?" I asked.

"Because me and Sam were the last people to leave. I mean, except for Lionel, but he was already passed out on the floor. I asked Sam if we should move him or bring him back with us, but she seemed to think he'd be okay." Alfred shrugged. "I didn't fight too hard because she was already touching me a lot, you know, so . . ."

"Gotcha. When was the last time you saw Dorian?"

Alfred paused, head and shoulders drawn back in suspicion. "Why are you asking this?"

"Because that's my restaurant too, and I want to know what happened in it," I said, flushing, unable now to keep the anger out of my voice.

"Oh, right." Alfred relaxed again and sat down next to me. "Well, I'll tell you what I can, but I was pretty drunk the whole time."

"That's okay; just do your best."

"I just came into town on the eight o'clock ferry. Danielle came to pick me up, and then we went to meet Sam and Dorian at the Anchor for drinks. At first it was just the four of us. Then some other girls joined us—about six of them, I can't remember all their names, but Dorian knew them. After that some guys from the kayak shop showed up."

"Naturally."

"And then there were maybe twenty of us, and the girls all decided they wanted to go dancing, except there was nowhere to dance 'cause it was Thursday."

"So the Eelgrass dining room was the next logical step," I said. "How did Lionel end up with you guys?"

"Sam saw him walking home alone and invited him." Alfred trailed off, staring into space.

"Anyway, after you got to the Eelgrass?"

"Right, right. Dorian went behind the bar to line up the drinks, and a couple of the girls from the fish-and-chips place went back to the kitchen to make something to eat. The girls came back to get Sam because they couldn't find any knives, and Sam went to the office and brought a couple out for them. Nice ones."

The surge of anger that burst red behind my eyes was only partially mitigated by the tiny pleasure of solving the mystery of how my knife got out of the office.

I must have flushed because Alfred again asked, "Are you all right, man? Your neck veins just popped up."

"I'm fine. I just don't like it when other people lend out my things."

"Oh, I hear that." Alfred gave a nod. "Sam loaned my lighter to Dorian, and that's the last I saw of it. It's a Zippo too, monogrammed. Did you see it there? When you found him?"

"It's not like I went through his pockets."

"Right. And there were a lot of people going in and out the back door to smoke, so I guess he could have loaned it to anybody."

"Why didn't you just smoke out front by the ashtray?"

"We couldn't. That big cop was sitting in his patrol car down the way. Speaking of smoking, though"—Alfred pulled a joint out of his pocket—"do you have a lighter I can borrow?"

CHAPTER THREE

Orca's Slough's lone diner, the Prospector, sat about four blocks from the Eelgrass physically but resided in another dimension temporally.

It wasn't old-fashioned so much as old. The late-seventies decor did not qualify as retro, as it had genuinely been installed forty years prior. Duct-tape repairs striped the vinyl booth seats silver and blue.

It served breakfast all day and hard liquor well into the night, and it was where Big Mac went after leaving the Eelgrass.

When I walked through the door, the waitress gave me a nervous, shifty look, which told me she knew who I was and what had happened.

"Excuse me, Deputy." I rushed up behind him before he sat down at the bar. "Can I speak with you?"

"Sure thing. But please, call me Mac." He turned from the bar with clear reluctance and gestured to a booth. He took off his mirror shades and his hat and raked his fingers through his hair, which improved his visual aesthetic. If I could somehow have removed the cop badge from my field of vision, he might have even been attractive.

The waitress automatically brought Mac coffee with cream and gave me an even shiftier look than before. I ordered two fried eggs and a Bloody Mary.

"Come here a lot?" I asked.

"Closest thing to a donut shop in town." He shrugged out of his jacket before taking a seat opposite me. Once again he'd defaulted to that deceptively quiet manner of talking. He took a drink of his coffee, stirred in a spoon of sugar, then tasted it again, all with agonizing slowness.

"Don't you want to know what I have to say?" I asked, unable to wait any longer.

Mac turned his full attention to me. A hint of a smile creased his cheek.

"I'm sorry. I was just getting comfortable. I've been on duty since six this morning. Please go ahead and tell me whatever it is." He retrieved his notebook from the pocket of his jacket. His pen looked small in his hand and somewhat awkward. The face of his watch also seemed like it had been owned by a smaller guy—his grandfather maybe?—

and I could just see the tip of a thick scar protruding from his right shirtsleeve just above his elbow.

I related my conversation with Alfred. Mac listened, nodding occasionally and jotting down notes.

"Alfred Tomkins," Big Mac clarified.

"Yeah, Danielle Tomkins's brother."

"He specifically told you that Dorian had taken his monogrammed Zippo lighter?"

"He didn't go out of his way to tell me. Just mentioned it in passing." Mac must have found the lighter. Maybe he'd hoped it would be the clue that busted the case open. "When I found out he had been at the party, I asked him if he knew what had happened to Dorian."

"What time did this conversation take place?"

"Right after I finished talking to you. Two o'clock maybe."

"I'm curious why you waited until five p.m. to contact me."

"What do you mean?"

"You had my number, you could have easily texted me right then, and I could have spoken to Alfred myself." Mac sat back to allow the waitress to set a plate containing a pretty good-looking Rueben sandwich down in front of him. She delivered my food without making eye contact.

"You seemed busy with the investigation, and I didn't want to interrupt you. Plus, I didn't want to seem weird." I slurped my Bloody Mary.

"Weird in what way?"

"Because I was asking people about the murder. Isn't that one of the giveaways of a guilty person—inserting yourself into the investigation?"

"That does sometimes occur, yes," Mac said. "If I were you, I would be more worried about my personal safety in questioning potential murderers than relating information to a member of law enforcement."

"Alfred is a suspect?"

"Everyone is a suspect," Mac intoned.

"And that includes you then, right? Because you were there too, sitting in a patrol car down the block."

Mac went quite still. "Did Alfred tell you that?"

"I'm not saying you killed Dorian." I put myself into full backpedal mode. "I mean, why would you?"

"Why would anybody?"

"Are you serious?" I leaned forward, lowering my voice to a whisper. "Who knows what he might have done to you? He's slept with practically every woman in this town. I mean, if you have a girlfriend, Dorian probably tried to bird-dog her at some point or other."

Mac also leaned forward, close enough for me to smell his aftershave.

"I don't have a girlfriend." He took his time having another drink of coffee before saying, "Drew, I'm going to ask you straight out: did you kill Dorian?"

"No," I spluttered, then childishly countered with, "did you kill Dorian?"

Mac laughed then, a full, unexpectedly melodious laugh. "You really are quite a comedian."

"I'm not trying to be funny."

"That's what makes it perfect." Mac flipped his pocket notebook to an empty page. "I'd like you to do me a favor. Write down the names of all the women you know Mr. Gamble had intimate relations with in the last year."

"It's going to be more than one page," I said.

"Take as many as you need."

Mac engaged his sandwich while I tried to put Dorian's conquests into a timeline. But as I mentally scrolled through the women I'd seen sitting at the bar talking to him, I kept getting distracted by the fact that Big Mac hadn't actually ordered a sandwich but one arrived anyway. He must be such a regular here that the staff started making his food when they saw him walk in.

Normally, when a person is a regular like that, their order never changes. Those kind of customers like their food to be just so, resist variation, and complain bitterly when their plates are even the slightest bit different. But when he dined at the Eelgrass, Big Mac ordered the daily special, which was always different.

I set down the pen and asked, "How's the sandwich?"

"Good," he replied. "Slaw's a little soggy today, but still good."

"Oh yeah?"

"Yeah." Mac glanced back to the kitchen. "Juan must have the day off. He's usually here on Friday."

"You keep track of who's cooking at the places you eat?"

"Don't you?" He seemed genuinely surprised.

"Not unless I know them," I replied.

"Well, I eat out a lot," Mac said. "Actually, I don't cook at all. Except spaghetti."

"So what's best in this town?" I asked. "Is it the sandwich you're having now?" It did look quite well made, and it smelled great.

"It's the best thing they serve here. But I'd say the best food in town is whatever you're cooking Wednesday night."

I am not immune to flattery. Also fishing for compliments is a persistent vice. "Just Wednesday?"

"Your Friday and Saturday night specials are good, but not as unique as Wednesday." Mac took another bite of his Reuben. "Actually, I have no idea where I'm going to eat my Wednesday supper now..."

"Fish-and-chips place?"

"I'd rather get a burrito from the gas station hot case."

"Ouch." For a split second I almost offered to make him dinner, just for being a valued customer. Then I came to my senses. I did not want him to think I was coming on to him, get scared, question his sexuality, and beat me up to prove he was straight. I went back to eating my eggs.

Mac finished his sandwich, then folded his hands in front of him.

"Okay, so what you're saying is that there is a witness who saw both Sam and the fish-shop girls handling your knives on Thursday evening."

"Right."

"And you think that puts me closer to finding the killer because . . ."

"Because now we know how the knives got out of the office?" I felt lame even uttering that sentence. He was right. Just knowing how the knives got out of the office didn't prove any single person's guilt or innocence.

"Ms. Eider mentioned that you and Dorian had fought earlier in the week. Can you tell me what the argument was about?"

"Business."

"Ms. Eider said the argument was about cocaine."

I felt my eyes go wide. How could she put our personal business out there like that? I clenched my jaw and nodded.

"What exactly were you angry about?" Mac asked.

I hesitated, feeling like a snitch. But Dorian was dead and Sam had already exposed herself, so it hardly mattered now.

"I didn't want him using our place to make drug deals, and I didn't want him selling to Sam."

"You weren't one of his customers?"

"No. I came here to get away from that scene, and I've stayed away from it. So I can't tell you much about Dorian's sideline business. I'm more of a hard-liquor guy." I rattled my ice cubes at him. This finally attracted the attention of the waitress, who asked me if I'd like the same again.

I decided to go for coffee.

"Was there a reason why you didn't want him to procure drugs for Ms. Eider in particular?"

"Would you? You saw how she partied. Would you want a bunch of random moochers coming into your business after-hours to drink for free, disrespect your belongings, and fuck up your kitchen?" I felt my cheeks flushing.

He nodded, then said, "I couldn't help but notice when I looked up your particulars that you have a criminal record. Malicious mischief and obstructing a law-enforcement officer."

"I was drunk and fell into the window of a bar and broke it. It wasn't malicious or even mischief, just clumsiness. I spent the night in the drunk tank and paid a fine."

"What about the other charge?"

"I tried to keep the cops from coming into a house where we were having a drag party. There was some swearing, and I was perhaps somewhat rude."

"You've got a temper, in other words."

"People have said that, yes." I didn't cross my arms in front of my chest, but it took all my willpower not to.

"Did your argument with Mr. Gamble turn violent?"

"Not even a little bit. He never even stopped smiling. He was that kind of guy. He never took other people's feelings very seriously."

"You know, Drew, my problem is that I want to believe you—that you had nothing to do with this—because I want to have my Wednesday night dinner back. But you are currently the only person who is known to have had a significant conflict with Mr. Gamble. So I want you to think hard whether anybody could have seen you after you left work last night."

"I don't remember seeing anyone."

"Did you text or . . . or log in to any websites from your home computer or pass by any ATMs or places likely to have security cameras?"

"I don't think so. I went home and went to bed by myself."

Mac sighed. "In that case I'm afraid you can't be ruled out right away so…best not to leave the island for the time being."

"For how long?"

Mac shrugged. "I guess until we find out whether or not you did it." He stood and started to pull on his jacket. "Thank you for contacting me. I'll be in touch."

Chapter Four

Saturday morning started off well. Still half in my dreams, I fantasized about creating a scallop special for Wednesday. Something classic like angels on horseback but paired with avocado and heirloom tomato . . . Could it be a sandwich? Or should it be more of a main-course salad with bruschetta? Mac would be there for sure.

Then my phone buzzed, and I sat up, coming to full consciousness. It was Mac, telling me the Eelgrass would remain closed today. I forwarded his message to Sam.

Six o'clock. I fell back onto my dank pillowcase.

Because housing on Camas Island was scarce and expensive, I'd taken the first place I could get: an elderly mobile home about half a mile from town. Originally, Sam had lived in the second bedroom here, but she'd moved in with Danielle after she realized that her booming social life often left her too bleary to make the trip back to her bed without ending up in a ditch.

Wan yellow light glowed through my bedroom curtains, indicating sunny skies ahead. I lay there for some time, trying to figure out how I would occupy myself for an entire day without work.

Pathetic, I know. Better people would walk down to the beach, or take a hike, or binge-watch some TV show all day, but that's not the way I'm built. I needed to get up and move. And in addition to that, I had no food in the house.

I dressed and headed down to the Prospector. My route took me past the Eelgrass, where I spied Evelyn standing outside on the sidewalk, peering in.

"Hey, Evelyn, how's the peeping?"

Evelyn gave me a rather savage side-eye. "I'm monitoring, not peeping."

"Thanks for the clarification."

Inside, technicians in white paper bunny suits performed activities that I hoped involved getting the DNA of the killer and not just my and Lionel's genetic markers. I turned back to Evelyn.

"You're up early."

"I wanted to see what was going on here." Even cocooned inside her puffy jacket, Evelyn shivered. "Dorian and I didn't always agree about what was right, but he was still family. He shouldn't have died like that. He was my brother's grandson, you know."

I nodded. I hadn't liked Dorian, but not even at my angriest would I have thought that he deserved to be stabbed to death in a dank basement.

"He came to see me Thursday afternoon. He told me he was going to pay back some money he borrowed from me last year, which shocked me half to death."

So he must have had something going on? That he thought would get him…

Aloud I said, "How much money?"

"Ten grand."

"That's a chunk of change. Do the cops know?"

Evelyn shook her head. "I tend to keep my trap shut around the fuzz. Our sheriff is a sexist and a bigot."

"Then talk to Mac instead. He seems okay."

"Mac's good-hearted, I'll give you that," she said. "But there's something else that doesn't look good for me. I'm the beneficiary of Dorian's will."

"What? Why?"

"I made him write one when I loaned him the money, so that after he got killed doing whatever idiot thing he was planning to do, I could at least sell his car and recoup part of my losses after he was dead." Evelyn spoke matter-of-factly, as though this were a perfectly normal thing to demand.

"Damn. That's cold."

"You gotta be tough. Otherwise a charmer like Dorian will run all over you." Evelyn took a quick breath, and I realized she was trying not to cry. She sniffed and regained her normal cranky composure. "I thought drawing up a will would be one of those . . . what do you call them? Wake-up calls? Teachable moments? Make him consider how dangerous it was for him to get involved with married women and big-time gangsters." Evelyn shook her head. "He agreed just like that. We went to the bank to get it notarized and everything. He just smiled the whole time, joking, acting like I was some dingy old bat. Now the poor kid's dead as a doornail."

"I think the police really need to know this," I said. "I can text Mac directly and let him know you want to talk to him."

Evelyn arched a brow. "I didn't realize you were on such friendly terms with the law."

"Mac's a regular customer at the restaurant," I said, as if that explained it all.

"All right, then. Do it."

I tapped out the message quickly, fingers already stiffening from the cold wind blowing off the choppy sea. The clear day was giving me a much-needed infusion of sunshine and vitamin D, but without the insulating layer of cloud, the sharp wind cut straight through my jacket.

"I was just going to have some breakfast," I said. "Do you want to come with me?"

Evelyn cocked her head as if I'd done something incredibly strange and unexpected.

"At your place?" she asked.

"No, the diner." I gestured down the street at the Prospector.

"Oh, God no." She sniffed. "If you're hungry, come back to the Beehive with me."

"The what?"

"The Beehive—it's where I live. I'll cook you an omelette."

◆◆◆

The Beehive was a women-only assisted-living facility situated in a long, green one-story building three blocks from the Eelgrass. As we walked through the door, I saw a comfortable-looking lounge with a television. An assortment of unmatched recliners, love seats, and sofas made the space seem snug. Several of these were occupied by old ladies. A couple of them worked crosswords. Another crocheted, while three others seemed glued to the TV screen.

All but one looked up as I entered.

"This is Andrew," Evelyn announced, waving her hand back as though I were some stray dog that had followed her home. "He's the chef at the murder restaurant."

To my surprise, only one of the old ladies seemed scandalized, and she appeared to be mainly irritated at Evelyn.

"I'm sure he doesn't want to be introduced like that." She used her cane to push herself to her feet and steady herself as she held out her hand. "I'm Julie."

She said the word Julie with a strong French accent, though the rest of her English sounded free of regional inflection. She wore stylish black slacks and a bold red blouse. Her white updo managed to be elegant without appearing stiff.

Julie's bones felt frail as a bird's and her skin fragile as paper. She certainly wasn't intimidated by Evelyn, though.

"It's nice to meet you," I said.

Evelyn headed to the side of the living area, where there was a small kitchen with regular residential appliances. I followed, trailed by Julie.

"Katie isn't going to like you in there," she said to Evelyn.

"Katie's not my mother." Evelyn found a skillet and some butter and eggs. "Only cheese here is Colby-Jack, I'm afraid."

"That's fine with me." At this point I was curious what she was going to do. Plus, I don't have anything against Jack, or any other food when applied appropriately. "I'm more of a food nerd than a food snob."

Evelyn nodded as though this was the right answer. As she began to beat the eggs, Julie made it to the small table inside the kitchen alcove and sat down.

"Are you going to make me one too?" she asked Evelyn.

"You and me can split one," Evelyn said. This seemed to satisfy Julie.

My phone buzzed. Mac had replied with a text:

Drew, I strongly advise you to stop interviewing people about the murder.

I texted back: *I'm not. I just ran into Evelyn, and she told me.*

Mac: *You are not to question Evelyn further.*

So I replied: *I will not. I'm just sitting here at the Beehive, having breakfast. But if she happens to start talking about it, I'm not going to stop her. That would be rude.*

Mac made no reply for so long that I thought he'd given up. Then finally, a message popped up:

You are impossible.

To which I sent a smiley face.

As Evelyn cooked, I found myself distracted by the deftness of her gestures. Though she was normally stiff, while she cooked her gestures became fluid and more or less perfect.

"That's a nice, classic omelette you're making here," I remarked.

"She's just trying to show off," Julie said. "Do you know that she cooked for Pierre Troisgros? Back in the day she worked in the best French restaurants."

"That I didn't know. I didn't think women were allowed back then."

"A few of us got in." Evelyn finished sliding the omelette onto a plate and set it before me. "But we had to be tenacious and willing to work twice as hard as any man."

"And it helped to be homosexual," Julie added. "You know, no family or children with birthdays to take off. No romantic interest in any of the men in the kitchen. No distracting boyfriends. Just work, work, work."

"Somehow they never noticed the distracting girlfriend." Evelyn started cracking eggs for the second omelette.

"They always thought I was dropping by to flirt with them." Julie laughed, and Evelyn grinned.

I tried to keep my eyes from popping at this revelation. It wasn't Evelyn being family that surprised me, so much as the notion that Evelyn had been such an adventurous person. She seemed like such a creature of habit now.

The doorbell rang, and Julie struggled up to look out the doorway.

"It's a flatfoot," she whispered toward Evelyn. "Big Mac."

"We've been texting since the murder," I said. "He eats at my place all the time."

I'm not sure why I felt the need to drop this information. Maybe I wanted to impress Julie with my inside track to the sheriff's department.

"Oh?" Julie hobbled back to the table, sat down, and leaned forward. "You know, I can't remember him ever having a girlfriend."

"You don't say." I tried to keep a neutral face.

"Not one. Ever," Julie reiterated.

"Here's breakfast." Evelyn brought the second omelette over. She had only one plate with two forks. As they began to eat, I listened to Mac talking with the old ladies, then to a younger-sounding woman, who I imagined must be the dreaded Katie. I couldn't make out any distinct words. Then came the sound of cop shoes disappearing down the hall.

I glanced up to Julie, and meeting her eyes, realized she'd been attempting to eavesdrop as well.

"I couldn't hear what they were saying," she whispered.

"Me neither," I said.

Julie gave a big smile. "Evelyn said you were interesting. I'm so glad you've finally come to visit, so I can look at you myself."

"You're welcome to come to the restaurant anytime," I offered.

"No, your place is where Evelyn goes to get away from me and read her paper," Julie said. "I'm a talker, you know."

"I didn't, but I'm gathering that now." I scraped up a forkful of my breakfast.

"So tell me about yourself, Drew. Where were you born?"

"Wyoming. But I moved to Washington State when I was a teenager."

"That must have been a huge change. I had a transition like that myself when I left Port-au-Persil," Julie said.

"In France?"

"Canada," Evelyn corrected. "Though Julie and I met in France."

"I went to study design." Julie spoke as though studying design was the single most provocative action a person could take, which I guessed it might have been at the time Julie did it.

I'll admit, I haven't spent a ton of time with elders—particularly not lesbians. But I didn't want to offend. Julie seemed nice.

"Did it work out?" I asked.

"Like it was my fate! Design led me to Paris, and there I met Evelyn. And we're married, aren't we? For two whole years now." Julie waved her ring finger under my nose. It sported an impressive rock. "Before, we'd been living in sin for decades and decades. Now I can finally hold my head up when I'm pushing my little trolley through the supermarket."

"You haven't been to the supermarket for anything but a *Vogue* magazine in forty years," Evelyn commented.

"Because of the shame." Julie put the back of her hand to her head like the heroine in a black-and-white film.

I wasn't quite sure how to reply. I'd only just started to perceive Evelyn as a whole person. Interacting with her melodramatic other half challenged my social capacity. Fortunately, Julie seemed to notice my discomfort and reined it in.

"Do you like living in Orca's Slough?" she asked, introducing a non-sequitur so breezily that I could easily picture her at home in any sixties' Parisian soiree.

"It's all right," I replied. "I admit I didn't expect it to be so murder-intensive."

"These tiny island towns are like dormant volcanoes," Julie said. "They sleep and sleep and sleep, but there's always a molten mass of resentment and secrets roiling like magma beneath the surface. The pressure builds, then KABLOOEY! The place erupts, and everyone is incinerated. Then the scar heals over, and everybody forgets until . . . KABLOOEY!" Julie emphasized her point by waving her hands in the air. "You've heard about Charlie Lindgren's murder, I'm sure. Fishing with his brother and then gone into the sea never to be seen again."

"Wasn't that ruled an accident?" I asked. Sam had only mentioned her cousin's death in passing, but it had sounded like an open-and-shut case of too much alcohol and rough waters.

"The Lindgren brothers competed over everything." Julie said it like sibling rivalry was damning evidence. "They even fought over how much more each of them could leave to Samantha. That may have been the breaking point."

I started to suggest that fondness toward Samantha didn't sound like grounds for murder, but Julie wasn't done.

"And there's Sean Mackenzie—"

"Big Mac's father," Evelyn provided quickly. "He was a deputy fifteen or so years ago."

"He should have been sheriff, but instead he vanished and that brother of his took over," Julie announced. "Of course, his children were heartbroken. The big one—"

"Mac," Evelyn clarified, and Julie nodded.

"Yes. He's been stunted ever since."

"He looks robust enough to me," I remarked.

"Stunted inside." Julie clutched the front of her blouse. "In his heart."

"Well, I think I hear his big feet clomping back our way," Evelyn commented, deadpan.

Sure enough, Mac poked his head around the corner of the kitchen door. Dark shadows hung beneath his eyes, but otherwise he seemed as crisp and clean as normal.

He acknowledged Evelyn and Julie with a slightly wary, "Ladies," then turned his heavy cop-gaze on me. Steady, unblinking, and—unusual for Mac—unsmiling.

"Can I have a word with you outside, Drew?"

"Sure," I said. "Mac."

Somehow we both made the use of our own names sound awkward.

Mac's cruiser was parked across the street, and I padded toward it, careful to stay out of his arm's reach. I wasn't sure he didn't plan to just chuck me in the back. I glanced inside and saw a sheaf of stapled papers on the passenger seat. The title page read: *Officer's Evidence Handbook.*

"Do you recall how you were worried that involving yourself in a police investigation of a murder wasn't a good idea?" Mac asked.

I suspected I knew where he was leading with that question, but it wasn't as if I was chasing down leads or conducting interviews. Not really.

"I do," I said. "It was right before you told me that I was a suspect and that I couldn't reopen my business until you worked out who killed Dorian. How's that going?"

"These things take time—"

"And information from the public. At least that's what the morning paper said." I planted my hands on my hips, feeling pleased at having put him on the defensive.

Mac offered me a silent, penetrating stare.

"You understand that whoever killed Dorian has already committed murder, right?" he asked. "If they ever felt any reluctance to take a human life, they're past that now. That's not the kind of person you want to corner."

I didn't want to think about that. Mac clearly read my discomfort because he offered me a sympathetic smile and his tone softened a little. "I suspect you don't like guys telling you what to do, but I'm not trying to do that at all."

"Yes, you are. You clearly are."

"No, I am requesting that you resist the urge to interfere. I am worried for you—"

"So you said, but that doesn't get me any closer to having my restaurant back."

Mac's expression darkened at my interruption.

"And I am also worried that you will wreck our case by doing something stupid," he finished.

"I'm not stupid," I said, bristling.

"No, you are ignorant. You don't know the rules of evidence or understand how admissible evidence can be outweighed by countervailing considerations."

"Countervailing . . . Did you just read that this morning?" I pointed to the manual on his seat.

"I did a little refresher. Let's say you actually hear some information or, God forbid, find a piece of physical evidence someplace: your ignorant actions could render that piece of information or evidence inadmissible, meaning that even if we had the right perpetrator, we couldn't use in court the evidence you tampered with. Is that what you want? What is your thought process here?"

"I want to be able to pay my bills! I want to open my restaurant!" The words came out with more force than I intended. "I want to make a scallop special. But can I? No. What's stopping me? We don't know who killed Dorian. What can I do, then? Find out who killed him so I can keep going with my own stupid life."

Mac cocked his head slightly and said, "Well, no one can say you're not proactive."

"You asked what I was thinking. I told you."

"What if I told you that you could go back to work tomorrow? Would you lay off the investigation then?"

"Can I?" Part of me thought this might be a setup. I leaned forward so we were eye to eye. "Will you let me back in?"

Mac said, "Yes. The basement will remain sealed, but you can resume business tomorrow."

Relief swept through me. "I am so happy."

"You're welcome." As Mac opened his car door, he turned back to me. "I'll be there for dinner."

Chapter Five

At seven o'clock Sunday morning I stuck a sign on the door announcing that the Eelgrass would open at five, and got to work.

It felt good to walk into the darkened space, turning on the lights as though I were some kind of wizard bringing the kitchen to life.

I unlocked the office and found my chef's coat but had to search to locate my apron. Eventually I found it in the bar.

Undoubtedly it had been worn by Dorian, who frequently forgot his own gear. As I tied the strings, I felt through the pockets for any detritus Dorian might have left.

Sure enough, I removed two corkscrews and a couple of ballpoint pens with the Eelgrass logo on them. But I also found a small, clear sandwich bag containing a photograph. An actual picture, printed on paper. It looked old, with faded Kodachrome colors and one bent corner. It showed two men and two boys on a fishing boat, holding up the homely bulk of a delicious pacific halibut. The final item was an Eelgrass bar napkin with Mac's phone number written on it.

I'm not in the habit of memorizing numbers, and I never added Mac to my official contacts, but I'd been seeing his digits pop up frequently over the last couple of days.

So before Dorian died, he had taken down Mac's number in addition to visiting Evelyn. What did I make of that? Had he feared for his life? Had someone threatened him? Did he ever get a chance to use this number? And why hadn't it been discovered when the police had searched the place? Wouldn't they have recognized Mac's personal number?

Then again, maybe not? Who actually memorized numbers these days?

Hardly anybody.

And a bartender having a phone number written on a napkin wasn't exactly an unusual occurrence. I knew I should call Mac and report it right away, but I didn't want the cops coming around again before I even had a chance to open. I slid the baggie into my back pocket.

I know it sounds selfish. And it was, but that's what I did.

I put the picture and number on the back burner of my mind and got to work prepping ingredients for my dinner service.

An emergency order phoned in to my purveyor the previous afternoon meant that one hour into my usual routine a grizzled old Indigenous guy arrived at my door, holding a thirty-pound box of live, local scallops.

Being superstitious (and secretly softhearted), I muttered a quiet apology to the shellfish, then set about shucking them.

I found myself saddened by the waste of removing the coral and mantle from the adductor muscle. When I was twenty-one, I'd gone to Japan on a whim, and there eaten a scallop—gonads, gills, and all—and it had been delicious.

It had been a revelation to me, and I wondered if Mac would be game to try it, since I knew few others on the island would be so inclined to experiment.

I set aside three large scallops for him and went to work on the others, leaving intact the sac of vivid orange coral (AKA gonads) curled around the familiar cylindrical white muscle. I wasn't sure anyone would come dine, really. But I felt like giving them a treat if they did—a reward for still believing in me.

Because that's how I like to reward loyalty: by providing surprise gonads.

I checked my messages. Sam hadn't answered yet. I wondered if she'd gone to the mainland. If she didn't show, I didn't know what I was going to do. There would be no front of house person—nobody to serve the food or pour drinks.

I texted Lionel to make sure he planned to come to work, and he replied with a jaunty: *Yeah, chief, still gonna be in at 5 like I said.*

It was around noon when Evelyn walked in through the open back door.

"You should get a lock put on that," she said. "Anybody could come in here anytime."

"Yeah, I know," I said. "Were you knocking in the front? I'm sorry if I didn't hear you."

"Doesn't matter. I could see you back here." Evelyn held a plastic grocery bag in one hand and a knife case in the other.

"What's up?" I turned my attention back to my parsley chiffonade.

"I came to help you."

I heard a rustling of plastic and saw that she'd pulled a white chef's coat out of the plastic bag and was buttoning it on. She tugged at the bottom and frowned.

"I think I must have shrunk," she said. "They say you shrink when you get old."

"Come on now, I can't expect you to come in here and do my work for me," I protested.

"I didn't think you did, or you wouldn't look so surprised," she said. "Give me something to do."

"I can't pay you," I said. "I can't even pay myself."

"Don't worry. You can trade me lunch credit." She glanced swiftly around the room and saw the piece of paper lying on the table behind me. "Is this your prep list?"

"Yeah."

"Looks small."

"I'm not expecting too many clients," I admitted.

"What's for dessert?" she asked.

"I don't know yet."

"Got apples?"

I told her I did. She then quizzed me on the availability of a few basic staples.

"I'll make tarte tatin, then," she finally announced. "It's easy, and people like the fancy name. Hopefully by the time I've finished that, you'll have found something else for me to do."

Evelyn set about peeling apples for the tarte tatin while I continued with my preparation.

"Julie wants to know if you're single." Evelyn started to place the sliced apples into the pan of bubbling caramel. "If you are, there's a physical therapist at the medical center, who she's been trying to set up for ages. Do you like massages?"

"Can we all get massages or just Drew?"

I glanced up to see that Sam had entered through the back door. She wore her usual work attire: black pencil skirt, spangled black sleeveless top, and patent leather clogs. The red streak in her black bob had turned purple, and her eyelids gleamed with crisp, freshly applied eyeliner.

I won't say I was astonished to see her turn up ready to work, but it definitely hadn't seemed like a sure thing. I decided to go for diplomacy and positive reinforcement.

"Sam," I said, "I'm so glad to see you."

Sam offered a tentative smile, though she frowned immediately when she saw Evelyn working over the stove.

"Evelyn's helping me out today," I said.

"I'm broke and need to work for my supper." Evelyn spoke without looking up from the pan full of apples.

Sam and I locked eyes. Her expression questioned my sanity. I answered with a helpless shrug. Sam went on her way.

We worked throughout the day, speaking occasionally. Sam had misplaced an invoice for an order of lettuce, something that normally wouldn't have fazed her at all, but I guess it showed how edgy we both were, because she couldn't seem to stop searching for it. Neither of us mentioned Dorian. Sam just tidied the bar herself. Evelyn took a couple of breaks, visibly fatigued but unwilling to admit it. I thought of cutting her loose, but the fact was I did need the help, and I sensed in her a need to help me—and also to dispense various criticisms of my technique. This rankled my pride, but I took it anyway because: elders. And because she was right.

Though I was glad Lionel wasn't present to hear Evelyn busting my balls all day.

Fifteen minutes before we were to open for dinner, Lionel himself arrived, cloaked entirely in the blue rain poncho he always wore in inclement weather. Beneath this he wore his usual uniform of baggy sweatpants and a t-shirt for a band I didn't recognize.

"Hey, chief, there's a whole line of people waiting outside to get in," he said in an excited rush.

"Really?" Glancing up, I saw that this was, inconceivably, the case. Though I felt a shadow of disappointment to see that Mac was not among them. "Damn."

"That's what I said." Lionel then saw Evelyn, and cocked his head theatrically before saying, "Hey, Granny."

"Hey, Fuzz Nuts," Evelyn replied. "Best get to work now. You're three minutes late."

"Yes ma'am," Lionel replied. But when he turned, he rolled his eyes so far, I thought he could use them to massage his brain.

Sam appeared at the food pass-through, looking happier than I'd seen her look in weeks.

"Did you see the line? Are you ready for me to unlock the doors?"

I made a point of surveying the kitchen in the manner of a king gazing out across his kingdom.

"Ready whenever you are."

◆◆◆

The dinner service was so busy, I didn't notice when Mac arrived. The only thing that clued me in on it was Lionel returning from bussing a table in the dining room, singing "Fuck Tha Police" under his breath.

Mac sat in his usual place by the window, his back to the wall, where he could see everyone on the sidewalk and everyone in the dining room.

How strategic.

Again, that dissonance slithered through me. There was no denying I found him attractive. Obviously. I'd set aside special shellfish just for him.

And yet . . . a cop? Really? The personalities of the cops I'd met ranged from rule-obsessed wiener to fascist sociopath.

Had I somehow become masochistic during my tenure at the Eelgrass? Had entrepreneurship warped me so completely that I'd begun to find authority figures comforting?

For a second I nearly gave up my plan of making his "special-special," then went into heavy rationalization mode. Even if this guy was just as diametrically opposed to me as I suspected him to be, it couldn't hurt to suck up to him a little. If I got him to like me, it might make him think twice before finding a reason to convict me.

So I stuck to the plan. I removed only the black sac of guts from the scallops and placed them back into their shells. I added some butter and a little soy sauce and left them to grill while I made the pasta that would accompany them—lightly dressed that with mentaiko citrus cream sauce and added a fresh vitamin-C-laden tomato salad on the side so that Mac would not die of scurvy before being able to clear my name.

"Are we serving this?" Sam squinted at the plates with grave suspicion. "He ordered the special."

"Tell him I decided to substitute something else," I said. And when Sam looked as though she might refuse, I added, "If he doesn't want it, he can send it back."

"What's it called?"

"Hokkaido-style scallops, pasta with mentaiko yuzu cream, and grilled tomato with sesame and ginger."

"Oh my God, are you into him?" Sam raised her eyebrows in alarm.

"Please just take it before it gets cold."

I tried not to watch as Mac received my gift—not because I didn't want to know what he thought, but because I didn't want to be caught watching. I spied what I thought looked like an expression of stunned delight, which could have also been shock.

Sam returned immediately.

"He doesn't want it remade, but he wants to talk to you when you have a moment. I told him I'd comp it, but he refused."

I finished my last two tickets and took off my apron. I left my chef's coat on, wanting to counter his uniform with mine, even though he had dressed in plain clothes.

"How are you enjoying your meal, Deputy?" I asked.

"It is so, so good. I've never even seen anything like this." Mac gave me a bigger smile than I'd previously seen on him. It made him look younger. "Sit down and tell me all about it."

It's not that this has never happened to me before. At certain venues, it's actually pretty common to be summoned to explain the intricacies of your culinary creations. But in my experience, the guys—it was always guys—who demanded explanations just wanted to show off their influence over the kitchen staff. I'd never been invited to sit down and talk about how and why I made a dish with a person who seemed so impressed with me or so deeply awed by what I'd created.

So I told him all about the ingredients—what they were and where they came from. Mac listened, nodding occasionally, but mostly eating.

It made me wonder whether dining with a companion was unusual for him. Come to think of it, I couldn't remember him ever being anything but alone. There were no new customers, so I stayed at the table, talking. I went on from the mechanics of the dishes to the first time I ate scallops prepared in this fashion—how I ordered them accidentally, then was too embarrassed to say so, but also confused about how to approach this weird food.

"It must be fun to travel," Mac remarked. He was almost at the end of his pasta.

"Yeah. I like it."

"Is that experience why you decided you wanted to be a chef?"

"Not exactly. I was the problem child. I got expelled in high school for fighting. So I went to work with my dad, doing construction. He had a job in the city doing renovations on this restaurant. Dad and I stayed with my oldest brother, who was in college, while we were doing the work on the restaurant. One day, the chef needed a dishwasher at his other restaurant, and the owner offered to pay me cash to fill in. I was sixteen years old. The rest is history. How about dessert? Evelyn made a fancy apple pie."

Mac brightened. "Absolutely."

I went back into the kitchen to plate the tarte tatin. I noticed that Evelyn hadn't dated the container—probably not that big of a thing in her day, but now an offense against the health-department gods. As I reached into my back pocket for a Sharpie, I touched the napkin and photo Dorian had left there.

I had to ask Mac about these, I thought. Yeah, it might ruin the mood, but I should still do it. I would just wait for the right time. Plus, I wanted a piece of this pie myself.

So I came back with two plates, reseated myself, and said, "But enough about me. What about you? How did you get into police work?"

At the change of subject, Mac shrank a little and shrugged. "I joined the sheriff's office to help my mom pay the bills after my dad wasn't around anymore."

Mac's change of demeanor when speaking about this didn't encourage me to continue along these conversational lines. But ultimately my curiosity won out.

"Did you not want to be a cop when you grew up?"

Mac paused, fork held in midair as he gazed out into the rainy autumn night—as if I'd asked a question too difficult to answer.

Maybe I had.

I gave him some space and kept eating my luscious slice of fancy pie. I was about to casually introduce a new subject when he continued.

"My dad was a really good guy and a great deputy. I guess I wanted to be like him, but I didn't necessarily want his job. Now I've been doing it for twelve years, though, so I don't know what else I'd do." Mac finally ate his bite of pie. "I can't imagine going to college now. I'd be so much older than everybody else."

I hadn't expected his answer to be so candid.

"Older people go back to college all the time."

"Yeah, but in this job I'm already halfway to retirement," Mac said. "I suppose I'll think about doing something crazy like going to school when I've finished out my twenty-five years."

I couldn't imagine doing anything for twenty-five years and said so. Mac just laughed.

"How long have you been cooking?"

"Fourteen years."

"See? You're more than halfway there." Mac gave a smile.

"Yeah, except there's no retirement . . . or really any other sort of benefits. The best thing you can hope for is to sell your place to somebody who invariably takes what you made and runs it into the ground."

"Wow. Outlook so bleak."

"Just realistic," I said.

"It might be precarious, but at least you get to live the life of an artist."

"Artist? Oh please, I spent an hour today making French fries."

"Fancy French fries."

"They're still fries. That's hardly artistic."

Mac gave a shrug. "I think you're an artist."

Normally I'm a sucker for a good compliment, but Mac's, delivered with such sincerity, made my shy.

"Listen, I'm going to have to go back to the kitchen soon, but I found something." I handed him the napkin and photograph I'd found in my apron. "That's your phone number, right?"

The napkin didn't faze him, but when he saw the photograph he became transfixed, turning it over and scrutinizing every part of it.

"That's Dorian's handwriting on the napkin. I think he might have been wearing my apron. I don't know what the photograph is of," I said.

"It's all right. I do."

"What is it?"

"It's nothing to do with the case," Mac said.

"If it's nothing to do with the case, can I have it back?"

"I think I'll keep it."

"Are you kidding? This could be evidence."

"I told you it doesn't have anything to do with the case." Mac met my glare with stone-faced refusal.

"Is it the reason you were outside the restaurant that night?" I demanded.

Mac ran his finger along the edge of the photograph. After a few seconds, his easygoing demeanor returned.

"Okay, yes. It's none of your business, but I'll tell you. Dorian called me and said he had something for me. At the time I thought maybe he'd decided to become an informant rather than get caught in a big bust. He asked me to meet him outside, but he never showed up." Mac's eyes returned to the photo, and his expression seemed almost tender. "He must have found this picture of my dad while he was going through his grandma's old photo albums."

I took this information in and said, "Which one is your dad?" Though looking closely, I realized the answer was obvious. The brawny man sporting a shock of dark hair and giving the camera a charming grin closely resembled Mac.

"The guy on the left," Mac said. "Next to him is Bill Lindgren. The boys are the Lindgren twins, Charlie and Troy. I couldn't say which is which."

I stared at the two boys, trying to pick out Troy's features in either of their youthful smiles. In their pre-teen androgyny, they reminded me of Samantha more than anyone else.

"Your dad looks nice."

"He was," Mac said. "Bill was his best friend. They used to tell all us kids stories about the hidden smugglers' loot buried in the old tunnels beneath the buildings. Sometimes they'd even take us down there to dig around in the dirt for old beer cans. Made my mother hopping mad."

"'Cause they were condemned tunnels or because of the risk of tetanus?"

"Probably both. Listen, I have to thank you for the excellent meal, Drew. Your best so far." Mac smiled at me, and then his gaze slid toward the photo, preoccupied and slightly melancholy. I took this as my cue to go, and excused myself.

As I receded into the kitchen, I felt a cold draft flow over me as the door opened to admit a new table of customers. Except it wasn't customers—it was the other deputy, Mac's cousin Chaz. He was yawning in a dramatic fashion. Mac quickly pocketed the photo and napkin as Chaz approached. The two of them spoke only a few words, and then they both departed.

My disappointment at seeing him go was mitigated somewhat by Sam's announcement that he'd left without paying.

Chapter Six

Sam locked the doors of the Eelgrass at nine p.m. and had her own work done by nine thirty—aside from never locating the elusive lettuce invoice. But that was probably long past recovering. We'd just have to trust our produce purveyor's monthly bill when it arrived.

Danielle's smiling face flashed up on Sam's phone, accompanied by a retro-disco ringtone. Sam spoke to her briefly, then glanced to me.

"You don't mind if I go, do you?" she asked.

This was a purely ritualistic interaction. I wouldn't say no, however much I could have used her help. I gave a nod.

"Me and Lionel will be another hour at least."

My statement elicited a groan from Lionel.

"See you tomorrow, then." Sam whisked herself out the back door.

"We're not really going to be here another hour, are we, chief?" Lionel tugged his yellow plastic gloves off.

"Why? You got somewhere to be?" I turned to start scraping char off the grill.

"Well . . . yeah. I was going to go with my friends to meet some girls."

"What girls?"

"The fish-'n-chips girls." Lionel sounded exasperated. "You're as bad as my mom. Hey, speaking of my mom, though, I was going to show you this the other day but forgot."

Lionel crossed the kitchen and showed me a photograph on his phone: a white plate with a dark-brown cube on it. In the background I could see another crock like the one that had exploded in the Eelgrass's basement the morning we discovered Dorian's body.

"What's that supposed to be?"

"My mom made salmon. I cannot tell you how tiny and burnt it was." Lionel pocketed the phone. "So I'm done with the dishes. Are you really gonna make me stay, 'cause I will, but those girls . . ."

Honestly, I had no reason for keeping him, except for the company. Not a good enough reason for depriving Lionel of the opportunity to court females.

"Go." I waved him away. "Be safe."

After he left, I tried to bury myself in rote tasks—making the prep list for the next day, rotating stock in the refrigerator—all the while aware of the building's eerie emptiness and of the yellow police tape that still draped the back stairs.

Is it any wonder that my subconscious mind chose that moment to remind Mac, via text, that he had forgotten to pay?

The man himself arrived fifteen minutes later, ghosting through the back door and scaring the hell out of me when he seemed to materialize in the dry-goods storage area.

I did yell, yeah. And brandish a skillet.

Mac held up his hands in surrender.

"See, this is exactly why you should lock this back door," he remarked. "Anybody could come in here."

"Yeah, Evelyn already chewed me out about it." I dropped the skillet back on the range with a clang.

"Is this door always unlocked?"

"While somebody's here, yeah. Fire codes require it."

"It is very, very unsafe," Mac said. "I cannot tell you the number of times I've investigated crimes that could have been prevented by taking the preemptive step of locking the door."

"Is one of those crimes dine-'n-dash?"

Mac's cheeks colored, and he hung his head. "I'm sorry for that. The matter was urgent."

"Was it to do with Dorian's death?"

"I'm not at liberty to say." Mac pulled his wallet out of his pocket and started thumbing through the bills contained therein. He pulled out a fifty and handed it to me.

"That's about ten bucks more than you owe—even accounting for the tip."

"Call it an additional finance fee."

I pocketed the money. "Pleasure doing business with you."

"How long do you plan to stay here tonight?"

"I still have the fryer to break down. Then it's just mopping. But I thought I'd stay to do some deep cleaning."

"By yourself in the middle of the night?" Mac asked.

"You make it sound so creepy."

"Hey—you said it, not me." Mac observed the mop bucket Lionel had left behind. "I was planning on driving up to Top Hat Butte. It's so clear tonight, we should be able to see the Milky Way right across the sky."

"You've got a date?"

"I mean we in the general sense. We being the residents of Orca's Slough."

"The Milky Way, huh." I placed my hand on the side of the fryer. It was still too hot to drain the oil without damaging the machine. "I haven't seen that since I was a kid in Wyoming."

"You should come see it, then—get yourself out of this building."

"I just barely got back in here," I said. "I think I'll pass."

"You're really going to stay here alone?"

"It's not like there's someone else here to close down for me."

Mac stood there for a moment, taking in the kitchen and then studying me. At last he said, "How about I help you out?"

"Doing what?" I asked to stop myself from thinking too much about why he might be willing to abandon gazing at the open beauty of the Milky Way to spend his evening cleaning a commercial kitchen.

"I can mop," Mac offered.

"Are you just worried that I'm going to violate the crime-scene tape and go downstairs?" I asked.

"To be honest, I'm worried that you won't lock the door after I leave." With that, Mac went to fetch the mop bucket. I stared after him, puzzled.

What was he playing at, anyway? If Mac hadn't been a cop, I'd have known exactly what was happening because nobody—nobody—hung around mopping a restaurant floor just to be matey. If Mac had been a normal guy, I would have instantly known he was trying to hook up. But Mac wasn't normal—even by cop standards. I supposed he could be trying to make friends. Or, was this some weird extension of being the "great cop" his dad had been?

I just couldn't figure out what he was going to do. Or what his motives were.

Because there he stood, dressed in his street clothes, churning up the greasy mop water as though it was what he'd expected to be doing this evening.

Mac glanced up at me.

Embarrassed to be caught staring, I said, "You don't have to do the dish room. Lionel's already done it."

"He has?"

"Yeah."

"Not very well," Mac remarked. "Your side isn't too much better."

"You're killing me here."

"My littlest sister mops like this." Mac tipped the old gray mop water out into the mop sink and started to refill the bucket. "She also used to hide her dirty dishes under her bed for no reason I could figure out. Once a week I'd go looking under there for all the little plates and bowls she squirreled away."

"How many sisters and brothers do you have?"

"There are six of us altogether. I'm the oldest." Satisfied with the new water, Mac went to work swabbing the deck in an efficient, fast manner. "A house can get filthy fast with six kids in it."

"Must be where you learned your sweet moves," I remarked.

"You can just call me Mop King," Mac said, then squinting into a dark corner, he added, "Lionel has a long way to go before he'll be challenging my title."

"Somehow I don't think that bothers him." I checked the fryer and decided that it had cooled enough to be cleaned. For the next fifteen minutes Mac and I worked in an oddly amiable quiet. He asked after my own family. I confessed to being the youngest of three sons. My mom often speculated that my defiant personality stemmed from constantly resisting my outgoing brothers. I didn't tell Mac that.

Mac paused in his mopping. "I guess I can tell you that Lionel's no longer a person of interest."

"No?"

"As you said, he would have been covered—absolutely covered—in blood if he'd assaulted Dorian, and there wasn't a drop on him. Photographs taken at the party show him wearing the exact same clothes he had on when we interviewed him the next morning, so lucky for him, he likes taking selfies with pretty girls."

"And what about the girls themselves?" I asked.

"The girls from the fish-and-chips shop? They all have alibis—and not just with each other," Mac said. "We're working on running down the whereabouts of a couple stragglers who went back to Seattle."

"That's good news, I guess. About Lionel at least." All at once I felt very light. Without being consciously aware, I'd been carrying that worry that Mac would arrest Lionel like an anvil lodged in my chest. But with the dissipation of that tension came a wave of fatigue. The idea of cleaning the restaurant all night no longer held that manic appeal.

"So how long will it take you to finish the floor?"

"Twenty minutes, maybe."

"I'll go get changed, then," I said. "Do you think you could give me a ride home?"

Mac smiled. "Absolutely."

◆◆◆

Apart from the contents of his phone, is there any space more personal than a man's car? My second-hand station wagon, for example, spoke of a life spent hauling giant boxes of paper towels and engaging in drive-through dining. The perennial occupants of my passenger seat were my unopened mail and stacks of industry magazines I meant to read someday.

In contrast, Mac drove a twenty-year-old silver Ford F-150. Very clean blue seat covers concealed what I could feel was cracked vinyl. But both seat belts functioned, and when he cranked the engine, the vehicle chugged to life with only a tiny hiccup. At midnight, the town of Orca's Slough was mostly asleep. Here and there a couple of raccoons ambled along the sidewalk, their eyes flashing yellow-green as they watched us pass by.

"Business at your place seemed to be fine today," Mac remarked.

"I'm pretty sure it was morbid curiosity," I said. "Once that wears off, who knows. Maybe I'll set up an 'Orca's Slough Underground Ghost Tour' like they have in Seattle."

"You are quite the schemer, aren't you?" Mac said, giving a sideways smile.

"I like to call it the entrepreneurial mindset."

As we drove, I grew relaxed and for a few seconds slipped outside my day-to-day. What would it be like to live life like a normal guy? To make time to go up and look at stars I'd already seen hundreds of times, in a tiny town on a little island in the middle of a dark sea? I found myself manufacturing a different trajectory for myself. Could I ever be the one going to barbecues I was not catering, attending weddings as a guest instead of staff? Paying for a room at a bed-and-breakfast instead of being the guy making breakfast? Regular activities that people with regular jobs did?

What was that like? How did people know how to behave socially without a function to complete? I almost asked Mac, but then realized it wasn't as though Mac had a regular job either. Probably a fair number of people hated him just for being the law. And I knew he worked weekends and holidays just like me.

What had moved him to invite me on a stargazing trip, anyway?

He was probably lonely. He'd mentioned a couple of times that his brothers and sisters were all gone. Did he think of me as some little brother replacement? Or was he one of those guys who'd grown up and forgotten to make new friends?

One more turn in the road and then the trees on either side thinned, revealing the ratty trailer I called home.

"I guess this is me," I said. "I've got an early morning. You?"

"I'm off tomorrow."

"Yeah? Where will you be having dinner?"

"Not sure yet. What are you cooking?"

"Chicken Provençal—that's with wine and mushrooms," I said. "And butternut squash. Haven't figured out the details yet, though."

"Butternut squash, huh?"

"I promise that even though it's a vegetable, you have nothing to fear."

"Maybe I'll give it a try." Like a gentleman, Mac waited until I'd gotten fully inside to drive away.

It was only as I was watching his taillights recede that I realized I'd never told him my address.

But he would know that, wouldn't he?

I drank beer in the shower, then at the last second remembered tomorrow was trash day. I struggled into a pair of sweats and took out my measly bag, only to discover my trash can had been stolen.

Chapter Seven

Monday I had a busier than usual lunch—now certain I was getting the rubberneck assist, but whatever; I was happy to take it if it meant revenue coming in—then got right into ordering food for the next week. I figured I'd get a bump in sales during the time of the investigation, just because people love to associate themselves with any kind of infamy, so I decided to increase my meat order.

I walked out to the alley to get a breath of fresh air while I placed the call. As I disconnected I noticed Lionel arriving for work. He hunched in the passenger seat of his mother's green Subaru, looking miserable while she told him off in Korean. I stood gawking, impressed by the volume she managed to produce from her tiny body. She put to shame a couple of chefs I'd trained under.

When she noticed me watching, she changed her tone to chirpy English. "Okay, I love you, bye, bye!"

Lionel exited the car, dragging his feet like a condemned man. His mother sped off down the alley.

"What's up with your mom?" I asked casually.

"She's mad at me for blowing up Grandmother's kimchee crock. Mom says it's irreplaceable."

"You used a family heirloom to make your bootleg pickle?"

"I didn't realize it was an heirloom!" Lionel insisted, actually going so far as to stamp his foot. "How am I supposed to know that? Nobody tells me anything about cooking stuff except for you."

To be fair to Lionel's mom, she was a nurse, not a professional chef. But obviously, fermenting kimchee was another matter, especially if the crocks she used were heirlooms.

As I stood there, wondering if I was going to have to go find some Korean antiques dealer to repair my relationship with Lionel's mom, a cop car drove up.

I'm not saying my heart skipped a beat, because then I would be a nine-year-old girl. But I can't deny that a childish excitement lit within my chest as I walked over, expecting it to be Mac.

The man in the driver's seat was not Mac. He was an older, shorter, more heavily mustached iteration of the Mackenzie line: Sheriff Scott Mackenzie.

Though I'd never personally had a run-in with the guy, he was well known in Orca's Slough as a staunch supporter of the middle-class status quo. He liked to keep the town a peaceful event-free tourist haven, and if that meant rounding up the town's few bums and personally ferrying them to Seattle to set them free, that was what he would do.

Like Evelyn, Dorian had hated him. It seemed sadly ironic that Dorian's murder was being investigated by a man who, in life, Dorian had routinely referred to as the "laziest fucking cop in Washington State."

Sheriff Mackenzie's son, Chaz, rode shotgun, looking like he was going for gold in a mini-me contest. Not for the first time, I wondered if policing Orca's Slough was some kind of hereditary position or if the dominance of the Mackenzies was just another gross display of small-town nepotism.

"Mr. Allison, how are you today?" The sheriff's smile seemed genuine and warm. A dimple creased his cheek in exactly the spot Mac had his. And yet somehow on the sheriff the expression struck me as manufactured—a professional facade.

Chaz looked like he was about to fall asleep, which seemed to be his factory setting.

"I'm good," I said. "How are you?" Out of the corner of my eye I watched Lionel slink into the safety of the building.

"Very well, thank you. I was wondering if you'd be kind enough to come down to the station for a little conversation with us."

"We could talk now in my office," I suggested.

"I'd rather we speak in private at the station, if you don't mind." The sheriff nodded to Deputy Chaz, who got out and opened the back door of the police car.

Now, I wanted to be cooperative—I genuinely did. But there was no way in hell I was getting into the back of a police cruiser unless I was under arrest.

"Am I under arrest?"

"Not right now." The sheriff's smile faltered slightly.

"Then I'll meet you down at the station in ten minutes. I could use the walk anyway."

"Ten minutes, then." The sheriff motioned Chaz back into the vehicle, and the car glided away.

When I went back in to drop off my chef's coat, I found Lionel lurking right beside the door.

"So I guess you already know that I'm going down to talk to the cops."

Lionel nodded, his silence betraying his fear.

"I'm not under arrest," I assured him.

"That's what they say to get you down there, but once you're locked in that little room, there's no way to tell what they're going to do."

"Right. I get that, but I'm also not too worried." Somehow putting on a brave face for Lionel helped me shore up my own courage. "But just in case I don't come back by five, I'm going to give you Evelyn's number."

"Granny? Again?"

"Yes, again. She cooked professionally longer than you and I have been alive." I copied her number from my phone and handed the piece of paper to Lionel. "If you don't piss her off, she could probably give you some real pro tips. She's even worked with Pierre Troisgros."

"Is he somebody famous?"

"He's the OG of French cooking. Serious, old-school, brigade-style cooking." I let that sink in with Lionel. After a moment he decided to be impressed, though I'm sure he had no idea what a brigade system really was. It probably sounded tough as hell to him, and in reality it was, especially back in Evelyn's time.

"She really was a pro?" Lionel asked.

"Yes, really. But don't call her unless I'm not back by five. I don't want to bother her for no reason. In the meantime, I need you to take over for me."

"By myself?"

"Yeah, you can handle it." I wasn't sure that was entirely true, but good enough for this situation. "Just finish the rest of the prep list and keep making orders till I get back. You'll be fine."

Lionel's chin lifted with pride, though the expression on his face remained dubious.

"Yeah, sure. No problem, chief."

Most of me did think Lionel could handle the slow afternoon business, maybe even the start of dinner service. And if he couldn't? Well, sink or swim—that's how the cooking life works. He might as well see how long he could dog paddle while it was still plausible for him to find a different calling in life.

As I walked down the street, I texted Evelyn to inform her that Lionel might be calling her to ask her to give him a hand at the restaurant. Which was my roundabout way of asking her for her assistance while avoiding actually stating why I wouldn't be there. Not that I fooled her.

She texted: *Call if you need a lawyer or bail. I'll see what I can do to keep Eelgrass from burning down while you're in the slammer.*

◆◆◆

I sat in the locked interview room for three hours before the sheriff bothered to come in. During that time I memorized every part of it, from its industrial blue carpet to its conspicuous camera.

When he finally trundled in, trailed by his still-drowsy son, I was exhausted from anxiety for my business. Or at least that's what I told myself to avoid panic.

"I'm sorry for the wait. We had some urgent matters to attend to. I guess I'm just curious to know one thing." Sheriff Mackenzie sat down opposite me in a great jangling of keys and other cop utility-belt gear.

"Okay," I said. I tried not to show my anger or give him a reason to beat me up, but it was hard.

"Why did you kill Dorian Gamble, Andrew? Did he reject your advances?"

"What?!" I didn't mean to yell, but seriously?

"Last night officers discovered a set of bloody clothes in your trash can, and I feel confident that the blood on those clothes will prove to be Dorian Gamble's." The sheriff folded his hands together and gazed at me with an understanding expression. "So what was the last straw? Did he make fun of you? Insult your food?"

"I did not kill him." Even as I spoke, my mind raced backward. Last night? Was that why Mac had stayed late at the restaurant helping me? To distract me while his cousin stole my garbage?

Or worse yet—had he helped his cousin plant evidence when he'd been called away? Or had the cousin planted the evidence there while Mac had me in his truck, reevaluating my life like a chump?

"If you didn't kill him, why did we find blood-covered clothes in your trash can?" Chaz roused himself to ask.

"I don't know anything about any bloody clothes in the trash can. I didn't put them there," I answered. "I couldn't put anything in my garbage can because somebody stole it. Wait—was that you?"

"Where did you put the clothes you were wearing when you killed Mr. Gamble?" the sheriff asked.

I didn't fall into the trap, but just barely.

"Am I under arrest?"

"Should you be?" the sheriff asked.

I glanced from him to Deputy Chaz, who now stood rubbing his eyes like a tired child. What the hell was going on here?

The sudden sound of the door opening startled me almost out of my skin. Mac walked into the room in plain clothes.

Sensing the opportunity for escape, Deputy Chaz staggered out.

Mac didn't look at me.

To say I felt betrayed at this point would be like saying Luke Skywalker felt "disappointed" when Darth Vader chopped his hand off. Still, I wanted to believe he might somehow be on my side, if only because it gave me hope of rescue.

"Am I under arrest?" I asked Mac directly.

"May I please see your shoes, Mr. Allison?" Mac asked.

Yes, I did want to physically assault him, thank you for asking. But I didn't. Not taking my eyes off him or his shitty uncle, I unlaced my Converse, removed them, and handed them to Mac without another word.

Mac turned them over, studied the soles, then said, "I'm going to need to keep these for now."

"Fine. Am I under arrest?"

Mac glanced to his uncle and shook his head. "No, Mr. Allison, you're free to go."

I don't know if I imagined it, but I thought I caught the shadow of rage cross the sheriff's face.

Mac opened the door and held it for me as I walked through. He didn't follow me as I walked, shoeless, out of the police station.

◆◆◆

I walked the few blocks to the Eelgrass in my socks, fuming with rage and humiliation. I wondered how Lionel had held out on his own. He was a good line cook but had a tendency to become overwhelmed when his emotions were running high, which they naturally would be for the entire time I was in the cop shop, so the dinner service would probably have been a disaster. Sam would be furious. But there was still time to help them clean up the carnage, at least.

As I drew closer I realized I shouldn't have worried. Sam sat out at one of the tables in front of the restaurant, smoking a cigarette. A CLOSED sign hung on the door.

Though it was only seven thirty, all the lights were off.

There had been no reputation-damaging business disaster because she had closed. Most likely as soon as she'd arrived at five. She looked downtrodden but also twitchy. I guessed she knew she shouldn't have closed the restaurant before even attempting to serve dinner, and maybe she was waiting there, half expecting me to storm up and tell her as much. But I didn't have it in me to feel angry or disappointed with her right now. After hours in a police station, facing claims of bloody clothes in my trash and having my shoes taken as evidence, the dark restaurant and the CLOSED sign seemed inevitable.

"Jesus, what happened to your shoes?" she said, by way of greeting.

"The cops took them—hopefully to eliminate me from the pool of suspects, but who knows? How did things go tonight?"

"I decided to cut our losses."

No big surprise. Despite my earlier thoughts, I found myself growing annoyed.

"If you never open, we won't have anything but losses," I muttered.

"Dorian's dead!" Sam rounded on me, eyes blazing with fury. "You were taken in by the cops. And you expect me to just go on recommending specials?"

"It's what I would have done. Or tried to do."

"We should sell this place," Sam said. "If I asked, Troy would buy it right now, and we could get the hell out of this rotten town."

"It's not like leaving town would make the cops less suspicious of me, you know," I said.

"Yeah, but it wouldn't have anything to do with me anymore."

Sometimes there is a silence that indicates the exact end of a relationship. During that silence it can feel like all the wind in the world blows between two people, eliminating the very last vestiges of amicability.

A breeze raised goose bumps across my arms.

Suddenly, Sam's expression turned horrified.

"Oh God, Drew, I didn't mean it like that! I just can't take any more stress. I was struggling even before Dorian was murdered . . ." She trailed off as her lip began to quiver.

I stared at her, fighting my reflex to comfort her and forestall her tears.

I currently faced trumped-up murder charges, and the only thing that concerned her was how much more stressed it made her feel. And before Dorian's murder, she'd been throwing parties in our business and snorting all our profits. How much of a struggle could that have been?

Sam stood trembling, tears streaming down her cheeks. Across the street I saw the old man from the souvenir shop watching us. Great. Now we were a spectacle, and I was the villain—making a woman cry.

"I know it's my fault," Sam gasped out between sobs. "None of this would have happened if it wasn't for me."

"You didn't kill Dorian," I told her but uncertainty rose in me. She could get pretty unbalanced when she was high. Dorian had joked about cutting her off on a couple of occasions—not that he would have, but still. Could Sam have murdered him? "I mean, you didn't kill him, right?"

Sam gave me a horrified stare, and her tears dried up at once. "No! Did you?"

"No," I said. "See? Neither of us is to blame."

"I was responsible for him being there. If I hadn't thrown the party, he might still be alive." Once again tears began to fill Sam's eyes. "And if I hadn't come back to Orca's Slough, you wouldn't have gotten mixed up in any of this. It's all my fault."

I wondered if she realized how self-centered this guilt of hers made her sound. Probably not.

"Listen, you're really tired—" I began.

"Don't patronize me." Sam wiped her face with the sleeve of her jacket. Her waterproof mascara didn't budge.

"I'm not patronizing you. I'm making a statement of fact." I rolled my eyes. "I'm tired too. That doesn't mean I want to throw our business away just because one bad thing happened."

"One bad thing?" Sam gaped at me. "Oh my God, how can you trivialize murder like that?"

"It's not trivializing—"

"Yes. Yes it is." Sam glared at me with glassy-eyed fury. "He was our friend, and you're not even sad that he's dead."

"Dorian was not my friend!" Now the roiling fury rose up in me. "And he wasn't your friend either. He was a lying, cheating, coke dealer."

Sam looked like she might argue, but then she seemed to deflate.

"At least he was fun to hang out with," Sam muttered. "Since we came to Orca's Slough, you've turned into some sort of dried-up old man who can't think about anything but money."

"That's not true," I said. "I also think about food. That's because I'm a chef. This restaurant is my whole life."

"But is that really a good thing?" Her tone turned from angry to weirdly sincere.

"It's not like I have anything else going on," I answered.

Sam nodded as though I'd spoken some great truth.

"But you should, Drew. You could do amazing things somewhere else." She reached out and squeezed my cold hand in her icy fingers. "If we sell Eelgrass now, nobody will think we failed. We had a personal tragedy and had to close the restaurant. That kind of thing happens. We could each start again someplace better. Please?" Her grip tightened, and she gazed up at me as if she couldn't fathom how our friendship had reached this all-time low. "Please, let's just sell."

I looked down at my socks, now filthy and wet.

"Okay. If Troy makes an offer, I'll consider it," I said.

I couldn't tell whether or not I was lying.

Chapter Eight

Tuesday morning I woke up in a different reality. I had agreed to consider closing the restaurant. I might be charged with murder. I didn't have a lawyer, and I wouldn't have a job for much longer.

I had never felt so alone. Nor had the island seemed so claustrophobic. I needed to get away, even for a day. Forget my life. Make some new friends. Get laid.

Fortunately, modern technology has created a cure for isolation and loneliness, and that cure is the hookup app.

I found a likely candidate in Seattle and immediately booked the next ferry to the mainland. During the ferry ride to Seattle I tried to put things together just for myself.

First, I had to face the fact that somebody was deliberately trying to set me up as Dorian's murderer. After working through the surge of fear and hurt at the notion that anyone hated me enough to want me to go to prison for something I didn't do, I tried to narrow the candidates to people who might hate me.

Sheriff Mackenzie hadn't seemed like a fan of mine, but it was hard to imagine him, much less his sleepy son, going to the trouble of planting evidence in my trash can when they could have just done it in the restaurant and saved themselves the drive out of town.

I wondered if Sam could have set me up. She felt like I judged her for being an addict—which, yeah, okay, I did—plus, she could find a way to sell the Eelgrass without my consent if I was convicted. But even as bad as our relationship was, I didn't think she hated me. Sam was too spontaneous and emotional to frame anybody. She might stab me in a fit of rage one day—and regret it the very next second—but she wouldn't frame me.

That left me with no one else to consider. I had so few connections on the island. Which was unlike me. Back in Seattle I'd had plenty of rivals and inspired more than a few grudges. But here I'd been so preoccupied with just trying to keep Eelgrass afloat that I hadn't made many friends, much less enemies.

Lionel and Evelyn were the very closest I'd come to making friends. Maybe Big Mac—until yesterday when he'd taken my shoes.

I scowled at the gray water of the bay.

Maybe this wasn't personal, or even about me.

Because no matter how much being framed offended me personally, framing me could not have been the murderer's initial goal—just an added bonus on the way to eliminating the primary target: Dorian.

That led me back to the question of who would kill Dorian who also didn't care about what happened to me… which brought it back to a very wide group of angry husbands and drug associates. Not for the first time, I revisited the pics of the party. There had to have been at least twenty people there. Had they all been identified and dragged down to the station as well? If they had, no one was mentioning it.

And although I didn't realistically think Sheriff Mackenzie would trouble himself with framing me, I doubted he would bypass an easy opportunity to close the murder case. Thinking about that put me right back in the interrogation room. And unwillingly, I relived that feeling of hope and then disappointment I'd felt when Mac came in.

In the transitional space of the ferry, I could admit to myself that being pulled into the police station had terrified me. And because of it, maybe I'd been unnecessarily angry at Sam, who only wanted, essentially, to quit her job and escape the small town where she'd grown up.

I should apologize to her. I would apologize to her.

But maybe not right now. Both Sam and I needed time to cool off.

The grim October weather didn't help my descending mood. Gray skies merged with a gray sea. The shoreline bristled with dark conifers.

I was not in the greatest mindset for a date with a stranger and was considering calling it off and going back home when I noticed that, seated among the passengers, in plain clothes, was Mac. He wore jeans, a gray wool Henley, and a blue rain shell. His attention was directed downward at his phone.

Now there was a coincidence.

Or was it?

Surely if Mac was surveilling me, he'd make more of an effort to hide.

I considered ignoring him and going about my business, then decided waiting and worrying wasn't my style. And that glimmer of recognition I'd felt when he'd been mopping my floor . . . Though even if Mac was gay, that didn't mean he wasn't playing the long game on behalf of his uncle.

Only one way to find out, I decided.

When I sat down next to him, Mac did not seem surprised, which meant he'd already seen me.

"Hello, Drew."

"Hello, Officer. Going to Seattle?"

"Not sure yet," Mac replied.

"How do you mean?"

"I'm going wherever you're going," he replied amiably.

"So you're following me?" Even though I had suspected as much, the certain knowledge ignited an ember of fearful anger.

"That's right. Where are we headed?"

"What the hell gives you the right to ask?"

Mac blinked. Then he reached into his jacket pocket and silently withdrew his shield wallet. The badge inside glinted at me.

"Touché," I conceded.

Mac flipped the leather case closed. "You realize that fleeing the island after your interview seems extremely suspicious."

"I'm not fleeing. I'm going on a date."

"That's a long way to go for a date."

"I find the offerings on the island to be somewhat limited."

Mac nodded his agreement, then asked, "Where's this date taking you?"

"He's not taking me anywhere. We're meeting at the Bantam Room for dinner."

"Not my favorite," Mac said. "Dull menu."

"Of course, I forgot you are Western Washington's foremost restaurant critic." My acid tone sounded catty even to me, and Mac colored slightly. Feeling like an ass, I offered a conversational olive branch. "Where would you have taken me?"

Mac's mouth curved up in a private smile he suppressed to bland professional friendliness by the time his eyes met mine.

"If it were me, I'd have taken you to that conveyor-belt sushi place by the convention center. Or Vietnamese.

Something we don't have on the island, anyway. Or a food truck."

While all those things did appeal to me, I wasn't ready to admit that.

"Well, it's not you, so you're going to have to settle for overpriced unimaginative appetizers and wood-fired pizza," I said. "Or you could just say you followed me, go get sushi, and meet me on the ferry back tomorrow morning."

"Can't do that, I'm afraid."

"Sure you can. Think of it as an undercover investigation you're performing on my behalf. Take some pictures. Bring me back a takeout menu."

Mac just shook his head and looked back down at his phone. I watched as he found the Bantam Room menu and started thumbing through his future dining options. The announcement came that the ferry would be docking shortly, and I stood to go. "I'm going to check in at my hotel. It's the Spencer on Second Avenue. I'll see you at the Bantam Room at eight."

◆◆◆

Probably the only thing more demoralizing than being on a boring date is the knowledge that there is a cop watching you tread water.

The guy—Erik—was nice enough. He was a tall, sandy-haired California transplant, who worked in tech (shocker) and had a nice condo in Belltown only a couple of blocks away from the dark, trendy restaurant where we sat. He sipped bourbon and told me about being new to town while I drank Rainier and struggled to find his conversation even remotely interesting.

Why had I thought I needed this? Why had I thought I could be attentive to another human being after having been interrogated by the police? Why a date and not the simplicity of an anonymous grope in the back of some dark bar?

And glancing over Erik's shoulder to where Mac sat alone at a table, I felt a weird need to go there and relax.

At least the guy knew what I was going through. Even if he was one of the people putting me through it. Was this how a person comes to welcome Stockholm Syndrome?

Mac pulled out his phone, texted something, and I felt a buzz in my pocket. Then another.

After the fourth alert, I finally excused myself to look.

Mac: *This guy seems nice.*

Mac: *Kinda boring, though.*

Mac: *You work in tech? You don't say . . .*

Mac: *I think he's going to regret ordering the mahi-mahi tacos.*

Struggling to suppress an unwanted smile, I typed: *Maybe you could come over and arrest me, and then we can both get out of here.*

Mac smiled when he got my text. Then, to my shock, he stood, walked over to our table, and said, "Drew! Wow, buddy, it's great to see you!"

I sat paralyzed for just one second before I stood and gave him a big, long-lost-friend hug. I meant it to be just for show, but when he wrapped his arms around me, I suddenly realized that this was what the child inside me wanted when I went searching online. I didn't want a date or dinner or even somebody down to fuck. I just wanted a hug.

Kinda pathetic, but that's what we monkeys are like. We get scared and need comfort even if it's wearing cop shoes.

Mac sat down uninvited, and without consulting Erik or me, directed the server to bring his duck prosciutto, chèvre, and fig pizza to our table.

Erik didn't last long once Mac started on a dull monologue of the least interesting aspects of island policing. He thanked me for my time, and I promised I'd text next time I was in town.

He left two of his three tacos uneaten on his plate.

Once Erik had gone, Mac said, "See? The mahi-mahi just didn't sound like a winner."

I laughed and finished my beer.

"I suppose being on duty means you can't have a drink," I remarked.

"Nah, it'll make it hard for me to keep tailing you."

"You really don't need to. I'm walking three blocks to my hotel room and spending the night in. Where are you going to be? Your truck?"

"I'm in an unmarked cop car," Mac said. "The seats recline pretty far."

"Now that's just ridiculous." I dismissed the idea with a wave of my hand. "Tell you what: I'm booked into a double room for tonight because it was the only one they had on short notice. Why don't we go to the convenience store, buy a six-pack, go back to my room, and watch something stupid together? You can even have the bed that's closest to the door, in case I try to creep out and murder somebody in the night. Unless you're scared of me. Then I guess you could sleep in your car."

"I don't think you're going to creep out and murder anybody." Mac sighed and folded his hands on the table. "All right, I'll come up. But you can't tell anybody I did this. I'm not even supposed to be talking to you."

"Fear not, I know how to keep my big gay mouth shut about who I've been in a hotel room with." I gave him a wink, which brought a little color to his cheeks.

Our walk to the hotel was mostly silent, punctuated with only perfunctory talk about who would pay for the beer. We got back to my room before ten.

I liked the Spencer Hotel because it reminded me of my first apartment—built around the turn of the century, heated by clanging radiators, and decorated in a shabby kind of hipster chic.

Mac sat down on the bed closest to the door, looking nervous, but also happy—like he'd been chosen by a television crew for a man-on-the-street interview.

"This hotel is my home away from home," I announced, spreading my arms out like I invented the place. "How do you like it?"

"It's nice. High ceilings."

"Right? I like to be able to stretch and not scrape my knuckles on the ceiling . . . or get whacked by some low-hanging fan."

We fell silent. The sludgy waves of awkwardness lapped at the shores of hospitality. What was I really doing here apart from wading into strange and murky waters? I needed to step back and think.

"I need a shower." I cracked a beer and handed it to Mac. "Please make yourself at home. Also feel free to search my overnight bag for any items you might need . . . or just to satisfy your curiosity. Whatever."

"I'm not going to search your bag, Drew."

"Just saying that mi casa es su casa."

With that, I took myself to the mostly hot shower. To be honest, I hadn't expected Mac to do something as inappropriate as agree to come to my hotel room. And now that he'd called my bluff and we both inhabited this neutral, rented space, I didn't really know what to do.

The way Mac vacillated between professional and those shy, private looks undid me in a way I found profoundly distressing. Mac was into me, certainly. Or was he setting me up? Or was he into me and setting me up? Or was he setting me up and not consciously acknowledging he was into me?

And above all, why had I invited him to my room?

I supposed I shouldn't have been so cavalier, but that's the story of my life. Low impulse control. I can't keep my mouth shut. I say something, make that joke, and then suddenly I'm bunking with the cop who's supposed to be following me.

I turned off the water and stepped out of the shower.

Mac had turned the TV on, but I couldn't tell to which channel.

I pulled on my boxers and paused before putting on my jeans. I hadn't planned to need loungewear as I'd either be sleeping alone or having sex—and in either case I'd be naked.

I decided the jeans would go back on, but I could leave the shirt behind. I emerged from the bathroom still toweling my hair dry.

Mac had removed his shoes and socks and left them by the door. He sat propped up against the headboard, legs straight and ankles crossed in front of him. If he meant for this to be sexy, I couldn't understand how.

I realized that maybe all my obsessing on whether or not Mac was attracted to me might actually be me finding my way to the terrifying knowledge that I wanted him. A lot.

I sat down on my own bed, and taking in the salient points of the on-screen cooking competition, remarked, "That guy's really in the weeds. Can't take the pressure."

"Yeah, I think he's gonna get cut." Mac glanced over at me, looked me over. "Good shower?"

"Yes and no. The pressure's lackluster, but the nozzle's high enough. Did you search my stuff yet?"

Mac sighed. "I told you I'm not searching you."

"Why not?"

"What do you mean why not?"

"Well," I said, "I watch a fair number of those forensics shows, and it seems like you should be rifling through my bags for evidence that would eliminate me as a suspect."

"I don't have to. I've already eliminated you."

"Then why are you following me?"

"My uncle hasn't cleared you." Mac turned off the TV. "Look, I know those clothes were planted at your place, but until the experts come back with their findings, my uncle won't rule you out."

"But what makes you sure they're not mine?"

"The shoes we recovered are too small. You've got feet like water skis," Mac said.

"Thanks for that."

"Well, you do, and the shoe impressions will confirm it," Mac said. "I volunteered to tail you because you don't seem to realize you're not safe."

"I'm definitely in danger of being wrongfully convicted by your uncle," I conceded.

"That's honestly the last thing you have to worry about." Mac spoke with more urgency than I'd heard from him before. "The real danger to you is that there's a murderer out there whose attention you've attracted. Probably with all the questions you keep asking. Once it becomes obvious they can't get rid of you by pinning Dorian's death on you, they may take more extreme measures. And it's not like they haven't already solved one problem with homicide. You could be in serious danger, Drew."

After the sting of Truth with a capital T wore off, I managed, "First a food critic, then an arbiter of men's fashion, now a bodyguard. You are truly a man of many dimensions, aren't you?"

"Everybody has a hidden side," Mac said.

"Like the side of you that secretly wants to get down with me?" I teased. Then, understanding the confirmation in Mac's complete silence, I continued, "'Cause that's not hidden."

"Well," Mac said slowly. "I'm not trying to hide it from you."

And this is why banter is not always a good idea. Nonetheless, I am not one to shirk. He'd met my challenge, and now I would have to escalate. Because I'm competitive. And because I wanted another hug.

I crossed the room, pulled the stiff orange curtains closed, then sat on the edge of Mac's bed.

"Have you ever kissed a guy?"

Mac let out a laugh. "I'm thirty years old."

It wasn't really an answer, but I leaned forward and laid one on him anyway. Gently. His lips parted slightly. I felt his hand on my thigh. I pulled back far enough to look him in the eye and said, "I only need to know one thing."

"What's that?"

"Your first name," I replied.

"Cormac," he said. "Cormac Patrick Mackenzie. You can stick with Mac, though."

"Okay, then, Mac." I swung my leg over to straddle his lap. "Wow me."

Mac stared unblinking at me for so long, I thought I'd made a grave error in judgment. But then he laced his fingers behind his head and said, "You're apparently the expert. Why don't you show me how it's done?" Mac's quick concession made me pause, but then he gave a challenging smile and added, "No pressure."

"Oh, it's on." My hands went immediately to his belt.

Mac lifted his hips as I pulled his pants and boxers, and then my own, down and off.

I stared at his half-hard dick with something approaching awe.

There was a long silence, and Mac didn't try to fill it, which was unusual enough to make me drag my eyes away from possibly the finest cock I'd seen outside of porn, to his face. His confidence was vying with something that looked like embarrassment or maybe uncertainty, which is a normal reaction to having your dick assessed by a comparative stranger. But with a cock like that, it made no sense at all. He should have been waving it at passersby. Still, something in his expression made me want to reassure him.

"Well, you're, um . . ." I cleared my throat. "You're definitely in proportion."

Mac blinked and blushed. He had lovely eyelashes. I hadn't noticed that till then. Or how nice his skin was. Or that his stomach looked like a laundry washboard.

"So . . ." I said, with an attempt at flirty roguishness, "are you going to let me suck it?"

Mac drew a visibly deep breath, and his cock jerked against his muscular thigh as it filled to full erection.

That'd be a yes, then. It certainly wasn't a no.

I leaned down and licked the silky tip of the now-swollen head. Mac groaned in disbelief. I pressed my mouth against the rigid length of his dick and smiled. The sense of control I felt was unbelievable.

"You still haven't said," I murmured against hot, taut velvet skin. "Do you want me to?"

"Are you kidding?" It sounded desperate. Outraged.

"No, Deputy, I am not." I blew on the wet stripe, scratched my fingernails through thick, dark pubic curls, and peered up at him with a try at polite interest.

But beneath the frustration I thought I saw . . . he looked lost, as if he didn't understand or enjoy the sleazy etiquette of casual encounters. I felt a melancholy hook land in my shriveled, jaded heart.

"Why don't you put your hands on my head," I said, "and just push down when you're ready to signal your complete consent."

His eyes widened. He looked about twelve years old. So I leaned down, took the head of his dick in my mouth, and began to suckle very gently. Tormenting him with it.

It didn't take long before I felt his hands in my hair, fingers opening and closing helplessly on my skull, but instead of trying to hold me in place, he cradled my head and let me set the pace. Which was really just as well, given the size of that dick. I don't know what I'd have done if he'd decided to go triple X on my face.

This could have been Erik, I thought randomly, but it wasn't, so . . . lucky me.

And then it escalated too fast. I was starving for release, too long without touching another body, never mind an attractive one.

In no time I was holding Mac's hips, jaw aching, as he tried not to fuck too far into my throat, and I was humping the puffy hotel comforter like a horny mutt. Mac kept saying my name, as if it added to his high. It certainly added to mine.

I love giving head. The smell and sound of it—the obscene sucking squelch, the panting and whimpering as I take someone else apart with my mouth.

Our stamina was frankly pathetic, but we came pretty much together, which is more or less the desired endgame, isn't it? It'd never happened to me before anyway, and it was crazy it happened now. I just knew that Mac felt and smelled and tasted perfect, and I shot like a fire hose.

I had needed it, and I think, probably he did too.

When I'd finally caught my breath, I rose, turned out the lights, and lurched into my own bed. I didn't look at Mac. Somehow I couldn't bear to see his reaction to what we'd done, now that the clammy chill of reality settled over my damp skin. If he didn't regret it now, he probably would once the sun came up.

But I couldn't help saying, "You can come to my side if you want. It's dry over here."

Mac said nothing, but a few seconds later I felt him slide into bed beside me. And just before I fell asleep, I felt him pull the crisp white comforter up over my bare shoulder.

Like some kind of romantic dork.

Chapter Nine

The next morning I had texts to reply to. I started with the one from Lionel, asking if he was supposed to come to work at five or if the bistro would be closed because I was in jail.

I glanced over at Mac, still asleep, arm draped across my abdomen. I considered waking him up and asking whether he thought I'd be taken in for questioning, then decided to err on the side of optimism. I told Lionel to report to work at five as per usual. Even if we didn't open, I wanted to tell him in person that we were considering selling the Eelgrass.

My second text came from Sam, apologizing for losing her shit and asking if I wanted to open the bistro for dinner. I told her that I did. After a few moments, Sam agreed. Then she informed me that Troy wanted to meet with us both at the restaurant at three to discuss a possible offer.

I'll see you there, I wrote. I hit the Send icon before I could rethink the decision.

I lay there for a few moments, feeling adrift. I ran my hand over Mac's arm, admiring its foreign solidity and wondering if I'd ever cook for him again. If the restaurant closed, would we ever see each other again? Naked or any other way?

My phone buzzed again, and a flurry of messages scrolled up my phone screen. All of them from Evelyn.

"Mac?" I patted his arm—very gently. He didn't rouse. Or even shift. "Mac!"

"What?" His eyes popped open, then seeing me perfectly fine, drooped closed. "What the hell?"

"There's been a break-in at the Beehive. A guy tried to choke Julie."

That got Mac's attention.

"Is she hurt?" Mac reached for his phone.

"I don't think so. Evelyn says it's not too bad."

"Do they have the perp?"

"No. Evelyn texted me to warn me that the sheriff was coming around looking for me because apparently I'm his favorite suspect for all crime on the island now." I leaned closer to try and get a look at Mac's texts. "Any official messages about that?"

"You don't have to worry about being charged with that." Mac shifted to prop himself against the headboard, where I couldn't see his screen.

"I don't?"

"Obviously not." Mac patted my shoulder but kept his eyes on his screen. "You have a really solid alibi."

"But do I really?" I had hoped not to broach the subject of whether or not Mac would have my back—at least not so early in the morning—but needs must . . .

Mac twisted his fingers through my hair and gently tilted my head toward him. If I were to deny a thrill went through me, would you believe me?

He looked me in the eye. "I know you were in a hotel in Seattle. Though I would prefer if we didn't go into great detail about it, for the sake of my professional reputation."

"Sure. But if we have to . . ."

Did I believe that Mac's sole concern about being revealed to have slept with me was police-integrity related? No. Not for a second. But I also didn't want to argue about it. Call me lazy.

"You have an alibi." Mac released his grip. "Did Evelyn say if anything was taken?"

"No, but I can ask." I started to tap out the question.

"No need. My cousin's already telling me about it. He wants me to verify your whereabouts, which I am doing right now," Mac stated firmly.

"So what actually happened?" I asked. Not only were Evelyn's texts uninformative, but their disjointed nature worried me. She was old and probably wasn't all that familiar with texting, but still . . .

"I can't tell you." Mac continued his laser-tight focus on his concealed phone screen.

"Oh, come on!"

"She's okay, all right?" Mac said. "But I can't tell you anything more, not before the sheriff has decided what information to release. That's for your own protection, Drew. So that you don't appear to have information that only the police and the perpetrator would have."

"Oh. Right."

"That said, I can't stop you from going straight to the source. I bet Evelyn would love to tell you all about it. She isn't the type to say so, but I think it would reassure her to have you visit her."

"I will do that." I tapped out a query and shot it out into the ether.

Evelyn didn't immediately reply, so I started my morning routine. When I emerged from the bath, I saw that Mac had already gone. But he left a note that read: Have to go talk with Seattle PD. Meet me on the ferry.

◆◆◆

The ride back to the island proved uneventful. We sat together, though once outside the hotel space, Mac reverted to his blandly friendly demeanor—his professional face.

It annoyed me more than I thought it would. But I couldn't stop myself from wanting to be near him, thirsty for his attention.

"What do you think the odds are of having a murder and an assault happen in the same week?" I asked.

"Good if they happened at the same place and time," Mac replied. "These were a few days apart. Still, the chances of them being related are better than average."

"Please, Mac, don't overstate it. I can't stand it when you're such a drama queen." Belatedly I noticed that more than a few of the ferry seats were occupied by familiar faces—not people I knew by name, but I'd seen them around town. I toned it down. "Are you going to go see Evelyn and Julie with me?"

"No, I'm going to the station before I pick up the investigation," Mac said. "What are your plans after that?"

"For the investigation? I'm not sure."

"Please be joking."

"I'm really not." I lowered my voice below the range of the gaggle of commuting snoops who surrounded us. "I need this thing solved, like, yesterday."

"I understand that. What you don't seem to get is that these things take time. And some crimes never get solved and you just have to live with that." Mac's deadpan delivery communicated more to me than mere words could. "A solution is not guaranteed, no matter how big a nuisance you make of yourself."

"That does nothing to reassure me that I'm not going to be wrongfully convicted, you realize," I informed Mac.

"I'm sorry I have to put it bluntly," Mac said, "but it's like you're not capable of perceiving that you're not a law-enforcement officer." Mac spoke without anger. More with incredulity at my arrogance. "Okay, let's say you do figure out who this murderer is. What do you think you're going to do?"

"Perform a citizen's arrest?"

"That's only for felonies committed in your presence. I'm assuming you weren't present for either of these felonies?"

"No." I felt a sulk coming on.

"Then you can't arrest anyone, okay? Just try to be patient. I'll find out more about it when we get back to the island."

"That won't help me, though, since you won't tell me about it."

"Just because I'm not telling you about it doesn't mean it's not ever going to help you," Mac said. "It just means you won't be in control of it, which is as it should be. You shouldn't be planning to confront a violent person. Ever."

"You can be surprisingly annoying," I said.

Mac shrugged as though his behavior was out of his hands.

The autumn morning was gray and foggy. Slate-gray seas and dove-gray sky. As we neared the shoreline, Camas Island seemed to coalesce into existence just in time for the ferry to dock. Deep-green conifers crowded the shoreline, punctuated by intermittent bursts of yellow leaves.

Finally, Mac broke the silence. "So from what Evelyn's texted you, what do you know?"

"Around three a.m., a man broke in and tried to smother Julie. Evelyn raised the alarm, and the guy escaped."

Mac nodded.

I continued, "My question is: why attack Julie? And even if you decided to do that, why would you think Evelyn would just lay there and watch you do it?"

Mac sighed. "Maybe the intruder didn't realize they'd be in the same bed. Neither of them is physically imposing. And in the dark it might be easy to miss that there are two old ladies instead of one."

Inspiration hit me like a flash.

"Which means we don't really know if Julie was the intended target. The guy could have been going for Evelyn, which makes more sense."

"How is that the next logical step?" Mac asked.

"Julie hardly ever leaves the Beehive, whereas Evelyn is always wandering around town, looking into people's windows and snooping. What if the murderer thinks Evelyn saw something on the night Dorian was killed? He'd think he needed to silence her. What—" I leaned closer to Mac. "What if she actually did see something?"

"If Evelyn had any information regarding this case, she'd have reported it," Mac said. "She may not be all that fond of the police department, but she's not the type to let anyone get away with murdering her family."

I had to agree with Mac on that point.

"So you really think the break-in and the murder aren't related?" I asked.

"I didn't say that," Mac replied. "I just don't believe that Evelyn would knowingly withhold information that could convict Dorian's killer."

"But unknowingly?" I suggested.

"Maybe," Mac allowed. "The reality is that it's too early

to be leaping to conclusions. At this point we still don't know why Dorian was killed. Was the murder motivated by jealousy? Rage? Greed?"

"Probably not greed," I said. "Dorian burned through his cash way too fast to have some big, hidden stash of money. As long as I've known him, he hadn't owned much more than an old Subaru Outback."

And the man-purse he dealt coke out of.

I paused, allowing myself to listen to my thoughts.

"Oh my God! His bag. I just realized. That thing was hardly ever out of his possession, but it wasn't downstairs with him when I found the body."

I pulled out my phone and went to Lionel's social-media feed. I scrolled back through dozens of new, virtually indistinguishable selfies until I came to the pictures Lionel had taken at the party that Thursday night. I spotted Dorian's bag sitting on the back bar next to the espresso machine.

"See? Here it is on Thursday night. But the bag definitely wasn't on the bar when I went in and discovered Lionel sleeping on the floor the next morning." I continued swiping through the photos until I spotted the bag again.

"Here! It's here!" My heartbeat picked up as I studied the picture and realized I recognized the man wearing Dorian's bag slung over his shoulder. "This is Sam's fuck-buddy . . . what the hell is his name? Danielle's brother . . ."

"Alfred Tomkins," Mac supplied.

When I turned to look at Mac, he pinned me with a vexed stare and said, "It's kind of amazing that you will break off a conversation with me to actively research a case I literally just told you to stop researching."

"I'm not just researching it." I wiggled my phone in front of him enticingly. "I'm solving it. This is your guy."

"You think Alfred Tomkins—the vegetarian surfer—killed Dorian to steal his bag?" Mac studied the picture with an unconvinced expression.

"There's nothing that prohibits a vegetarian from committing murder; just from eating the body," I responded. "And he's got Dorian's bag in this photo."

"And after he stole the bag, he broke into Evelyn and Julie's place . . . why?"

My triumph deflated, but I clung to the fact that I had discovered something fresh. Alfred Tomkins had stolen Dorian's bag. Though that didn't make him a murderer and it didn't give him a motive to accost Julie or Evelyn.

"What if the person who killed Dorian and the person who attacked Julie are different people? What if when Alfred stole Dorian's gear, he set off a chain reaction?"

"Hold on." Mac held up his hand like he was directing traffic and I was doing forty in a school zone. "Tell me exactly what you think was in the carryall."

"Cocaine," I said. "And probably MDMA. At least that's what was in it the last time I saw him open it up."

Mac raised his brows. "You saw it. Right. So Dorian was in possession of a carryall full of drugs at the time of his murder. It would have been helpful to have this information earlier." I could hear the edge of annoyance in his voice. "Certainly points to one strong motive for killing him."

"Right, except like you said, it wouldn't make sense for the person who had the bag to bother with a break-in." I pondered the problem. "Unless someone else had the same idea—to rob Dorian. Maybe they went to the Eelgrass and killed Dorian, but then they couldn't find his bag?"

"Because Alfred had already stolen it," Mac finished.

"And then when they heard that Dorian had gone to see Evelyn before he went to Eelgrass, they broke into her place, looking—"

"Wait!" Mac cut me off again. "Dorian visited Evelyn directly before he was murdered? How was I not informed of this?"

My blood ran cold. In my rush to impress Mac, I'd blabbed Evelyn's previous confidence.

"Evelyn just mentioned it offhand . . ." I trailed off.

I could see the flush of frustrated anger rise in Mac's face. He glared past the railing at the green-gray water. Slowly the tension drained from his expression. He took in a deep breath, then released it very slowly and turned back to me.

"Is there anything else you've been holding back from me?" Mac asked.

"I wasn't purposefully omitting information. I just didn't know you then."

"But you do now?" The direct challenge in Mac's voice surprised me, but I held my nerve.

"I know you're more than a pair of cop shoes."

"That is true." Mac's voice warmed fractionally. "So now that you've gotten to know me with my shoes off, you're going to tell me everything, right? Because you can understand how knowing that Dorian had been to see Evelyn might have given us a heads-up. It might have helped us prevent the assault on Julie."

I hadn't thought of that, but hearing Mac say it, I realized why he'd been so angry.

"Yeah, I do now," I admitted. I hoped Evelyn would see it the same way.

I spent the remainder of the ferry ride detailing all I could remember of my conversation with her about Dorian. After the ferry docked, Mac didn't offer me a ride. I hadn't expected him to, since I had my own car, but still felt disappointed anyway.

Because I'm an idiot.

Chapter Ten

For the first time since I'd stepped off this ferry two years earlier, I considered the nature of Camas Island. It had both real and conceptual borders and barriers. There were less than seven thousand residents on the whole rock, and Orca's Slough was home to half of them.

In this kind of close environment, people couldn't hide nearly as much from each other. Everyone knew everyone else's business—or thought they did. Gossip and grudges couldn't dissipate across vast distances. But people could also be close, in the best way. Nowhere else would I have found myself hanging out daily with an oldster like Evelyn and a kid like Lionel like some kind of three-generation advertisement for family of choice.

I needed to see Evelyn and Julie, if only to apologize for being off in Seattle the one night they needed help. And for taking the only trustworthy cop on the island with me.

When I stepped into Evelyn and Julie's room at the Beehive, the first thing I saw was a large cardboard square covering the hole in the room's one window. Autumn cold seeped around the makeshift patch. Next I laid eyes on Julie's battered face, and immediately and without reservation wanted to murder whoever did that to such a small, frail old woman. I couldn't stop myself from looking down at Evelyn's hands. Two of her nails were torn, and her knuckles were red and swollen.

"I'd say you should see the other guy, but I barely scratched him," Evelyn said glumly.

"You did your best. You're just not the bruiser you once were." Julie's voice was slurred.

"Did he give you a concussion?" I knelt down beside Julie's overstuffed red armchair.

"No." Julie's exasperation with my question was obvious. "And I'm not having a stroke either. I sound funny because my lip is split. That's all."

"You really didn't see him at all?" I asked.

Evelyn patted my shoulder. "Drew, we can barely read the subtitles on the television, and it's sixty-five inches."

"I think this has to do with the murder," Julie said in a stage whisper.

The fact that the assailant hadn't knocked the theatricality out of her comforted me. And made me want to cry, and to strangle the guy who had hurt them. I hadn't expected to be such a mess. I had to pull myself together.

"I agree," I managed to say.

We both looked at Evelyn, who sighed.

"Yeah, that's what the Five-O said when he phoned and gave me business for not telling him that Dorian had visited me." Evelyn sighed again and then gave me a sidelong look. "I think I need you to give me a ride to the bank."

"What for?"

"On that day, Dorian asked to put some things in my safe-deposit box. Most of it was just junk he'd picked up and a couple photos of his grandma's. But he had a sealed envelope too. It's probably time I looked inside it," Evelyn said.

Julie nodded in vigorous agreement.

"Wait . . . what? You didn't tell this to Mac when he called just now?" I demanded.

"Look, this morning the sheriff trotted in here and started squealing at me about how I brought this on myself and how Dorian deserved what he got." Evelyn glared at the empty doorway as if she could still see the sheriff standing there.

"We're not used to having a friendly relationship with Sheriff Mackenzie," Julie explained. "And that envelope could contain absolutely anything."

"Dorian trusted me with it. I can't just hand it over to some pig before I know what's in it." Evelyn gazed down at her bruised hands. "Dorian had his faults, I know. But I can still remember what a sweet little boy he was. He used to make me laugh. And when he got older and realized about me and Julie, he didn't care. He was the only member of my family who didn't care."

I nearly responded that Dorian's open-mindedness probably resulted from having literally no morals, but stopped myself. Of course they cared about the one person who seemed to accept them as they were. And who knew? Maybe he had. What did I know about it?

Nothing. Nothing at all.

"I can give you a ride to the bank, but . . . what about this?" I gestured at the broken window. "Why isn't there someone here fixing it?"

"The handyman's on the other side of the island at the other facility. He says he can be here tomorrow." Evelyn crossed her arms over her chest.

"So what? They expect you to just stay here in this freezing, broken-into room overnight? What if the assailant comes back? What if you get fucking hypothermia?"

"We've got electric blankets," Evelyn said.

"And we can snuggle close." Julie threw Evelyn the sort of playful, blatantly sexual look I was not used to seeing outside of a black-and-white movie. Though charming, it was not convincing.

"That's just not good enough. Who's in charge here? Katie the kitchen cop? They could at least put up some plywood instead of this." I flicked the cardboard with my finger.

"Don't be mean, Drew. Katie does her best," Julie said.

"Who is Katie's boss, then?" I pulled out my phone and started to search the Beehive's website.

"Drew, don't cause trouble," Evelyn said. Then Julie laid a hand on her arm.

"Go on. Let him. I like this new butch persona he's trying on," she said.

"I'm not trying on a new persona!" I returned to my regular tone. "I just don't want anybody to think they can push you around."

"Anymore," Evelyn added.

Never again, I promised them silently.

For the next forty-five minutes I harassed the management until they finally agreed to let me hire a handyman myself in Orca's Slough. Then I spent another hour finding a handyman willing to be hired by me on short notice, in the rain.

His name was Cliff, and his fee drained what was left of my savings, but by three that afternoon, the broken window at the Beehive had been secured and Julie was resting beneath an electric blanket cranked all the way up to nine.

With the arrangements around the window, I hadn't had time to worry about Mac. Now I wondered if I should tell him I was taking Evelyn to the bank. I decided that although I should, I wouldn't. The envelope could contain anything or nothing, and it was Evelyn's call whether we would, in her words, "involve the law."

The safe vault at the Orca's Slough branch of the Island Federal Bank was small, well lit, and exactly like every other bank vault I'd ever seen. After we retrieved the box, the bank manager escorted us to a private room. I looked away as Evelyn opened the box, feeling that the contents were none of my business. But then Evelyn just upended the thing, spilling out a dozen or more old photos as well as numerous corroded antique coins. A piece of tarnished silver skidded across the table and fell to the floor, and I snatched it up. It turned out to be a battered and dirty cuff link that looked like it had been buried for years.

"Dorian was always hoping he'd uncover some piece of treasure," Evelyn commented. "When he was a little boy, I used to tease him for being such a magpie. He'd grab anything shiny."

I remembered Alfred lamenting his lost lighter and nodded.

The collection of photos looked similar to the one Dorian had intended to give to Mac. The Lindgren twins peered at me from most of them, no longer boys but now men. I recognized Troy by his dress shirts and suits. Charlie, who'd drowned before I even came to town, seemed tired and worn down despite his crisp white chef's coat.

"Why would Dorian have so many pictures of Troy and Charlie?" I wondered aloud.

"Those would have been his grandmother's. She was a Lindgren before she joined our family." Evelyn picked up a photo and considered the group of people gathered around a boat. Then she tossed the photo down. "She never once spoke to me."

Evelyn fished a white business envelope from the pile.

"Here is what we came for." Evelyn tore the sealed flap open and pulled out a yellow piece of paper. I recognized it at once as a produce invoice, the kind that pulls out of a three-part carbonless copy. It detailed the contents of a vegetable delivery that had been received a couple of days before Dorian was killed. "Recognize this?"

I nodded. "Sam tore up the whole office looking for this the other night. What's written on the back?"

"Don't know. Didn't bring my glasses." Evelyn handed it over to me. The writing was neat, feminine, and definitely not Dorian's jittery script.

"For and in consideration of the three-hundred dollars," I began to read aloud, "the receipt of which is hereby acknowledged, Samantha Eider does hereby sell and convey to Dorian Gamble all the assets, property rights, and interests of the Eelgrass Bistro—" I stopped speaking and skimmed to the end. "It's a bill of sale."

Evelyn's eyebrows shot up. "Is it signed?"

"Yes, by Sam and Dorian and witnessed by Lionel and some other guy I've never heard of—Adam Vukoja. So I guess . . . Sam had a reason to kill Dorian after all." At first my shock was so complete, I couldn't feel anything. I expected rage—hurt—but all I felt was a deep paroxysm of contempt curling like an anaconda through my guts. She had sold out. And for what amounted to pocket change. That couldn't be right, could it?

"Vukoja's one of Dorian's coworkers from his other line of business." Evelyn's disapproving expression spoke volumes. "Some Croatian person from Portland. Dorian's main supplier, I think. Do you think Sam was, you know, too high to remember?"

"The handwriting looks like she's sober. And why would she have been looking for a paper she couldn't remember? Once we get out of here, I'll call Lionel and ask him if he remembers signing this." As I glanced at my phone, I saw a text from Sam telling me I was half an hour late for our meeting with Troy.

"Damn it," I muttered.

It's not like me to forget a major commitment—even one I didn't want to meet. But since the murder, it was like my mind had come unwound and with it my ability to prioritize had gone. But when your life is all just pissing on one dumpster fire after another, that's what happens.

"Bad news?" Evelyn said.

"I forgot about an appointment. Sam and Troy are waiting for me at the restaurant. Sam was arranging for us to sell Eelgrass—"

"What?" Surprise bordering on loss showed in Evelyn's face. "Why would you do that now?"

"I don't want to," I said hastily. "And with this receipt, I'm not even sure that she can. But it's obvious that I need to talk to Sam and straighten this whole thing out."

"Seems pretty clear what she's doing: selling up. Twice. Doubling her money," Evelyn said.

"For three hundred bucks?" I shook my head. "Her share of Eelgrass is worth way more than that." I didn't want to speak ill of Dorian to Evelyn, knowing that she cared for him, but I was pretty certain of how this bill of sale came about.

"You know, this Vukoja guy may have coerced Sam into signing this." I turned to see Evelyn gazing at me with blatant skepticism. She probably realized Dorian would have had to be in on it as well. Neither of us wanted to say as much, though. I could see Evelyn weighing the possibility of just locking the receipt away again.

"You need to take this to the police," I told her. "It could be a big part of why someone—maybe Mr. Vukoja—murdered Dorian."

"On the way over here you said you thought he was killed for his supply," Evelyn said, but I could tell she wasn't putting up a real argument. She just didn't want the sheriff to be right about Dorian playing a part in his own murder.

"Maybe Vukoja wanted both, and Dorian refused to give him what he wanted," I said. "The thing is that if Vukoja did play any part in Dorian's murder, then this receipt is the only physical evidence pointing to his involvement. Mac needs to know about it. If he doesn't, then how is he gonna have any chance of getting justice for Dorian?"

"You think any of them in that flatfoot family care about Dorian?"

"I think Mac cares about justice and the law. And I think he cares about you, Evelyn."

"Yeah . . . maybe." Evelyn absently poked at the cuff link I'd picked up earlier.

"I tell you what. I'll text Mac directly to say you're bringing something important to him. I could ask him to meet you outside, or better yet, I'll ask him to come here and meet with you. That way you won't have to go to the police station or even look at Sheriff Mackenzie."

I held out the receipt and Evelyn took it, but she didn't look happy.

"You'll call him?" Evelyn asked. "Just him?"

"Yes. Just Mac."

"Okay, then," Evelyn decided. "Go on and phone the fuzz."

I pulled out my phone and nearly dropped it when it buzzed in my hand. Mac's now very familiar number flashed up as my ringtone of "Hey Good Lookin'" wondered what I had cookin'.

"Hey," I answered. "I was literally just about to call you."

I wasn't sure if the brief silence that followed was alarmed or dismayed, but I quickly realized the last thing Mac probably wanted was me calling him at work after we'd . . . gone on a date? Or was it a one-night stand? I didn't want it to be, but at the same time . . .

"I don't mean calling you personally," I said quickly. "I mean I was about to call the police, and you're the only one I know and also the only one Evelyn likes—"

"Mr. Allison, we'd like you to come in to the police station at your very soonest convenience. In fact, if you give me your present location, I can come and pick you up." Mac's formality made me feel certain that either his uncle or his cousin—maybe both—were listening to him.

"I'm with Evelyn at the bank. Why do you want me at the police station?" I had a terrible feeling I knew why.

"We have a few questions we're hoping you could answer. Routine questions."

"Routine questions that I can't answer now over the phone?"

Mac was silent for so long that I thought maybe we'd been disconnected. Then he whispered, "A witness is claiming he saw you break into the Beehive."

"What witness?"

"I'm not allowed to say," Mac replied. "And please don't go around town trying to hunt him down because—"

"I thought I had an alibi!" My voice echoed through the room.

"You do, but this is a very credible witness—"

"More credible than my alibi of being pinned naked next to you all night in Seattle?" I demanded.

Evelyn raised her brows at me.

"Look, Drew, you aren't being arrested." Mac sounded like he was trying to calm a rabid dog with soft tones and meaningless words. "But I would really like you to come in, for your own safety, if nothing else."

"But I'm not under arrest."

"No . . ."

The way his voice trailed off did not fill me with assurance. How shoddy of an alibi had he given me?

"Well, I was going to feel kind of shitty about not telling you what I was doing here at the bank with Evelyn, but now I hope it really pisses you off," I announced.

"What? Why would it—"

"We just opened up her safety-deposit box. It seems we forgot to tell you that the last time Dorian visited her, he asked her to put some things of his away."

"Forgot?" Mac muttered something else under his breath. "So you thought that instead of telling me, you needed to take it upon yourself to go check it out?"

"I would have hated to waste police time," I snapped. Next to me, Evelyn chuckled.

"You know, it's for the police to decide whether our time is being wasted—" He cut himself off, and I heard his cousin's drowsy voice mumble something. Mac assured him that he had everything under control. His voice was again formal and clipped when he spoke to me. "So you believe you may have discovered something important?"

"Yes, and Evelyn is willing to share it with you. But she won't talk to the sheriff and she's not stepping foot in the police station."

"All right." Mac sounded resigned. "I will be there in a few minutes. We'll work this out—"

I hung up without telling him I wouldn't be there when he arrived.

◆◆◆

I paused outside the bank to call Lionel and confirm that he had been the one to sign the bill of sale.

"Yeah, chief, I did sign something. I didn't read it, though. Am I in trouble?" he asked.

"No, not at all. I just wanted to know—was Sam sober when she signed it?"

"Oh yeah. Dead sober. And crying. I got out of there as fast as I could, for real," Lionel said. "Anyway, I'll see you at five, right?"

"Right." Even to me, my voice sounded strange.

"Do I still have a job?" His plaintive tone jabbed me right in the heart. "You haven't been arrested again, have you?"

"I haven't been arrested at all, and yes, you still have a job," I replied firmly. Who knew how long I'd retain my liberty or if Lionel would be working for me after today, but I tried to reassure myself that Troy wanted to keep the restaurant going. Neither Lionel nor the rest of the staff would lose their jobs. "I'll see you later," I said and disconnected.

When I came within sight of the Eelgrass, I stopped walking and took several breaths till my heart stopped racing. Better to go into the situation late but calm, than to race in shouting angry accusations in front of Troy.

I decided to let myself in the back door and walk through my kitchen, like I normally would have done. There was something relieving about the familiarity of stepping into the dark, quiet back room. It was my ritual moment of calm before I faced the challenges of a day filled with rush orders, sharp objects, and grease burns.

Through the dim shadows of the kitchen I saw Sam standing in the dining room. I guessed the dapper suit with his back to me was Troy.

They'd gone ahead and started arguing without me.

"I cannot take this!" Sam's shout echoed around the dining room. "I know you're trying to help me out. And I know I screwed everything up, but the place is worth more than that."

"I'm sorry, but I don't have that kind of money just lying around." Troy's lugubrious whine rolled back toward me with so much force that I practically had to sidestep it.

Sam crossed her arms over her chest and curled down as if in agony.

"Drew's not going to accept less than twenty thousand," she said. "That's what he put into this place. He deserves to get his money back."

"I can't pay what I don't have," Troy responded. "If you're worried about Drew, then maybe you could sell your half for less."

I'll admit, I was torn. After so long, it felt good to hear Sam arguing in my defense. But only a dick would have allowed her to accept less than a fair deal for her half of Eelgrass. Not after she'd already been intimidated into signing it over for a pittance once.

So I took that opportunity to flip on the kitchen lights and crank the radio. Sam jumped, and Troy spun around to glower at me.

I strolled up to them and then walked behind the bar toward the espresso machine.

"Hey, guys, sorry I'm late. The ferry was delayed."

"What ferry? Where did you go?" Sam's surprise turned to bewilderment.

"Seattle," I said. "I had a date. Do either of you want a coffee? I need about twenty shots, I think."

"I'm fine." Sam seated herself at the bar.

Troy took a seat next to Sam's. "I'll take a quad half-caff low-fat tall latte with extra foam."

It took all my strength of will, but I smiled instead of rolling my eyes.

"Sure." We didn't have decaf, but he'd be long gone by the time he realized that. "So you're no longer interested in entering our noble industry, Troy? I can't say I blame you."

"It's not that I'm not interested; I'm just not made of money. I don't know why you and Sam can't seem to understand that." Troy raked his fingers through his hair so dramatically that I could vividly imagine him spending hours perfecting the move in front of a mirror. "We all know this place isn't going to make me anything. When Charlie had a restaurant here, it was a complete failure, and now nobody's coming to this place either."

"Well, that's partially due to the fact that it hasn't been open." I shot Sam a meaningful glance, then returned to assembling Troy's ridiculous beverage. "But also it's not the tourist season. Your store hasn't exactly been rocking the customers. No business on the island is booming this time of year. But to my thinking, that would make this the perfect time for you to learn the ropes."

"What ropes?"

"Learning the recipes, for one thing. Or did you plan to hire a different chef?" As the espresso shots poured out, I pondered the correct vessel in which to build Troy's monstrous latte. I settled on a paper to-go model. That way he could have a mountain of foam and I could get rid of him without giving up one of my cups . . . at least while they were still mine.

"Well, I wasn't planning on using any of your recipes, Andrew." Troy pulled a wry smile at the notion. "If I do buy the business and building from you, I'll probably reopen it as something more commercial. Orca's Slough needs a place like a chain but better. A great burger and a fancy cocktail. The people in this town can't appreciate real cuisine. I told Charlie as much, years ago."

"Poor Charlie." Sam nodded and wrapped her arms around herself tighter as if feeling the chill of her cousin's ghost passing over her.

"I've found that the people here are generally excited about quality food that's prepared with real skill and care." I handed Troy his drink without touching his hand and then tamped down the grounds for my own shot of espresso. "And it's not like I don't have a great burger on the menu."

"Listen, I understand the position you two are in." Troy sipped his drink, and I wondered how he could possibly think we would believe he understood our situation.

"You're obviously not going to last now that this horrible crime has occurred. No one is going to buy this business off you lock, stock, and barrel either, not with it sinking further and further into debt every day."

"Maybe it would be better to just tear this whole place down," Sam muttered.

"It's a historic building. We're not allowed to tear it down," I reminded her. "And we're not sinking further and further into debt. We've been closed, but when we did open, the customers came."

"That's true." Sam's expression lightened a little. She offered a warm smile to Troy, which I didn't feel he deserved. "We made good money. Drew's recipes are popular—"

"Maybe before he was dragged away by the police, but now . . ." Troy trailed off.

"Oh, right." Sam's expression sank further.

I kept my face turned away, focusing on the shiny espresso machine. I wondered if this had always been Troy's angle with other people. Feign interest in their well-being, using a front of concern, while constantly shooting down their every word.

What did Troy really plan to do with this space? He had no discernable interest in feeding the people of Orca's Slough. An expansion for his clothing store maybe? The building alone was worth a cool two million. Never mind the business.

"Thirty thousand," Troy said.

"Each?" Sam sounded painfully hopeful.

"Thirty total. That's all I can offer. Take it or leave it." Troy waved a dismissive hand.

"Then we're going to have to leave it." The words were out of my mouth before I even knew I was going to say them.

But I'd had enough. I turned to Sam, whose face showed a weird mix of alarm and amazement.

"Sam, things are rough right now, but we don't have to put up with your asshole cousin jerking us around." I glanced back to Troy, watching as his bland expression turned fully hateful. I drank it in, happy to have spited him. "No offence, Troy, but you're a fucking idiot if you think you can pressure me into jumping at some lowball offer."

"You won't find anyone in this town who'll give you better," Troy thundered, his true inner bully finally showing himself.

"Even if that were true—and I don't think for a second that it is—I'd rather let the bank seize this place and everything in it to sell at auction rather than sign it over to you. Now take your coffee and fuck off. I need to speak with Sam privately."

Troy's face went from red to purple. He picked up his coffee, and pointedly ignoring me, turned to Sam.

"You know I'm being incredibly generous offering you anything, Samantha." He pretended to straighten his cuffs and then turned and huffed across the empty dining room. With a sense of satisfaction, I watched the front door fall closed behind him.

It was then that the oddness of Troy's words struck me. Why would he feel that offering Sam any money for her share of the business was an act of generosity? Unless... Could he know Sam didn't actually own her share anymore?

I turned back to Sam, who just sank her head down to the bar in tears. And no wonder. With family like that, of course she wanted off the island. Had Troy been treating her like this her entire life?

"Come on, Sam, it's not as bad as that," I coaxed. "Yes, we are in a fucked-up situation right now, but we're not beaten. Eelgrass is still getting customers, right? We did amazing business Sunday. We'll be able to survive until a deal comes along that's worth taking."

"I just don't see how this can be fixed." She lifted her head, and I saw that her face was pale and streaked with red. Her eyes bloodshot. "I can't sleep. I can't eat. I've wrecked everything."

Did I agree with her? Mostly. But telling her that wouldn't do either of us any good. I took her hand.

"Sam, no one person can wreck everything. It takes a whole team to wreck a team."

"Oh yeah? What did you do to contribute to this disaster?" She waved her hand around the spotless dining room as though it were filled with the carnage of some massive battle, which is probably how she saw it in her mind.

"I could have tried to talk to you instead of just checking out." I said it offhandedly, but listening to my own words, I knew the truth in them. "I never even attempted to confront you about what was going on here, even though it enraged me. I was too passive."

"Nothing you said could have made me stop," Sam said.

"Maybe not, but at least I could have tried. I could have stepped up and stopped the business from becoming the main venue for Dorian's coke-dealing operation."

We were both silent for a few minutes after that. Thinking of Dorian made me angry and frustrated. Even dead, he was still causing people pain. Then I remembered the fondness in Evelyn's voice when she'd described Dorian as a child. I remembered how Julie had smiled because he had accepted her. It was strange how the impression left by a single person could be so fractured—bouncing between the twin poles of good and evil at the speed of light.

"I wish I could go back to the day I hired Dorian and stop myself." Sam turned toward the kitchen. "I don't think I can ever go into that cellar again. I don't see how you can be here alone."

"I'm not afraid of ghosts, I guess." I shrugged and took a drink of bitter espresso. "Listen, I know you signed over your part of the bistro to Dorian."

Sam froze, seemingly afraid to even look at me. "How do you know that?"

"I found the bill of sale. That lettuce invoice you couldn't find. Evelyn had it."

"I didn't want to do that, but I owed Dorian money. Then his friend came, and he—he's terrifying, Drew."

"Vukoja?" I asked.

Sam nodded. "They went away and talked and came back and said they wanted part of the business. I didn't want to be involved, so I just signed my part over so I could leave."

I nodded and thought it over.

"Whose idea was it to steal Dorian's stash?" I asked after another bracing drink of espresso. "Yours or Alfred's?"

"Freddy's. I was supposed to leave the island with him the next morning. We were going to sell the coke and use the money to go live in Bali. Just get away from everything we grew up with here on the island. But then . . . everything happened. I got stuck here. Freddy left without me. I haven't heard from him, and he isn't answering any of my texts."

"You don't think he . . ." I let the question hang as Sam nodded.

"Yeah, I think he must have killed Dorian. Not on purpose, but everyone was really drunk. Lionel had passed out, and Dorian had wandered down into the cellar to dig around for more junk like he always did."

"Okay." That directly contradicted her previous statements to everyone. "What then?"

"Freddy went to get his lighter back from Dorian while I tried to wake Lionel up. But it was so late, I figured I should just let him sleep. I knew you'd be coming in soon and you'd take care of Lionel." She dragged her hand across her eyes, wiping away tears. "Then Freddy came back up in a rush. He said Dorian must have already taken off because he couldn't find him down there . . . I didn't know until after

I was talking to the cops, figured out they must have gotten into a fight. Freddy was so mad at him . . ."

"Just over a lighter?" I asked, but of course it wasn't just a lighter. It would've probably been a lot of other small slights and frustrations that had built up over the years.

Hadn't that been how Julie had described Orca's Slough: a cauldron of resentments and secrets roiling like magma beneath the calm surface?

"The stupid thing is he didn't even take his dumb Zippo in the end." Sam stared past me at the bottles of infused vodkas Dorian had concocted. "God, why am I always so stupid about people? That Vukoja guy is probably going to come after me for Dorian's stash and my half of the restaurant now."

"If he tries, we'll call the cops on him," I said.

It gave me a feeling of bitter satisfaction to realize I'd been right, back on the ferry. Vukoja must have been the one who broke into the Beehive. He'd probably been after the bill of sale. Maybe he'd thought he could get it signed over to him? Maybe he'd forced Dorian to sign a will and then belatedly found out that Evelyn had too?

"That's what Troy said. He thought that if I sold to him, he'd be in a better legal position to fight Vukoja's claim. But then I guess he took a big loss in the stocks and couldn't afford to buy us out . . ." She shook her head, exposing remnants of red in her purple-streaked hair. "It feels like I'm cursed, like everyone I get close to just falls apart or goes crazy or gets killed or. . . or leaves me. You're the only one who's stuck it out with me. I'm sorry I've been such a shitty friend, Drew."

"It's okay." I said it out of reflex, but her apology did seem to wash away a lot of my resentment. "And I'm not sure who made you think that everything was your fault, Sam. But you aren't to blame for all of this. You definitely aren't responsible for Dorian's murder."

"I don't know," Sam said quietly. "I feel like he's haunting me. Like he knows he'd still be alive if I hadn't agreed to try and steal his stash. And he probably would be."

"No one is responsible for his death except the guy who killed him."

"Yeah, but Freddy's gone and that just leaves you and me here with Dorian's ghost," she said.

"I don't believe in ghosts," I said. Sam's gaze faltered. She didn't share my skepticism. "But if this is going to be a problem, then we can have the basement exorcized or cleansed or whatever you do to evict ghosts."

"I probably just need to tell him I'm sorry," Sam said. "And that I hope he can move on."

For a moment I wondered what Mac would think of all this.

I had to call him and tell him everything Sam had said to me, but I really didn't want to talk to him right now. Then again, if I could hand him the solution to Dorian's murder, well, I probably wouldn't have to talk to him or any other member of his family again.

"Sam, I need to make a call. But I'll come back here after, okay? We need a real plan if we're going to get this place running again."

◆◆◆

Outside, the crisp autumn air felt bitingly cold. I was about to call Mac, but then stopped myself. If I called him directly, there would be a record of me contacting him. I wasn't certain that would be a good thing, especially with me having not come to the station as he'd requested. Plus, I was still mad.

I texted Evelyn instead:

Is Big Mac still with you right now?

Yes, she wrote; then another text popped up from her: *He's sorting through Dorian's collection. I told him it's all sentimental junk, but I guess he needs to feel useful.*

A third text bubble: *He wants to know if you're texting me right now. I told him he can't see my phone without a warrant.*

I laughed: *Tell him Samantha admitted that right before they left, Alfred went down into the basement after Dorian to get his lighter. He claimed Dorian wasn't down there, but Sam's pretty sure Alfred and Dorian fought and that Alfred killed Dorian.*

There was a long pause, then the response: *Okay, I'll tell him.*

A few seconds later a text from Mac popped up: *WHERE ARE YOU?*

It was petty, I know, but I didn't answer him. Instead I deleted his message and texted Evelyn: *Tell him I'm at Eelgrass, but we aren't open for business today. Sam and I have a lot to work out before we open up again.*

Evelyn: *You're not selling?* A series of smile emojis and fireworks flashed up on my screen.

Me: *Nope. You're not getting rid of me that easy. I'll come by the Beehive later. If Katie will let me in.*

Just as I pressed Send, Mac started blowing up my phone:

WE

NEED

TO

TALK

I deleted each single word bubble as it arrived. It gave me a childish pleasure, and maybe in some corner of my heart it did me good to know he was annoyed enough for all caps:

I KNOW YOURMAD ATME BUTYOUAREIN REALDANGER.YOU ARE NT A SUSPECT ANYMORE

My finger hovered over the reply arrow. Before I could inform him that I was perfectly fine and just hashing out things with Sam, another message from Mac popped up:

IM SERIOUS DREW DONTBE A FOOL

Deleting a text never felt so good.

My ringtone sounded, and Mac's number appeared on my screen. I declined the call, turned off my phone, and strode back into my restaurant with a renewed sense of purpose.

Inside, Sam had dimmed the dining-room lights and turned the music to the ChillWave station we both found relaxing. I peered around but couldn't pick her figure out of the gloom.

"Sam?" I called over the hazy melody drifting from the sound system.

"I'm down here." Sam's voice rose from the basement.

"What are you doing down there?" I tried not to sound alarmed. But what the hell was she doing in the basement? I peered down and saw the beam of a flashlight sweep up toward me. Sam stepped closer to the dry-goods shelf. The small overhead light made her hair look glossy as a raven's wing.

"I'm telling Dorian I'm sorry," Sam announced as if it were obvious. "I won't take long."

As much as I didn't want to descend into the basement, I recognized that Sam was genuinely trying to face not only her fear, but her past actions. I made myself walk down the concrete steps and pace into the deep, musty gloom to stand beside her.

Sam moved the beam of the flashlight across the cracked cement floor, revealing several scuff marks and a crumpled wad of police tape.

"Where was he found?" Sam whispered.

"Over to the right and farther back." I lowered my voice as well despite knowing that Dorian's immortal spirit wasn't lingering around our old cellar. He'd much prefer to haunt the liquor cabinet of some adventurous divorcee.

Sam linked her arm with mine and edged slowly farther into the darkness. I moved with her. Her hands shook. The white beam of the flashlight trembled as it exposed a dark bloodstain. A blue latex glove lay a few inches away.

A disturbing chill rolled out from the pitch-black depths ahead of us. It carried a humid, dank smell that instantly roused the thought of moldering old corpses. Realistically, I knew it was just the ghost of kimchee gone wrong.

Sam's fingers dug into my arm.

"Dorian," Sam whispered, "if you're here, I want you to know I'm sorry. I never wanted anything like that to happen to you, no matter what I ever said. I'm so sorry I didn't pay you the money I owed you and that I let Troy and Charlie call you white trash. I'm sorry I said your mom was a crack whore. And I'm sorry I left you here on the island when I ran off to Seattle." Her voice caught, and she shuddered.

I'd known she had grown up here and that she had some kind of history with Dorian, but until now it hadn't truly struck me that the two of them had shared so much of their childhood. No wonder Sam was such a mess.

I squeezed her shoulder, and she leaned against me.

"I guess that while we're clearing the air, Dorian," I addressed the darkness, "I might as well tell you that your yuzu-infused vodka was actually really good. And your black-walnut bitters were amazing."

"They were, weren't they?" Sam's voice lifted. "That charcoal-flavored ice-cream was terrible, though." She gave a laugh that sounded a little like a sob.

"Don't forget the gluten-free, salmon-infused Sea Breeze," I reminded her. This time Sam laughed out loud.

"You know, half the time he was just trying to impress you, Drew. You were the classiest person he'd ever met, and you didn't even have to try."

I took a moment to let the idea of that sink in. Part of me didn't want to think warmly of Dorian—not now when he was dead and it was too late for us to ever be friends. But at the same time it seemed pointless and petty to keep holding on to the idea of him as some one-dimensional dude. I might not have liked the side of him that I knew, but obviously I hadn't known all aspects of him.

"I'm sorry you're gone, Dorian," I said.

Sam hugged me, and I returned her embrace. The stale scent in the air seemed to lift, and I could have sworn a warm breeze wrapped around us.

"Did you feel that?" Sam whispered.

"I . . . did."

"I think Dorian's okay. I think he's moved on."

I nodded, but there was something about the heat and hint of air freshener that made me think this breeze had more to do with a draft blowing through the basement than it did with the gates of paradise opening up to admit our skanky, deceased bartender.

"We should go upstairs—" I began, but then a faint grating noise sounded from far back in the rough wall of the basement. Sam and I both jumped.

"Probably mice," Sam said.

Or rats, I thought, but mice sounded cuter.

Then a very metallic noise rose up and was followed by an earthy scrape. Shhhhick. Thup. Shhhhck. Thup. Over and over. Digging?

Sam's body went rigid.

"Oh no," Sam whispered. She pulled away from me and started after the noise.

"Wait, Sam, where are you going?"

Darkness closed in around me. I stumbled after her and the bouncing beam of her flashlight. The concrete floor broke off into packed dirt, and I nearly fell.

"I think Freddy has come back for the safe." Sam stilled for a moment as she shone her light on a rough section of the rocky basement wall. Shards of Lionel's kimchee crock littered the ground at her feet. Sam looked frantic as she scanned the random pieces of basalt protruding from the sandstone wall.

"What safe?"

"Uncle Bill's safe. Dorian thought it was buried in the floor, but it's actually back in the bootleggers' tunnel that Charlie and Troy's dad cleared out to connect his two properties. Like a fucking idiot, I told Freddy about it. Damn it, where is—"

More glints of jagged ceramics caught my attention. How probable was it that Lionel's crock had cracked apart on exactly the day Dorian was murdered? What if instead, someone using this tunnel had knocked it over and broken it while making a fast escape?

Suddenly Sam reached out and shoved her shoulder against one of the basalt stones. It sank back into the wall. What had appeared to be an outcropping of sandstone swung inward, revealing a narrow black seam. Warm, perfumed air gushed from the opening. I recognized the fragrance now. The swank "room cologne" that perfumed Troy's shop.

The digging noise grew louder.

Sam shoved the false stonework farther open.

"Sam, I really don't think we should go in after—"

"I let that fucker kill Dorian. I won't let him rob the family too!" Samantha darted through the crack. Her flashlight illuminated a low, uneven ceiling and a rocky dirt floor.

I knew I'd regret the decision, but I followed her. If she was going to confront the man who'd murdered Dorian, I wasn't going to let her do it alone. My shoulder smacked against a stone, and I felt cobwebs clinging to my head. The beam of Sam's flashlight ricocheted erratically off the clammy rock walls.

I dug my phone out of my pocket and prodded it blindly. The screen lit. A string of glaring text notifications rolled up. I squinted against the light as I turned my phone away and hit the flashlight function.

The blue-white beam illuminated what looked like a small rocky chamber and part of a roughhewn staircase. Ahead of me, Sam gave a startled shout. Then she dropped suddenly out of sight—like the ground just swallowed her whole.

I shone my light across the dirt floor as I rushed ahead. I sidestepped a mound of freshly dug soil, and a gaping hole came into view. Maybe five feet square but it looked much deeper.

"Sam, are you down there? Are you okay?" I knelt at the side of the hole. The blaze of Sam's flashlight swung up, burning into my eyes. I shifted my head to see Sam sprawled across disturbingly familiar shapes. An arm curled under matted, filthy hair. Legs tucked up in an almost fetal position, pale bones jutting out from a badly decayed suit.

"There's a body down here, Drew." Her voice came out in a hoarse whisper. Her eyes were wide with horror.

"Are you hurt?" I asked again.

"I don't think so."

I reached out to her. "Take my hand. I'll pull you—"

A shadow loomed over me. I tried to lurch aside, but a boot caught me hard in the back. My phone went flying as I crashed down into the grave with Sam and the corpse.

A pained whimper escaped Sam. I scrambled off her. My knee burned and my wrist throbbed, but nothing was going to stop me from bounding up and reaching for the edge of the grave. My heart pounded deafeningly as adrenaline raced through my body. I heaved myself up.

The beam of a headlamp flashed on, and the silhouette standing at the edge of the grave swung a shovel down. I jerked my hands back and fell just as the shovel slashed a deep gash into the soil. Gritty, damp dirt sprayed across my face.

"Stay down." Troy's voice floated from the dark figure standing above us.

"Troy? What are you doing?" Sam called out. "It's us! Sam and Drew!"

"I have eyes in my head, Sam," Troy snapped. "Goddamn it, Samantha, you just can't stop screwing things up, can you? What are you doing down here?"

He raised the shovel, and I thought he was pondering taking a swing at my head. I tensed. If I had the chance to yank that thing out of his hands, I would. But then Troy stepped to the right.

"If you'd taken the damn deal, we could have all gone on just fine. But you had to fuck it up." His headlamp shone across the mound of freshly turned dirt. He scooped up a shovelful.

"I'm sorry," Sam whispered. "I'm so sorry."

Troy hurled the dirt down onto us. A terrified gasp escaped Sam.

I spit out a mouthful of dust, scooped up a fistful of dirt, and hurled it back at Troy. No fucking way was I just going to let him bury us alive. I grabbed another handful of dirt, compacted it, and hurled it hard. This time the mass of damp grit slammed into Troy's head.

"You little motherfucker!" Troy hefted his shovel. "Do that again and I'll take the top of your head off."

"You don't have to do this!" Sam shouted. "Whatever happened here, Drew and I won't say anything about it. You can have Eelgrass. We'll just go."

"If it was just you, Sam, maybe I'd believe that." Troy scraped up another shovelful of earth. "But we all know Andrew is trouble."

"I'm trouble?" It was a minor slight, but at that moment it filled me with outrage. "You're attempting to bury us alive! And you have the gall to claim that I'm trouble? What? Because I wouldn't let you con Samantha out of her half of Eelgrass?"

"The restaurant isn't hers! It's mine!" Troy shouted as he hurled the dirt down onto me. "I was going to help her set it up and run it just how it should have been. But then YOU came along!"

The light of Troy's helmet burned into my eyes.

"Everyone loses their minds over you, because YOU'RE a hot-shot Seattle chef. I was a chef! They just turned up their noses and kept stuffing greasy burgers and fries into their faces while I lost more and more money!"

Troy slammed his shovel into the heap of dirt and leaned against it. He struck me as agitated and exhausted at the same time. And what was he talking about? When had he ever been a chef?

"I was up to my neck in debt. The bank was foreclosing on my house," Troy went on, and I wondered why he was telling this to Sam and me. Then I realized. He was in the process of justifying killing us. He was explaining everything—as if we'd somehow concur with his reasoning and lie down and let him bury us. But the more he talked the more our chances improved because these slow shovelfuls of dirt would eventually provide me with enough ground to get out of this hole.

"That's the business," I replied. "It's tough."

"No one gave a damn. And Troy! Troy just laughed at me. Wouldn't give me a penny, but he offered to help me fake my death. What a brother, offering me a fucking penniless fresh start at forty-six. He deserved what he got."

Any time any guy speaks about himself in the third person, it's a sign of insanity, but Troy didn't seem crazy. Just furious. So if "Troy" deserved what he got, the man singing me a dirt nap lullaby must be . . .

"So you're Charlie." I stole an instinctive glance to the corpse at my feet. I thought I saw the glint of a cuff link. Probably a match to the one Dorian had locked away in the safe-deposit box. "After Troy kept his part of the deal and reported you dead, you lured him down here?"

"I didn't lure him. I was hiding down here in Dad's old man-cave, and he came to show me the blueprints of the improvements he'd make to my place. The joke was on him." Charlie gave a dry laugh. "I'm running his shop better than he ever did, and not a single goddamned one of the people in this town even noticed the switch."

"I did," Sam whispered.

"You did not," Charlie snapped.

"I did. I thought I was going crazy. At first Dorian teased me about how I kept confusing you with Charlie . . ." Sam bowed her head and then sank to the ground.

"And then he realized you were right," I finished.

"You should've kept you mouth shut, Sam." Charlie swung the shovel and hurled dirt across us, then swept up another mound and tossed that after quickly.

I watched Charlie closely, trying to sync up to the rhythm of his movements. If I could grab the shovel and give it a hard enough yank, I felt pretty certain I could pull him down. Or at least take the shovel from him.

Sam remained hunched with her head down, as if she'd withdrawn entirely into herself to await her fate. Then I saw light flickering beneath her hands. The whisper of tapping sounded just beneath the noise of Charlie scraping up more dirt.

Sam had my phone. And it looked like she was getting a signal—talking to someone. Most likely Mac. I put my plan to grab the shovel on hold and tried to do what I could to keep Charlie from noticing Sam.

"So I guess it was you who killed Dorian as well."

"I don't have to answer that."

"Why did you do it? Did he discover this grave? Who are we standing on? Your brother?" I asked.

"No, he did not discover the grave," Charlie corrected me. "He just found some junk that fell out of Troy's pockets three years ago when I was dragging his corpse back here. A cuff link. He took it to the sheriff. Scott and I had a good laugh over the whacked-out little kook's paranoid delusion."

Charlie tossed another mass of wet earth at me, but it fell short. He was getting tired and distracted. I edged a little nearer.

"But if the sheriff didn't take it seriously, then why did Dorian have to die?"

"Because he just would not give it up. He contacted Mike's nephew Big Mac." Charlie gave a frustrated, snarling noise. "He's dumb but persistent."

"Mac's not dumb," I spoke without thinking.

Charlie gave a derisive snort.

"What? Are you some kind of boy badge bunny? Dream on. He's a Mackenzie. They're not trash like your lousy employees. Fucking Dorian . . . The one time I come back just to make absolutely sure there's nothing left here that he could have used against me, what happens? All of you show up to have some idiot after-hours party. And he comes traipsing down the stairs with a chef's knife and starts laughing at me."

"That's when you took the knife away and killed him."

"Yeah. He looked pretty surprised by it too." Amusement sounded in Charlie's voice. "If he really thought I'd murdered Troy, what was he expecting me to do to him? He never did think things through."

"Chief?" Lionel's voice sounded far away.

Charlie switched off the headlamp immediately. "You call him for help and I swear to God, I'll take him out," Charlie hissed at Sam and me.

"Chief, you down here?" Lionel quieted, and I think we all strained to hear if he was coming any closer. For his sake, I prayed he wouldn't.

"I have a new crock of kimchee. This time my mom told me . . ." His voice trailed off in a curious way that made me feel certain he'd encountered the open door to the tunnel.

Charlie sighed. He hefted his shovel up.

I had to stop him from taking a swing at Lionel, I realized, even if it meant taking a blow from the edge of that shovel.

I bounded forward, caught the edge of the grave, and heaved my chest out of the hole. I swung one leg up and looped an arm around Charlie's leg to drag him down.

Charlie spun on me and kicked me off. I fell back into the grave with a heavy thud.

Then suddenly a huge dark mass burst up from behind Charlie and wrenched him back and off his feet.

"Mac?" Even through the dark I knew there was no one else that size on the island. But where had he come from? How long had he been here? Then behind him I glimpsed the light of the staircase that must have led up to Troy's shop.

Charlie swore and cursed as Mac slammed him into the dirt and mechanically Mirandized and cuffed him.

Then Mac pulled out his flashlight and shone the glaring beam on me.

"Are you hurt?" Mac demanded.

"No." I pulled myself up out of the grave and tried to brush the dust off.

"Ms. Eider?" Mac called.

"Present." Samantha stood up, shading her eyes from the flashlight's full force. I reached down and helped her climb up.

"Very quick thinking calling us, Sam. Maybe next time don't ask Lionel to provide distraction, though."

"He was on his way over anyway. There were like a million texts on Drew's phone." Sam handed me my phone. "You really should read these, Drew. Mac totally called Troy trying to murder us and told you to stay in plain view from the street until he got here."

"Nice." I brushed a glob of dirt off Mac's shoulder while

Sam stepped gingerly around her prone cousin, heading for the staircase up. "But did you also figure out this asshole on the ground is really Charlie, the twin?"

"Yes, I did." Mac switched off the flashlight and pulled me into a crushing hug. His arms felt comforting, and his breath was warm against the side of my shoulder. He kissed me, and I kissed him back, my previous anger swept away by a rogue wave of relief.

Over Mac's shoulder I saw Lionel standing goggle-eyed, holding a celadon pickling crock in front of himself like a shield.

"Whoa, chief," he said. "Get a room."

RECIPE FOR TROUBLE

Chapter One

On Wednesday night at six forty-five Deputy Cormac "Big Mac" Mackenzie walked into my restaurant. He was tall, just over thirty, dark-haired, handsome in a "rough-hewn from solid oak" way. Except for the days that some idiot had committed a crime, for the last six months he'd darkened my door at this same time every Wednesday then sat at the same small table in the front window with his back against the wall and waited.

Without taking his order, the waitress, Savannah, brought him a beer. Likewise I started cooking, since I knew his order by heart—his order was whatever I cooked for him AKA the Wednesday night special.

Today it would be crispy duck breast with tamarind rice and green papaya salad. It seemed summery and exotic without being aloof. I hoped he would like it.

It had been eight months since I started secretly sleeping with this cop and I still got nervous making him a plate of food.

I shouldn't have worried. Three hours later I was laying beside him on the ruckled, twisted sheets in his dilapidated old mansion on the hill, taking in the warm summer night, breathing heavily, sweaty, nude, limp as a fish. Mac's chest heaved and he reached to lace his hot fingers with mine.

A pang passed through my chest. I tried to figure out when I started wanting him to fall in love with me. It wasn't right away. At first I just enjoyed the novelty of his massively strong body and was fascinated by his stoic, self-deprecating nature. Then, gradually I started wondering what he thought of me. Did he like me back? What could be my appeal, apart from convenience and proximity? Camas Island was not so big that other gay guys were a dime a dozen. So I tried to keep the conversation light and focus on an area where I felt comfortable—the twin carnal pleasures of food and sex.

Mac seemed happy to follow my lead and over the weeks we fell into the habit of simply meeting on Wednesdays. There was no prior agreement and at first Mac didn't text if he wasn't showing up. A couple of months later Mac began appearing on different nights—giving me rides home from work, mostly. We both worked all the time so neither of us ever spent the night at the other's place.

At some point I started getting disappointed if I didn't see him and that's when I knew I was in trouble. Like an idiot, I'd fallen in love with a cop who I was pretty sure was in the closet—or if he was out, only he knew it, which amounted to the same thing.

When I was alone in my crappy trailer I could access my self-respect and resent him for taking up so much space in my brain. But when he lay beside me in the hot timeless present, I didn't even know what the word 'pride' meant, I guess.

I'd never been a sucker like this before. Ever. I needed to know our status, because if he thought of me as the sexual equivalent of the gas station burrito then I needed to take some evasive action before I became completely pathetic.

So I rolled over onto my side and leaned my forehead against his shoulder. I thought maybe it would be better if I took some initiative and just asked him if he was my boyfriend now. I could absorb the blow if he said no . . . probably.

And then his phone rang.

And then he let go of my hand and answered it.

And then he had to go.

"There's a fire." Mac gently pushed me away before he jackknifed into the seated position. "It's a big one out in the county."

"It's your day off! And why are they calling you for a fire anyway?"

"They found a body." Mac turned and glanced at me. His eyes were shadowed in the thin, silver moonlight. "I guess I might not see you for a few days. Good luck with the cooking contest if I don't see you."

"Thanks." I wasn't surprised he remembered the contest. Mac didn't forget anything ever. It was both a good and bad quality that he honed daily in his work. "They've got a famous chef to judge this year."

Mac nodded. "I've seen him on TV. He seems like a cinnamon roll." He pulled on his discarded tan deputy uniform shirt then tossed me my own clothes. "I bet you can wrap him around your little finger in no time."

Would it bother you if I did?

That's what I wanted to ask him. But I didn't have the guts.

◆◆◆

The next morning I did a quick search for news of the fire and only found a short article on the local paper's website. A disused barn ten miles out of town had gone up in smoke in the early hours of the night. But the owners of said barn turned out to be none other than Copper Kettle Confitures.

Copper Kettle was one of the sponsors of the Strawberry Days cooking contest that I was about to compete in. It was a startup run by NYC exiles with great PR. They'd already been featured in several national magazines despite having been in business for less than a year.

I'd be lying if I said I wasn't jealous of their success . . . but saying that I liked their product would also be a gross inaccuracy. Good press and graphic design. Mediocre flavor profile. Any of the old ladies who resided at the Beehive Assisted Living Center could definitely have given the owners of Copper Kettle some solid lessons on what good jam should taste like. And one old lady in particular probably already had some intel on the dead body by now too.

Evelyn Olsson was eighty something, an island native and the champion jam and pickle maker of Camas County seventeen years running. She was also a police scanner addict and possibly the nosiest person in Washington State. She lived at the Beehive with her wife Julie, a retired fashion designer who wanted to make sure everyone on the whole island was as happily married as her. They were exactly the right people to consult on everything bothering me that morning.

I swung into the Beehive parking lot and slotted the car into the visitor parking. The long, one-story building had been an elementary school in the days before schools had gymnasiums. Now it housed twenty elderly ladies, including my favorite lesbian soul mates. I passed through the common room, nodding to the other ladies assembled there, and signed the unattended visitor check-in book before heading down the wide hallway to the propped-open door.

The room contained a double bed, two cushy chairs and a large, tabletop computer. Julie sat there, watching some kind of fashion video, with headphones on. She glanced up at me and gave me a friendly wave. Her towering white chignon and bold red clothes made her seem larger than life—or at least larger than the five-foot, slender eighty-year -old that she really was. She glanced up at me and gave a friendly wave. Her perfect French manicure glinted in the morning sunlight.

Julie and Evelyn had met in Paris back when their love dared not speak its name. When I'd met Julie she'd been using a walker, which had made me think she was at death's door, but it turned out she'd just had a hip replacement. She now sported a stylish cane and religiously attended the community rec center's aquacize program, which seemed to be supercharging her.

Evelyn sat in the armchair, scowling at her phone. She looked up when I entered. She was about the same height as Julie but with short, gunmetal gray hair and a compact flat body. She wore jeans and a printed t-shirt—though whatever had originally been printed on it was now cracked and illegible from endless trips through the tumble dryer.

"What are you doing here? Shouldn't you be at work?" Evelyn said, by way of greeting.

"I'm the boss. I can come in late if I want." I sat down in the empty armchair opposite her.

"Not if you want to keep your clientele," Evelyn said.

"Anyway, I was wondering if you'd been looking at the police scanner this morning." I deftly sidestepped the unsolicited entrepreneurial advice and shifted the conversation to one that would bring us mutual pleasure.

"Not yet," Evelyn said. "Should I?"

Julie finally stopped the video and took off her headphones. She pranced to the door and closed it before turning around.

"Is there something juicy?" Her eyes lit up.

"Mac got called to a fire last night." I leaned back in my chair.

"What time?" Evelyn thumbed through her phone.

"About one am," I replied.

"He shouldn't keep you up so late on a school night," Julie whispered. "And here I thought he was a gentleman."

Did I mention that these two know about me and Mac? They keep it to themselves though, being old school homos from the bad old days. But they tease me about it mercilessly behind closed doors.

"Found it. Wait—is that the location for the cooking contest?" Evelyn's brows rose in alarm. "Oh shit! It is, but looks like the fire was contained pretty fast. What did they call Mac for?"

I shrugged and gave my most innocent look.

"You know he can't tell." Julie nudged Evelyn. "Not as a confidential informant. We have to follow the breadcrumbs."

I didn't bother to point out that I was a leak, which was exactly the opposite of a police CI but whatever.

"There was a deceased person found at around the same time," Evelyn remarked, not looking up from her screen. "No deaths have been announced on the island though."

"Oh poor thing, I wonder who it was." Julie raised one hand to her lips.

"Did you stop by just to have me look this up for you?" Evelyn asked. "You could have just texted. Or downloaded your own app."

"I don't like stuff cluttering up my phone," I said.

"No, he's clearly upset," Julie chimed in. "Did you fight with the lawman? Does that good-natured façade hide the face of a depraved maniac who is secretly cruel behind closed doors?"

Being naturally dramatic, Julie could be counted on to find the most absurd way to phrase any sentence. It made me feel better somehow.

"Secretly cruel? More like secretly dumb," Evelyn put in.

I rolled my eyes. "You know Mac's not dumb."

"Then what is it?" Julie reached out and touched my shoulder. "Why did you use such a facile excuse to come by?"

"Nothing. I just made myself sad," I said.

From Evelyn, "So then the dumb one is you?"

"Hush darling," Julie admonished her. Then, she wrapped her thin, silk-clad arms around my shoulders and hugged me, which was what I'd wanted and why I'd come here. Not consciously, of course, but as humans we tend to gravitate towards people who fulfill our needs. These two had become my queer support network in the last year. I'd be lying if I said I didn't like the attention they gave me.

"Put your troubles out of your mind," Julie said. "This weekend is about tasting the sweet nectar of triumph when you crush your competition at the cooking contest."

Evelyn looked at her watch. "I mean, if you ever go to work. You're ten minutes late already."

"Fine." I stood to leave. "I'll go."

"Good." Evelyn went back to her phone. "I'll be there at eleven for my lunch. I'll see if I can find anything else out about the fire before then."

◆◆◆

My day at the Eelgrass Bistro started with first apologizing to my second in command, Lionel, who'd let himself and Savannah the waitress in and started without me. Shortly thereafter I received a delivery of one hundred and twenty pounds of local, organic strawberries. Twelve ten-pound flats stood in two, fragrant columns. Their red skins glinted and shone.

"Are these all for dessert?" Lionel asked.

"They are for everything!" I swept a hand toward the towers of strawberries, "Apps, entrees, salads, desserts. This year it is I who shall be the true Queen of Strawberry Days."

"You wish, chief," Lionel said. "You're just gonna be cheering on the sidelines as I ride by in the convertible."

For the first year ever the Associated Berry Growers (who fronted Orca's Slough annual strawberry festival) had elected to modify Strawberry Queen Beauty & Talent contest to allow males to compete for the gender-neutral title of "Strawberry Sovereign."

My favorite teenage employee, Lionel, had entered in the spirit of smashing the status quo and also to impress the girls at the fish-n-chips shop. He had been awarded first place for his essay, "Strawberry Dreams: A Camas Island Childhood," wherein he detailed his own biographical interaction with the Strawberry Days parade, from marching dressed in a small, foam berry suit as a kindergartener, to playing trumpet with the middle school marching band. It touched upon the alienation of his high school years but brought it back to his newly emergent civic pride (and welcome change of eligibility rules) that caused him to aim at the top honor.

It had narrowly edged out the top runner-up's piece, "Equality is my Jam," by one vote.

Before I moved to Orca's Slough I wouldn't have given much thought, much less respect, to a small town's berry celebration but after a couple years here I'd learned not to underestimate the draw of these kinds of events. Island businesses are made or broken by the infusion of tourism dollars during Strawberry Days. And I wanted to make absolutely sure that the Eelgrass Bistro would be positioned to succeed. Even the newly-minted legal pot store was in the spirit, introducing a limited-edition gummy edible called, "Strawberry Daze."

The festival also featured a parade, and cooking contest—judged by the sheriff, the mayor and usually one special guest—this time celebrity chef judge Michael Xavier who just so happened to be my ex.

Had I failed to mention that to Mac? To Evelyn and Julie? To . . . everyone?

Yes. But it wasn't that huge an omission. He'd achieved fame after we parted ways.

Michael had moved to Los Angeles and won a talent call for the next new celebrity chef. He now appeared regularly on the cover of cooking magazines—featuring his personal take on high-end Mexican cuisine. I had to concede that maybe he'd been right when he'd said my criticism had been holding him back.

Our relationship could have been described as: Opposites Attract, "In a Bad Way" Edition. Michael was dynamic, good-hearted, and had a knack for juxtaposing flavors and textures that daily made me jealous. He was also the worst judge of character I've ever met. Every single psycho that came through our kitchen suckered him in and he failed to think ill of all of them, routinely tolerating any and all infractions.

A guy stole from us? Maybe he needed the money.

Waitress who insulted customers? Did the customer do anything to provoke her?

Bartender who insulted me to my face? You're just taking everything too personally, honey.

All of which left me in the position of having to reprimand, apologize for and fire every problem employee all on my own. At the end of every day, I'd be fuming from having to be the heavy over and over while Michael got nothing but smiles. He was a ray of sunshine and I was a drizzly cloud that came between him and his fans. Then he'd get high and I'd drink and we'd get along well until we were sober and the whole cycle started again.

It was for the best that we broke up, there was no denying that, but it stung a little that it seemed to have been so much better for him. Sure, I'd moved up from management to being the co-owner of an upscale restaurant, but he was making big money on TV. Go figure.

I wondered how Michael would feel about seeing me again, then I realized I didn't have to be worried because his innate moral relativity would apply to me too.

"Oh, by the way," Lionel broke into my reverie. "Some lady called while you were out yesterday and the celebrity judge wants to come to the Eelgrass for lunch. Six people. They'll be here in an hour. I told them okay. Oh look Granny's here." He waved at Evelyn who had just entered and was taking her regular seat at the bar.

I thought of throwing something heavy at Lionel but I didn't want to disable him before he'd finished his shift.

So, exactly fifty-eight minutes later I caught my first glimpse of Michael Xavier 2.0: beloved television personality. He was walking through the front door and, of course, talking into a camera.

I couldn't hear what he said, but he looked like the same old Michael. Muscular and dark-haired. Just slightly paunchy, which relieved me. He'd only ever been thin while living off party drugs and vodka. I much preferred dealing with the sober edition.

Before any of us could even move to welcome him, the camera swung around in a wide panning shot, taking in the entire of Eelgrass Bistro and everyone in it.

Evelyn looked like she'd been suddenly hit with a fire hose while Lionel and Savannah the waitress struck instantaneous gorgeous poses like only the generation raised on selfies can.

Michael stepped in front of the lens.

"This is where the newest magic is going to happen." Michael flashed his pearly whites then said, "Okay cut. Thank you everyone. I'm just going to have a word with Drew."

He jogged back to the pass-through window and said, "Hello chef, you look well."

"Hi chef." I peeled off my latex glove and offered my hand. "So do you."

"Sorry about the cameras. I'll send my assistant Ainsley around to get everyone to sign a waiver." He pointed to a thin, blandly attractive girl with straight blonde hair who appeared utterly occupied with rapidly thumbing a text into her phone, then made a show of surveying the room. "Sam said this place had potential. But the décor—wow! I can't tell if this is retro or dated."

You know the feeling when you accidentally come in on the second episode of a TV show? That's how I felt about this conversation. What had our mutual friend, Samantha, been telling him? Also, when and where?

"Maybe just go with 'historic' then," I tried to keep up the pretense of knowing what the hell he was talking about, but the bewilderment in my tone was evident.

Michael gave a little frown. "So, when was the last time you talked to Sam?"

"Not for a while," I admitted. "A couple months."

"I see." Michael leaned across the pass-through and I leaned forward to meet him. "You're probably confused about why I just came in here with a camera."

"Cause you're on TV now?" I guessed.

Michael gave a bright smile. "Sam and I reconnected at Rancho Esparanza."

"Right," I said. So Michael had been in a high-class rehab. That was par for the course for our industry. "And?"

"She said she was having some trouble and so I bought her half of this place. I'm your new business partner."

I wasn't shocked to hear this, but I've heard this term—incandescent—that's when you're so filled with some emotion—in this case the emotion was anger—that you glow from within like a light bulb. Maybe this was the reason I had nothing to say. I worried that if I opened my mouth a beam of pure rage would shoot out like a laser and burn the entire restaurant to the ground.

Michael, in his innocence, apparently took my silence as shock and awe.

"I know—it's a lot to take in but I'm not here to change a single thing about your menu. You're an artist and I love what you're doing."

I also noticed a subtle change at this announcement. I could no longer hear the sound of Lionel loudly chopping away. I turned to see him staring at Michael with exactly the awe I failed to feel. I could see the kid bathing in the light of Michael's celebrity starshine. He sensed the heavens aligning—providing us all with an opportunity for greatness.

And . . . he wasn't wrong. But he also didn't know the price of greatness.

"Okay hold that thought," I told Michael. "I've got to go grab something out of the walk-in before I forget."

I pivoted and strode briskly into the walk-in refrigerator all the way to the back. Then I opened the second door to the walk-in freezer. As I closed the door firmly behind me a howl of absolute rage ripped from my chest. It took the form of the word, "MOTHERFUCKER!"

No one really knows how many lives have been saved by the invention of the decompression chamber known as the restaurant walk-in. Probably too many to count. So many customers, staff, even delivery drivers owe their continued existence to this escape zone where well-armed cooks can safely retreat to collect themselves rather than stabbing someone to death in a fit of total rage.

Front of the house staff generally use the walk-in to cry, but the 'pulling yourself together' aspect of the room remains the same.

I took a deep breath of icy air, forcing myself to confront my situation before I froze to death. Sure, I could storm out and rant at Michael, but would that actually do me any good? It wouldn't change the fact that he now owned half my restaurant; it would only mean our new business partnership would start with the same betrayed anger that had ended our previous romantic one.

Or I could phone Sam and leave a couple dozen angry messages in her voicemail, but again it wouldn't change anything. What was done was done. Right now the only thing I still had a say in was my own response. So, I needed to find a way to reframe all of this.

I focused on my options going forward. I hadn't been consulted about this change of partnership but that didn't mean it had to be bad, right?

Had Sam sold me out? Yes. Undeniably. But not for the first time or even in the worst way. And it wasn't as if she'd been contributing anything as a business partner other than being absent. So there was certainly room for improvement. Because whatever other history Michael brought with him, his success could not be denied. He might very well be that spark that the Eelgrass needed to pull in crowds of patrons. That could level me up to finally overcoming the blow dealt by the previous year's body in the basement.

I grabbed a case of pork shoulder and strode out of the walk-in. As I put it into the sink to thaw I sensed Michael watching me carefully. The friendly smile on his face showed some strain.

As a fellow chef he knew what walk-ins were for too, after all.

"So you came to Orca's Slough to have a look at your new business venture?" I managed.

"To help out a couple old friends." Michael said it like he thought he was still being filmed. "That and I want to get back in the game. I've been doing these TV gigs for a couple years now and I feel like I'm needing to go back to my roots, you know? A real restaurant in a real town with real people. When they say people in LA are fake, they're not kidding. There's this whole superficial nature to the place. And then they call what I do 'reality TV.' Nothing could be less real than the shit you see on TV."

"You were born in LA though. That would make you one of those fake people," I remarked.

"But I want to be better, Drew." He gave me a deep smile. "I want to be real."

I glanced to the bar. Evelyn openly monitored our every move.

"So you wanted to buy into this place because it seemed . . . wholesome?" I wondered if Sam had told him about the murder. Or if he understood that Orca's Slough was a tourist town and so its wholesomeness was just as curated as LA's glitz and glamor.

"Exactly." Michael nodded. "But not in a cheesy way. Just a nice, local joint in a place where people still know how to be kind to each other."

I decided then that he definitely didn't know about the murder . . . and probably a huge number of other details.

"So, where is Sam now?" I asked.

"She stayed behind in LA but she's coming to meet us on the weekend."

I locked eyes with Lionel, who stood silently shaking his head. I gave him a nod, acknowledging our simultaneous insight. Michael clearly didn't know Sam the way we did if he didn't recognize that classic kiss-off line of hers.

Sam wasn't coming back.

Whatever Michael thought, she'd slipped her neck out of the noose of ownership of this place. Likely none of us would ever see her again.

"Look I know this seems strange, but we can make it work." Michael reached out and, to my horror, took my hand. Tenderly. "It's good to see you again Drew."

"Um . . . chief?" Lionel's voice shredded the already awkward moment. "Can I talk to you in private?"

I slipped my hand out of Michael's and followed Lionel back to the alley. The sun was at its zenith and clouds of gnats hung in the humid, early summer air.

"What's up?" I asked.

"Why are you letting that dude sexually harass you?"

I rolled my eyes. "He's my ex. And it's fine. He's just a touchy guy."

"What is wrong with you, chief! You already got one guy on the down-low, which none of us approves of, by the way," Lionel added before I could speak. "My aunty told me never to get into a secret marriage. And my aunty knows things about life."

Lionel had been the only person to witness Orca's Slough's most fascinating specimen of manhood, Deputy Cormac "Big Mac" Mackenzie, lay one on me late last fall. He hadn't mentioned a word about it before this and I thought he'd forgotten or somehow not seen.

"I'm not in a secret marriage."

"You're definitely in a secret something."

"I appreciate your concern," I said.

"Granny Evelyn thinks the same thing," he went on.

"Please don't tell me you two are talking about this in public."

"Only when nobody's around," Lionel said. "She and Miss Julie are worried about you too."

"There's no reason to worry about me."

"But what if Big Mac sees you with this other guy and gets jealous and disappears you?" Lionel leaned close. "That kind of shit happens."

"Then I'm sure you and the old ladies at the Beehive will all join forces to bring Mac to justice," I whispered back.

"If you can't think about yourself can you at least think about me?" Lionel appeared to be serious, so I didn't laugh out loud.

"What does it have to do with you?"

"Because Mac's little sister Abby is back from college for the summer and she already came in here and cornered me and asked me about you."

For an instant I froze up at the shocking thought of one of Mac's relations knowing about us, but then I forced myself to relax. Mac was the one in the closet, not me. I had nothing to hide. At the same time I didn't want to be the reason Mac's family life imploded.

"Why don't you just tell her you don't know," I suggested.

"You don't understand how hard it is to lie to her. She's like a goddess. I can't keep spilling water on myself and running away every time she gets close to me."

I considered Lionel. He wasn't normally clumsy or shy. So Mac's sister must have something on him.

"You two are friends?" I asked. Of course they were. This town was tiny.

"We were on student council together. She's a year ahead of me and smart." Lionel's leg bounced with nervous energy. "I hate lying to her. And I'm bad at it."

"I'm sorry. Next time she comes in send her over to me and I'll just introduce myself okay?" I held out my arms so Lionel could bring it in for a brief, back-slapping hug.

"You're going to tell her you're dating her brother?"

"Who I'm dating isn't any of her business and it isn't any of yours either." I tried to be firm but kind and it seemed to work. Lionel straightened his headband and stuck his hands deep into the pockets of his checkered chef's pants.

"Yes, chief."

When we walked back in Michael said, "Everything okay?"

"Lionel was worried you'd be wanting to make staffing changes," I lied. "I told him you wouldn't."

"Oh, no need to worry about that. Seriously. Drew and I worked together before. I trust his instincts better than my own. Particularly when it comes to staffing." Michael offered Lionel a winning smile. "Now that the Eelgrass is part of my restaurant family, we're all on the same team—"

"Lionel," I supplied.

"Lionel," Michael finished with a smile.

Just then I felt a ghost of the old camaraderie that had fueled our once-successful professional relationship rise up. But I also knew Michael well. He grew anxious easily and didn't enjoy being on the line during actual service. If I could hold out for six months he'd be tired enough of Eelgrass and Orca's Slough that he'd be happy to leave the place to me while he jetted back to LA. I figured I could probably get some promotion, new tables, and stylish light fixtures out of the deal, if nothing else.

Then Michael's assistant barged into the conversation.

"Okay, Michael, I just need to run down tomorrow's schedule if that's okay."

"Sure." Michael laid a hand on her shoulder. "Drew meet Ainsley. She's a miracle worker. If there's anything you need, she's here to get it for you."

Ainsley turned her blue eyes toward me and I swear I saw cogs whirring behind them. "I have some papers—"

"Order up." Lionel slid a couple of Caesar salad plates up on the pass-through. I took one look at the papers in Ainsley's hands and decided I didn't want to deal with them right then.

"Gotta run this." I sidled past Ainsley and her dubious paperwork and threaded my way through the scattered film crew to gently set the plates down in front of a couple in matching boating gear. Then I went to see Evelyn at the bar.

"Dirk Van Weezendonk," Evelyn pronounced.

I snickered with involuntary laughter. "Wow. What a name."

"It's the name of the stiff from the fire." She folded her *Wall Street Journal* and tapped the side of her coffee mug. "I need a refill."

I sobered right away, feeling like a tool.

"How did you find out?" I turned away to grab the coffee carafe to pour Evelyn another.

"His mother lives at the Beehive. Room 14. He'd only come back to the island recently. His cause of death was a gunshot wound to the back of his head."

"Oh wow." I guessed I wouldn't see Mac for a few days. Homicides were rare on the island—the last one had taken place just twelve feet below us in the basement of this very building. "And he was found on the Copper Kettle Confitures property?"

I wondered if that would affect the contest.

"Correct." Evelyn laid her fork aside and began to cut her toast into small squares. "His people are in raspberries over on the other side of the island but he grew up right here in Orca's Slough. Volunteered at the local nursery in high school. After that he worked at the bank but didn't last long."

"Do you know why?"

"He cracked up." Evelyn shrugged as though this was regular.

"From working in a bank?"

"You might not know this since you're not from here but there were a few years that people couldn't get enough of robbing Pacific Northwest banks. Dickie got robbed and the next day he resigned. Couldn't face going back to work. Anywhere apparently. He's just been drifting for more than a decade working construction and jobs like that."

"So he didn't come back to take over the family farm?"

"I don't think so," Evelyn said. "But who can say? Anyway that's all I know, so far. What's up the with the celebrity judge?"

"What do you mean?"

"You obviously know him," Evelyn said. "And yet you've held out on us for the entire twelve weeks that we've known about him coming. You got something to hide?"

"We used to be a thing before he was famous," I said it off the cuff. "And I just found out Sam sold him her half of Eelgrass."

Evelyn's attention darted to Michael, and she fixed him with the assessing gaze of an exceptionally experienced professional cook.

"Looks sober, which is a step up from Sam." She returned her attention to me. "And it seems like you're still on good terms."

"Yeah, well its easy for him to be magnanimous since he's literally coming back to judge me."

Evelyn snorted with laughter. "Bet you haven't told Mac."

"Nope."

"You're too chicken, huh?" She ripped open a packet of sugar and poured it into her mug.

In fact I wasn't scared, I just didn't want to talk about the kind of dissolute party life me and Michael had lived together. I wanted Mac to see me as the better person I pretended to be these days.

So I just shrugged and left. I didn't have to justify myself to her. And anyway Mac wasn't even my boyfriend so what did he care that my new surprise business partner was my ex? So long as I kept being free Wednesdays and didn't break any laws he didn't seem to mind anything I did the other six days of the week.

Which was as it should be, I supposed. Why had I been wanting to pin him down, anyway? To get to the next level? But next level of what? And toward what endgame?

He was a member of a local law enforcement family. None of whom were likely to welcome me with open-arms, if Mac's uncle was anything to go by. And to be fair I regarded both Mac's uncle and his cousin as lazy bigots. Even if Mac did care for me, I didn't feel at all secure. They were his family. Naturally they would come first.

How could I fit into a world like that? And where could he integrate into my world?

Probably this arrangement we had was as close as we could be, given the people who we were. From experience, I knew that if I could stay detached, this relationship would end gently and bloodlessly when some new, better suited person entered one or the other of our lives.

If, on the other hand, I started competitively treating Mac as mine, I could wreck both our lives and become the spectacle of the town I was slowly starting to enjoy living in.

No, I had to keep it together and let this thing run its course, in the way that did the least amount of damage to both of us.

It was the only smart decision.

Chapter Two

I didn't see or hear from Mac all Thursday, but I saw his cruiser in front of the Beehive Friday morning when I arrived to escort Evelyn and Julie to the Strawberry Days Cooking Contest. Mac was probably speaking with the murder victim's mother. I looked, but didn't see him before Evelyn, Julie and I had to leave.

Day one of the contest required an early start. Not only did we have to complete an orientation and competitor interviews but the actual jam making portion of the event would take place today as well. Because the jam making process could be lengthy and involved allowing the product to completely cool in order to set, it had to be completed a day in advance. Our jam maker was Evelyn, our team representative was Lionel because he enjoyed talking to cameras. I wouldn't enter the field of play until Day Two when the cooking began. The jam made today would stay on the Copper Kettle property to ensure it hadn't been switched out for a different product.

We picked up Lionel then drove out to the county, passing row after row of dwarf fruit trees in full leaf.

When Copper Kettle opened, there had been a news article about how the site, a defunct, overgrown farmstead, sheltering hundreds of neglected but mature Italian prune plum trees. Those sorts of old-time fruit trees were everywhere in the Pacific Northwest as they weathered the climate well and produced reliable fruit. But faced with competition from showy tropical fruits the prune plums had declined in popularity in the mid century, demoted from tasty treat to being known primarily as a good source of fiber to ease the troubles of the constipated.

Now, with the resurgence of artisan preserves geared toward the upscale cheese market, the prune plum was getting another chance in the spotlight.

So the trees had been tended and the farmhouse painted and fresh gravel had been laid on the road.

It all looked idyllic from the outside.

"You think they're gonna say anything about the dead body or the fire?" Evelyn asked.

"Wait, there was a dead guy here? Are we going to a crime scene?" Lionel met my gaze in the rearview mirror. Orca's Slough's previous murder investigation hadn't been a walk in the park for either of us.

"But of course, Lionel. It's an old estate. Who can say how many crimes of cruelty and passion have been hidden away here over the generations," Julie responded with a gentle smile. "We are always walking through crime scenes, we just don't know it most of the time."

Oddly, that did seem to relieve Lionel.

We turned down the long gravel drive into the orchard. A guy in an orange vest directed us to park at the newly built event center.

"Why does a jelly company need an event center?" Lionel asked.

"These days agritourism is all the rage," Julie answered. "Most farms around here have vacation rentals on their property now, although—" She leaned forward and dropped her voice to a whisper. "I've heard that most of the clients are middle-aged people from town who only stay a couple of hours."

"What's up with that?" Lionel asked.

"They're people driving out where they think no one will see them to knock boots," Evelyn said. "Cheaters cheating on their husbands and wives."

"At a farm?" Lionel's lip curled in disgust. "Gross."

The property had a number of outbuildings—some historical, others brand new. There was the original two-story farmhouse that served as the front office as well as the dilapidated, burnt and half-collapsed barn. A lone crime scene investigator in a white paper bunny suit stood outside removing crime scene tape from the door, only to be followed by a tall girl with aqua and purple dyed hair in a Copper Kettle t-shirt who was stretching "do not enter" tape in its place.

Had they really finished investigating the crime scene that fast? Or had the company just asked for the tape to be removed for the weekend's event to avoid the bad publicity?

We moved down the winding gravel path, passing by a new industrial structure that presumably housed the modern production facility. Beyond this was a beautiful new building in the classic Pacific Northwest timber frame style. It had huge plate glass windows that overlooked a massive veranda and a stretch of well-maintained lawn bordered by more fruit trees.

"What a perfect place to hold a wedding," Julie remarked. Then, to Evelyn, "Darling! We should renew our vows."

"As far as I know they haven't expired," was all Evelyn had to say on that subject.

Stymied, Julie sunk into a mock pout that I knew from experience was only fifty percent fake.

The scents of boiling sugar and freshly cut grass drifted over us as we filed in to register. A fair number of contestants were already there, mingling and gossiping and admiring the facility while simultaneously eyeballing the newly arrived competitors.

Next to a massive stone fireplace stood one of the three judges: Mayor Sheila, a stocky blond in her late forties who was the town's sole orthodontist. She was speaking to Carmen Foti, owner of the local yoga studio, and Eugene Wang, owner of Copper Kettle Confitures.

Carmen was a local girl who journeyed all the way to Nepal to secure her yoga teacher training, then taught in Miami and Las Vegas before bringing her knowledge and experience back to her hometown. She looked to be in her mid-thirties and had long, dark hair and wore high-end athletic gear. She sat in a folding chair holding a set of crutches casually in one hand. She'd seemed nice enough and hadn't ever given me the side eye like so many other people in Orca's Slough. As for Eugene Wang, his normally sleek black hair hung lank and his complexion was waxy. He stared at his surroundings like he hadn't slept in a week. I sympathized. Having your business become the site of a murder investigation was no fun. I personally rated it one star—do not recommend.

I wondered how much of his equipment the fire had destroyed and whether or not he could recover from it.

I very much hoped he had insurance.

Michael lingered by the door along with the members of his camera crew, who with the exception of one single older woman, seemed to all be around thirty years old, white and male.

Then the doors of the grand ballroom opened and we were allowed to enter the competition floor.

Normally the Strawberry Days cooking contest was held in the town's rec center gymnasium as it was the only place big enough to accommodate all twelve cooking stations. Copper Kettle's event center was a dramatic improvement from the gym's ambiance of aged locker rooms and humming florescent lights. Walking into the ballroom was like walking on stage. A massive bronze chandelier hung like a crown over the polished wood paneling. Twelve identical gleaming cooking stations had been set up in two rows. At the far end of the room stood the judges' table.

A Copper Kettle employee stood at each station already, each holding a sign displaying the team's name. I and my fellow Pickle Queens had been assigned the second station on the right. Our volunteer was that same tall young woman with long hair dyed in a purple and aqua ombre style that I'd noticed earlier. Her strong jaw lent her face an androgynous quality, like a high-fashion model. She, like the rest of the staff, wore a lavender Copper Kettle polo shirt.

"Chief—see the girl with mermaid hair?" Lionel murmured.

"Is she your girlfriend?" Even from this far away I could tell the girl was taller than Lionel—close to my height.

"I wish," Lionel sighed. "No, that's Abby Mackenzie. I warned you she was trying to find out about you."

Honestly, I can't say I was surprised she'd insinuated herself into the contest. If she was even half as tenacious as Mac she'd probably already found out my shoe size and where I got my GED.

I followed Lionel to station number two and gave Abby my big, gay salesman smile.

"Abby, right? I'm Drew Allison. I own the Eelgrass Bistro on Main Street. Lionel tells me you two were on the student council together." I offered my hand and she shook it.

"Lionel's great." Abby's smile was bland and somewhat artificial, but I'd come to expect that from her family. "My brother says he loves your restaurant."

I couldn't tell if she was messing with me or fishing for information. Either way I wasn't going to crack.

"I'm so flattered, Mac's got great taste," I said.

"Wow, chief, hype yourself much?" Lionel muttered under his breath.

"They say charity begins at home." I gave a bright laugh. "So Abby, you're working here?"

"Just started last week," she said. "They've got a great seasonal program that includes room and board since it's so far from town. It's a fun crew so far. Chill."

"So if you're staying out here it means you must have seen the fire," I remarked.

Abby's gaze shifted and her smile weakened by about fifteen percent. "Yeah, it was nuts. Everybody was worried the whole place would burn down and we'd all lose our jobs. But practically my whole family showed up as first responders so that was fun."

"Nothing like an impromptu family reunion," I agreed.

Evelyn and Julie arrived at the station and, seeing that Julie still limped, Abby excused herself to go find them chairs to sit on.

The members of other teams located their own stations around us. I recognized two of the hairdressers who belonged to Team Berry Beautiful as well as a couple staff members from the local brewery who were competing as Team Straw-Brewery.

You might think that I'd dismiss all these people as serious competitors right away, but the fact is anything can happen when you're cooking. Disaster is always one second away. Plus, anyone can be a hidden expert who can pull off a dessert of mythical deliciousness that renders your carefully crafted creation just so-so. The food gods are fickle like that.

As more people filed in, I glanced around the periphery of the room and caught sight of my least favorite person in Orca's Slough—Sheriff Mackenzie, Mac's uncle. He was a friendly-looking guy in his late fifties with graying blond hair and that same gregarious professional demeanor that Mac cultivated. As he scanned the crowd our eyes met for one moment and his eternal bemusement faltered.

Part of me knew I should cast my eyes down and not provoke him, but another, larger part of me still wanted to tell him to fuck himself for that time when he detained me at the police station without adequate cause. So we stood there, eyes locked, neither of us moving.

Out of the corner of my eye I saw Evelyn's arm begin to rise, middle finger thrust obscenely out. I quickly stepped in front of her. Refusing to back down from a staring contest was one thing but openly provoking Sheriff Mackenzie could escalate badly. And not just for me and Evelyn but for Mac, as well.

It's not illegal to flip off the cops, but it doesn't help relations with them either.

"Chicken," Evelyn muttered.

"Now don't be that way," Julie said sotto voice. "Drew has a right to try and keep the peace. He might well be a Mackenzie someday. As his supporters we should save our defiance for special occasions. Just think of how much more awkward it will be if we salute the sheriff's hypocrisy on Easter Sunday instead."

"You're right." Evelyn lowered her long, boney middle finger with a smile. "I might need to pull it out for Drew's wedding."

Lionel began to snicker.

"If I asked you to stop talking about this in public, would it matter? I just want to know before I bother to make the request." I tried not to look around to see who might be listening to us because what did I have to hide?

Other than everything from Mac's family, which included that sister of his.

In the end I couldn't help but glance shiftily about—which is when I discovered that Ainsley had been silently standing behind me for God knows how long. And Abby was just a couple of yards behind Ainsley, approaching fast with two folding chairs.

The two young women gave each other the once over then Abby executed the Mackenzie smile and set out the two chairs.

Julie sank down, somehow managing to make a metal folding chair look as glamorous as a chaise lounge.

"Thank you my dear," she said to Abby. Then, to the world at large, "I just love to witness the first blush of fated love. You know, I knew Evelyn was the one for me the instant I saw her—on a small Paris street, hurling stones at the gendarmerie. So strong. So accurate. So sexy." Julie's eyes softened, presumably reliving the vision of Evelyn's excellent throwing arm.

"You were still holding that can of spray paint," Evelyn returned. "I don't remember what you'd written."

"*Il est interdit d'interdire* 'It is forbidden to forbid.'" Julie's hand went to her heart.

They gazed at one another for a long, sweet moment. While witnessing their decades long old-lady love was slightly cringey, I still felt deep gratitude that they'd stopped talking about me. And, not gonna lie, there was some envy. Who didn't want what they have?

Ainsley stared at the two of them as though she'd never seen a person over the age of thirty speaking in real life.

"Okay lovebirds, take it down a notch, you're intimidating the children," I murmured. "Ladies, let me introduce you to Ainsley. She's Michael's PA."

Evelyn stuck out her hand and Ainsley gave it a limp shake.

She said, "Elders have so much knowledge to gift the community," then, hand to earpiece, "I'm sorry, I'm getting a call."

Ainsley drifted away, weaving through the crowd, listening to some tiny, far-off voice.

Evelyn raised her eyebrows in sheer bewilderment. "What a weird little girl."

"Right?" I said. "I think she might be an artificial life form."

"I think she's great," Lionel opined, eyes narrowed to condemn our slanderous commentary. "We're going to get together later and read *Das Kapital.* She's been corn-free, no soy, no GMO, gluten-free and vegan for six months."

The two elders nodded and smiled at him, making no remark on the relative admirability of restrictive dieting while I marveled at the sheer flexibility of Lionel's go-to strategy of reading aloud to get close to prospective girlfriends.

Abby just rocked back on her heels, silently watching Ainsley's retreating back. Then she pulled out her phone and tapped in her code, which I noticed only because it was the same four digits as Mac's: 1028.

I'd never wondered why Mac had chosen those four numbers before, but seeing Abby replicate them, I couldn't help but think they had some significance. Noticing me looking at her she smiled and said, "Do you mind if we take a selfie to post?"

"Sure." I snuggled up against her, trying to look cute and not old and haggard next to her dewy freshness. "Tag the restaurant, okay?"

"Oh, don't worry." Abby's thumbs were already flying too fast for the human eye to see as she added at least two dozen tags and @'s to our simple image.

"Evelyn," Julie suddenly asked. "Is You Know Who in this contest too?"

"Most likely—unless she's died," Evelyn replied.

"Who are you talking about?" I asked.

"My cousin Joyce." Evelyn hooked her thumbs in her belt loops. "If she knew how to cook she'd be our team's main rival but since she can't she's just a permanent pain in my ass."

"Every year she tries to start something at the county fair." Julie leaned in toward Evelyn as if proximity alone could protect her. "Mark my words, she'll have something up her sleeve during the contest."

Evelyn nudged me and silently directed my attention to a woman who could have been her evil twin.

Where Evelyn's hair was close-cropped and gray, Joyce's still blond bob recalled the helmet-hair of the mid-Eighties. She wore khakis, a tasteful cream-colored sweater and as much gold jewelry as a low-level rapper. Her manicure was perfect. I'd never seen her before, which was odd in itself, given how small the island was.

Lionel tapped my arm and directed my attention to the judges' table.

Michael stepped up to the microphone, flanked by Mayor Sheila, Sheriff Mackenzie, and a few minor dignitaries from the county council. Ainsley stood behind Michael, fingers resting gently on her earpiece, like some sort of secret service agent.

No sooner had Michael introduced himself than Joyce stood and let out a voice so similar to Evelyn's that the hair on the back of my neck stood up.

"Excuse me, but this lack of basic fairness is shocking!"

Her objection blindsided Michael, who actually glanced to me as if I would leap up on stage and rescue him. Back in the day, I would have. But not anymore. Instead it was his producer who walked forward, casually putting herself between Michael and the irate Joyce.

"Pardon me?" Michael asked.

"Here we go," Evelyn whispered.

Lionel glanced between Evelyn and Joyce then moved closer to me.

Joyce continued, "You can't expect us to believe that any contest can be fairly judged by the business partner of one of the contestants." Joyce flung out her arm, but somehow managed to avoid looking in our direction. "Not to mention having the Strawberry Queen on their team."

Ainsley stepped up to the microphone.

"Strawberry Sovereign," she corrected. She gave a brief nod toward Lionel then stepped automatically back, mission accomplished.

I believe it was at that exact second that Lionel fell in love with Ainsley. His chest swelled and his shoulders straightened.

Michael wasn't wrong-footed for long. Even before he'd worked on television he had mad diplomatic skills.

"You know, I can see your point Miss—"

"Joyce." She leveled an imperious glower at him.

"It's a pleasure to meet you." Michael gave the warm, irresistible smile. "So why don't we even the odds then? What if I joined a team?"

"Joined a . . . team?"

"Perhaps yours, maybe? If you'll have me. I'd much rather be down there competing than standing up here judging anyway." Again came the smile, this time broadly expansive, like sunrise breaking over the horizon. "If that's okay with everyone?"

From the rest of the contestants came a variety of shrugs and acknowledgements, even faint laughter.

"Old Joyce didn't see that coming," Evelyn whispered in savage good humor. "He's a smart one, that Michael."

"Yeah." I narrowed my eyes as he walked down and accepted a souvenir "Strawberry Days" apron from a member of Joyce's team who seemed relieved to give it up.

That left a gap at the judge's table, but fortunately it was quickly filled by the yoga teacher, Carmen Foti, who'd apparently already agreed to cover should any of the judges fall ill or have an emergency.

As Michael had joined the competition, the duty of reading out the rules fell to the mayor.

"As we all know the jam and preserve contest is the highlight of Strawberry Days." Sheila waited while the audience clapped politely. "You've each been provided with twenty pounds of strawberries for both the jam making and cooking portions of the contest. You're free to use the facilities here until nine p.m."

She then passed a sheaf of papers, which turned out to be filming waivers Evelyn insisted on actually reading before she'd let any of us sign.

"You two hull those berries while I have a look at this," Evelyn told us. Then she took a seat beside Julie.

"Yes, Granny." Lionel hefted up a crate of local berries and I joined him washing them and slicing off the green tops. We worked fast and had prepped all twenty pounds by the time Evelyn finally signed her name to the waiver. Lionel snapped a few selfies holding our selection of berries, while I moved aside to let Evelyn begin her jam magic.

Just then I caught sight of Mac. How long had he been there, lingering in the doorway with a weird expression on his face? While I wish I could say I caught him staring longingly at me, he was plainly trying to catch the sheriff's eye.

No doubt he had information to report. Maybe about the murder.

"I'll be right back," I told Lionel.

Lionel looked up, also saw Mac and replied, "Tight," in the most deadpan tone imaginable.

When I approached Mac noticed me right away. Maybe he'd been paying a little attention to me after all?

"You're looking good," I said.

This seemed to please him, though it was hard to be sure. Mac's public face had the perpetual slight smile.

"Why is my sister at your station?" he asked.

"She's our helper from Copper Kettle. Each team has one."

"What a coincidence." Whether Mac's dry remark was aimed at Abby or myself, I could not say.

"Did you find out who it was in the fire?" I whispered.

"Yes," Mac said. "But I can't tell you so don't even ask."

I started to protest that I wouldn't have presumed but stopped because we would both know that was untrue. And anyway, I already knew Van Weezendonk's name, so I said, "Okay, I respect that."

Maybe a little of my smugness showed because Mac narrowed his eyes.

"Let's say I actually told you the identity of the deceased," Mac began.

"Are you saying you will?"

"No, but let's say I did. What do you think you'd do with that information?" Mac's lips curved up from his resting dolphin face to an actual smile. "Go solve the crime?"

"So you're saying that a crime has been committed then?" I pounced on the statement like a cat on a vegan fur mouse. "Was it arson? Murder or . . . both? One to cover up the other?"

"Oh my God." Mac closed his eyes in that long-suffering way that I'd come to find adorable. "Drew, is it possible for you to not mistake yourself for a member of law enforcement?"

"I don't think I'm a cop—"

"Then quit asking cop questions," he said.

"I just think I might be able to help you ta—"

"Help me? With . . . what? Your extensive knowledge of forensics TV shows?" His full attention rested on me now.

"Real cops use those too you know."

"Listen I get why you kept butting into the investigation when your bartender was killed but you've got to let this go. I don't try to enter cooking competitions—" Mac began.

"I wouldn't mind if you did. Not that you'd win." I put in. "But I get it. You want me to stay in my lane. Well, you don't have to tell me the identity of the deceased because I already know. Dirk Von Weezendonk. Island native with a history of depression. No wife. No kids. He'd been drifting until recently but returned in order to visit his mother who—"

"—is a resident of the Beehive," Mac finished. "Did you go harass her or did your fairy godmothers do it for you?"

"I haven't harassed anyone," I said primly.

"You are just . . . terrifying."

"I thought that too when I first met him but then I found out that Drew is a pussycat inside." Michael's voice cut into our conversation. At the same time, I felt his hand snake around my waist.

Sometimes there's a moment when your whole perspective seems to go upside down through a prism to a new revelation. First, I knew that despite Michael's extensive knowledge of me, he had not guessed Mac and I had a relationship. He'd seen me, quietly arguing with a cop and come over to offer solidarity and maybe to try and repel Mac with an overt display of homosexuality.

Mac's reaction took me completely by surprise.

He laughed.

Not just a smile—a full laugh. Right in our faces.

"But he's not a real detective though," Mac wiped the corner of his eye. "Drew you didn't tell this guy you're a detective now did you?"

Mac was exhausted, I realized, and slaphappy.

Michael looked askance at me.

"This is Chef Michael Xavier, my new business partner." I said it quickly, as if it wasn't a revelation I was still struggling to accept myself, then turned to Michael. "Deputy Mackenzie is a regular at the Eelgrass. One of our most loyal customers."

Mac's easy smile slipped for just an instant, as he absorbed the revelation of my new business partner.

Michael's hand dropped away from my waist, only to be offered to Mac a moment later, creating perhaps the most awkward handshake seen on the island this year.

"I look forward to serving you in the future," Michael said.

"That's . . . great news. Well, I need to speak to the sheriff now." Mac turned his eye on me. I could tell he wanted to say something else, but Michael's presence stopped him. He brushed a fleck of something off the shoulder of my chef's coat. "Good luck out there."

He acknowledged Michael with a gentle, smiling nod then strode off.

"He does look good walking away," Michael said. "But honey, am I imagining it or are you into him?"

Our eyes met and held. One of Michael's greatest qualities was his ability to unquestioningly go with the flow. He was like one of those dogs that learns to surf—he doesn't know why he's doing this crazy thing but doesn't care as long as people are smiling and clapping.

Basically perfect for television. And in a way perfect for a person like me, who didn't like to admit anything out loud to anyone ever. In our own way, we'd been a good team once. Although it was because of this same dynamic of not communicating and avoiding pursuit of communication, that we'd managed to starve our previous relationship to death, so I guess maybe neither of us was so smart after all.

We'd probably have to work on developing protocols for honest dialogue together if we were going to be business partners.

But not today.

"Shouldn't you be getting back to your team?" I asked.

We both glanced to Joyce, who was glaring at us—probably worried that we were now in collusion. Michael gave her an apologetic wave.

"I guess I'm going to get a crash course in jam, right fucking now." He gave a rueful shrug.

Now that the waivers had been signed, the producer had started circulating through, talking to the contestants—getting that extra biographical information that would help viewers get to know us all. One of them stood in front of Evelyn asking something. She drew herself up in the stiff posture she used when dispensing some great gem of wisdom. Julie beamed from beside her.

And then I caught a strange aroma.

One thing that's not fully appreciated by the non-food industry public at large is how attuned professional cooks are to scents. Even the smallest whiff of certain odors will send us on full alert.

"Do you smell something burning?" I immediately looked to my team and felt relieved seeing that Evelyn, Julie, and Lionel were in no danger, nor was their jam. Evelyn and Julie seemed to be flirting over the confectioners' sugar, while Lionel observed with an expression that was both embarrassed and amused.

"Oh yeah." Michael cocked his head.

"It doesn't smell like food," I scanned the other workstations, but didn't glimpse any smoke or panic there either.

"No, like plastic maybe?" Michael covered his mouth with his hand. "It's foul."

"It's garbage." I realized as a breeze from the door behind us brought more of the stench wafting my way. "That's a garbage fire. It's this way."

I strode through the largely featureless side doors that led out to the public restrooms. I zeroed in on the fire right away—just outside the door a plastic can stood smoldering. Then in an instant, yellow flames leapt up as the fire truly caught hold, licking against the wall.

"Dios mio!" Michael darted back into the ballroom.

No fire extinguisher seemed handy and I wasn't about to use my jacket to smother it—especially not when there was an exterior door less than six feet away.

Yes, the door had a sign that said: EMERGENCY EXIT. DO NOT OPEN. DOOR ALARM WILL SOUND.

But I had a can of flaming garbage. I grabbed the lip of the can and started pulling. It was pretty light and I crossed the distance to the door in an instant.

"Drew! I've got—" Michael's voice was cut off by the piercing claxon that started when my ass hit the door. I pulled the can out across the damp grass and kicked it over. The flaming lump sizzled and died against the damp earth. I stomped on it a couple times for good measure.

Despite the smell I crouched down to have a look at the glob. A scorched matchbook lay beside something that seemed to be a toilet paper roll stuffed with paper. It smelled like nail polish remover. It was half burnt and plainly the source of ignition.

A shadow fell across me. Lionel. Phone raised and aimed at me.

"What are you doing?" I asked.

"Recording you killing the garbage, chief," he said as though it was the only reasonable thing to do. "Do you mind if I post it?"

"Don't you dare," I replied.

Behind Lionel I saw Mac and his uncle rounding the corner of the building, followed by several others, Ainsley and Michael's camera crew among them.

Inside, someone shut off the claxon. I waved Mac over and he jogged closer.

"Can you please stop filming?" I asked Lionel.

He silently shook his head as Mac stopped at my side and scowled at the smoking remains of the trash. Mac only glanced to Lionel, and he lowered his camera.

Mac then turned to me. "Come talk to me in my cruiser."

Chapter Three

"Go ahead and sit in the front." Mac opened the passenger side door for me.

"Your sister, your uncle and half a dozen other people are standing right there watching us." I ducked down into the passenger seat and waited for him to climb into the driver's side before asking. "What are you going to tell them we're talking about?"

"The fire," Mac said. "Because I want to talk to you about the fire."

"Which fire? The garbage can one? It seems like it was deliberately set, doesn't it? But that's a good point—"

"I didn't make any point," he said.

"But I could tell that you were going to. You were going to say that it could be related to the other fire."

"Was I?" Mac took off his sunglasses and rubbed his eyes.

"Weren't you?"

"No. I would never assume two fires were connected without any evidence whatsoever." Mac then removed his hat and scratched his flattened hair. It looked like he'd just showered and slammed the hat back on top of it. I wanted to reach over and mess it up—just to give it some style. I didn't though, and not just because Lionel and Ainsley were standing there on the sidewalk, blatantly gawking and stalwartly recording the whole interaction.

"But two fires in two days in the same location?" I said. "It has to be connected."

"You think they're related because you knew about two fires. But Drew, things burn down all the time. That's why the fire department exists."

"Do things that burn down all have murder victims inside them?" I countered.

"I'm pretty sure the garbage can didn't have a body in it," Mac said. "Anyway, what I wanted was to caution you against picking up and disturbing things that are on fire but I didn't want to do it in front of Lionel and your crew so that's why I asked you over here."

"And here I thought you just wanted to cozy up to me," I teased.

"Your new business partner seems to have that covered today." Mac's gaze slid down my torso to where Michael's hand had rested, glaring as though it had left a visible stain on my waist.

I hadn't expected him to bring up Michael. The hint of jealousy thrilled but also annoyed me.

"He's just a touchy-feely guy," I said. Inside the closed confines of the car, I could smell the fatigue radiating off Mac—a particular blend of stale coffee and acrid, exhausted sweat. "So, is that it?"

"No, I want to make sure you get it about not messing around with flaming objects."

"Mac, I've put out so many fires in the kitchen. Seriously. I'm not an idiot."

"Those were in your own kitchen though, not fires of mysterious origin. When you were binging your marathon of forensics shows, did you fast forward through all the ones about arson?" Mac finally turned sideways in the seat and looked me dead in the eye.

"No . . . I mean, I don't think so." Now that he asked, I couldn't think of any specifically about arson. Had I skipped those after all? "Maybe?"

"When people deliberately set fires, they often use a kind of ignition device that ensures that the fire is exacerbated by trying to put it out. What if, for example, there had been a gallon of gasoline or kerosene in the bottom of that trash can when you dumped it out? What would have happened to you?"

"I'd have gotten fried?" I guessed. "And have to get airlifted to the Harborview burn ward?"

"In total agony," Mac added. "You'd be in the burn ward in agony with a bunch of your skin melted off."

"Lucky me then," I didn't mean to be flippant, but I didn't want to get schooled any further by Mac either.

"I'm only telling you this because I don't want you to get hurt. That's all. If you see another random fire don't physically interfere with it, please. Use a fire extinguisher. From a distance."

"Then . . . you really do think the two fires are connected? And that there might be more?" I couldn't help bringing it back around to this.

Mac gazed at me, his eyes blank with fatigue and, I thought, a faint glimmer of disappointment.

"It's none of my business though," I hastened to add.

"I can't say there's no connection between two fires in the same location," Mac said. "But if they were both deliberately set then I do know that there is at least one, possibly two people who are setting fires."

"And Van Weezendonk?" I asked. "Do you know who killed him? Just shake your head or nod. I won't ask any more details, I'm just trying to figure out if you're going to make it to the contest on Sunday."

Mac gave me a tired smile. "At this point I don't know if I'll be there," Mac said. "If it's not resolved, I might not. I'll definitely let you know."

◆◆◆

Back inside the air was now full of the sweet piquant smell of berries and sugar. I located my information packet, which included the competition rules and team lineup, signed my waiver and returned it to Michael's producer, a plump, heavily-mascaraed woman who seemed always to be having two conversations at once. She appeared happy to accept my paperwork with a wordless smile, while making some sort of travel arrangements with the person on the other end of her phone.

At the work station, Evelyn stared down our pot of jam as if daring it to displease her while Julie seemed to be having a good time chatting with contestants from Team Berry Beautiful. They speculated about Joyce employing Clear Gel to set her jam as if adding modified cornstarch to a recipe was tantamount to an Olympic doping scandal. Lionel stuck to Ainsley like glue. Abby and the rest of the helpers from Copper Kettle had been released and were walking back to their regular duties tending the orchard and jam production facility.

I was left with my own ruminations. For example, why had Mac been so reluctant to speculate that both fires could have been set by the same person? Certainly there couldn't be two separate arsonists interested in burning down the same jam company at the same time? Right? Unless—did firebugs work in teams?

I took a minute to sit on the counter at our station and do some cursory research on arson. Even the most lackluster keyword search returned one interesting fact. Most people who set fires stayed to watch them burn, so it was likely that the person who set the garbage fire was still present. There were at least seventy-five people in this ballroom, including the event center staff, contestants, and TV crew. So which one of them was guilty?

The next logical step would be to see if the event center had security cameras, so I went to the front desk and asked. They verified that this was true, but only on the exterior to prevent break-ins. The fire had been started inside near the entrance to the restrooms, which I thought was clever. No one would be filming people going in and out of the bathroom.

So I went back to my station and ran down the roster of the members of each of the eleven other competing teams. All the member seemed to be still present except for a woman named Linda Jansen, who hadn't been able to attend the first day at all.

I had no idea how to spot an arsonist. Nobody here seemed to be incessantly flicking a lighter or mumbling crazily about the beauty of fire.

But a pool of a few dozen people is better than a pool of everyone in the world, so it was a start. So, what now?

I tapped the sheaf of papers wondering which people could have potentially been at both fires. Eugene Wang? He'd been present the whole day, probably worried that the murder on the property would be announced any second.

A stressful situation for sure. And didn't my fifteen seconds of research say that stress is a factor with people who set fires?

I had first-hand experience in how nerve-wracking it was to be in the proximity of a murder. How much more anxiety would a person feel if they were responsible for the murder? Especially if they were guilty?

I looked back at Eugene Wang. He chewed his lip and texted relentlessly, elbows tucked in against his body, like he was freezing to death in the early summer heat.

Then a body posted up next to me. A muscular tan hand wrapped around mine.

"I didn't think corporate casual was your type, honey." Michael snuggled up against me. "But he does look sweet in a neurotic kind of way."

I smirked and removed Michael's grabby hand. Not too harshly, but also decisively. He'd always been a smooth gremlin when it came to getting in close.

"Enough with the hands," I warned.

"I'm just excited to see you." He nudged against me with his shoulder. "I get it though. You're probably still angry on some level."

"No." My tone was more swift and decisive than I expected it to be, so I went on, "We were right to end it. We weren't doing each other any good."

"I know. And I want to make amends," Michael said. "Not just in a 'recovery' way but man to man. I want to help you make your place successful."

"I thought you said you wanted to get back to basics," I remarked.

"It's not just one thing or the other," Michael said. "So I was going to say—think about things that I can do. Like, do you want to clean house and start again? I can take care of that. Rebrand? Redecorate? Any changes that the staff doesn't like can all be my fault. Anybody who gets pissed off can come to me."

I couldn't help my obviously skeptical stare at Michael. In all the time I'd known him he'd never been the one to confront problem people or be the 'bad guy'.

"Okay not to me personally," Michael admitted. "But I have staff who can handle it, for both of us."

"If I wanted to clean house or do any of those other things, I'd do it myself." I sighed. Michael was always like this. Big on promises, but when it came down to bringing the hammer down, I'd always had to be the one to do every termination, reprimand, and complaint. Because it hurt me less than it did him. On some level I just cared less what people thought about me, so being the heavy came easily. Naturally, even. "The only thing I want from you is to actually invest in the place . . . and if you can't do that let me buy you out."

"What kind of money are you talking? I mean about investing in Eelgrass." He leaned in.

"Right now? Nothing. I mean your time, your effort. I want to take a day off, you know? And know that someone has my back. I want a partner." Somehow the word came out with an embarrassing aching resonance.

Was I even talking about my restaurant anymore?

Michael once again rested his hand on mine. "I know, honey. I'm here to do my best."

Waves of ambiguity sloshed over me, but I managed to kick my way to the surface, take a deep breath and remove Michael's hand again, just as Ainsley arrived to capture Michael's attention with a slew of questions about his upcoming new series.

I gazed across the ballroom, noting that Sheriff Mackenzie and Mac had converged upon Eugene Wang. From the bewildered expression on his face, I guessed that they were speaking to him about the murder.

Honestly, my heart went out to Eugene. I knew exactly what it was like to be in his position. How the panic would be choking him then churning itself into anger and helplessness. The sense of injustice at having been drawn into someone else's problem.

The similarities between the murder at Copper Kettle Confitures and my own troubles at the Eelgrass were numerous. The properties where the murders took place had both changed hands within the last five years and been purchased by newcomers to the island. Both Eugene and I were outsiders to the small island community and were ignorant to the histories, grudges and hard feelings that came with purchases that felt fresh and new to us.

Now, I wondered if what Eugene's company website described as a "forgotten and abandoned farmstead" had ever really been either of those things. Roots on the island went back generations. Who had been displaced by Copper Kettle's new venture? And were they angry enough to light the place on fire?

My phone buzzed. It was a text from Mac with a link to the sheriff's department press release. It named Van Weezendonk as the deceased and ended in a statement that the investigation was ongoing.

I thanked Mac. Then I texted him an eggplant to demonstrate the vigor of my gratitude.

Because I'm classy like that.

Across the room I could see Mac smirk as he received my suggestive vegetable. Then he glanced up and our eyes held for just an instant before he again turned away.

Half an hour later our fragrant, deep red jam cooled in a refrigerator and the interviews were complete. My little crew gathered at the ballroom door, waiting for me to drive them back into town. I noticed Michael lingering nearby.

"We'll be heading back to Eelgrass." I thought of the promise Michael had made me about our partnership and then asked. "How about you?"

Michael shook his head. "I have to stay to talk to my producer. You go ahead. I'll meet you all there."

Chapter Four

Michael never arrived at the Eelgrass, but he sent Ainsley to help with hosting. The fair weather meant business was slow, so she spent most of the night hanging around by the food pass-through showing Lionel pictures of places she'd traveled with Michael. By the end of the night Lionel had decided to personally introduce Ainsley to the entire under-25 population of Orca's Slough, the majority of whom were gathering in some field off Top Hat Road to have a bonfire—the standard entertainment in a town with no nightclubs and only two bars.

The last diner left an hour before we were supposed to close so I sent the remaining staff home as well and settled into running out the clock by prepping for the next day's lunch. Since it would be Saturday, we'd be busy with the sailing crowd.

Just before nine p.m. the door opened and Mac walked in. He often came by at closing time—a holdover from the previous investigation when he'd been convinced I was in danger. To be fair, he had not been wrong.

He took up most of the doorframe. And, from so far away, his features obscured by a shadow cast by the brim of his hat, and recognizable only by the line of his jaw and his uniform, he seemed iconic in his masculinity.

The icon checked his watch—this was a show—he clearly already knew what time it was or he wouldn't be here. But it was a kind of ritual for him, so I accepted it.

"You want me to flip the sign?" he asked.

"Sure. Lock the door too, if you don't mind."

He did so and then walked to the bar and sat down. I ambled up to the other side.

"Deputy Mackenzie, are you suggesting I serve you liquor afterhours?" I teased. "Because if that's the case I'd be happier getting a six pack and drinking it with you in your living room." I leaned against the bar in a way that I hoped was casual-yet-sexy. Since it had been a slow night, I felt relatively confident in my looks.

"I'm still on duty," he said. He took out his phone and turned it around to show me the screen. On it was a photograph of me and Michael holding hands in the ballroom that afternoon. I stood stupefied, not understanding what I was looking at. But once I grasped it, instant rage exploded though my chest.

"What the actual fuck?" I tried to snatch the phone out of his hand, but he was too fast. "Who sent you that?"

"My sister."

"Why would she—" My hands shook in affronted anger. "Well, I guess she knows about us 'cause why else would she be sending you her shitty stalker pics?"

Mac tapped the photo. "The interesting thing about this picture is that these two individuals definitely know each other well."

Oh. So that's your takeaway from this? Fine. Let's go.

"Yes, we know each other, all right?" I snapped. "He's one of my exes."

"And yet you chose to introduce him as your new business partner," Mac remarked.

"Because that's what he is now." I turned around and grabbed a towel to wipe the bar, deliberately forcing Mac to remove his elbows and lean back.

"Fill me in on how that happened, again?" For a second I thought Mac would bring out his cop notebook and start taking notes but he just folded his hands on the now-damp bar.

"No," my response was automatic.

Mac's eyebrows shot up. "Why not?"

"Why should I?"

"Why wouldn't you?" his voice was calm and practiced, like he had me locked in that little room at the station making me confess my crimes.

"Because my business is none of your business. What makes you think you have any right to amble in here and start interrogating me because your sister—a woman who just met me, by the way—is sending you pictures of me holding someone's hand? How do you know Michael didn't just tell me he has stage four cancer and I'm comforting him about his imminent death?"

"Does he have stage four cancer?"

"Whether or not he does isn't the point, Mac! What's going to be next? Spyware on my phone? Photographing the license plates of everyone who comes to my trailer?"

Mac held up his hands. "Okay, Drew this is really escalating quickly. I just wanted to ask you what was going on."

"No, you didn't. If you wanted to ask me what was going on you would have called me and told me what happened instead of confronting me with this so-called evidence." I threw the towel down into the sink. "You wanted to catch me."

"I didn't—"

"Then why the dramatic reveal of the picture?"

"I thought you would laugh because my nineteen-year-old sister is acting like a mean girl from middle school," Mac said. "Instead you got angry and defensive so . . . now it seems like you have something to hide."

"How can I have something to hide from a man who has never even asked me to sleep over at his house? Even if I was sleeping with someone else—where's the obligation to tell you anything?"

"What?" It was Mac's turn to be incredulous. "I don't . . . you always leave. Every time. It's what you do. That's not on me. You don't like clingy people. You don't like being told what to do. I stay in my lane. I don't make any demands of you at all. Ever. You can't just change the goal posts like this."

Have you ever been so embarrassed and angry that you want to disappear? This was how I felt realizing that Mac had me dead to rights. My cheeks burned in shame but I couldn't argue.

"And anyway," Mac said. "Now that I know he's your ex I kinda want to beat him up for making you weird like this."

"Michael didn't make me weird. I was already weird when I met him," I replied. "If you want to beat someone up you can just go beat up the entire city of Sage Springs, Wyoming."

"What? All of them?"

"Yeah. Everybody right down to the babies. Dogs, cats, alpacas, miniature horses," I said. "You ready for that?"

"It seems easier to just invite you to sleep over. I'm off at midnight."

"But it's Friday." I sounded sulky even to myself.

Mac nodded. "Sure is." He pulled an enormous key ring off his belt then carefully worked a single key off and set it on the bar.

I eyeballed the thing warily, not willing to take it in front of him. I'm not saying I didn't want it. Just that I couldn't make myself pick it up while he was staring at me.

Because I'm a coward, I guess.

"Don't you want to know about Michael anymore?" I asked.

Mac stood up and stretched. "I'm sure you'll tell me all about him when something goes wrong." He started to leave.

"Hey, wait." I didn't have anything to say. I just didn't want him to leave like this.

Mac turned back. "Yeah?"

"I was thinking: I don't think the murder has anything to do with Copper Kettle Confitures. Eugene Wang's products were featured in high-end cooking magazines even before the glue on the labels was dry. He has so much to lose from bad press."

Mac studied me in silence for a moment, then his expression shifted a little. I wasn't certain if he looked more amused or long suffering but he didn't leave. He took a step back toward me.

"Just because it would hurt his marketing scheme to be involved in a homicide doesn't mean Eugene Wang is not involved." Mac gave a slight smile.

"I know but let's say he isn't—just for the sake of argument. Then why did Van Weezendonk go to the property?"

"I don't know," Mac said. "But I feel like you've got a theory to share."

"Because he was meeting his murderer," I said.

"That's just a statement of the facts of the case. But I get where you're going with this. You're suggesting that someone arranged to meet Van Weezendonk on the property and then, for some reason, killed him."

"Yes," I said. "So then the question is: why did they meet at that place?"

"Because it was known to both of them." It was clear that Mac had already been down this line of reasoning but seemed to be humoring me—possibly for the sake of dissipating the lingering tension in the air.

"Which means that both the murderer and Van Weezendonk must be connected with the property in some way because they both felt safe meeting there." I picked up the key and slid it into my pocket. "Do you know who owned the property before Eugene Wang?"

Mac gave a helpless shrug. "You know I can't tell you that. But the previous owner of the property is a matter of public record. You could always go down to the courthouse and satisfy your curiosity on Monday."

"Then you're still investigating Eugene Wang?" I asked.

"He's—" Mac's shoulder radio crackled to life, informing him he was wanted somewhere and had to go, like always.

I locked the door behind him. Only when he reached his cruiser did it occur to me to say, "Be careful."

And by then he couldn't hear me.

I leaned against the locked door and watched him drive away. I ran my finger along the edge of the CLOSED sign where Mac had touched it, thinking that it was cute that Mac thought I had to wait till Monday to find out who had owned the property where Van Weezendonk's body was found.

One text to Evelyn later I had a name: Margaret Simmons.

Me: *Does she have any connection to Van Weezendonk?*

Evelyn: *Don't know. Wife wants me back in bed. We'll look into it in the AM.*

◆◆◆

Closing up didn't take too long. I slid into the driver's seat of my car by 9:25. Plenty of time to go home and pack my toothbrush in anticipation of my sleepover at Mac's place.

I'd just settled back into the seat when my phone started to buzz and buzz.

Lionel texted me seven times, but provided no information except that "really, really, really, please, please, chief I need a ride" and the address where he was at.

So I agreed, thumbed the location into a navigation app and found myself routed up Top Hat Road.

Away from the town's streetlights the night became very dark. Silvery stars twinkled above me while I followed a series of switchbacks up the bluff.

Then I spotted a strange glow to my left. Orange light pushed between the black silhouettes of tree trunks. Then other lights. Strobe blue and flashing red and yellow.

"Your destination is on the right," the app informed me, but I had already guessed as much. Not necessarily because of the fire truck, sheriff's cruiser and burning barn, but from the sight of two of my employees standing among a group of young people huddled near the fire truck. A huge white cloud of vape, slipped from between Lionel's lips then he passed the pen to a girl I didn't know who passed it along to a person I did: Ainsley.

Good to see she was already melting into the Eelgrass family, I supposed.

But the burning barn . . . would damage my plans for a night with Mac.

I put the car in park and opened the door. The roar and smell of the fire hit me the second I did.

As I trudged up the hill I caught sight of a big, muscular man in a flat-brimmed deputy's hat. The conflagration cast leaping shadows across his face as he talked into a radio at his shoulder. I changed my trajectory and headed for him instead.

Mac glanced up at me. A transient expression of bewilderment crossed his face then he seemed to work it out.

"You're here to pick up Mr. Fogle, I assume?"

"Yeah. What the hell happened here?"

"According to Mr. Fogle—" Mac flipped open his notebook and began to read aloud. "'We were all talking about our pageant outfits and chilling around the bonfire and cooking hotdogs when we noticed the barn going up.' You can see what's left of their bonfire over there." Mac pointed to a sodden area just in front of the burning barn. In the jumping light I could see very little. Maybe a bag of marshmallows and what looked like a case of beer. Definitely no weenies. "Unfortunately, some sparks seem to have traveled from the fire and ignited this structure. Or at least that's the working theory."

"Is anyone hurt?"

"Everyone's accounted for but several of them are not in a fit condition to operate a motor vehicle." Mac turned and gave them a look. "It is also my opinion that they could all use a refresher course in fire safety."

"So you don't think this is connected too?"

Mac gave a noncommittal shrug. "Maybe?"

The heat from the structure suddenly intensified. As I watched, the firefighters seemed oddly complacent about the conflagration. Two stood spraying while another couple of them held long poles with hooks on the end.

"What's that all about?" I pointed at them. "They look

like they're harpooning a whale."

"I think they're getting ready for an exterior attack; they'll try to pull the remaining walls down." Mac watched them. "I guess the interior was just full of old farm stuff—wooden plows—that kind of junk. Tinder dry. That's why it went up so fast. I'm glad no one was inside. It would be easy to get disoriented if you were inebriated."

Instinctively, I drifted closer to him, reaching out to surreptitiously brush against him in the dark. Mac gave me a smile and I automatically relaxed.

"Are you going to issue tickets?" I asked, under voiced.

"To the minors in possession?" Mac asked. "I'll pass today. Wouldn't want to take out the whole pageant crew before the big parade. Anyway, they have parental permission to be on the property."

For a moment, we both watched the firefighters sink their hooks into the burning building and heave. The barn wall bowed outward but didn't collapse.

"Just in case you're still wondering, I wanted to tell you that it won't be a problem," I said. "Working with Michael, I mean. Interacting harmoniously with people you once slept with is part of the basic criteria for working in the hospitality industry. Everyone's slept with everyone always."

"I don't think that's technically possible," Mac said. "And it sounds like a recipe for disaster. But I mainly see what happens when relationships go really wrong, I guess."

"I'm just trying to make the best of what Sam left me with," I said then I took a couple of minutes to explain what had happened with Sam, and that it hadn't been my plan to reconnect with Michael and that unless I wanted to sell my half of the Eelgrass too it was wholly out of my control.

"Honestly, I had assumed that when Sam sold me out, she'd do a worse job," I finished. "At least Michael's solvent and sober."

Mac frowned but didn't argue.

"So you're okay with me working with Michael?" I wished I could see his expression better through the darkness.

"Who you work with isn't my decision. And in this case it doesn't seem to be yours either so . . . good luck, I guess."

Would it have killed him to act jealous? Forget charmingly possessive, I would have settled for vaguely concerned. But then if he had, what would I have done? Blown him off and told him he wasn't the boss of me, probably.

Down the hill, I saw a state highway patrol car pulling up behind mine. A young, dark-haired guy got out and made his way toward Mac and me. His face, bearing, and general attitude were eerily familiar. He could be nothing but another Mackenzie. But what sort? Cousin? Brother?

I moved an appropriate distance away from Mac.

"What idiot did this?" the newcomer asked by way of greeting. Mac silently pointed at the kids. The state trooper nodded. "Anybody getting arrested?"

"Don't think so. The kids had permission to be here. That structure was decrepit and the owner was going to pull it down this summer anyway so for her it's almost a win." Then seeing the trooper giving me the once-over he said, "This is Drew Allison. He's the chef at the Eelgrass. Drew, this is my brother, Remington."

"Just Remy's fine." He held out a hand, which I shook. "Mac got takeout for us from your place once. It was so good! I still think about that fried chicken sandwich. I told my girlfriend she had to learn how to make it. She told me where I could go, of course." Remy gave a laugh. "I guess we'd better get started with traffic control?"

Mac looked toward the dark two-lane road.

"So I can take Lionel?" I asked.

"Yeah, they're free to go so long as they're not driving," Mac said. I could tell he wanted to say something more, but

Remy stood there being a clueless third wheel. Served me right for trying to talk to Mac at work anyway.

I started to say goodbye when the night was split by an explosion. I felt the intense surge of heat and the pressure wave against my skin. A high-pitched scream pierced the flickering darkness. One second I was standing, the next I was on the ground in the damp leaves end debris. Mac lay on top of me. I lay there stunned, taking in the scene from shoe level.

To my left Remy crouched, shielding his face with his hat. The firefighters shouted to one another and the bystanders "Is anyone hurt? Is anyone hurt?"

Mac's hat had come off and he breathed heavily into my ear. I craned my neck to look at him. His eyes were wide with alarm.

"You okay?" he asked.

"Yeah," I shrugged him off me and sat up. "What the hell was that?"

"I'm going to guess there was an old propane tank in there," Mac said. "You all need to clear the area."

Remy had already regained his feet and was looking down at us smirking. I smiled back at him and gave an awkward laugh while slapping the dust off my shirt. He offered me a hand up. Mac found his own way to his feet then bent to scoop up his hat. All three of us moved farther downhill, away from the fire zone.

"Jeez, Mac why didn't you pick me to save from the deadly shrapnel?" Remy said, with a snicker. "I feel so betrayed."

"You're not a civilian," Mac's gruff tone telegraphed his embarrassment. "How many of those people do you think you can fit in your car, Drew?"

"I only have four extra seat belts," I said. "But I could probably jam seven of them in there." Then to Remy, "It's a hatchback."

Another massive bang broke through the roar of the flames and again I found myself smashed into Mac's chest—though not on the ground this time. It was touching and, if I'm honest, comical how Mac just couldn't stop himself from attempting to shelter me.

"You're breaking my heart, bro." Remy, half-crouched over, gave an exaggerated pleading look.

"Just get everyone out of here." Mac ignored Remy's remark, but I could see his neck reddening. "I'm going to say the urgent evacuation trumps seat belts at this point."

"Plus, every highway officer on duty in this sector is here right now, so as long as you promise not to crash, I can look the other way," Remy put in.

I raised a solemn hand, "I swear to do my best to keep it between the ditches."

"Good." Remy nodded then looked pointedly between his older brother's retreating back and me. "It's been very nice to meet you, Drew."

◆◆◆

Not since my high school days in Wyoming had so many people crammed so illegally into my station wagon. Seven partygoers piled in: two in the hatchback, three in the back seat. Lionel called shotgun but let Ainsley ride on his lap while he stretched the seat belt around them both. Had the car flipped over several of them would have pinballed around like mice in a coffee can. Fortunately, I was able to get them all back to their respective domiciles. I dropped Ainsley off last.

The house Michael had rented for himself and his crew sat on the outskirts of town. It was owned by a couple in Seattle who let it out as a vacation rental most of the year. Since most of the front wall of the house was made up of the kind of high-end windows that entirely blocked out the roar of the surf below, I could see Michael inside, sitting on the couch texting. Ainsley was also texting. A quick glance at Ainsley's screen confirmed that they were texting each other.

Ainsley had been so absorbed in this that she didn't even notice I'd stopped the car.

I considered mentioning that this was her stop but decided, on the whole, that it would be funnier to honk.

Two little beeps, just to say, "Hey Michael, come get your drunk PA so I can go home."

So that's what I did.

Remember that Dad joke "instant karma?" The ear-splitting shriek that Ainsley emitted was so shrill and so loud that it left my right ear sore and ringing. She clutched her chest as though I'd actually given her a heart attack. I glanced inside the house, but Michael just kept texting away, which I guess proved that the sound-proof windows really worked.

I turned back to Ainsley.

"Your stop," I said, as blandly as I could.

She shot me a petulant glare.

"Michael says you should come in and say hello." As she spoke, she flinched as if relaying the request physically hurt her. She screwed her ear buds more tightly into her skull.

Through the window I could see Michael beckoning me inside.

I don't know how you feel about your exes, but I try to avoid mine, just as a precautionary measure. I don't like conflicts that end with me having to admit uncomfortable truths about myself or my ability to love and be loved.

Unfortunately, fate had saddled me with Michael as a new business partner, which meant that I would be working with him day-in, day-out. We might as well try and set a few ground rules at the outset.

The first one would be no pawing me in public. Or in private, for that matter.

So I followed Ainsley up the stunning path of beautifully placed boulders and lush fruit trees to the architectural gem where Michael awaited me. Inside was warm, quiet, and scented with the unmistakable fragrance of freshly-baked tres leches cake—my favorite of Michael's vast baking repertoire.

Ainsley stalked off deeper into the building, leaving us alone in the great room.

Michael watched her go with an expression of slight concern tinged with amusement, before welcoming me with open, cashmere-clad arms. The softness of them contrasted sharply against the cheap fabric of Mac's uniform.

I kept the hug brief.

"You're covered in leaves," he remarked, picking a couple bits of debris from the sweater.

"I got hurled to the ground." I gave a brief summation of how I'd come to be Ainsley's taxi ride home. Michael listened, nodding.

"Yeah, Ainsley texted me already. Is everything in this town always burning up? It's worse than California," he said.

"Not until recently." Though as I said it, I could feel the deeper truth tugging at my consciousness. The fires had coincided with the arrival of Michael's film crew. "Did you have a bunch of unexplained fires back in LA recently?"

"Drew, almost the whole state was on fire," Michael said.

"But no garbage cans or anything strange like that?"

"What are you trying to say?" Michael asked.

"Nothing. Sorry." I bent to peer through the window of the gleaming silver double wall ovens.

"No problem. Are you hungry?" Michael gave me a smile. He had nice lips. Perfect lips, even, and soft brown eyes with dark lashes.

"If you're offering me some of that cake, yes."

Michael gave his big smile—the one that had landed him a television contract and said, "Sure thing."

He rounded the plinth-like expanse of the kitchen island and started opening up cabinets, searching for a couple of bowls. He found them on the third try.

"You know I was worried about seeing you again," he said, with post-rehab frankness. "I didn't know how you would react to the news that Sam had sold her stake in the restaurant."

"I'd say I was shocked but . . . I've lost the ability to feel anything at all regarding Sam." If he was going to be forthright, I might as well be too. "I'm not unhappy to have a new business partner. Especially not one as successful as you are. But I do wonder why you agreed, given how you feel about my influence on your creativity."

Michael stalled for a while by focusing his attention on cutting and scooping out two pieces of the moist dessert. "One of the things you do when you're in recovery is to try and make amends for your past actions."

"I'm not in recovery."

"I know, Drew, but since I am, I'm telling you that I'm sorry about saying that you were holding me back."

"It's okay. It seems to have been true." I gestured around at his grand rental property.

"No, it wasn't. I was just pissed at you for wanting to quit partying. I felt like you were putting yourself above me and rubbing my nose in the fact that I was drug-dependent. But that's not what you were doing. You were acting on your own behalf, which is your right."

While I had known that this might be the case, I found the statement gratifying nonetheless—which was how I was supposed to feel, I guess. So far so good amends-wise. The problem with this transaction was that it required me to offer up some atonement of my own.

I am not a good apologizer. I don't know if it's a deficit of remorse or loathing for looking into the rearview mirror but I'm terrible at all aspects of personal recompense.

"I could have been more supportive of your dreams, though. Focused on the positive. Thought a little bigger. Gotten out of my own head." I took the tres leche cake Michael offered.

"That's true, but I think somehow coming to this town was the right thing for you." Michael grabbed his own fork.

"Oh?" I took my first bite of the ultra-sweet, cinnamon-topped cake. The heady flavor transported me back to the time when I was still in love with him and fascinated by every aspect of his sugar and spice existence.

"I couldn't imagine the Drew I used to know going out of his way to drive a bunch of drunk teenagers home. 'Sink or swim,' that was your motto."

"I guess it was. But hey look at me now. I'm practically a soccer mom."

"You're so full of shit," Michael said, but he was smiling. "What about your new boyfriend?"

"Who says I have a new boyfriend?" Was it possible that Lionel had already somehow managed to blab about Mac?

"Come on we both know you do." Michael drifted closer. "What's he like? Another married guy? Or some kind of priest?"

"None of your business," I spluttered. "And priest? What the hell?"

"You have weird taste." He shrugged.

"You realize you're talking about yourself as well, right?"

Michael had been married to a woman when we'd first hooked up—though I hadn't known that and in retrospect should have been paying more attention to the red flags.

"Is he a . . . merchant marine?" Michael relaxed back against the counter, gesturing airily with his fork. "Or no, wait—how about longshoreman?"

"Now you're just listing macho jobs," I said. "And Orca's Slough is a tourist town. We don't have longshoremen. If it wasn't for UPS, we wouldn't even have teamsters."

"It's gotta be something like that," Michael's eyes gleamed with mirth. "You don't want no suit and tie guy."

"Please stop."

"Does he have a big lumberjack beard? Oh, is he a lumberjack?"

"I'm not doing this—" I set down my empty bowl.

"I bet he's broke."

"He's not broke," I snapped, then cursed myself for rising to the bait.

"What kind of car does he drive?" Michael kept on. "Is it the kind with flashing lights on the top?"

So he had known. Probably through Lionel via Ainsley. Through the transparent front wall I could see the lights of Orca's Slough glittering against the dark water.

"You're the worst," I said.

"I know," Michael gave a sigh. "But I had to tease you. I miss you, you know? People in LA are so serious and secretive and sensitive. You're just all out there. What you see is what you get."

Flattering as this statement was, it filled me with alarm. Was Michael just nostalgic or could he really be trying to rekindle the flame? Or, and this was much more likely, he was scared of the new life he was making and wanted to see a familiar face.

Michael leaned closer to me.

In my pocket my phone buzzed, giving me the excuse to move away apologetically, yet quickly.

"Is that your man now?" Michael asked. "Tell him Hi from me."

Let it never be said that Michael didn't have a knack for accuracy. It was Mac:

Did you get home safe?

Me: *Dropped off all the kids. Now at Chef Michael's rental, talking shop.* (I mean, it was sort of true in that how we related to each other would affect the Eelgrass.) *What's up?*

Mac: *I won't be home tonight. Sorry.*

Me: *Roger on that.*

"Not the text you were hoping for?" Michael asked, reading the disappointment in my face. "You could stay here tonight. If you don't mind that there's no booze in the place."

I pulled back, inadvertently shifting my shoulder, which was still sore from when Mac hurled me to the ground.

The blatant come-on astonished me. What the hell could he be thinking? We'd barely come back into contact. No idea could be worse than having sex with each other. He had to know that didn't he?

He must be lonely. My heart went out to him but ultimately his dislike of solitude wasn't my problem anymore. Maybe if it had been a year ago when I'd been feeling lonely and at a loss too, I might have given it a try—maybe. But now I knew what I wanted, and I had the key to Mac's house in my pocket.

"Thank you for the offer but let's just try and keep our business together for a while." I patted him on the shoulder, turned, and left.

Chapter Five

Saturday morning saw a massive influx of tourists to the island. As Lionel was riding on a convertible in the Strawberry Days parade, I prepared to face lunch service armed with only one waitress and a fifteen-year-old dishwasher named Gerald. I went upstairs to the office and found the door already open. Had Michael come in? A ribbon of dread slithered through me. As much as I knew I could use the help, last night's casual come-on left me feeling slightly uneasy about working in close quarters with him.

But I needn't have worried. It turned out to be Ainsley. She hunched in the narrow confines of my closet-like office, rifling through my desk, completely oblivious to my presence in the doorway.

"Is there something I can help you find?" I asked.

The scream that erupted from her mouth, though piercing and viscerally irritating, was at least exactly what I expected. She whipped her head around, hand still deep in the drawer, sneering so hard I thought she might actually hiss at me.

I held up my hands in surrender.

"What? I'm only trying to help you search my desk faster," I said.

"It's not really your desk," Ainsley snapped.

I won't lie, I was astonished at just . . . the nerve of her.

"Whose desk is it then?" I inquired. I'm pretty sure through gritted teeth.

"It belongs to the company." Ainsley straightened up and recovered her regular android demeanor. She smoothed her blonde bangs away from her face. "So it's at least half Michael's."

If I had been nineteen years old when she fronted a line like this, I'd have lobbed a rubber spatula at her stupid face. Fortunately, I was thirty-one and had learned to avoid assault charges—even ones as justifiable as bouncing a utensil off Ainsley's forehead seemed right then.

I took a big step back. So far back that I was outside of the tiny office.

"I'm gonna ask you again: what are you looking for?"

"The key to the bar closet." She lifted her hand out of the drawer to display the very key, dangling from its Hall of Mosses souvenir bottle opener fob. "Last night Lionel said I should come in to help you since it's going to be busy . . . since I work here now."

"Don't pour any liquor," I said. "Unless you're licensed in this state."

"Heard, Chef." She exited the office with her head held high, not giving me another look.

I stepped into my office—yes it was mine, not anyone else's—and studied the drawer that she'd been rummaging through. It contained odds and ends: a few spare keys and pens, an Allen wrench, a couple of dead butane lighters, some spare Canadian change left over from when Mac and I went to Vancouver for the weekend. Standard stuff.

Could she have actually been looking for the key after all? Why look so suspicious then?

Michael and I would have to have words about his PA. If we were to remain partners, she had to go.

I returned to the kitchen where the dishwasher and I slung all manner of burgers—beef, chicken, salmon, veggie—until we closed at two before re-opening for dinner at five.

Normally during the break I would do paperwork while the employees prepped but the tension of the last few days made it impossible for me to even sit down, much less concentrate. So I decided instead to drive our equipment and supplies for the contest out to Copper Kettle as the venue would be open until seven to allow teams to set up their stations in advance.

Only a couple of members from other teams were present—apparently most of them had already been in first thing this morning, which checked out as most of them were women over the age of fifty.

After I finished dropping off the knives and cutting boards and hotel pans we'd be using, I ambled outside. Because of all the festivities available in town, few employees lingered on the Copper Kettle grounds.

Of course, I drifted toward the burnt barn. How could I not? There was a sign on it warning me to keep out, therefore, naturally I wanted to go inside. I could almost hear Mac inside my head, voicing his opposition to my persistent contrary urges. So, I lingered just outside peering in through a broken window.

Three of the exterior walls still stood. The fourth had been broken through. The inside of the barn had been subdivided into rooms . . . offices perhaps? There seemed to be a front office, then a hallway with four doorways, and an exit at the end. A pervasive odor of burnt metal and wood emanated from the place, bringing with it a sudden profound sense of pathos.

Someone had died right over there, only yards away and nobody knew who had done it much less why.

I really wanted to go inside but I knew Mac would never let me live it down if I crossed the barrier and fell through the damaged floor and had to be rescued. I was about to turn and go when I saw a familiar combination of aqua and purple in a ponytail moving down the hallway inside.

I ducked halfway behind the window frame. What the hell was she doing here? Granted, she worked on the property but still . . .

I peeked around the window frame to see if Abby was gone yet and, through a partially charred wall I saw her crouching down. It looked like she was shoving something into the floor. Then she stood and I ducked again out of sight until I heard the door at the end of the hallway clang shut.

You already know enough about me to know that I investigated immediately. I shoved my hand into the exposed joist beneath the floor. I felt around for a few seconds, hoping not to encounter anything living, then my fingers brushed against something cool and smooth.

It was a phone, but not the phone I remembered seeing her with before. This phone was old.

I quickly entered the passcode I'd seen Abby use before and it opened to the home screen. Nothing unusual. Why hide it then? And in a condemned building too?

I'd like to be able to say that I felt a moment of shame as I thumbed through the screens to see which apps were open, but I did not. The curiosity was just too strong. There weren't many apps on the phone and it seemed to only use wi-fi with no cellular carrier. Only one app had been used recently and it was a social media platform. Interestingly, the app logged in not as Abby, but a person named Amy Carmichael.

"Amy" had a rather generic feed full of inspirational memes. Checking her DMs I saw only one name, but that name stopped me short: Dirk Van Weezendonk.

There were dozens of DMs.

The first few seemed to be the two of them renewing their acquaintance from high school. Then the messages got strange. Dirk began to talk about feeling ashamed of something he'd done in Orca's Slough. Amy coaxed and consoled him for weeks but Dirk never said what the terrible thing he'd done was—only that he wanted to make it right and apologize. Amy said she was going home for Strawberry Days and offered to be there for him if he wanted to come back. Dirk had agreed. In the last message, Dirk said he'd arrived.

I pocketed the phone and headed straight for my car. Just as my butt hit the seat I saw Abby jogging toward me, waving me down.

My heart was in my throat and my foot flexed over the gas pedal, ready to gun it the second she started to do or say anything crazy. Instead, Abby smiled brightly, even winded and bent over.

"I heard from Remy the other day that you and Mac are friends," she said, between breaths.

"Yes?" I forced my hands to not grip the steering wheel.

"We're having a big barbecue at our place for Fourth of July and we wondered if you wanted to come?" Abby straightened up and flipped her marvelous ponytail over her shoulder.

"I'll have to talk to my partner before I can answer," I replied, deliberately using the word 'partner' to potentially muddy the waters and obscure Mac and I's relationship. "But thanks for inviting me."

"No problem." Her smile faltered somewhat but recovered. Then she turned and jogged back the way she came.

I did feel bad stealing her secret phone after that, but not bad enough to say nothing about it. I texted Mac and fifteen minutes later he met me in the parking lot behind the hardware store, which was closed so that the employees could take part in the festival.

As per standard I exited my car and sat down in the passenger seat of his cruiser. My heart hammered and my hands shook. I really didn't want to have to show him what I'd found. I must have looked terrible because he put his hand on the back of my neck and started gently massaging.

"What's up, Drew?"

I unlocked the phone and handed it to him. "I needed to show you this."

Mac's expression as he scrolled through the messages to and from Van Weezendonk changed from worry to controlled horror.

"Drew, what have you been doing?" he finally asked.

"It's not mine," I said. I explained where I found the phone and who I'd seen using it. "Abby's code is the same as yours—that's how I opened it."

Mac leaned back in his seat and stared out the front windshield for a full minute. "Did you read all of these?"

"Sort of? I got the basic gist." The pressure in the car was like a deep-sea submersible, like innumerable tons of water pressed down on my chest. "Who is the Amy Carmichael person? Is she real or is Abby catfishing Van Weezendonk?"

"Amy Carmichael was in the same year of high school as Van Weezendonk. She was very popular in her time. Strawberry Queen a couple years running. The year before you arrived, she converted to Buddhism, shaved her head, and moved to Thailand." Mac recounted the information so quickly that I wondered if she'd played some part in an earlier investigation of his. "So, I'm ninety-nine percent certain that none of these messages actually came from Amy. I think Abby was impersonating her to get a confession out of Van Weezendonk."

"What confession? How did she even know him? She would have been a little kid when he . . . did whatever he did." A sudden horror rushed through me. "Did he do something to Abby when she was small?"

"No, nothing like that." Mac's voice was tight. "He was the last person who saw our father on the day of his disappearance. He claimed he witnessed Dad board the ferry and leave."

"And so 1028 is?"

"The day our dad vanished." Mac leaned back in his seat, eyes pressed shut. "I just filed the paperwork to access Van Weezendonk's social media accounts this morning. It's not going to be long before the fact that Abby sent these messages becomes common knowledge at the station."

"I mean, I guess that depends on whether you share what you find out," I suggested.

Mac's eyes snapped open. On his face was a look I'd never seen before: scorn.

"I don't know what Abby has or hasn't done, but I would never, never cover up a crime for anyone. Who do you think I am?"

"Easy, Mac." I held up my hands in surrender. "I'm only saying that if you find out who killed Van Weezendonk and it wasn't Abby, then you might not have to reveal Abby's shady hobby, that's all."

Mac relaxed back into his seat, still giving me painful side-eye. "I'm going to call a family meeting to get to the bottom of it."

"Wise decision." I patted his arm.

He laid his hand over mine and in a deadpan voice said, "I want you to be there."

"Oh, hell no." I won't say the speed at which I removed my hand was supersonic, but it was pretty damn fast. I recoiled, plastering myself against the passenger door in total panic. "What the fuck, babe?"

Mac turned and leaned toward me then broke into a wide, somewhat malicious smile. "You know, that's the first time you've ever called me babe."

I wanted to hit him, but I didn't. But I did unstick myself from the passenger door. How could I never stay cool when he provoked me? No one else could make me react in such an absurd way.

"Thank you for bringing this to my attention," he continued moving back into his smooth, professional tone. "I'm not off till midnight but if I can I'll come for dinner tonight."

◆◆◆

I still had an hour before I had to be back for the dinner service so I decided to swing by the Beehive and give Evelyn and Julie an update. I resisted the urge to share what I'd learned about Abby with anyone except Mac, so I focused on informing them about the third fire. Predictably, Julie had an entirely different takeaway from the story.

"Mac introduced you to his brother last night? And invited you to his family meeting today?" Julie's hand fluttered above her heart. "I might as well start researching fabrics for the wedding attire right this instant."

Evelyn rolled her eyes. "I can't believe that's what you're focusing on. He obviously did it to get a rise out of Drew."

"For the sake of his pride, of course he would have to play it off as a jest," Julie responded. "But in the depths of his heart the desire must have been growing there already like a rising tide, building and building until he could no longer hold it back! He had to express it."

"I feel like the only desire growing in his heart is the need to solve this before anyone else gets killed or any more buildings go up in smoke," I said, attempting to bring the conversation back to a more comfortable subject. And yes, I get that it reflects badly on me that I felt less vulnerable and awkward discussing murder than venturing into the realm of where things could go for me and Mac, but I am who I am.

"What do I care about arson and murder when I can hear wedding bells sounding in the distance?" Julie countered. "Oh, Drew, speaking of flowers, which are you partial to?"

"Don't answer that," Evelyn said. Then to Julie, "You're not going to start planning Drew's wedding."

"Oh, certainly not. That would be meddlesome and completely inappropriate." Julie set her chin on her palm and gazed glassily into space so clearly envisioning the event that I could practically see it myself.

I suppressed a shudder and silently congratulated myself on not telling them about also receiving a house key.

"After I got home last night I did a little research on Copper Kettle," I said. "Eugene Wang is the owner of the business but not the property. He leases it from Carmen Foti, the replacement judge. She inherited it from her grandmother five years ago. That's why Carmen was at the competition in the first place."

"I guess that explains why she was so willing to be a last-minute participant as well," Evelyn said.

"It does," I said.

"It's a good connection, but she couldn't have started the fire then gotten back to the judge's table. She's on crutches, poor thing. She can barely hobble faster than me," Julie said. "I'm in her Aqua Yoga class. She can't even manage downward-facing dog paddle right now."

"So she's out of the running for being the pyromaniac." My hope for a quick solution sank slightly but not completely. "But Carmen is still a local and she'd have been in high school at the same time as Van Weezendonk so she might have known him, at least in passing."

"Oh, she knew him all right," Evelyn said. "She even came to visit his mother here this morning to give her condolences. The two of them were friends, it turns out."

"Really?" I did my best to quash my excitement about this news since the fact was that the school here was so small that basically everyone would know everyone. "If they were close then maybe Carmen would have some insight about why he'd have been at her grandmother's property? Maybe he thought it was still abandoned? He hadn't been back to the island in years. I wonder if there's any way to ask her about it."

"You'd need to be careful." Evelyn put her espresso cup down on the table and leaned close. "Shirley—that's Dirk's mother—is beside herself and very defensive about people slandering her son. If Carmen told her you'd been asking questions she'd be on the phone to the sheriff's office lickety-split. We're only able to talk to her because Julie does her hair."

At the sound of her name, Julie roused herself, "Oh yes, that's true. She favors an updo for church."

Evelyn continued. "From what we've been able to gather, Shirley couldn't figure out what possessed her son to come back to town after being gone for so long."

That, at least, I knew, even though I couldn't say.

"And then she didn't even get to see him before he was killed." Julie raised her hand to her mouth. "It's tragic. It would almost be better if she never knew he'd intended to see her."

"How's that?" Evelyn asked.

"Because there's the question of what he might have said," Julie said as if it were obvious. "Imagine if Drew said he was coming to say something important then got murdered—wouldn't it be so much more agonizing than if he simply got murdered?"

"I think Drew getting murdered at all would be the main cause of that agony," Evelyn said. "But I acknowledge that the burning question would also bother you a lot."

"Thank you, darling." Julie reached over to pat her hand.

This casual exchange of theirs somehow made me teary and I excused myself right away.

◆◆◆

When I got back to work, a line of sunburnt tourists were already queued up in front of the restaurant giving their names to Savannah and waiting to be fed.

Michael arrived just after me with his producer in tow. They ate at the bar, then the producer departed and Michael set up his laptop.

Perhaps anticipating that I'd have some words to say about her, Ainsley hovered near Michael the whole dinner service, deflecting all my attempts to initiate a private conversation.

Dinner went by in a blur of "catch of the day" plates then, shortly before seven, Mac arrived. As he came through the door I ducked into the employee bathroom (read: mop closet) to check my look. It was not good. I splashed some water on my face, raked my flat hair back into some kind of shape and ditched my apron. I left the chef's coat on. I liked to match a uniform with a uniform when I could.

I wondered if he'd had a chance to talk with Abby or if he'd really decided to convene a whole family council over it.

When I came back out I caught sight of Mac standing near the bar looming over Michael. It was the first time I'd ever seen Mac flex on anyone who was not actively committing a crime. He didn't seem angry so much as displeased to an extreme degree. His arms were crossed over his chest and his jaw jutted forward slightly.

I had no idea what he was saying to Michael, but I knew I either had to go break it up or else leave out the back door and never come back to this restaurant or even this island ever again.

After one brief glance at the back door, I strode across the dining room and carefully grabbed Mac by the shoulder.

"Why don't you get settled at your usual table?" I gestured to the small round table in front. "And I can start your dinner."

"Wow, I never would have thought you'd evolve into a domestic goddess," Michael commented. His tone was excessively catty—almost a parody of himself.

I felt Mac's arm tense and I gave it a firm squeeze.

"Come on, go sit down," I said.

Mac finally looked at me. Then, with great reluctance he turned and stalked toward the front window. I rounded on Michael.

"You prick what did you say to him?"

"I didn't say nothing." Michael couldn't keep the smirk off his face. "Look at you all in my face protecting him, though. You never protected me like that."

"I did, you were just too drunk to remember," I said.

"That's low."

"More like just accurate," I said. "Tell me."

"All I said was that it looked like we were going to be sharing you." Michael made a grandiose gesture of innocence. "Who knew he'd get the wrong impression?"

"Why?" I leaned closer to Michael. "Why would you do that?"

"I bothers me that he comes here pretending like he's your husband looking for his dinner." Michael gave an airy wave of his hand.

"But, again, why? He pays full price so what the fuck do you care?" I could feel my neck getting red. "I get that you live for drama, but can you not drag Mac into the perpetual soap opera of your life? It's okay when it's me. I fully expected to be exploited for the purposes of entertainment but can't you leave my boyfriend alone?"

"Honey, he's so not right for you. He's way too . . . uptight." Michael slouched over his laptop.

"He's not uptight. He's just mad. At you. For saying that shit to him." I sighed. "Stop trying to get attention this way. It's pathetic."

"Don't use that tone with me. I'm not your employee. And speaking of that, you have to start talking to OUR employees much more nicely. When you yelled at Ainsley it triggered her anxiety so bad she had to go cry in the walk-in. Did you know?" Michael asked. "It's not like the old days when you could just treat people like trash. You're just lucky she doesn't go online and accuse you of being a toxic employer."

"Yell?" I turned back to him. "When did I yell?"

"When she went into the office to get the bar key. She was only trying to help."

I narrowed my eyes. "First of all it's my office, not the office. Secondly, I asked her what she was doing in a normal tone."

"I think it's at least our office now." Michael gave me a smile. "Isn't it?"

"Oh my God, is that what this is about? You think I picked on Ainsley, so you go wind up Mac?" Even as I said it, I knew it had to be true. "Can you please stop being petty? Please?"

Michael smiled. "You know I miss our arguments. You always have a comeback. Other people aren't as good at it as you are. I miss this—it always made me feel so alive."

"Maybe you should take up boxing, then." I snapped "Because I did not miss this in any way."

I stalked back to the range and fired up a skillet. Incredibly, Michael decided to follow me onto the line to slouch against the salad fridge. I didn't have a lot of energy to get incredibly creative while sparring with Michael at the same time, so I decided to make Mac some alfredo. It was fast and he liked it. I could serve it with grilled shrimp and green salad and Mac would be happy. I continued to ignore Michael, who had apparently decided to stick to me for the purpose of providing unhelpful commentary.

"You didn't put enough garlic in that," he remarked. "It won't have any punch."

"I put in as much punch as he likes."

"You even nerf your recipes for him? You've really lost your edge. No wonder this place loses money, oh my God . . ."

With that last shot, Michael peeled off, leaving me to finish Mac's plate and fume silently over the belated realization that owning the Eelgrass with my ex and his weird, entitled PA was never, ever going to work in the long term. Orca's Slough was my territory, and he was a hostile invader.

I had to get him to go back to LA.

But in the meantime, I picked up Mac's plates, walked them out to his table, and sat down opposite him. He still looked angry but accepted them. He had the old-fashioned habit of always taking his hat off at the dinner table and his hair sat flat against his head. Even with that, he was still the most handsome guy I'd ever seen.

"I'm sorry about Michael. He's always been an instigator," I said.

Mac nodded and twirled the pasta around his fork. "I've called a family meeting—about Abby."

"You're going to confront her?"

"I don't know if confront is the right word." Mac moved a shrimp onto his fork. "More like gently inquire."

I gave a mirthless snort of laughter. How did a person gently inquire about whether or not your younger sister lured a man to his death? Only Mac would think this was possible. Then as I considered the restraint and tolerance he'd demonstrated toward me and even Michael, I decided that it might be possible for Mac to do just that thing.

Chapter Six

Finally, around nine-thirty, the last ticket had been made. Gerald had left hours before, replaced by Kaden, my newest protégé, freshly graduated from the culinary program at Seattle Central College. With only half an hour to go, I turned the place over to him and headed straight to Mac's place. I already had fresh clothes from my aborted mission the previous night and I figured I'd shower when I got there.

I'd been on my feet for twelve hours and felt swoopy—almost drunk with fatigue. I wanted to get a good night's sleep before the contest, but I also wanted to see Mac. Like for good luck. Was that a thing? Good luck sex? If not, I intended to make it so.

The light was on in the kitchen, so I tried the door and it opened. I swept inside and saw five sets of eyes looking at me. Human eyes.

Five people sat around the small, round kitchen table. Each held a hand of cards. Red, white, and blue poker chips lay in a pile in the center.

These people were mostly tall, mostly fit and mostly dark-haired with the exception of one teenager whose hair had been dyed a kind of sea-foam green to violet ombre in the "mermaid" style.

"Hi Abby," I said. Then to the off-duty highway patrol officer who sat next to her. "Remy."

Holy hell, I thought, how could they all have been summoned to the family meeting so quickly? It didn't seem to have started yet, though.

"Mac's not home yet." Abby cracked a big, shit eating grin which told me she had no idea what was about to happen to her.

"Hey Drew," Remy gave me a professional smile, such as the Mackenzies were apparently born with the ability to produce. "Mac said you might be crashing here tonight."

After another moment of stupor I realized the other three poker players must be the remaining siblings: two brothers and one sister. The brothers and oldest sister regarded me with various degrees of suspicion. As Remy introduced them, I privately gave them my own monikers: Cowboy Clayton, Morose Mason, and Charlotte the Friendly Spider.

At times like these there are only two choices: bold advance or bold retreat. To cringe or equivocate is death. Here, facing Mac's whole family in their family home I, of course, chose advance.

"I really need to take a shower. When Mac gets here tell him I already went to bed, okay? Got a big day tomorrow." I gave them all a tight-lipped smile. "Nice to meet you all."

I walked up the stairs, resolutely not looking back down into the kitchen as I turned on the grand staircase's landing. I went straight to the shower. As the water hit me, so did the stupidity of my decision. I stood practically shaking in anger at myself as I realized that I might have just outed Mac. Then again, he'd obviously alerted Abby to potentially expect me so maybe not? Still, if all the Mackenzies were here, where was I supposed to be sleeping?

What the fuck was wrong with me that I was like this? I should have just turned around and left. Or claimed that I was just dropping by for a beer.

I rested my head against the white and gold tile shower-surround, letting the limp shower with its terrible water pressure flop down the back of my neck, wondering: is there anyone who can screw me as well as I can screw myself?

As I pondered whether or not I should now attempt to climb out the window, slither down the drainpipe and disappear into the night, a light knock came at the door. Then it opened a crack.

"I'm coming in." Mac's voice was sweet relief. I didn't even care if he was going to be mad at me because: I mean, he might. At least I wouldn't be alone in this idiot predicament.

I pulled the shower curtain slightly aside and peeked at him. He still wore his uniform and looked more tired than I'd ever seen him. I didn't intentionally pull puppy-dog eyes. But I noticed, glancing in the mirror, that my face was doing that anyway.

Mac started to snicker. "You have the worst luck of anybody I've ever met. You're like an awkwardness magnet."

"I know!" I slumped against the shower wall.

Mac locked the door. Guilt began to creep over me. As bad as the situation was for me, how much worse did all of this have to be for Mac?

"Your brothers and sisters, do they know?" I'm not sure why I was so awkward but I couldn't seem to help myself. "I mean about you—us?"

"Well, they do now," Mac replied.

My heart began to pound in my chest. This could go so very badly. It certainly had for me. Coming out had been the death knell for my already-distant relationship with my family. But at least I'd been prepared for the rejection. I'd been able to console myself with the knowledge that they hadn't ever been all that close with me to begin with. But for Mac . . .

I suddenly felt both protective of him and terribly guilty. As in, I should have protected Mac from my own dumbass bravado, and thoughtless actions.

"I'm so sor—" I began only to have my agonized apology cut off by Mac.

"I mean they just learned about us," Mac said. "About six months back I started talking to each of them about me."

"Really? How did it go?"

"Better than expected," Mac shrugged. "It'll probably be worse when it comes to my uncle, but it helps to know that my brothers and sisters are all right with it. With me."

He started to unbutton his shirt.

Were we really going to shower together with his whole family downstairs?

"Wait," I spotted a smear on his shoulder. "Is that blood?"

"Yes. Not mine though. I had to help drag a dead deer out of the road. You finished?" Mac sat down on the toilet and started unlacing his boots.

"Just have to wash my hair."

So this wasn't going to be one of those romantic showers. Good thing, 'cause I probably couldn't take it. Also the shower wasn't really that big. In fact the whole bathroom was so small that our chests scraped together as we shifted places in the tightly confined space. I gave him a sheepish half-smile and he patted me on the shoulder and kissed my cheek. Chastely.

Like I'd been demoted to younger brother status.

Out of respect for my own rank I grabbed his ass, which prompted him to say, "Yeah, yeah. I'll be done soon. Just wait in the bedroom, okay?"

I'd have defied the instruction if I hadn't been so relieved to see him. As it was, I slipped out of the bathroom and down the hall to Mac's room without fuss. From below in the kitchen I could hear murmuring but no distinct words.

Mac's bedroom was clean and contained very little. He had recently painted the walls mid gray and the ceiling, with its elaborate crown molding, white. Dark blue blackout curtains hung over the single sash window. Most of the small space was taken up by a double bed that we both barely fit on. This was covered by a handmade pinwheel-patterned quilt that looked very old. There was also an antique chestnut dresser with nothing on top of it, and a black gun safe that if it were open would be shown to contain a Glock 9mm pistol, a Remington pump-action shotgun, as well as a kid-sized .22 bolt-action rifle that had Mac's initials burnt into the stock.

I dropped my bag near the door and climbed into the far side of the bed staring up at the old brass light fixture with its frumpy, square glass shade that, although not my style, was probably original to the house.

Mac entered only a couple of minutes later, wearing only sweatpants, still toweling off his hair.

"So I guess you met everyone?" he began.

"Not really, just learned their names."

"I'm glad you decided to come." Mac sat down on the bed next to me. "We're going to talk to Abby as soon as I get dressed."

I rolled over on my side and rubbed a hand up his wide, well-muscled back. My mind went a million directions. Did he really expect me to just intrude on this intimate family conversation? Mac reached around and caught my hand in his, patting it lightly as though to tell it to quiet down and quit moving around.

He must be really tense, I thought. I went limp and watched his profile.

I had only the sketchiest grasp of the events surrounding the disappearance of Mac's father. Julie aside, everyone in town who had been an adult at the time had accepted that he had, for whatever reason, abandoned his family. I could see how that explanation would not appeal to his children though.

"I think Abby may have inadvertently gotten Van Weezendonk killed," Mac said.

"What? How?"

"I'd always thought he'd lied about seeing my dad leave the island, but I could never find a way to prove it."

I pulled my hand out of Mac's and sat up. "Wait, back up. So for all this time you've been looking for a way to prove this guy lied?"

"Wouldn't you?"

"I—well, I guess I would." I filled in the blanks pretty fast. "Why did you think Van Weezendonk lied in the first place?"

"Either because he was involved or because he wanted to cover up for the person who was actually responsible for my dad's disappearance."

"And that person is?"

"I don't know." Mac's shoulders slumped as if this admission physically weighed on them. The rims of his eyes were red from fatigue and maybe something else. He pushed himself to his feet. "Anyway, I have to go talk to Abby now. Are you coming?"

"You know that would be beyond inappropriate. If I'd have known everyone was here I would have never come over tonight."

Mac smirked. "I know. I just wanted somebody to hold my hand while my little sister gets real mad at me. Deep down, I'm a coward."

"You can hold my hand when you get back." I leaned forward and smacked his butt. "Go get em, Tiger."

Mac took a deep breath and pulled a t-shirt over his head and turned to plant a kiss on my lips. "Don't wait up."

After he left, I set my alarm for five, since I had to be in makeup at six. I waited for a few minutes, listening, but apart from the low rumble of Mac's voice the warm summer night remained quiet. Without knowing it I fell asleep, only to be awoken hours later as he coiled his legs with mine, curling into me.

He didn't need to say anything; I could feel that whatever transpired downstairs during the family meeting had hurt. Need radiated off him, a desperation, and I realized with a start that he wasn't entirely joking about the bit about me being there to hold his hand.

I carded my fingers through his hair, as I'd been longing to do all day. Then I jerked his head lower and kissed him.

His tongue surged into my mouth, big hands cradling my face, and I was at once thrilled and overwhelmed by the sheer size of his desire. When a man the size of Mac wanted you, you felt it everywhere.

He rolled on top of me, our cocks grinding together, and I moaned loudly.

"Shh," Mac whispered in my ear. "Remy's sleeping downstairs."

I pressed on Mac's shoulders. "Are you saying we should stop?"

He smirked. "Just try not to be so noisy for once."

Of course, that's easier said than done when a hundred and ninety pounds of heavy male heat presses you into a mattress and directs all his attention on getting you off.

It was a dance we'd gotten good at but being quiet added a challenge that I enjoyed for its novelty. Mac wasn't particularly loud in bed, but I was. I had to bite my arm as he pulled my length into his mouth, hand gripping my testicles with gentle firmness, pulling me deep enough that he gagged on his first go, then went back for more.

My arm was bitten raw by the time my pleasure crested. He never immediately let go; he liked to continue to nuzzle me afterward, licking me clean.

After, he crawled up my body and we kissed sloppily. I tasted myself in his mouth, felt him rutting against my leg. Precum was forming a slick on his hairy chest as his own cock begged for attention, so I figured it was time to see if I could get Mac to break his mute streak.

I pushed at his shoulder and lay him on his back, then scooted down to return the favor.

His cock was a blowjob challenge, but I was nothing if not persistent when I set my mind on a goal. Mac had already worked himself into a state, so it wasn't long before I felt him shaking, hips stuttering under me, desperate to push deeper but too polite to do so.

I glanced up at him. His eyes were glazed, watching me, mouth open, lips flushed red.

"Do it," I whispered.

"Are you—"

"Come on, babe. Wreck me."

Mac let out a guttural groan. He gripped the sides of my head, turned us slightly, and then let himself go.

I had a moment of thinking, oh shit, what have I just agreed to? Because Mac wasn't small by any standards, and he was strong. He started fucking my mouth with fervor.

But he was also still Mac, incapable of ignoring his macho protective streak. So a battle waged in my mouth between his cock's need to be rough and his heart's desire to be gentle. His cock was winning. And I was fine with that. Moments later a loud cry filled the air as he filled my mouth.

His hands released my hair and switched to caressing my head. He urged me up, and I sleepily climbed his body once more, resting my head in the crook of his neck.

"Are you all right?" Mac whispered, panting. "I didn't hurt you, did I?"

I grinned. "Try not to be so noisy for once."

I was rewarded with a flush that he quickly hid by pulling the covers over both of us.

"Go to sleep, Drew."

Mac lay beside me when my alarm went off at five.

He shifted and grumbled but didn't wake up as I slid from beneath the quilt.

I thought I could slip away unseen. Instead, I found Remy at the kitchen table, stirring a cup of milky coffee, wearing his uniform.

I gave him a smile. "Don't you have a home to go to?"

"Stayed here last night after the big ol' family meeting." He slurped on the coffee, a thoughtful expression on his face. "Mac said you wouldn't say anything about finding out about Abby's little catfishing expedition. Is that true?"

"I've turned the phone I found over to a member of law enforcement, like any good citizen would." I took a drink of the too-hot too-cheap coffee then went to the refrigerator to find some half and half, understanding for the first time why Mac felt it was necessary to add it. If ever I were to be in a position to sleep here a lot, changing the brand of coffee served would be among my first priorities. "It's up to him what to do with that information."

"Mac seems really close to you."

"Not all the time," I said wryly. "But we do have moments where we're more or less inseparable."

"Has he told you about what happened to our family?"

"That's such a broad, ominous question." I decided to stall for time on this one. The energy coming off Remy wasn't the same as before. He'd dropped both the Mackenzie affability and smile. His expression had gone flat as a mask. I made it my mission to compensate for his lack of friendliness. "Do you mean how your father disappeared? He hasn't told me much. That he went missing is about all I know."

"Well, about a year before it happened Mom was sick for the first time," Remy said. "She had chemo and the doctor said she was cancer-free, but she never completely recovered and we were all struggling with that, but Dad had a hard time asking for help, you know? He was very depressed. After he left, Mac became obsessed with proving that he'd been murdered and finding his remains."

"No big change in Mac's personality since then I guess." I gave Remy a swift smile, which, as it turned out was exactly the wrong thing to do.

In hindsight, I guess I should have figured that out, but I was thinking my own thoughts, feeling nervous about suddenly having so much that was obviously still painful revealed to me before I'd even finished my first cup of coffee. The irony is that I'd gone with a breezy response thinking it would give Remy the opening to just blow me off and change the subject to something that wasn't obviously still hurting him and the rest of their family.

"Is this whole thing a joke to you?" Remy's eyes were bright and hard as polished stone. "You don't know what Mac was like after Dad left."

"No. But I guess you could tell me." I did my best to backpedal after badly misreading his mood.

"Tell you?" Remy spoke as if I'd made the most outrageous request on earth. "I don't have time to tell you about my brother's whole life. I just want to know if you understand that you're not doing him any favors by encouraging him to go back down that rabbit hole."

"Why would you think my encouragement is something that can affect Mac at all?"

Remy set down his mug with a heavy clunk. "Every single person in LE in this town knows you think you're some kind of amateur detective."

"How do they know that?" I tried to recollect any time I'd talked about my morbid fascination with crime with anyone other than Mac.

"Because Mac is always repeating great ideas you had," Remy said. "It's always, 'Drew down at the Eelgrass' was saying this or that. And how cute you are when you're being so serious about telling him stuff you saw on some true crime show."

I was stunned. Mac had actually talked about me. Bragged about me. Called me cute! The revelations made me want to defend Mac, and by extension myself, from his argumentative little brother. Despite my earlier intention of not getting further involved in a painful family history, I couldn't keep from responding. "I listen to what Mac tells me and I offer my thoughts about crime or whatever else he wants to talk about. So what?"

"Do you ever think that maybe some of the things that you say are very irresponsible? That maybe he needs to try and come to terms with the fact that there are some things we'll never know and start to live his own life instead of being stuck in the past? Do you know that he still follows up every single unidentified body in our Dad's age range? Chaz said he saw Mac running a search of the police data base just last week. He can't be doing that at work." Remy glowered at me. "Now Abby is doing this crazy shit too. Dragging us all back into the past. Both of them need to accept that their father was just a sack of shit who left them. And move on."

I almost said something really mean then I managed to see around my defensiveness to onboard the obvious: Mac's dad was Remy's dad too.

I know, I know.

Please feel free to nominate me for Dumbass of the Year for ever engaging in this conversation at all, much less with the flippancy that I did.

I looked at the floor and for a while said nothing because nothing was what I had the right to say about this. I wasn't going to apologize—Remy had clearly intended to ambush and blindside me. But I ceded the battlefield to him.

Remy appeared to accept my capitulation.

"Why are you telling me any of this?" I asked.

"Because I want you to stop condoning Mac's obsession," Remy said. "You're his first serious boyfriend. Be a better influence."

I don't know where Remy got the idea that Mac somehow asked for my permission to do anything, but that was beside the point. His choice of words had given him away.

"Bullshit." I stepped close and dropped my voice to a whisper. "This has nothing to do with me encouraging Mac, does it? You're pissed off because I caught your kid sister getting into trouble and you blame Mac for being a bad influence on her. But you're scared to tell him yourself so you're trying to get me to rein him in on your behalf."

Remy gave me a stare so blank I thought for a second that someone had switched the lights off in his mind. Then the Mackenzie smile reappeared on Remy's face, just like that.

"You're one of those guys, aren't you? A straight shooter?" Remy's professional smile widened.

"And you're one of those guys who likes to get other people to do his work for him," I replied.

"That's just common-sense delegation. You should understand that since you're so full of great ideas. Think of this as your initiation into the family," Remy spread his arms expansively—to include all the Mackenzies in the world in his welcome, I suppose. Then he turned and started for the door. "I believe in you."

"I'm not joining your family, dickweed," I hissed at his retreating back.

"Good luck making it through the probationary period," he called back sweetly.

I spun on my heel and saw Abby and her older sister Charlotte standing in the kitchen doorway. Charlotte wore blue plaid pajamas but Abby was completely dressed for work. Of course she would be. We were going to the same competition. I knew they couldn't have been standing there long. Probably only since the point that Remy had put his professional smile back on again.

So I took a cue from him, flashed them my pearly whites and said, "Who wants coffee?"

◆◆◆

I'm not sure how I managed it, but I convinced Mac's sisters that my argument with Remy had been about who would tell Mac that, for the sake of the world, he needed to buy a set of odor-destroying insoles, and got to the front doorstep in less than five minutes.

It had rained during the night and droplets beaded every surface, edging them with a surreal glow in the early morning sun. I should have been focusing on the contest but worry over what Remy had said left a knot in my gut that would not dissipate. If the Van Weezendonk murder didn't get solved before access to the dead man's social media accounts was granted, Abby's catfishing expedition would have to be investigated. She'd have to be treated as a real murder suspect. That would be hell for Mac. For their entire family—but Mac had my personal vested interest and concern. The fact that I'd discovered the phone and handed it over to Mac was a persistent needle of guilt.

I'd barely gotten my keys in the car door when Abby jogged across the lawn. "Can I ride with you?"

There wasn't a diplomatic way to say no.

As soon as she ensconced herself in the passenger seat Abby began to smile and cringe.

"Mac told me that you were the one who found my secret phone," she said. "I'm sorry you got caught up in this. I'm not a creep usually."

"I'm sure you're not," I assured her. Main Street was still empty as we passed through, populated only by a couple of early morning runners. "I guess I just don't know why you didn't tell your brother."

"My cop brother who's certain our dad was murdered, who is deep-down filled with sorrow and rage? Or my other cop brother who thinks our dad's still alive and is also really angry?" Abby gave a weak laugh. "Or do you mean the other two who pretend like nothing happened?"

"Fair enough," I conceded. "I am curious about something though."

"Go ahead. Ask me anything." Abby twirled her ponytail in one hand while gazing out the window at the passing orchards.

"How did you even get the idea to do this?"

"I saw it on a true crime show," Abby replied. "The investigators used a dummy social media account to break the murderer's alibi."

"I think I've seen that one too," I admitted.

"I knew Mac suspected Van Weezendonk, so I thought I'd friend him online. I used the name and picture of a classmate of his I knew wouldn't be online because she'd gotten religion and moved to Thailand to turn her back on the secular world. Van Weezendonk accepted my friend request and I just started watching him." Abby spoke as if all these actions were the next logical step. "He belongs to a music appreciation group where they post pictures of their ticket stubs for various shows. And one day he posted a ticket with a date that contradicted his story about being an eyewitness to Dad leaving."

I wasn't sure if I should be more impressed or frightened by Abby's sleuthing. At her age I was still struggling to keep track of my work schedules and excuses I made up for late rent checks.

"But anybody can get a picture of a ticket stub. How did you know he was really at the show?" I asked.

"I verified it with Van Weezendonk."

"In the guise of your girl-next-door catfishing persona?" I was impressed, sure, but that didn't mean I wasn't going to tease her.

"I wish you wouldn't call it that, but yeah. We chatted about the concert and he had a lot of details about the date and the venue and the weather. I believed him. After that we started talking. He told me a lot about his life, which hasn't been great. He had a lot of regrets. He'd been an alcoholic and his kids didn't know him. He said he'd done something really wrong that he wanted to make right. So . . . I decided to push my luck. I asked him. And he told me. He said he'd lied about seeing Deputy Mackenzie disappear and that looking back, it was a cruel thing to do to his family."

I was momentarily stunned. With this information Mac might actually have legal grounds to investigate his father's disappearance. But then I realized the flaw in that. Van Weezendonk's admission hadn't come to light through means that Mac would want to share. I wasn't even sure if the testimony would be considered reliable considering the circumstances.

"He didn't tell any of this to you though, did he?" I had to clarify. "He confessed to your fake persona, Amy Carmichael?"

"Exactly. So I, in my fake persona, told him that he could still atone for that mistake and he said he'd think about it. I sensed I was losing him so I told him that I'd be back on the island for Strawberry Days and . . . if he wanted, I would go with him to confess. He said he'd try. The next day he phoned me, and said he was on the island and asked me to meet him . . ."

"And?" I prompted.

"I agreed," Abby said. "I thought that once I confronted him with everything he'd already confessed to me that he'd realize he couldn't take it all back. I hoped he'd agree to talk to Mac. But he never showed up. I figured he'd lost his nerve."

"Until the orientation day when you found out he was dead and that you needed to get rid of that phone," I finished.

"Yeah. They'd already finished processing the crime scene so I thought it was the safest place to hide it until I could figure out what to do with it," Abby said. "But I didn't count on my brother's super good friend Drew from down at the Eelgrass catching me and ratting me out."

"I can't apologize for that, I'm sorry." I turned down the long lane which led to Copper Kettle's production facility. "You're just lucky it was me."

"I guess." Abby's tone was sulky, though her expression remained calm.

"Is your family mad about the catfishing thing?"

"Remy is, but not for the right reason." Abby heaved a sigh. "Mac's just disappointed I didn't include him. Clayton and Mason were both annoyed to be called to a meeting for something this stupid. And Charlotte thinks I need to get grief counseling. Everybody thought it was funny that we finally caught Mac with a boyfriend though. Except for Mac. So overall it was worth it."

"So you all knew he's gay already?"

Abby rolled her eyes. "He's thirty, he's never ever had a girlfriend and he has two gay hookup apps hidden in a folder on his phone. Like, what else could he be?"

I decided that I was, justifiably, intimidated by Mac's super-sleuth little sister and also that I could not, under any circumstance, let her realize that I was.

"Bi? Pan?" I said airily. "An amateur anthropologist studying the culture of hookup apps?"

"Wow, so random," Abby laughed.

"I do my best," I said.

"Honestly, if Mac hadn't actually come out to them, Clayton and Mason would probably have believed the anthropologist thing." Abby gave an amused sigh. "Charlotte would've found a way to use it as an excuse to break up with her current boyfriend. And Remy would've pretended to believe it while giving Mac shit about it at the same time."

I laughed, though Abby's insight into the Mackenzies piqued my interest.

"What about your uncle?" I asked.

"Oh, so long as it doesn't make more work for them, good old Uncle Scott and our sleepy cousin Chaz will believe just about anything," Abby sounded more than a little bitter. "It's kind of like deciding to believe dad abandoned them."

It was telling that she said them and not us, but I didn't call her on it. Though she must have noticed something because a moment later she explained.

"I was only four when he died so I don't remember him very well. Really the person who took the place of my dad was Mac, which I know sounds weird because he's only eleven years older than me but he's the one who went to all my soccer games, picked me up when I was sick, chewed me out when I skipped class. He was just . . . always there, you know. I didn't even realize how much of a burden that must have been for him. Especially after Mom died and he became my legal guardian. He was the same age I am now, and he already had a job, a house, and a kid to take care of."

She flashed a melancholic smile that was eerily similar to Mac's as she leaned against the passenger side window. Only a moment later she recovered herself enough to give an almost convincing laugh and said, "Not anymore though. As of last year I'm legally an adult. I'm free, and so is he."

"Congratulations to you both," I said, but all I could feel was a kind of sorrow for how hard those years must have been.

A moment later I rolled up to the employee entrance at Copper Kettle and Abby bounded out of the car and off to work. I continued down the lane, feeling a little stunned by the sudden knowledge of what Mac's daily existence must have been like until only one year ago. The same year he'd become an adult he'd also become head of household and the de facto father of five. By contrast I'd left my family entirely at the age of seventeen and led a more or less responsibility-free life of casual adventure for more than a decade. I didn't consider my family in any decision I made. My interaction with them amounted to a couple of phone calls a year.

Mac's life and mine couldn't have been more different.

A conversation we'd had the previous October right when we'd started to be interested in each other came vividly to mind. I'd been talking about my experiences in Japan, and he'd replied that it must be interesting to travel.

He hadn't been making small talk, I now understood. He'd been making a sincere statement of desire because before that he'd never been anywhere or done anything, because his youngest sister had left home to go to college only one month before then. No wonder he'd seemed so delighted when I'd taken him to Vancouver and shown him all the sights I knew so well.

Some genius sleuth I am.

But my cluelessness wasn't all on me. Mac rarely talked about his brothers and sisters, and they had never been at the house when I was there. When he and I were together we talked about our day, the weather, food, the petty crimes of Camas County—we talked about now.

But everybody has a past.

And Mac's was heavy. And saintly.

And over, because I'd decided that I was going to take him more places, share more experiences with him. I couldn't give him back his parents or the years he'd spent raising his siblings. But I could and I would share with him the best of the discoveries I'd made during that same time. I couldn't do anything about his past. But I wanted to give him a better future.

Finally, I pulled up next to a gold town car that turned out to contain Evelyn's cousin Joyce. She'd already put on her face and sprayed her updo to meringue-like stiffness and was applying another layer of mascara to her eyelashes, which were already so thickly coated that they looked like spider legs sticking off her eyelids.

I knew Evelyn and Julie hated her, but who knew what her life had been like? Maybe she'd lost both her parents and labored in silence for years to bring up a household of dependents. Or maybe she carried a secret grief for some impossible love? Maybe she just needed an opening to feel welcomed and wanted. How did the saying go—before you judge anyone first walk a mile in their ugly knockoff Chanel pumps?

Inspired by Mac's goodness and filled with the spirit of humanity, I knocked on the car window and gave her a smiling thumbs up.

"Break a leg," I said.

"Go to hell," she replied.

Chapter Seven

I mounted the stairs of the event center two-by-two, invigorated by the opportunity for triumph. Or if not triumph, at least the chance of defeating Joyce and Michael's team. I'd like to claim that a healthy spirit of competition energized me, but honestly I'd had about enough of both of them. I was feeling just petty enough at the moment to enjoy the two of them losing as much as I would look forward to my own team winning. Don't judge me.

That was what Carmen, the yoga teacher was here for. I spotted her just ahead of me on the path that led to the event center, moving slowly and carefully on her crutches, staring down at the sidewalk in front of her. Seizing the opportunity to speak with her alone, I jogged ahead to get the door before she made it there. When she looked up, I saw her eyes were edged with red.

Why was everyone in such a bad mood this morning? Had there been some sort of new tragedy that I was not aware of?

"Are you okay?" I asked.

"I'll be all right." She moved herself forward another step, wincing.

"There should be a wheelchair inside," I remarked. I'd scoped it out earlier in case Julie might need one.

"No, it's just a sprain." She gave an unconvincing smile. "You caught me at a bad moment, that's all."

Carmen turned to gaze at the burnt-out building.

"To tell the truth, the man who was killed the other day used to be a friend of mine." She took a shuddering breath. "We hadn't seen each other for a long time, and I didn't think it would affect me this much."

"I'm sorry," I offered. At the same time, I reconsidered my callous plan to interrogate her further about the death of her old friend.

"Thank you." Carmen seemed to regain her composure Then she gave me an assessing look. "Didn't I see you talking to Big Mac the other day?"

"He's been a good pal," I replied with a tight smile. Mac might be out to his siblings, but I wasn't about to share our relationship with the public at large. "We talk a lot. Ever since he solved the homicide at my restaurant."

"So then do you know—does he have any idea what happened?" Carmen asked. "We were all interviewed about where we were and what we all saw, which was nothing, but he didn't say if he had any leads. It's driving me crazy not knowing. Why did it have to happen?"

"Even if Mac had an idea of what happened he couldn't tell anyone." I relaxed a bit. Because of my recent experience I could relate to the feelings of fear and helplessness that must be assaulting her on every level now. "You shouldn't take it personally. They can't make accusations until they have proof."

"I don't understand."

"Even if Mac knows exactly who's guilty, he can't go ahead without real evidence," I said. "So he won't be telling me or you or anyone anything until they make an arrest."

"If they make an arrest." Carmen's expression turned glum.

I nodded. Solving a homicide wasn't as simple as picking up a can of soup at the grocery store. Gathering evidence, and testimonies, then combing through everything for the smallest clue could be time-consuming and exhausting. There was a reason the police were always asking for anyone with information to come forward. Gathering every possible piece of information would be particularly important in this case since there was no knowing what small detail might help Mac finally discover what had happened to his father.

So, I decided to just go for it and ask my questions. Sure, I might be offending a woman who was about to judge my cooking—and the Eelgrass Bistro by extension—on national television, but right now Mac's happiness mattered far more than that.

"If you don't mind me asking, what was he like—your friend I mean?"

"He'd had some struggles." Carmen began hobbling slowly through the door. "Went to LA then drifted up and down the West Coast. But when I knew him, he was really a sweet guy. Quiet. Good listener. He had a crush on me, but I wanted to live a more adventurous life. Look at me now, back here in Orca's Slough teaching Aqua Yoga."

"At least it doesn't put any strain on your ankle."

Carmen gave a slight laugh then took a step and winced. I was about to offer to go and fetch the wheelchair for her again when she turned back toward the parking lot with a deep frown. I followed her gaze to see Ainsley, Michael, and the producer pile out of a rented SUV.

"Could you do me a favor?" Carmen reached into her bag and removed a small metallic bento lunchbox. A piece of masking tape on top of the box read: 'Ainsley, GF DF VEGAN'. "Would you mind giving this to that PA? She must have left it while the crew was filming the promo for the jam company. I know it's a strange favor to ask but I really need to sit down and that girl she . . . she's sort of creepy and I don't really want to talk to her."

"Of course." I responded automatically. As I took the box I felt something shift inside. Cutlery, maybe? It seemed heavy. "I get it. Ainsley can be pretty challenging. I'll give it back to her."

Carmen smiled and then made her getaway. Though I noted that she seemed to be moving much more easily now that she'd been unburdened of having to speak to Ainsley. I headed to makeup where most of the other contestants were gathered, chatting. Generally, the attitude was congenial.

Everyone wanted to win, but most people were just happy to have the opportunity to be on television.

After we'd been powdered, sprayed, and rigged up with mics, we reported to our cooking stations. Because Michael had joined one of the teams, we were short one television personality. Fortunately a local travel show host had been fished out of his vacation cabin at the last second to talk to the camera and to do his bit for Pacific Northwest tourism.

He, Carmen, Mayor Sheila, and Sheriff Mackenzie approached the head table, which held eight identical mason jars, each containing one team's preserves.

It was time to judge the jam. This step wouldn't take too long, and then we'd get right into cooking our berry-forward appetizer, entrée, and dessert.

Since none of them were professionals, I knew the technical aspects of the jam wouldn't be judged too harshly—which would be a benefit to the other teams. I glanced over to Michael, who gave me a happy smile and a wave.

I watched as the judges reached Evelyn's jam. They dipped. They tasted.

They didn't look happy.

Lionel leaned in. "I thought that was yours, Granny."

"It is." Evelyn's voice dropped to a whisper.

As we all watched, Carmen and the two other judges spit the jam out. Evelyn started forward but then seemed to remember that she was being filmed.

"What happened to it?" Lionel asked, undervoiced. "It tasted great yesterday."

"Sabotage," Evelyn said. "Same thing happened at the Blueberry Bake-Off back in 2017." Evelyn glowered across the workstation to where Joyce stood looking smug.

"How could she even get away with it with this many cameras?" I didn't bother to ask "why" or "who" we all knew it had been Joyce.

"They were playing with our hair most of the morning," Evelyn said. "Anybody could have walked up there and switched our jar."

"Does this mean we're out of the competition?" Lionel asked.

I looked under the table. The extra jam jars were still there. I opened one and tasted it. "This one's fine. We should have enough to make it to the next round." I patted the flat of jelly jars. "So we still have a chance."

"Why aren't you saying anything though?" Lionel's expression was stricken.

"Wouldn't be classy," Evelyn gritted out. "When you lose, you lose, no matter why."

"Oh hell no." Lionel rushed forward toward the judges. "Stop the competition! We know someone is cheating!"

All three judges turned to stare at him as he rushed to the table and plonked the unadulterated jar down in front of them.

"We've been sabotaged!" Lionel proclaimed, straight to the camera. "I demand a re-taste."

The cameraman grinned from ear to ear and scuttled toward us with his Steadicam.

"What's going on?" This from Michael, who had sidled up to me while I stood stock-still, entranced by Lionel's flair.

"Drama," I said.

"Oh, fantastic! That's good for ratings." He stuck his hands in his pockets and rocked back on his heels.

"For the love of Pete . . . ." Evelyn sat down heavily on her folding chair.

Lionel remained standing with his arms crossed over his chest like a nightclub bouncer. Evelyn sat shaking her head at him and pretending to frown, but I could see she was secretly impressed by his ballsy attitude, regardless of her old-school "suffer in silence" stance toward unfairness.

The producer stopped the show for a moment and gathered all the teams around her. I instinctively looked to

Michael for the low-down. Had we screwed up the filming? More importantly, could we be fined for breaking some contractual agreement in that long waiver we'd signed? But Michael did not appear the least bit alarmed. If anything, he was enjoying the show.

The producer gave us all a long, narrow look then said, "Okay, that was cute, but if one of those judges gets sick from . . . WHATEVER was in that jelly, I'm going to get sued and shit rolls downhill, okay? So stop screwing around. We will review our footage and figure out who is responsible. In the meantime, we're going to judge the Pickle Queens based on a new, untainted jar. Everyone good with that? Great. Let's get back on track, then."

Then she gave the bright, hard smile of a person who is ten seconds away from rage-killing everyone in the room.

I leaned over to Michael and whispered, "Does she know you're quitting TV yet?"

Michael frowned. "Who said I was quitting TV?"

"Didn't you say you wanted to work at the Eelgrass? You know, in a real town?" Had I hallucinated that part?

"I said I wanted to have a place that was real. I'm not going to—you know, work the Thursday lunch shift. Executive chef—that's what I was thinking. That'll give me plenty of time to travel and you space to do your thing." Michael gave me a wink.

"Right. Makes sense." I nodded slowly and returned to Team Pickle Queen's station. Michael was already planning his escape from the drudgery of serving actual customers. Part of me wanted to be angry, but in truth, the only feeling I could summon was that of heady relief that he'd planned his own obsolescence. I didn't even care about the fate of the stylish new light fixtures I'd been hoping for.

The judges re-tasted all the jam and Evelyn's once again won the competition as it had for the last few years. Although the victory surprised no one, I'd be lying if I said Team Pickle Queen didn't feel vindicated when the judges presented Evelyn with her oversized for television blue ribbon. Even Abby grinned like a maniac as she leaned over to say, "You're pretty cool, dude," in Lionel's ear.

After that the second competition began. It was my turn to take the lead. We had thirty minutes to turn out an appetizer. To my eternal shame, Michael took the first round with his strawberry, chevre and balsamic bruschetta, Team Pickle Queen hit back hard during the entrée competition taking first for our salmon glazed with strawberry reduction garnished with strawberry-basil salsa then, quite unexpectedly, dessert went to Team Berry Beautiful, a group made up of island hairdressers who, I have to admit, nailed their strawberry Charlotte Royale.

At this point the producer had the brainwave to have a three-way run off the next day. We all agreed and started packing up.

It was only once I got home that I remembered Ainsley's lunch box. Sitting alone in the dank living room of my mobile home I gave in to temptation and opened it.

Inside was a kitchen torch wrapped in fiber-fill, like the kind you'd find in a pillow. I put the lid back on, took a photo and texted it to Michael:

Did Ainsley lose her lunchbox?

Michael: *Omg yeah where'd you find it?*

I didn't answer. Instead, I drove over to Mac's house. I parked in the driveway and texted him to come meet me in the car.

Less than one minute later, Mac sat down in my passenger seat.

"You know you really don't have to be scared of my family," Mac remarked. "They're not going to say anything to you."

"I'm not scared of your family." This was a lie, I was scared of everyone's family, including my own. But that wasn't the reason I wanted to speak with Mac alone. "I think

I found something important. Look at this." I offered the lunchbox. Mac didn't take it.

"Is this something I should potentially be wearing gloves to handle?" Mac took a pen out of his pocket and used the tip to lift and maneuver the box so that he could examine the bottom. "I only ask because you've got that crazy expression you get on your face when you think you're solving crimes."

" . . . probably?" I could feel my cheeks getting red. "Carmen Foti gave it to me to return to Ainsley."

"And?"

"Guess what's in it?"

"A gluten-free, dairy-free vegan lunch?" Mac glanced up at me. "For someone named Ainsley?"

"Nope, it's a kitchen torch." I couldn't help but beam. "And some pillow stuffing."

"Hang on." Mac returned to his house and re-emerged wearing a set of black nitrile gloves and holding a paper bag which he held out to me. "Put it in here."

I complied then watched while Mac neatly folded the top of the bag shut and made a few notes on the outside.

"Okay, tell me what you're thinking," he said.

"Carmen said that on the day of the murder, Michael, Ainsley, and the production crew came to film promotional stuff at Copper Kettle Confitures. Later on she found this lunchbox, which she asked me to return to Ainsley because she didn't want to talk to her because she's weird."

Mac shrugged. "Everyone is weird. Did Ms. Foti tell you what was inside?"

"No, she didn't. I don't think she looked, which is strange now that I think of it."

"No, that's not strange. It's completely normal for people to not look inside boxes that have other people's names clearly written on them." Mac seemed to be suppressing a smile. "You just have poor impulse control."

I would have been more sullen about the unsolicited criticism if Mac hadn't looked so happy giving it. Sometimes you've got to acknowledge a fair assessment.

"I mean that lack of impulse control works out for you though, doesn't it?" I reached over to squeeze the thick muscle of his thigh. I didn't deliberately give him a lewd smile, but I'm sure that's what was going on with my face. Because I'm arrogant, thirsty scum, especially when I've just discovered the identity of a murderer.

"Sometimes it works out. Sometimes . . . not." Mac turned to look over his shoulder to the house where Abby could be clearly seen staring out the window at us. When our eyes met, she quickly ducked below the window sash. I gave a shallow laugh. Though her sleuthing skills were top-notch her surveillance skills remained age appropriate.

Mac's cool, nitrile-encased fingers removed my hand from his person. He then returned to his notebook.

"Okay, from the top. Tell me everything that you remember about the conversation with Ms. Foti."

I dutifully recounted the conversation as far as I remembered it, while Mac made notes. I expected him to look happier about this than he did. I'd cracked the case, hadn't I?

"But why—doesn't it fit? There have been three fires in this town since Ainsley arrived and she was present at each location either before or during those fires."

"How does Van Weezendonk's murder figure in then?" Mac asked—not with aggression, just opening up the line of conversation.

But I had no answer so naturally I started speculating.

"Long lost estranged daughter who sets fires to get her drunken trash father's attention?"

Mac rolled his eyes. I realized that there had to be something about the crime scene that made my discovery and speculation less damning than it seemed at the outset.

"For a second I thought you might have actually solved it." He snapped his notebook closed.

"What if Van Weezendonk caught Ainsley setting a fire and she killed him for it? Or what if Van Weezendonk is not involved in the fires at all? What if he was coincidentally dead in there when Ainsley started the fire?" I knew I was grasping at straws, but I didn't want this lunchbox arson kit to be a meaningless discovery.

"You still don't have any real proof that Ainsley is the firebug."

"I bet I do." I pointed at the bag. "I bet that when confronted with this evidence Ainsley will admit that she started at least the fire at the community center."

"That evidence may not be as strong as you think. It's been through a lot of people's hands," Mac said. "But let's circle back to your theory that Ainsley accidentally burned down a building that coincidentally contained a dead body. You're suggesting that Ainsley came across Van Weezendonk's dead body, took a look at the corpse that had been shot in the head at point blank range and decided to, for reasons of her own, douse it with gasoline and directly set it on fire?"

"So what you're saying is that Van Weezendonk's body was doused in gas and set on fire and that's how the building burned down?" I pounced on this information. "That means Van Weezendonk wasn't killed because he caught the arsonist torching the barn. Otherwise, the fire wouldn't have started with his body, right?"

Mac caught himself, realizing that he'd just given me information that he'd been carefully avoiding revealing for several days. "Yes."

"Okay. Well, I guess that does make my accidental arson theory sound ridiculous." I sat back in the driver's seat, deflated.

"That part is, yeah." Mac patted my arm. "It doesn't mean that she didn't set the other two fires though. It's worth checking out, since what's inside that lunchbox looks like a genuine arson kit. You say this Ainsley is your business partner's PA?"

"Right."

"Do you know how long she's been working for him?" Mac asked.

"A couple of years I think. Since the first season of Michael's show at least."

"Right, the show," Mac said. "I checked that out the other day. Have you seen it?"

I shook my head. "I didn't want to see my ex being really successful without me."

Mac nodded. "It's one of those shows where some guy travels around and features the cooking of local chefs. Seemed mainly to be about the diversity of Latino cuisine in the US."

"Makes sense," I replied.

Mac pulled out his phone and scrolled through some pages then said, "According to this psych paper I was reading earlier, female arsonists are usually seeking attention or responding to stressors in their lives."

"Entertainment is a stressful industry," I said. "Also, why were you already reading a psych paper about female arsonists?"

"I wasn't. I was reading about arsonists in general and females are a subcategory. Did you know most arsonists are never caught?"

"No, I didn't," I said.

"It's because their motivations aren't something that you can see as an outsider. But what you can see is the location of the crimes and work toward suspects using geographic profiling."

"So you're thinking that if Ainsley set fires here then she might have set fires in the locations of those other shoots?" I grabbed my phone.

"Exactly. We have the locations but it's a TV show so we don't have the exact dates, which would make searching a lot easier."

"I could ask Michael for his schedule," I offered.

"But why would you be asking for something like that? It might not be her. If the arsonist truly is a member of his crew, it could be the producer or any other person who happened to have found that lunchbox lying around. This town's population almost doubles during the festival weekend. Lots of people come back. There's the yacht crews, the Berry Growers Association—almost always at least one high school reunion." Mac gazed out at the summer evening. "There are too many variables."

He was right about the normally sleepy streets being lively. It was a fine evening and everyone in town seemed to have chosen to come outdoors. Kids rode bikes. Middle-aged guys stood by smoking grills. Clouds of shining gnats glowed golden in the oblique sunlight.

Mac continued, "What about Michael's social media accounts? Does he post a lot of selfies?"

"I mean, he must, right? Don't all TV people do that?" I pulled up my social media accounts and searched Michael's profile and discovered an image bonanza. I kept my fingers crossed that he had not stripped the location data from his photos and a few minutes later was rewarded by a wealth of data about the time and location of each and every one.

Mac gave me a wide smile, and then a pat on my head. "We can cross reference between those dates and the locations of the featured restaurants. Then it should be easy to inquire about suspicious fires."

"It doesn't solve your problem though." I slumped glumly in the driver's seat. "We still don't know who killed Van Weezendonk, or why."

"Well, at least we have alibis" Mac gave me a smile. "That's two people eliminated."

"Yeah. And seven billon more to go." I kicked uselessly at the floor mat.

"Don't be so dramatic. The highest number it could plausibly be is six thousand."

"Why six thousand?"

Mac's response was characteristically pragmatic. "That's all the people this town has, hobos and houseguests included."

"I expected you to be much, much more interested in this whole lunchbox thing." I reached across to lay my hand on his shoulder. "Did something happen?"

"It's the social media profile Abby made using Amy Carmichael's name," he said. "I've been monitoring it. There's a complication."

"Did the real Amy Carmichael find out and report it? It's not illegal—I looked it up. She could sue Abby though, and maybe you, if you've taken over," I said.

"No, Amy doesn't seem to have noticed. And even if she did she's unlikely to win a case against me, given that I am a law enforcement officer attempting to find a missing person and solve a murder. And the account hasn't been used to defame her publicly." Mac lapsed into silence staring at the dashboard for so long I though the conversation might be over.

"Mac?" I prompted. "Are you gonna tell me what's bothering you?"

"Today I got a message from Van Weezendonk's account," Mac finally said.

I sat straight upright. "What?"

"Someone direct messaged from his account to Abby's fake account late last night." Mac shifted back in his seat. "I'm guessing it's the person who killed Van Weezendonk since we didn't recover a phone from the crime scene."

"What did they say?"

"That they knew I was lying and a catfish and advised me to stop digging up the past, or else," he said.

"Do you think they know your real identity? Or Abby's?" I couldn't help but whisper.

"I doubt they'd make contact if they knew it was me on the other end, but I'm not certain about Abby." Mac took the phone out of his pocket. "Do you want to read the messages? The sender's account has been deleted but I took screenshots."

I sat straight up in my seat. "Hell yeah."

He passed the phone to me and I keyed in the passcode, which at least made him laugh. "Can't you at least pretend to not know that?"

"I don't see why I would. It's the same as yours." I thumbed through the photos until I found what I was looking for. There were only two messages. The first had come in at 2:15 a.m:

You're not even on the island so stop digging up the past, you whore.

Then at 7:38 p.m:

I know you're a fake and a liar. Stop or you'll be sorry.

"Huh." I looked back to Mac. "I think this might be an empty threat."

Mac nodded. "I think in the first message the sender thought that they were addressing the real Amy Carmichael then thought about it—or investigated and realized that it couldn't be her."

"Right." I handed the phone back to him. "Which implies that whoever it is, they are familiar enough with the island to easily figure that out." Then it struck me. "Since the killer has activated Van Weezendonk's phone after his death there's a new opportunity: find the phone and you find the killer. Right?"

"Correct." Mac nodded.

So why was he looking so glum?

I said, "Can't the mobile carrier tell you where the phone was? Couldn't we narrow down the suspects just by that?"

"They can. I've got them working on it. If the phone is turned on again after this we'll know." Mac shifted his gaze to the window of his house. Abby's shadow flitted past the curtain. "If this is the chain of evidence that leads us to the killer then the social media account, Abby's involvement, our dad's disappearance–everything could come out in the trial."

"But if it means catching a murderer then . . ." I prompted.

"I wouldn't hesitate," Mac replied. "I'm not hesitating. I'm just worried for Abby. She was too young to remember what it was like when Dad first went missing. The things people said about Mom and us kids, and him. I don't want her to have to go through that."

I studied Mac's profile. Abby might have been too young to remember it all, but he clearly did, as did Remy.

"I'm sorry that people back then were so shitty," I told him.

"It was a long time ago." He shrugged. "And not everyone was shitty. The guys at the hardware store were really nice."

"Yeah, well if anyone tries that shit now I'll . . ." I didn't know what I could do. "I'll serve them expired clams."

Mac laughed at that. Then shook his head. "No, you wouldn't. You're too good of a chef to do that."

I frowned but Mac had me there. I'd flat out refuse to serve anything before I'd give anyone bad food.

"It's ok. I'm all grown up now. People gossip. It doesn't matter," Mac said.

But it clearly did matter.

"Stop acting tough," I murmured.

"It's not an act," he replied.

I'd run out of words so I pinched him. Not on the nipple. Just the closest piece of skin to my hand. He at least had the good manners to yelp and grab my hand.

"It's illegal to assault a law enforcement officer, you know," Mac said.

"Even one who's deliberately being a dick?"

"I mean . . ." Mac trailed off. "Especially then."

"I'm serious, Mac," I said. "You don't always have to take responsibility and shoulder everything all on you own. I want to help you. I'm trying to help you."

"Really?" he asked.

"Yes, really," I stated firmly.

A genuine smile spread across his face and he pulled me into a hug. I hugged him back, accepting comfort and giving comfort at the same time. It felt good—like everything I'd been missing all day long. I didn't want to let him go.

Then I noticed Charlotte leaning out from the front door of the house. She was still dressed in pajamas and held her phone in one hand.

"Mac, Uncle Scott wants to know if you can cover Chaz's shift this afternoon. He's not feeling well again," she called out.

I felt the heavy sigh Mac released blow across my ear. Then he pulled away.

Despite the fact that we had an audience I kissed his cheek before he got out of the car.

"Be safe," I told him, and he nodded.

After he'd returned to his house, I did a quick check of my phone to make sure the restaurant hadn't texted me with some question. It was then I noticed Michael's message. The producer had reviewed the footage, and she was ninety-nine percent sure that the saboteur of our jam was Ainsley.

Chapter Eight

"All I want to know is why," I stated.

Ainsley sat in the corner of the massive sectional sofa in Michael's vacation rental, knees drawn up against her chest, face buried in her knees. She shook her head.

Michael rubbed her shoulder. "It's okay."

"It's not okay," I said. "You adulterated food. You're 86'd from the Eelgrass. If you set foot in that building again, I'll have your arrested for trespassing."

"Come on, Drew," Michael began. "She used a food-safe bitterant."

"So what?" I could accept someone like Joyce tampering with a product that someone was going to eat. She wasn't a professional and was not required to adhere to our code of ethics. But a member of our own staff who fully understood how dangerous it was to introduce random substances into food without telling anyone?

Unforgivable.

Never mind the disloyalty to our team—that, again, I could handle—but the disregard for the safety of complete strangers could not be overlooked. What if someone had been allergic to it? What then?

"Fire her right now, Michael," I said.

"You can't tell him what to do." Ainsley finally lifted her face. I had expected her to be crying but she wasn't. Her eyes were clear and dry and full of contempt. She jumped up to her feet.

"For the last time—why did you do that?" I didn't shout, but total rage added heft to my voice.

"Because you're losers and I wanted you to lose," Ainsley said. "I don't want Michael to have your stupid restaurant dragging him down. I want to go home to LA."

Michael's producer appeared in the hallway, looking a lot less steely and a lot more afraid. She wore pink bunny onesie pajamas and clutched her phone in one manicured hand. I ignored her.

"And is that why you set the fires too?" I gave up trying to control my voice and settled for controlling my hands, which dearly wanted to strangle Ainsley.

Her eyes widened in sheer terror, and she shrank back toward Michael again.

"How many fires have you set with that little kitchen torch of yours?" I demanded.

At this Ainsley's expression turned to confusion then a weird little smile quirked the corner of her mouth.

"You're a very sad and toxic person," she said. "I don't own a kitchen torch."

"What the fuck, Drew?" Michael stared at me aghast, his mouth hanging open in stupefaction.

"She's the one who started the fire at the event center," I told him. Then, to Ainsley, "Did you burn down that barn on Top Hat Road too? Did you kill that guy at Copper Kettle Confitures? Just to go back to La La Land? It's an unusual way to express homesickness, but I suppose you're a complicated woman."

Ainsley was smiling her little smile again, as if she'd somehow beaten me. The smugness of it caused me to waver. She'd looked guilty and afraid when I accused her of arson but started smiling when I'd mentioned the kitchen torch. Could it be that I'd gotten it wrong?

"I don't know where these wild accusations are coming from but I'm afraid I'm going to have to ask you to leave, Mr. Allison." The producer stepped out of the shadows. A couple of cameramen had appeared behind her, backing her up in case they had to throw me out, I guess.

"Fine. That's fine." I swallowed hard. Then, to Michael. "Just don't ever let me see her again."

◆◆◆

Before I went back to work, I called Mac to tell him about who tampered with the jam and how the conversation with Ainsley had gone.

"She's at least got the mindset of a poisoner," I said in summary. "And even though the torch probably isn't hers, I don't think we can rule her out as the arsonist as well."

His response was a long silence followed by, "There's this thing called de-escalation—have you ever considered it?"

"I just lost my temper," I said. "I'm sorry. I also wish I knew how to take it down a notch."

"Just stay away from her," Mac advised. "You don't want to have her accusing you of harassment."

"I don't have any desire to go near her," I glanced at my watch then at the small, but growing, group of people gathering on the sidewalk outside the Eelgrass. "It's time to open the doors for dinner. I have to go."

"Be careful," he said. "Don't get hurt."

"Right back atcha," I replied.

◆◆◆

That evening after the Bistro closed, the Pickle Queens assembled at the Eelgrass to discuss our strategy for the cooking contest tiebreaker. Evelyn looked sleepy, whereas Lionel seemed too awake—hyped by participating all day in the festival events.

My first order of business was to break the bad news about Ainsley sabotaging the jam to Lionel. All things considered, he took it pretty well, only excusing himself for a minute to go punch the crap out of one of the bags of flour in dry storage before returning, sweaty, winded but more or less calm, which was good because we needed to win to remove the pall of shadiness that had fallen over the Eelgrass.

Since Evelyn was most familiar with all the other competitors, I yielded the floor to her analysis.

"Dorothy Kokoschka—she's always been a contender at the county fair, but I didn't expect her to make something so retro. A charlotte? That's something we were making in the sixties."

"Which means hardly anybody under the age of sixty has seen one, which allows her to use a classic tried-n-true recipe while still having an element of surprise," I pointed out. "Great strategy."

"What about making strawberry sando?" Lionel showed us his phone screen. "They're popular now."

"Too simplistic," Evelyn said. "But I like the direction you're going. Asian patisserie is a trend that the other oldies probably haven't had much exposure to since they stopped talking to young people thirty years ago."

They both went into deep dives on their phones. I followed suit but wasn't looking up recipes.

My pride still stung from my earlier sleuthing defeat.

I realized I'd gotten too hung up on pinning the murder on Ainsley—partially because I disliked her and wanted her to be guilty so I wouldn't have to work with her.

An ignoble motivation if there ever was one. Plus, she'd now been removed from my life for other reasons.

So . . . win-win?

Except it didn't feel that way.

I decided to run down the circumstances again.

Van Weezendonk was shot to death and then burnt, on the property owned by Carmen Foti and leased by Eugene Wang of Copper Kettle Confitures. Of those three people, only Carmen was local and had known the victim. She had also been the person to produce evidence that implicated Ainsley as the arsonist, which I now realized might have been fabricated for exactly that purpose. Because, now that I was thinking about it, I remembered that the fire at the event center had not been started with the torch and fiber fill found in the lunchbox. It had been started with a matchbook.

Which is why Ainsley's expression had changed when I mentioned the kitchen torch. Before that she'd been terrified. But afterwards she'd known I didn't have any evidence against her because she hadn't used a torch to ignite the fire. I took a few moments to suppress the surge of frustration I felt about that entire interaction. Then I considered what the planted evidence revealed, excitement lighting within me as the connections came thick and fast.

Carmen must have witnessed Ainsley setting the event center fire. Maybe she'd been going to or coming out from one of the bathrooms. But instead of reporting it, she took the opportunity to frame Ainsley for the murder? But if she wanted to do that then why not just give the torch to Mac directly? The answer: because she'd seen me and Mac together and had done the math about our relationship and therefore knew that I would do that for her, keeping her one step removed from the investigation.

I went to dial Mac, and as I was thumbing through my contacts I realized that he had probably already thought of this. All of this. Which was why he hadn't been surprised at all to hear the torch didn't belong to Ainsley.

I wished I could talk to him about it.

Then suddenly, I realized I could. I could talk to him all I wanted. He might not be able to answer me—but that didn't mean he couldn't or wouldn't listen to me.

Evelyn and Lionel were still scrolling through their phones, occasionally showing each other photos, deep in deliberation on our dessert strengths and weaknesses.

I excused myself to go sit at the far end of the bar, out of earshot, and dialed Mac.

"I think it must be Carmen," I opened, without preamble.

"Because she gave you the lunch box?" Mac picked up the conversation seamlessly, having become acclimatized to my tendency to open a new topic of conversation without any context, early in the relationship.

"Right. Plus, she's the owner of the property. But the question is why? What could she gain by killing a guy who had been gone for years and years."

"No, that's not the question," Mac said. "The question is always how can you link the suspect to the crime scene in a way that cannot be explained in any other innocent way. Why a person committed a crime is not always relevant. And sometimes even if you know, it's hard to understand."

"So you already know it's her—never mind—I know you can't answer that." I used my breeziest tone. "What about Ainsley? Were you able to find any other fires that she might have set? Do you still like her for the garbage fire?"

"Drew it's been two hours, what do you think?" Mac said.

"Back to Carmen then. I still want to know why she would have done such a thing. And on her own property too. That's just stupid. She could have lured him anywhere on the island and she chooses her own place?"

"Why do you think Van Weezendonk was lured anywhere?" Mac asked.

"Because he was murdered at the end of it. Why would a person willingly go someplace to be killed?"

"Because they did not realize they would be killed when they decided to go there," Mac answered.

It was a fair point.

"Okay then why would he go to that property of his own volition at all? The only thing we know for sure is that in order to impress an old classmate that he reconnected with online, who was really your little sister catfishing him, Van Weezendonk was planning to come back to the island for Strawberry Days to confess to providing false information to the police about your dad's disappearance."

"Correct."

"And Abby hoped that in discovering why Van Weezendonk gave a false statement, you would all find a new lead in your father's missing person's case," I continued.

"False." Mac's voice wavered.

"No?"

"Partially. There is no missing person's case open for my father. She was hoping we could open one based on Van Weezendonk's statement." Deep notes of fatigue and sadness rang through Mac's voice.

"Didn't your mother report your father missing?"

"Yes, but my father called my uncle after that to apologize and to say not to look for him." Mac paused for long moment. "Allegedly."

Allegedly? I considered the full implication of that single word choice on Mac's part.

"So you . . . you suspect your uncle?" I couldn't bring myself to talk above a whisper, even though I was in my own restaurant. I didn't like Sheriff Mackenzie at all, but I'd always assumed he'd at least be good to his own family.

"I know he isn't telling the truth," Mac said. "I don't know why he's lying, but I know that he is definitely lying."

"So this is really two different problems." I leaned over the empty bar and pulled out a beer mat and a pen. "There is the problem of finding either physical evidence or an eyewitness who can connect Carmen to the murder and subsequent arson at Copper Kettle Confitures. And there is also the problem of discovering why Van Weezendonk lied about seeing your dad leave the island all those years ago."

"Correct."

"You can't talk about what you know about Van Weezendonk's death, but you can tell me all you want about your dad's disappearance, right?"

"Sure."

"Then let's talk about that," I offered.

"Why?" Free floating irritation condensed around the word, saturating it with uncharacteristic hostility. "Why are you making me have this conversation right now? Don't you have a contest to win?"

"Because it's bothering you, that's why. I don't like seeing you suffer," I said. The sincerity in my voice surprised even me.

"I've been living with this the entire time you've known me. Nothing's changed except now you know about it." Mac's tone softened somewhat but it remained firm and unyielding. Mac did not want to continue this conversation but how could we not?

I said, "Okay, fine, then what's changed is me. I've fallen in love with you, and because of that I want to help you.

Now will you please just answer a couple of questions for me?"

Mac remained silent for so long that I thought he'd hung up on me.

"Me too," he finally said.

"What?"

"I love you too," he said.

Sometimes, in the grip of full curiosity, I forget about emotions—mine, and also those of other people, and so Mac's statement of reciprocated feelings completely blind-sided me. Yes, I'd just told Mac the true fact that I loved him, and cared for him and wanted to help him, but that had been mainly to get him to keep talking to me so that I could love him and care for him and, most of all, help him. I hadn't expected him to say anything back and felt suddenly shy, at a loss.

"Well . . . good." I grasped at any kind of appropriate reply. "I'm glad to hear it."

"Don't get back together with your ex," Mac added. "You won't be happy."

"I was never going to do that, but okay, I promise to not get back together with Michael," I said. "Can I please now ask you a couple of questions about your dad? I'm tired of getting cryptic, secondhand information from Remy and Abby."

"All right, ask me anything," Mac said.

Suddenly placed on the spot, I almost couldn't think of anything to say so I just started trying to work it out in real time, slowly tapping the pen on the bar as I spoke.

"Your dad disappeared fifteen years ago?" I asked. Absently, I jotted the number down.

"Right," Mac replied. "He was last seen October twenty-eighth."

"Can you remember anything else about that year? Or the year before?" I was thinking about the fact that Mac's dad had been a deputy. If someone had wanted to kill him out of revenge for wrecking their business or arresting their kid or whatever, Mac might remember something about it. Or it might even be on public record as an arrest.

"I was on the swim team, then mom started chemo. Everything else just kind of went away after that. I was only a kid then," Mac's tone had softened.

"There weren't any big arrests that your dad made?" I asked.

"Not that I remember." Mac said. "But I don't think his disappearance had to do with anybody my dad arrested because if it did, why would my uncle cover it up?"

I thought about that for a moment.

"Because he was somehow in on the crime—whatever it was?" I drew a dollar sign in the corner of the beer mat. "Most crimes seem to boil down to money in some way."

Mac gave a gusty sigh. "I know that seems like the next logical step, but I've never seen my uncle go that far. I mean, sure, he's lazy. But he's not taking payoffs. I've checked."

"Okay, then say your uncle isn't lying. That means that either your dad did call—under duress—or that someone impersonated your dad over the phone and your uncle, wanting to believe that your dad was still okay, chose to believe that instead of investigating his disappearance."

Again a long silence. I glanced back into the kitchen to see if Evelyn and Lionel seemed to be making any progress. They appeared to be sketching out something on the back of an old ticket.

"Okay," Mac said, but his voice held a note of uncertainty. "I guess either of those could also be true."

"Which leads us to the one person who has admitted that he helped to cover up your dad's disappearance—Dirk Van Weezendonk. Why might he do something like that?"

"Because he was involved in it?" Mac answered.

"Let's say yes. So, if you were involved in the disappearance of a police officer fifteen years ago and were about to come clean, what would you do?"

"You mean if I were Van Weezendonk?" Mac was quiet a moment and I let him think in peace. "If I were him, I'd apologize to my family, whose reputation I'm about to wreck."

"That's very admirable of you, but wouldn't you also maybe give any accomplices that you had a heads up? Just out of professional courtesy?"

"Criminals don't have professional courtesy. That's myth." Mac snorted. "But I see where you're going with this. You're trying to say that Van Weezendonk went to see Carmen Foti because she also had a part in my dad's disappearance. It's a good line of reasoning. Except she was out of the country at the time."

"Damn it!" I slammed my hand down on the bar in frustration. "I really thought I had something there."

"It's okay. I salute your determination and spirit," Mac said. "You just haven't been thinking about this for fifteen years."

"Yeah, I guess I wanted there to be someone still alive for you to question," I said.

"Me too . . . anyway, I have to go. I'm getting a call from the dispatcher."

"Another suspicious fire in the vicinity of Ainsley?" I asked hopefully.

"We should be so lucky," Mac said, laughing.

I returned to the kitchen in good spirits to discover Lionel and Evelyn were already prepping ingredients. I felt light on my feet. I hadn't managed to solve anything, but Mac told me he loved me, which when combined with giving me his house key could only mean one thing: I had a boyfriend. Officially.

"Nice of you to come back to class, boss," Lionel muttered.

"Hush, Lionel," Evelyn chided. "He had to call his boyfriend for moral support. You'll understand when you're older. Sometimes when two grown-ups are in love they get sloppy and formless without each other. Like gelatin without a mold. Just a hot, runny, protein-filled, smelly mess."

From Lionel, "Please stop being so gross, Granny."

"Are we really making Jell-O?" I glanced over the ingredients assembled on the counter.

"Mirror glaze," Evelyn corrected. "Lionel's been perfecting it to impress girls, or so he claims."

I was already familiar with Lionel's adventures in dessert-based seduction. In terms of successful strategies, mirror glaze mousse cakes ranked second only to reading aloud while snuggling in warm pajamas. "So, we're making mousse cakes?"

"Entremet cake." Lionel looked exceptionally pleased with himself. He handed me a diagram of the various layers, cake, jelly, mousse, and ultra-shiny coating. "We're making a demo now."

"You know that glaze is going to be all on you, right?" I leaned back against the steel prep table. "I have zero experience with that stuff."

"Yeah, I know." Lionel also folded his arms and leaned back against the table opposite me, eye to eye, which—had he grown? Since when could he look at me eye to eye. And yet, there I was staring directly into his light brown, extremely large and flat peepers.

"It'll be a lot of pressure on you," I continued.

"Come on, Drew, you can't fight every battle." Evelyn patted me on the shoulder. "Especially not when you're just thinking about your man eighty percent of the time now."

Lionel cringed and snickered; hand curled over his mouth.

I rolled my eyes and did my best to stifle a sigh. My best

wasn't good enough though and the sigh made it out.

"There's a lot more than that going on right now," I replied.

"Like what?" Evelyn returned to stirring the pot of jelly on the stove, watching it bubble, but clearly listening to me.

"Well, murder and arson, for a start," I said.

Evelyn waved a dismissive hand at me. "Sure, sure. We all know about that. Why don't you get on making the sponge cake. We're thinking Joconde."

I nodded and gathered the ingredients, measuring them carefully. Then set about whipping the egg whites.

"I met Mac's family," I remarked.

"All of them?" Lionel's attention snapped right to me.

"What did you think?" Evelyn's tone remained neutral.

"They seemed all right. Not as conservative as I thought they'd be. It's just that there's enough of them to make their own volleyball team so . . ." Then I recalled the barbecue invitation that Abby had extended to me. Between the murder, arson, and food tampering I'd nearly forgotten about it.

"Kind of intimidating?" Evelyn remarked.

"Yeah. I'm supposed to barbecue with them all tomorrow after the contest."

"Well, if you feel outnumbered, me and Julie can come along too. If they start being mean, Julie can fake heat stroke to get you out of there." Evelyn turned off the flame on the range. She started to lift the heavy pot but her hand shook and she set it back on the burner and stepped aside. "Pour this out for me, will you? You get weak when you get old. I'm afraid I'll burn myself."

"Sure." I rotated into position to pour the bright red jelly out into a silver hotel pan to cool.

"That sugar'll stick to you just like napalm," Evelyn went on. "Carmen has a hell of a burn on her foot from it."

"Carmen Foti?" I clarified, as though there were some other Carmen she could be talking about. "I thought she sprained her ankle."

"No, not at all." Evelyn sat down on her stool. "It's a burn. She said that's why she can't get in the pool. Can't get the bandages wet."

"Did you see it?"

"I saw the bandage when I went to get Julie at the aquatic center. All up her ankle. She's lucky to be walking."

My heartbeat started to pick up the pace. Inexperienced people who set fires often burnt themselves in the process, so that injury could be the crucial link between the perpetrator and the crime.

I texted Mac this information immediately but got no answer. Maybe he was driving? Or more likely he was occupied by whatever cop business had pulled him away from our conversation in the first place.

Lionel and Evelyn laid out several plates while the mousses set up in their individual molds.

How to decorate the plates? A swirl of deep red sauce? What about a white chocolate cage?

I tried to concentrate on the plating deliberations, but I couldn't keep my eyes away from my phone for longer than a few seconds.

Maybe it was all the earlier talk about Mac's father being killed, but the longer I went without a response from Mac the more uneasy I grew. It wouldn't be all that difficult to lure someone like Mac into a trap. Coming to the rescue, regardless of the cost to himself, was like a reflex for him. Dread swirled through me, settling in my neck, like a fist clamped around my throat. But this fear was irrational, wasn't it? I couldn't seem to quell the distinct feeling that Mac was in danger. Was this what it had been like for Mac and his family when his dad had disappeared? Mac had a dangerous job but I'd never felt afraid for him until now. So what? Why was I, with no evidence, slowly becoming convinced that he was going to die?

Had countless hours of true crime television finally brought me to a tipping point in my awareness that triggered a deep understanding that human lives can be taken away in an instant? Was it because I'd finally admitted that I loved him and he'd said he loved me too; the happiness of that felt so wonderful, so precious, that, on an unconscious level, I was suddenly terrified of losing him?

Was this panic?

I took a deep breath and tried to sort out my thoughts. I definitely was panicking, and I needed to calm down. It would be okay.

The feeling of suffocation returned along with a wave of dizziness, and I crouched down to keep from falling over.

"Are you all right?" Evelyn asked. I felt her hand on the center of my back. "It's just a barbeque. You'll be okay. Mac wouldn't let anything happen."

"I know. I'm overreacting. Just give me a minute. I'm going to get some air." I straightened up and somehow made it out the back door into the alley.

I leaned against the rough brick wall and tried to think away my anxiety over Mac.

Since cooking didn't seem to be helping me, I turned my racing thoughts to the case.

Evelyn's comment about sugar burning like napalm came back to me. Yes, a jelly burn was much different from a burn caused by gasoline. It would be easy to tell one from the other.

Did Carmen know that? Maybe that was why she'd gone out of her way to insinuate herself in the investigation and place the blame on Ainsley. But Ainsley hadn't been arrested, and if Carmen didn't already know that, she would soon. Fleeing would be admitting guilt at this point, but she had to be nervous that the police were closing in, otherwise why try and push the blame onto Ainsley?

And I still had no idea what her motive for the murder might be. It might not be that Van Weezendonk was even the target. Could he have just been in the wrong place at the wrong time? Could he have interrupted Carmen committing some other crime? Had she been attempting to sabotage Copper Kettle Confitures for some reason and Van Weezendonk wandered in to say hello to his old friend? He would not have known that Carmen had leased the property, so . . . maybe?

But the concept of old friends sounded a tiny bell somewhere in my memory.

Carmen had said that she and Van Weezendonk were old friends who had lost touch. And Evelyn had told me that Van Weezendonk had suffered a nervous breakdown due to PTSD after being involved in a bank robbery.

No, that wasn't right, he wasn't involved, per se. He'd been the victim of a bank robbery by a single armed gunman unless . . . could he have been involved? And hadn't Carmen left the country right afterwards to travel the world in search of yoga-based transcendence? How had she financed that trip? Could she have been the gunman and Van Weezendonk an inside man at the bank?

But even if it were true that Carmen and Van Weezendonk had robbed a bank together what did that have to do with the disappearance of Mac's father several months later?

Unless Mac's father had solved the robbery and Van Weezendonk and his accomplice had killed him rather than be arrested. But Carmen couldn't have been involved in the disappearance because she was out of the country.

Why kill Van Weezendonk then? Why set fire to her own property to cover the murder when she could have just dumped his body in the woods? It wasn't like Camas Island didn't have plenty of places to dump a body, including the entire Salish Sea that surrounded it.

I tried Mac again but got no answer. I wished I'd been smart enough to link our phones so I could find him. When I saw him again, I thought, I'd do that. But in the meantime, how could I locate him? Who would know? The police dispatcher, for sure, but she wouldn't tell me.

But she might tell Remy.

I dialed his number. He didn't pick up but did text me.

Remy: *Can't talk now. What's up?*

Me: *Do you know where Mac went?*

Remy: *No.*

Me: *Can you find out from the dispatcher?*

Remy: *No.*

Me: *Please?*

There was a short pause before he answered. I waited, listening to the thin calls of bats flying between the buildings. At the far end of the alley a family of raccoons rifled through the garbage behind the fish and chips shop.

Remy: *Mac isn't answering.*

Me: *I know. That's why I want to know where he went. I'm worried he's doing something dangerous.*

Remy: *That's so cute.*

I almost threw my phone away. I could easily visualize that smug Mackenzie smile on his big, stupid face. Why did their whole family have to be this way?

Time to pull out the big guns.

Me: *Okay, well, thanks for nothing.*

Again, there was a delay.

Then from Remy: *Don't be like that. He hasn't been dispatched anywhere. He's probably in an area with poor coverage. I'll see if I can get him on the radio.*

Me: *Okay*

So, Mac had lied about getting a call. Or maybe he'd just received a regular call instead of been dispatched. Now my heart raced so hard I couldn't hear anything but it.

Could he be going to meet Carmen?

Carmen wouldn't be able to lure Mac someplace to kill him because Mac wasn't born yesterday, and he already suspected she'd killed Van Weezendonk, so he'd never go to meet her alone.

Except . . .

Maybe Mac wanted to meet her alone because he had other questions for her that had nothing to do with the Van Weezendonk case.

The idea of Mac strong-arming a hundred-and-ten-pound woman into giving up information didn't fit with what I knew about him, but what I knew about him wasn't really all that much. For example, I'd only learned I was Mac's first real boyfriend because Remy told me.

I didn't know Mac well, actually. I loved him and felt a resonance with him that I'd never felt before. I wanted to please him and be next to him, but I didn't know him. Not deep down.

For all I knew he could be tying Carmen up with duct tape and beating a confession out of her.

I mean, it didn't seem likely or consistent with any of his previous actions, but it wasn't impossible.

So I decided to take stock of what I did know. I knew that Mac had strong habits and preferred to be indirect in most things. Despite the guileless front he liked to put on, Mac was not dumb.

If he was going to see Carmen, then I knew where the meeting would be—the crime scene. He would want to observe her there.

Pulse pounding in my ears, I ran to my car and headed toward Copper Kettle Confitures.

Chapter Nine

As I drove, I didn't know what I hoped for—that Mac would be there or that he wouldn't. And when I drove down the long gravel drive and saw his cruiser parked at the end, relief that I'd found him crashed through my chest only to be immediately replaced by dread.

Mac wasn't here to arrest Carmen. If he had been, there would be more than one cop car.

He had come here alone, like an idiot.

This impulsive act was something that I would do, not something a smart guy like him should be engaging in.

I parked my car near Mac's then turned it off and got out, barely remembering to leave the door ajar so as not to start or alert anyone by slamming it.

The night air was cool and thick with humidity. The smell of damp earth rose up from the gravel as night winds moved in from over the sea. As I took a step toward the partially burnt building, my phone buzzed. I jumped straight in the air like a cat.

Evelyn had texted to find out when I planned to return to the war room.

Me: *I'm out at Copper Kettle looking for mac*

Evelyn: *What the hell*

Me: *If I don't text back in 30 minutes please call the cops.*

Evelyn: *I will. But you better be ok.* (Followed by a glowering face emoji.)

I silenced my phone, then crept as quietly as I could toward the single entrance. The door had been broken open by the firefighters and I could see a beam of harsh white light coming from inside.

Holding my breath, I peered around the doorframe. The burnt-out interior was harshly illuminated by an orange construction light that hung from the ceiling. Some interior walls still partially stood, creating gaps I could see through. Rubble littered the floor. The ceiling had burnt entirely so that looking up, I could see the Milky Way just above the ruined walls.

I didn't spot anyone nearby but I heard the rumble of Mac's voice.

I slipped inside and crept closer, hugging the wall. The rancid smell of the burnt timbers and gasoline was thick and choking. I moved down what must have been a hallway then peered around a corner. This time I caught sight of Carmen's back.

She wore expensive red and black yoga pants and a matching sports bra. She'd accessorized with black running shoes, a red scrunchie, and a gold fanny pack which was probably how she'd carried the gun she was holding to the meeting.

I don't know what made me want to punch her more, the fact that she was threatening Mac or that she was doing it while dressed like a trash super villain.

I carefully lifted my phone to contact Evelyn:

nvmd call cops NOW

I pocketed the phone and leaned farther out until I could see Mac. He wore his deputy's uniform and had his hands up. I didn't know if he could see me or if his attention was solely taken up by the weapon pointed at him.

"You don't have to do this," Mac's voice was gentle. "I'm not here to arrest you. I know you're scared and acting out of instinct. That's completely understandable, so nobody has to know you pulled a gun on me so long as you put it away now."

"Bullshit!" Carmen hissed.

"I am not trying to deceive you," Mac said. "I only want to know what happened to my dad. You can understand that, can't you? I'm willing to let you walk out of here if you'll just tell me what you know."

I stopped dead in my tracks at the words. Would Mac really do that? Allow a murderer to escape just for personal closure?

The sincerity on his face must have been causing Carmen to waver because she said, "It wasn't me. I wasn't even in the country. I didn't have anything to do with any of that stuff that happened to your dad."

"I'm not trying to put the blame on you." Mac's voice was barely a rumble now. "But there has to be a reason Dirk Van Weezendonk claimed to have seen him. Anything you know can help me and my brothers and sisters find him and move on."

Mac's mouth curved into that guileless Mackenzie smile. A little of the tension seemed to ease from Carmen's shoulders.

"Okay . . . okay. Dirk came to me and told me that he was going to tell you that he fabricated that story about your dad getting on the ferry." Carmen shifted from side to side, like a runner who was about to break into a sprint. "He didn't actually see your dad at all that day."

Mac's face showed some surprise that I imagined was reflected on my own. My theory about Van Weezendonk killing Mac's dad to evade capture on bank robbery charges was blown.

Of course, Carmen could always be lying about this as well.

"So, Dirk didn't have anything to do with my dad's disappearance?" Mac asked.

"No. Nothing." Again Carmen shifted. The hand holding the weapon dropped a little bit.

"Do you know why he lied about it then?"

"Because someone put him up to it." Scorn rang through Carmen's voice. "You never were very smart, were you?"

"No," Mac agreed easily. "Basically I'm just a trained monkey."

Carmen let out a short laugh—the exact opposite of the rage that had ignited in my chest. How dare she? How dare she insult him? And how dare he stand there and take it?

"You got that right," she said. "You haven't even arrested that weirdo assistant of Chef Michael's yet and I actually gave you the fucking evidence."

"I know," Mac said. "We're closing in on her though, so like I said, you don't have to be scared that I'm coming for you. I know who is guilty and who isn't."

"Liar." Carmen raised the gun again. "I know you talked to Dirk's mother about the bank robbery."

"The statute of limitations has passed on that," Mac soothed. "Which I'm sure you know. That's irrelevant. I don't care about any of that right now. What I want to know is, if neither you or Van Weezendonk had anything to do with my dad's disappearance, who asked Dirk to lie about it? Please, I'm begging you." Mac's voice turned rough and I realized he was on the verge of tears. "I don't care about anything else but this."

Carmen was silent for a long time.

"The guy who killed your dad, I guess," she said.

"What do you mean you guess?" Mac dragged a hand across his nose.

"Dirk said he knew who killed your dad and . . . he was going to tell you," Carmen said.

"So my father is really dead?" Mac's hands slowly fell to his sides. "He was murdered."

"That's what Dirk said." Carmen shrugged as though this information was meaningless. To her I suppose it was, but Mac flinched. I realized he'd been holding out irrational hope all this time—even he knew intellectually that his father must be dead.

"Do you have any idea who killed him?" Mac asked.

"Dirk didn't tell me. He only said that he'd made a deal with this guy—they each knew what the other one had done. So they made a deal to cover for each other. But over the years it had started eating at him—once he had a kid of his own that was your age—he started to feel bad about lying and it affected his mental health. He came here to tell me that he was going to tell you everything."

"What happened then?" Mac asked.

"I told him it wasn't his secret to tell," Carmen said. "I told him he should just send you an anonymous letter. He didn't have to bring up that crazy thing we did in the past. But Dirk said that once he told you, the other guy would definitely know he'd broken their deal so he might as well come tell you in person, man to man."

"Meaning what?"

"Testify, maybe? I don't know. I don't care." Carmen shrugged again. "I didn't have anything to do with any of that. Why did he have to wreck my life just because he felt bad about something he'd done? He didn't have the right to do that to me! I didn't do anything wrong, and he had to push me into a corner."

And there it was—the reason Van Weezendonk had to die. Part of me wanted to point out that she had, in fact, done something wrong—more than one thing: first robbery and then murder plus arson. She wouldn't see it that way though. In her mind she had only protected herself.

I allowed myself to be smug for just one second that one of my theories had been correct, then I realized that Carmen's posture had changed a little. She'd put both hands on the butt of the gun.

"You know, it feels good to talk about it," Carmen went on. "Dirk wouldn't listen to anything I said. He'd made up his mind for both of us."

"I'm sorry," Mac's tone turned from sorrowful to gentle again. "He should have considered your feelings more."

"Damn right he should have. He thought it would all be fine but even if you wouldn't have arrested us, I still live here. What would everyone think if they knew?" Carmen's arms drooped again, slightly. I wondered how long she could hold the gun on Mac. She worked out for a living so she was fit and full of adrenaline, but she'd have to rest her arm eventually.

"He was selfish," Mac intoned.

Was Mac hoping to wear her out to make his move? I wondered if he knew I was here in the building as well.

"So yeah," Carmen finally said. "I asked for him to wait for me to change clothes so I could go with him to talk to you, then I went and got my gun and shot him. He didn't see it coming at all because that's how little he even paid attention to me. Some friend."

Mac said, "I can see how you would feel let down."

Carmen nodded. "I was so disappointed. But it's all over now. I'm glad I got to talk to someone about it."

"You can keep talking," Mac said. "I'm ready to listen to whatever you have to say."

"It's okay, I'm done," she said.

At that time it became clear to me that she was going to shoot Mac. Maybe not this second, but eventually, because now Mac not only knew that she'd murdered Dirk but also what Dirk had been killed for knowing. She wasn't a kind, free-spirited entrepreneur who people ought to look up to but a conniving thief and murderer.

I had to draw her attention away from Mac. I scanned the room for anything to throw and, to my astonishment, I saw Remy. Carmen wouldn't have been able to spot him from where she stood, but I could clearly see him crouching behind a half-wall and giving me the evil eye.

He gestured roughly and rudely (though still silently) that I should get the fuck out.

So, Mac hadn't come alone. He'd brought his little brother and Remy had pretended he didn't know where Mac was to keep me away.

It was at that moment that I realized that I had made a terrible mistake. I tried to back away and stepped on a weak part of the floor. It gave way with a crack and I stumbled forward into the line of Carmen's vision.

"What the hell are you doing here?" she screeched.

"I . . . I followed Mac. I thought he was cheating on me." I gave her as big a smile as I could under the circumstances.

"Drew?" The incredulity in Mac's voice said it all.

I gave Carmen a cringing smile. "I guess he's not."

Mac's expression—it resembled how a person's face might look if he was watching two roller coasters crashing into each other. Disbelief, horror, as well as a kind of awe that such a thing could ever happen.

Carmen just seemed annoyed by my intrusion. "Get over there." She jerked the gun toward Mac. I crept forward in slow, sheepish steps, hands up, until I stood alongside my boyfriend.

A twisted lump of a copper preserve-making pan hurtled forward out of nowhere. It sailed past Carmen and crashed into the far wall.

Carmen spun toward the sound and two things happened at once. First Mac pulled me down just as he had when the propane tank had exploded in the burning barn. At the same time, Remy lunged forward to grab Carmen's hand, twisting it violently sideways. I heard a snap and she screamed in agony but didn't drop the weapon.

Mac and I fell backward into the burned and decrepit wall. Then, with a sickening creak, the wall gave way and we just kept falling with it. The ruined timbers crashed down. I rolled sideways into the opening of a doorway and the wall fell around me, but it came down hard on Remy and Carmen. The construction light fell sideways onto the floor yet continued to illuminate rubble in a bizarre oblique angle.

"Remy!" Mac scrambled up to where his brother lay partially under the debris. "Remy?"

"Are you hurt?" I asked.

"I don't know," Remy replied. "Maybe?"

Mac gripped the scorched timbers. I reached out as well. Together we heaved. The wood bit into my trembling hands. The weight was incredible, pulling at my shoulders. Remy crawled free then turned to pull Carmen out. She wasn't unconscious but she wasn't moving well.

"Where's my gun?" she asked groggily.

"We'll find it later," Mac said.

"I want it now." She slurred and then began to turn but Remy pushed her onto her face and cuffed her.

That's when she started crying.

Remy pushed himself up to his feet. He gave me the once-over. "You're pretty strong."

"Yeah." Now that Remy was out of danger, I took the opportunity to rub my shoulder while giving Mac an accusatory side-eye. "Jesus, you pulled me down hard enough."

"You're lucky you didn't get shot," Mac said, but took over rubbing my shoulder anyway.

Outside I could hear the sound of sirens coming up the drive. Red and blue flashing lights illuminated the burnt and collapsed timbers. Mac and Remy exchanged a confused look at the sight of them.

"I called the police because of the whole Carmen pulling a gun on you thing," I told Mac. Then, to Remy, "When did you get here?"

"Right about the time she said that Dad was . . ." Remy's voice seemed to catch, then he simply gave a shrug. He'd taken his trooper's hat off and his hair stuck up in sweaty spikes. He looked much younger than he had before, almost like a child. "I guess you were right all along. I owe you an apology."

"No, you don't." Mac put a hand on Remy's shoulder. "Until now, neither one of us knew for sure. We still don't. She's not exactly the most reliable witness."

Both brothers nodded, then turned their attention to Carmen who sat on the floor, crying and occasionally swearing at all of us.

"Can I kick her?" I asked.

Mac gave a short laugh. "No."

"What if you're not looking?"

"I'm going to go out and meet the responders. Don't go anywhere." Mac leaned a little closer and gave me a peck on the cheek. "And leave Carmen alone. She's going to get her ass kicked plenty of times after this. Your contribution is unnecessary."

"Yes, sir." I gave him my least sincere salute.

Mac shook his head then suddenly pulled me into his arms. "Thanks for helping me lift that wall."

"No worries. I'm pretty sure it's my fault it fell down in the first place." I pushed my face against his shoulder. "I'll try to get better at my rescues. This one was definitely two out of five stars. Cannot recommend."

Mac pulled away, taking my face between his hands. "You always have to get in the last word don't you?"

I admit, I almost fell for it. I opened my mouth for a final zinger, but then just used it to kiss him instead. Mac's surprise was evident, but he also seemed shy.

Maybe it was because Carmen was still cursing us.

"I'm going to be here all night," Mac said. "But they should let you go right away. Good luck in the contest tomorrow."

Contest? What contest? What did the word 'contest' even mean to me anymore? How could I possibly care about that now? What did winning or losing matter compared to what had just happened in front of me? Compared to how Mac must feel right now? But then I realized I did care. Not for myself, but for Evelyn and Lionel and even Abby. We were all on the same team.

I felt noble. Courageous. And humble. But not so much that I wasn't still the opportunist that I'd always been. I said, "If I win can I skip your family barbecue?"

Mac smirked and answered with a succinct, "No."

"Oh, absolutely not," Remy chimed in. He stood, dusting himself off a couple of feet away from Carmen. "You've got a roasting coming after these shenanigans." Then, to Mac, "I think next time you should just include Drew in the big plans so he doesn't decide to come up with his own parallel strategy and accidentally kill us all trying to help you. They say communication is key to a healthy relationship you know."

"Shut the fuck up, dude," I muttered.

"You're not so smart either," Mac told his brother. "Just randomly throwing some hunk of junk as a distraction?"

"That wasn't random. I knew that our suspect would turn away and then you'd protect Drew, leaving me free to apprehend her." Remy shrugged. "Easy-peasy."

◆◆◆

Eight a.m. came way too early the next morning, but I did manage to haul myself back to Copper Kettle Confitures to the event center in time to participate in the three-way tie breaker battle.

Evelyn and Lionel were already present along with Julie, who had dressed all in red, right down to the stop sign lipstick. As I approached them I felt myself shriveling up internally. Whatever good I had done last night had been undone by the fact that I had conclusively failed my team. I'd run off into the night and left them high and dry.

I'd get no air kisses from Julie this morning. No awkward side hug from Evelyn and especially no cheerful salutation from Lionel. I approached the table fully expecting a heaping portion of silent treatment and for just one second, I got it. The three of them stood there staring at me.

Then Julie rushed forward and threw her arms around my waist—it was as high as they reached—and hugged me.

"Oh thank goodness." She gave me a squeeze. "I'm so glad you're all right."

"What did you think happened to me?" It belatedly occurred to me that the oldsters might not have spent the entire night cursing my name, but rather had been worried for me.

"Well, the damn building you were in collapsed, didn't it?" Evelyn stepped forward and put her hand on my shoulder. "I heard it on the police scanner. Can't you stay out of trouble for five minutes?"

I glanced to Lionel and he only smirked then mouthed, "busted," at me.

I won't lie, after being love-bombed like that, it was hard to generate the competitive bastard, winner-take-all fighting spirit that the cameramen loved, but at least I was there for my team and—just as importantly—my team was there for me.

Plus, Lionel looked fierce enough for all of us. His eyes swept over the old ladies in the gymnasium with the commanding glower of the protagonist in some fantasy RPG, only instead of wearing magical plate armor, he wore a red apron with a strawberry embroidered on it.

That's the difference between fiction and reality, I supposed.

The next three hours passed in a blur of grunt work—chopping, blanching, toasting, cleaning up. Just like Evelyn had said, I wasn't the star of this show and I felt . . . fine? Good, even. A kid who I'd taught was battling it out against masters and it looked like he might even win. Was this maturity? Had I finally become an adult? Or was it only that the consequences of this contest paled in comparison to what had happened the previous night. Here, either we would win or we would lose, but last night Mac had received confirmation of his father's death and now whatever faint dream he'd held of a reunion was gone.

More than that, Carmen had confirmed that the cause of death was murder.

How could making unbeatable dessert matter after that?

And yet, I still felt proud when the judges said our name. As I shoved Lionel forward to receive the prize and watched the elation on his face when Michael raced across the gymnasium to shake his hand, I realized that I must have leveled up somehow.

As I was thinking this, I felt a hand on my shoulder. Mac had his typical haggard, "I've been up all night" look.

"Why so glum, chum?" he asked. "Looks like you won."

"He won." I pointed at Lionel. "I was a mere functionary. How are you?"

"Exhausted."

"Why don't you go home?" Some amount of annoyance crept into my voice. Why was he like this? He was gonna die of drowsy driving one day.

"I wanted to see your team win." Mac flashed a faltering smile. "And I didn't want to go home alone."

My ice-cold heart melted at these words, but I still managed to maintain my chill. I said, "How could you be alone? Your house is crammed full of younger Mackenzies."

"Yeah, but my bed's still empty." Mac sat down on the bleachers, stretched out his legs and closed his eyes. "Wake me up when you're ready to go."

Epilogue

The Mackenzie barbecue turned out to not be that bad. I hid behind the grill with Remy the whole time, keeping the fish and fowl separated while maintaining a tiny square in the corner that was suitable for vegans.

Everybody drank a little too much but not so much as to end the party in tears. As the meal wound down, Remy told me that it wouldn't be too bad to have me around to help him cook breakfast on Christmas morning, which I supposed was his stamp of approval. So I accepted it, even though assuming I'd be playing out this scenario was making a lot of erroneous presumptions about every single aspect of my personality, as per his standard. The notion that any chef would happily bound out of bed at sunrise to spend his precious day off cooking was certainly some wishful thinking. But there was plenty of time ahead of us all for these truths to reveal themselves.

Carmen was arraigned for murder then immediately lawyered up and zipped her mouth shut. Mac questioned her several times, but she had nothing more to say, so Mac's search for his father's killer stalled as quickly as it began. However, it was discovered that Van Weezendonk had not been her only partner in crime and not the only one she'd killed either. He'd only been the most recent. During her travels she'd left a string of men dead as she worked her way around the globe stealing and killing, all with that benign yoga-teacher smile.

Mac turned his attention to incoming information about Ainsley's reign of tiny terror. Investigators were able to connect her with at least nine fires in six states set while traveling with Michael for his show.

Michael was heartbroken, but not surprised.

"Oh honey, doesn't it just go to show, my taste in assistants is just as bad as my taste in men." He shook his head slowly at Lionel, who snickered.

"I'm standing right here," I muttered.

"Seriously, I don't know what I'm going to do without her." Michael rubbed his temples. "There's just so much going on with the new series."

"A new series already?" I asked hopefully.

"*Michael Meets Mexico,*" he said, as if I should have known. "It's only a working title but we're supposed to start shooting in six weeks."

"So where does that leave this restaurant?" I asked.

"You were doing fine without me so let's just say I'm a silent partner for now." Michael gave me a wink.

"What if I wanted to buy you out?" I asked.

"Do you have the money for that?" Michael raised a well-groomed eyebrow.

I hung my head. "No."

"Then we can talk again when you do." Michael gave my shoulder a squeeze. "Anyway, honey, I don't want to step on your boyfriend's toes. You can tell he already wants to knock me out."

I rolled my eyes. "He does not."

"Drew, look at him." Michael pointed to the door that Mac had just entered through. He did, indeed, appear to be highly irritated at the sight of Michael's hand on me. "That man is not casual about you." Michael picked up his laptop and walked away, pausing only briefly to give Mac a smirk on the way out.

Mac ambled over and seated himself at his usual table and started scrolling through his phone.

A few seconds later I felt a notification.

From Mac: *Is he going someplace far away?*

Yep, and for a long time too.

Mac smiled and looked up at me before replying.

Good

HOMICIDE AND HOSPITALITY

Chapter One

In the restaurant industry, December is an onslaught of cooking for year-end parties, reunion dinners, people back in their hometowns for the holidays, as well as the packs of ravenous holiday shoppers. As early as November, our tiny tourist town of Orca's Slough had busted out all the seasonal decorations in hopes of promoting travel to a quaint seaside Christmas destination. Swags of white lights strung across the six-block main street lent cheer to the short, dark, rainy days.

After our crew won a television cooking show competition, business at the Eelgrass had rocketed to a near-frantic pace.

Customers in slick rain gear lined up outside before opening and packed our dining room until we flipped the sign over to say 'closed.' And best of all, the inclement weather reduced property crime rate significantly, as no one wanted to be out prowling vehicles or committing acts of porch piracy in the bitter, sheeting rain, which meant I got to see my cop boyfriend Mac more often.

At three p.m. on Wednesday I'd normally be dreaming up some needlessly extravagant dinner to feed him. Sadly though, earlier that morning he had been called to the marina to investigate a woman's body found in the water, so I wouldn't be seeing Mac. The identity of the deceased unknown—to me anyway. It hadn't been announced.

I hoped she wasn't a local. I hoped she wasn't a tourist.

Actually, it was just sad that anyone would end up that way, to be honest, regardless of their personal relatedness to me.

Somebody was going to have a not very merry Christmas.

The last lunch customer left and I locked the front door and flipped the OPEN sign around. At this moment the volume on the stereo went up to eleven as K-pop blasted through the whole restaurant. Back in the kitchen, the line cooks, Lionel and Kaden, had both tidied their stations and started prepping for reopening for dinner at five.

Up in the office our new GM, Lupe, crunched the numbers so I could focus on the creative aspects of the menu.

Standing at the front window I saw fat snowflakes the size of frosted breakfast cereal beginning to drift down. Then more and more of them began falling, fast and thick. The snow alighted on the towering cedars, the Christmas garlands that we'd hung across the front window, and on a tall, dark-haired figure approaching the door. He wore beige slacks, a bomber jacket, and the flat, wide-brimmed hat of a deputy. Even from a distance I could see Mac was cold and tired.

I unlocked the door immediately and hurried him into the empty dining room. Cold radiated off his jacket.

It doesn't snow very often on Camas Island, but when it does the entire town goes into instant hibernation. I'd need to tell Lionel and Kaden to stop prepping. Chances were we wouldn't even be open if the snow continued. But the expression on Mac's face told me he'd come to see me specifically, so all that would have to wait.

"Something up, babe?" I'd taken to calling him babe during the last couple of months. He seemed to like it, or at least didn't ask me to stop.

"The identity of the victim this morning has been confirmed." He paused for a moment and then added, "There's no easy way to say this so I'll just say it: the deceased is your previous business partner, Samantha Eider"

"No." The word came out as a reflex, as though I had the authority to countermand any unappealing reality. Samantha was much more than my ex-business partner. At one time she'd been my best friend, then a growing source of resentment, worry and guilt. We'd worked together, nearly died together in the basement of this very building and then parted ways with a lot left unsaid. Not the least of which had been the fact that she'd decided to sell her half of our business without informing me.

Mac just shook his head, his expression one of pained sympathy.

"She's not even in the state," I protested. "Are you sure—"

"It's her." Mac laid a hand on my shoulder. Then before I could even ask what had happened, he said, "It's homicide."

"By what—I mean . . . how do you know it's murder?"

"She received several blows to the back of her head with an object like a hammer or a club then was dumped in the water—we're not sure if it was from a boat or if the body was dumped on the shore somewhere and was pulled out then brought back in by the tide. We had to stop because the snow is coming down hard now. We're supposed to get more than six inches overnight." Mac looked into my eyes as though studying them. "Are you all right?"

"I'm . . . shocked," I said. "But also not shocked. She had problems and made a lot of bad decisions, but she didn't deserve . . . I think I'm . . . sad. Just . . . very sad."

Mac nodded. "I've just been on the phone to inform Charlie."

"Charlie her homicidal cousin who's in the State Pen?" Just thinking of Charlie sent a shot of anger through me. He was the one who had attempted to murder Sam and me in the basement. If anyone ought to have been bludgeoned it was him, not her.

"He's her next of kin." Mac gave a sigh. We both stood in silence. Snow continued to fall outside, quietly blanketing everything beneath a soft white shroud. At last Mac pointed to the specials board. "Do you happen to have a Wyoming chili plate left? I haven't eaten for a while."

His question offered me a release from the turmoil sloshing through me. I nodded then sat him down at the bar and went into the back. Lionel and Kaden were each focused on their own chopping boards, maybe having some sort of competition? I found Lionel's phone and turned the stereo off, giving them time to look up from their work and see the expression on my face.

I don't actually know what my expression was, but I know that I felt serious and sad and it probably showed. Kaden said nothing, but glanced askance at Lionel who said, "What's up, chief?"

"Mac wants the special," I said.

". . . okay." Lionel didn't move, his face frozen in suspicion.

"I'll get it." I walked around him, went into the walk-in and brought out a carrot, which I peeled and cut into sticks. I placed these, and a large, unglazed cinnamon roll on a plate and scooped chili con carne into a separate bowl. I topped it with a sprinkling of house-made queso fresco and extra cilantro.

Mac really liked cilantro.

"Is that your extra-special lunch for bae?" Lionel asked. He'd resumed chopping onions but kept side-eyeing me.

"That's right. He didn't eat yet today. Also he just told me that Samantha was found dead in the ocean this morning," I finished. Then, to Kaden, "Samantha was my original business partner here."

To say that Lionel stopped chopping would misrepresent his actions. He stepped back, clenched his jaw and threw his knife down so hard the tip embedded itself in his cutting board. It stood there at an acute angle, trembling from the impact.

"Oh my God, what the hell, chief? Is there a curse on you? Tell me who cursed you," he demanded.

In contrast, Kaden stood stock still, eyes wide in shock. At both of us, I think.

"There's not a curse on me," I said, though right then I wasn't certain I believed it. I kept myself as calm as I could, trying to separate myself from the feeling of loss. But every single pot and pan, every plate, every wine glass reminded me of how hopeful Sam and I had been when we built this business together. "Also, it's snowing pretty hard so we'll be closed tonight. You guys can clean up and go home. Thanks for your work today."

I returned to the dining room and slid Mac's food down in front of him. As I sat next to him, the music in the kitchen resumed but at a much lower volume. I could just make out the clatter of the two of them back there, talking in hushed voices as they cleaned up.

"Do you have any leads at all?" I asked.

"You sure you're okay to talk about this?" he asked.

Was I? The news seemed to have left me too stunned to really think of anything else, so I nodded.

"We don't have much yet. But it's early," Mac informed me. "According to everyone she's not even supposed to be on the island now."

"Right, she actually works for another of Michael's LA restaurants—worked I mean. Do you want me to give you the number?" I picked up my phone and started to scroll through the contacts.

"I've already talked to Michael." Mac carefully unwound part of his cinnamon roll while observing the plate I'd given him. "Carrot sticks, huh?"

"The addition of carrot sticks turns this plate into an exact replica of my favorite school lunch," I said. "I wish I had a carton of chocolate milk to add. That would make it perfect. Most people dip a piece of the cinnamon roll into the chili and eat it that way."

"For real?" Mac said, with evident skepticism.

"You don't have to but that's how we always did it. At some schools they even served the cinnamon roll sitting right on top of the chili." I put my phone down. "I think that takes it too far though."

"I'll stick to keeping them separated." Mac took a bite of the sweet, cinnamon scented bread. "This is delicious. Everything you make is good."

"It's Evelyn's recipe. I'm not much of a baker." I reached across and poked one of his carrot sticks. "Make sure to eat your vegetable too."

I stared at the golden spiral of the cinnamon roll that was so emblematic of everything carefree and delightful about my childhood. I recalled that I'd really wanted to share those memories and feelings with Mac when I'd been making this special. I'd wondered what his favorite school lunches had been and whether he'd snuck off campus to sneak burgers like I frequently saw students here doing.

Now all that seemed distant—almost alien to the reality that had settled over me.

Someone had beaten Sam to death.

The breath caught in my throat and I tried desperately not to imagine it—her dying that way. Or Mac having to identify her body.

It suddenly occurred to me that I shouldn't make Mac talk about murder when he was just trying to eat a meal. I ought to give him a chance to get away from the horror of it. Just let him enjoy the innocent sweetness of his cinnamon roll in peace.

He glanced at me but didn't say anything. Then he ate a couple of spoonfuls of chili while I sat still, reeling from shock.

Outside, the snow continued to fall. Inside, I felt an inescapable pang of loss at Sam's death—even though we'd fallen out and no longer communicated. Maybe part of my sorrow came from the fact that we hadn't spoken—not to reconcile or even argue—and now we never would.

I glanced at Mac. He wasn't finished eating. I wondered what more he knew that he hadn't told me yet, but there was still half a cinnamon roll left so I had a minute to wait.

I considered what might have brought Samantha back to town.

Christmas would have been the obvious answer but she had no one to spend the holiday with here anymore. Then again Sam could easily be described as one of those people who never escaped the event horizon of their hometown, so maybe inertia or force of habit had simply drawn her back?

I had no such problem. Even the amicable connections with my own family were distant and faint. The less we knew about each other the better we all got along. Because of this I had thought that there was no place where I would ever become part of the community. And then I'd started a relationship with Mac.

He came with a whole town—every historical building and every decorative crosswalk. All the rhododendrons and basalt cliff faces and the whole green expanse of the Salish Sea was included in the package called Mac. Every heron and salmon, geoduck and orca, stray cat and dog in town was attached to him. Plus, all the cops and all the criminals too.

Even the staff at the hardware store inquired after the details of his life and he theirs.

And Mac came with a big family. Leaving aside the uncle and cousin whom he worked with in the sheriff's office, there were three brothers and two sisters who had become regular fixtures in my life ever since Mac had given me the key to his house six months before. Only last week I'd sublet the awful single-wide trailer that I'd lived in for the past three years to Lionel, who needed some 'space away from his mom' (read: a place to take girls) and taken Mac up on his offer of freedom from rent in his shabby mansion on the hill.

The night I'd moved in the Mackenzie siblings had all crowded together around the dinner table, leaving a place for me on Mac's right. I sat there even though I still didn't exactly understand what the responsibilities of occupying the chair adjacent to Mac's included. At least his siblings all seemed to believe that I belonged there and owned that space now.

Even now, sitting at the bar in my restaurant, I took that same position.

"I was thinking," Mac said. "I want to invite Evelyn and Julie to our place for Christmas."

"You mean invite them to the Mackenzie house?"

"The Mackenzie house, yeah." A slight smile curved Mac's lips upward. "You know—it's the big blue building where all your clothes are now."

"Right," I said. "But Evelyn and Julie—I don't know. Will it be just your siblings or will your uncle's family be there too?"

"We celebrate on our own. Aunt Jenny throws a huge party every year and we attend that but Christmas Day will be just us. We keep it casual."

I nodded. 'Just us' in fact meant Mac, his sister Charlotte (recently returned from New York after breaking up with her orthodontist boyfriend), his brother Remy, and Mac's youngest sister Abby, (who was on break from her studies at the University of Washington). Neither Clayton nor Mason, Mac's two other brothers, would be attending this year as they'd both decided to go home with their respective girlfriends. That was a lot of players already. I doubted the two old ladies who had more or less adopted me would be ready to shuffle into the game but didn't want to shoot Mac's offer down.

"You can invite them, but I don't know if they'll come. They can be weird about traditional interactions with society," I said. "I think it's because they lived as outsiders for so long."

"Sure, I get it." Mac finished the last of his cinnamon roll and dusted the crumbs off his hands. He looked worn down and wary. "Listen, I have some bad news."

"Worse than the news about Sam?"

"I think . . . yes. It's related to the news about Sam but involves you." Mac stared directly into the mirror behind the bar, not making eye contact. "We need to interview you—just a routine thing—accounting for your whereabouts for the last couple of days since you're a known associate that might have a grudge."

"Okay." I had a cold premonition of what he was about to say. "I've been either here or at your house. I've literally gone nowhere else and never been alone."

"Right. I can't be the person to take your statement though because I'm in a relationship with you, so I'd like you to come with me to the station and give that information to the officer on duty." Mac finally looked at me. "Please."

"I am . . . actually pretty impressed that you ate that entire bowl of chili before even approaching this subject." I couldn't help but smirk. "Were you scared?"

"I was worried that you wouldn't feed me if you knew."

"I'll always feed you." I patted him on his big meaty shoulder. "Finish your carrot sticks and we'll go. I want to get this over with as fast as possible."

Chapter Two

Growing up, as I did in the High Plains, the mythos of the Old West looms large in every aspect of life. Everywhere you see the Wagon Wheel Café here and the Frontier Playhouse there. Cowboy boots are regular, rather than fashion-conscious footwear. Rattlesnakes abound. And if you drive a truck of a certain size, roads are merely suggested routes.

In that environ no figure loomed larger than the sheriff in terms of ultimate authority. To this day the sheriff's departments are often the only law for hundreds of miles in vast areas west of the Mississippi. I grew up revering those guys and the gunslingers who fought with and alongside them in equal measure. I suspected that the imprint of the good lawman which had been branded into my childhood psyche had been the reason I'd been able to overcome my fear of cops to date Mac at all.

Camas County had a sheriff too.

I don't think those old-time sheriffs were necessarily better people than the current sheriff of Camas Country but I'm pretty sure none of them could have been as lazy and survived.

Sheriff Scott Mackenzie was my boyfriend's uncle and the current patriarch of their clan. He did not like me and I did not like him but because we had to interact—sometimes for whole minutes at a time—we'd both tacitly agreed to pretend that we weren't both aware of our natural antipathy.

Sometimes, though, I wondered if I had been unfair to him. My impression of him was based mainly on hearsay and on what he'd said when interrogating me during the investigation of Dorian Gamble's murder the previous year. He'd provoked me—basically asking if I'd killed Dorian in a fit of horny gay rage—but deliberately flustering a person you're questioning in a murder investigation wasn't uncommon or necessarily personal.

According to Abby, though, 'Uncle Scott' had been good to Mac and his siblings. After their father had disappeared and their mother passed away, he'd allowed the six orphaned Mackenzie kids to continue living in their old house together. Only Mac had been of legal age at that time—and even then just barely—but Uncle Scott hadn't obstructed him when he'd decided to become the legal guardian of his siblings. I privately wondered if that great act of compassion hadn't had more to do with not wanting to have five extra kids living with him than empathy but then . . . I routinely suspected the worst of Uncle Scott because I really couldn't stand him.

I'm unfair that way. It gets me in trouble a lot.

This time I was not led to an interrogation room, but to Uncle Scott's office and Mac sat down in the chair next to me while we waited for him to finish his phone call.

Uncle Scott was the senior edition of a typical Mackenzie. He was big and bulky with lots of thick hair on his forearms and a bristling gray moustache. He wore gold-rimmed aviator glasses and had an expression that other people probably found affable but I knew was just the same old mask every member of this family wore when walking out in the world.

"Thanks for coming in, Drew," he said. "I heard you moved into the old house. How are you liking it?"

"Good," I said. Then, realizing I needed to be friendlier I added, "It's nice to be able to walk to work."

"It is," Uncle Scott agreed. "So, unfortunately I have to ask you some questions about Samantha Eider."

"I haven't been in contact with her since she sold her half of the Eelgrass to Michael Xavier." I hoped I could just get this over with.

"But she worked for another restaurant in your same group. Didn't you ever talk to her at all? See her at a meeting? An online meeting maybe?" Uncle Scott tapped his pen slowly on his desk.

"Our GM, Lupe, is the person who attends the meetings and does all the corporate-facing work. I focus on the creative side of the business, so no, I never saw Sam at all." I glanced past him, out the window. The snow was coming down even harder now, covering the lines in the parking lot. "I wasn't part of her life anymore and she wasn't part of mine. I don't know who would have wanted to hurt her like that, much less why."

"See, I think that's strange," Uncle Scott said.

"Come on, Uncle—" Mac began but Uncle Scott raised a hand to silence him.

"It's strange because everyone in our entire family knows that you're a little bit of an amateur sleuth and just chock full of ideas about crime on the island but you're not even advancing a single theory to me right now. I'd have thought you'd have a hundred ideas about what had happened to your former business partner but nope. You've got nothing. Not a peep." Uncle Scott gave a short laugh. "Are you that nervous to be here?"

"I think I'm just in shock," I replied. "And I really don't know anything."

"If you had to guess why Samantha came back to the island, what would you say?" Uncle Scott asked.

I shot a glance to Mac, who was scowling in deep irritation but keeping quiet.

"If I had to take a wild guess I'd say that she got nostalgic because its Christmas and thought she should come back to the island," I said. "Or it could be that she wanted to apologize to me or to someone else here in town. She's a big apologizer. She once made me go with her to the basement of our restaurant to apologize to Dorian Gamble's ghost for being mean to him a couple of times when they were children."

"What did she ever do to you that she'd need to apologize for?" Uncle Scott kept his question slow and even.

What did she ever do?

Uncle Scott and his baiting line of questioning was getting on my nerves. He knew what she'd done. He had everything right here on record as part of the investigation of Dorian Gamble's murder.

She'd burned through our restaurant's profits to fuel a drug habit, left me scrambling to keep the business afloat, signed over her half of Eelgrass to a drug dealer named

Vukoja, and then attempted to ditch me and flee to Bali with a bag of drugs she stole from the same drug dealer. All while I was being set up for the murder of her cousin Dorian by her other cousin, Charlie.

But I wasn't about to mention any of that. Partly because I didn't want to set myself up as a suspect again but also because all of it felt . . . like ancient history that I'd left behind. Thinking back, some of it was almost funny now.

Almost.

"She sold her half of the restaurant to Michael Xavier without telling me . . . as you already know," I said.

"And there was nothing else?" he asked.

"Isn't that enough?"

"Okay." He smiled and put his pen away. "If you get any wild ideas or hear anything, be sure to let Mac know."

I gave my sincerest fake smile. "I always do."

Chapter Three

I started talking the second we got in Mac's cruiser. "Do you really not have anything on Sam's case?"

Mac just shook his head, which shocked me since under normal circumstances he was evasive about giving me information. Or at least he put up more of a protest before allowing me to slowly wheedle some detail out of him.

He put the car into gear and started driving the few blocks to his house—I didn't consider it ours yet even though I lived there. It remained the Mackenzie family house—proven most recently by Charlotte's abruptly returning and taking up residence in her old room without informing either of us in advance.

"In terms of Sam's case we have both jack and squat," Mac said. "We haven't even found her phone."

"It's weird that your uncle called me out so directly about investigating things," I remarked. "It's almost like he asked me to help."

"It could be that he's trying to be friendly since you live with me now." Mac gave a shrug. "Uncle Scott is the kind of person who goes with the flow. When he brought you in over Dorian's death he was targeting you because you were an outsider. You're an insider now."

"Doesn't it disturb you that he doesn't seem to have any personal ethics or interest in objective fairness?" I couldn't help but ask.

"It does, but I can only do so much and still keep working the cases that need to be worked and solving the problems that need to be solved." Mack sighed. "At least he believes in keeping the peace."

"Sometimes the peace needs disturbing," I muttered.

"But most of the time it doesn't." Mac shot me a full smile. "It's a mindset that a troublemaker like you wouldn't understand."

"I don't want to understand it," I grumbled. "And before you ask, I don't want to go to his house for some Christmas Party."

"Did I ask you to?"

"No, but you were going to," I said. "You want me to go everywhere with you now."

"So? What's wrong with that? Can't I show you off?"

The feeling that moved through me was so complicated then. It wasn't as though I'd never been part of a public couple. My ex-boyfriend Michael and I had been, at times, like conjoined twins but the places we had sashayed through together were, for lack of a better term, gay spaces. Everything about Mac's world was limned with robust masculinity and instilled in me a profound awkwardness because I could not match his effortless ease navigating the boy's clubs of this town.

How could I feel at ease with a bunch of guys who, in high school, would have been trying to kick my ass all the time?

Yet everywhere we went no one challenged us. Even the crabby, ancient waitress at the Prospector spoke to me now—because I was with Mac.

But didn't that mean that the reverse could also be true? If we broke up would I have to leave town?

Most of all, why couldn't I just enjoy it? Wasn't this the rom-com dream? The only way it could have been more American as apple pie would have been if Mac had been the quarterback of the football team—not that I didn't know for sure that he wasn't.

"Did you play football in high school?" I asked.

Mac took the non-sequitur in stride. "No, I was on the swim team. But my main sport was track and field. I threw javelin. I quit after my junior year though."

"Right." Of course he had. Everything had stopped with his father's disappearance and his mother's death. I sank back into the cruiser seat, briefly letting myself be mesmerized by the windshield wipers endlessly clearing away the slush splatters of snow.

"By the way, was Samantha one of those people who wears a rubber band around her wrist to snap herself to try and break a bad habit?" Mac asked.

"Not while I knew her but she could have picked it up during rehab. I've heard that's a rehab thing."

Mac nodded slowly to himself. "Do you have time to come with me somewhere?"

"Is it somewhere sexy?" In truth I didn't really feel like jumping into bed but a certain sleazy reflex kicked in automatically whenever I was within the radius of Mac's aftershave.

"Gonna say a hard no . . . sadly." Mac drove slowly down Main Street and pulled into the parking lot behind the Prospector, which I couldn't even believe was still open. Another LE cruiser was already parked there—this one was State Highway Patrol.

"Is that Remy's?" I asked.

"Yeah." Mac parked and we went inside.

The Prospector contained exactly four people. One cook, one waitress, one guy drinking a beer and eating pancakes at the bar, and Mac's younger brother Remy. He'd taken off his wide-brimmed hat but kept his coat on as though he didn't plan to stay very long.

Remy seemed unsurprised to see me slide into the booth next to Mac and acknowledged me with a slight wave. The waitress, who I now knew was named Tilly, arrived and slid two cups onto the table in front of us, filled them and departed without saying anything more than, "Let me know if you need anything else."

"How did it go with Uncle Scott?" Remy asked me.

"Same as usual." I gave a shrug.

"I disagree. I found his behavior highly suspicious," Mac said. "He didn't even ask Drew for an alibi."

"That's bad," Remy remarked. "Real bad."

"Why is that bad?" I asked. "Isn't that just his way of accepting me into the family?"

"Uncle Scott hates you, Drew," Remy said. "If he could arrest you for something he would. Then he gets the opportunity to put the screws on you and he doesn't? Completely out of character."

"You don't have to be so harsh you dick." Mac kicked Remy under the table.

"It's not like Uncle Scott liked my girlfriend—when I still had one." Remy rubbed his leg dramatically but didn't fight back. "Sugarcoating it won't change anything."

"Wait, though. Back up. So what are you two saying—that you actually suspect your uncle of . . . what?" I hunched forward and lowered my voice. "What the hell is going on?

Why are we meeting up at some deserted diner in the middle of a snowstorm to talk about this?"

"The snowstorm is coincidental." Remy poured two sugar packets into his coffee then leaned forward, keeping his voice barely audible above the decades-old pop songs playing overhead. "Uncle Scott's investigation of this homicide . . ."

Mac's expression turned grim and he nodded.

"He was on edge all morning but when we got the call about the body—Sam—he actually seemed sort of . . . relieved." Mac wrapped his hands around his coffee mug but he only scowled down at it. "His behavior at the crime scene was way too brusque even for him. He made no effort to preserve the scene and had her body hauled off way too soon."

"He was going through the motions but just barely." Remy nodded. "Even Chaz has noticed."

"You talked to Chaz about this? What the hell?" Mac shook his head.

"I didn't tell him. He brought it up to me," Remy said. "Said that if Sam had any family left to complain the department could end up looking at a lawsuit."

The truth of his remark stung deeply, sending a cold chill all the way through me. I couldn't believe that the two of them were speaking so freely about this between themselves. Moreover, neither of them seemed shocked or hurt. Was the idea of negligence in the Orca's Slough Sheriff's Department really so banal that neither of them even felt disappointed?

"Chaz might be concerned but I don't want to bring him in on this—for obvious reasons," Mac said.

"No reasons seem totally obvious to me," I broke in, leaning forward into the huddle. "What are you afraid will happen? And what do you think is happening now?"

Mac took a deep breath. "What I think is happening now is that Uncle Scott knows a lot more about Sam's death than he's letting on. Him not asking you for your whereabouts? It means that he knows you weren't involved. That implies that he knows what really happened. I don't want to bring Chaz in because I don't trust him to hold out against Uncle Scott or to cover up for you and me and I also don't think it's fair to make him have to try."

"But what exactly would Chaz have to be holding out about and covering up?" I persisted.

"Mac has decided to investigate Sam's death independently, without reporting to Uncle Scott," Remy said. "I'm helping him where I can and, I guess so are you? Because otherwise I don't know why you're here, to be honest."

"Does that mean . . . I'm being deputized?" I asked. "Oh my God, I'm so excited."

"That's not—" Mac began.

"I need to get my own tiny notebook," I said.

"I can't tell if this is cute or sickening." Remy took out his phone and took a picture of us. "It's worth putting in the scrapbook though." He turned the phone around to show me my expression, which I recognized from another photograph snapped decades before. In that other picture I was standing in front of a Christmas tree, holding the handlebars of a bike that Santa had brought me. Mac's expression was one of both affection and suffering. He reached out and ruffled my hair.

"And with that it just became sickening so I'm out." Remy stood and threw a few bills down on the table. "Call me if you need anything."

Mac just gave a curt nod. I waited till he left then leaned in close to Mac.

"Do you really think that your Uncle had something to do with Sam's murder?" I asked in a whisper.

"I don't . . . know. There could be something else going on with him. Trouble at home or his health," Mac replied. "But I'm going to make certain that Sam's murder gets properly investigated whether he's involved in it or not."

"So does this mean that if I were to ask around at work about Sam's recent activities it won't piss you off this time?" I searched his expression for approval, still not quite believing that he'd chosen to officially confide in me. "It's just that I don't think anybody in our restaurant group is going to be comfortable talking to cops. We're not traditionally pro-cop in our industry."

"I've gathered that, yeah," Mac said. "I try not to embarrass you when we're out though."

I rolled my eyes. "Mac everybody knows the embarrassing one is me."

"No, you're nervous about being seen with me. It's okay." Mac leaned back in the booth and closed his eyes. He had a handsome profile. Strong jaw. Straight, dark brows. The slight crookedness of his nose only emphasized his masculinity.

"It's not being seen with you it's . . . being so publicly upstanding in broad daylight is weird. I guess I'm more used to being one of the nighttime people." I hoped he understood. "Also, a lot of the people you know scare the shit out of me."

Mac nodded. "Same."

I rolled my eyes. "Oh bullshit, who in my circle of acquaintances scares you?"

"Apart from all of your antifa employees?"

"Point taken," I conceded. "But you never answered my question. Should I call the restaurant where Sam worked?"

"Under normal circumstances I'd caution you against nosing around, but I think you're right. No one is going to talk to me or any of my counterparts in LA." Mac rubbed his face as though he could scrub the fatigue from it, then opened his eyes. "So I'd appreciate anything you could find out. Do you want me to drop you off at the restaurant where you can hide out or would you like to go back home where my sisters are lying in wait?"

"In wait for me? Why?" I couldn't imagine why. Neither of them showed any interest in food or cooking and Charlotte the model had only limited interest in even eating.

"They want to get to know you." He gave me a smile. "You know—bonding. Uncle Scott wants to wait until tomorrow to release Sam's name to the media but if you want, I can tell Charlotte and Abby that your former business partner died and they should leave you alone."

I looked at my watch. It was a little past five p.m. and the dinner service would have already started at the restaurant where Sam worked in LA. After that the employees would be surly and potentially also drunk. It would be better to call them in the morning when their answers would be more coherent.

"No, I think someone trying to console me would just make me even more confused. I need a distraction so go ahead and take me to the ambush," I said. "I mean, how scary could they be?"

◆◆◆

The second I walked through the door Charlotte and Abby were on me. They each seized one of my arms in a kind of pincer maneuver of holiday cheer and before I knew it, I stood sandwiched between them in the big kitchen at the Mackenzie house. Together we all stared at the floor to ceiling cupboards that lined two walls. These cupboards had been installed in the house in the thirties and were made of deep golden varnished wood and sported round gold pulls. Now every one of these doors stood fully open, revealing the densely packed contents of dozens of shelves.

Charlotte, twenty-nine, the oldest sister, stood on my right. She wore non-matching holiday separate pajamas and kept her long, bleach-blonde hair pulled up in a candy cane striped scrunchie. Her long slim build, flawless complexion and elegant features had allowed her to travel and work as a high-fashion model for nearly a decade. Though recently she'd been talking about finding other work.

Abby, nineteen, the baby of the family, stood on my left. Equally statuesque to her runway-model sister, but with ombre mermaid hair, a baggy anime t-shirt, and jeans.

"Do it," Charlotte whispered into my ear. "Be a hero."

"Yeah, we'll totally back you up." Abby leaned in close on the other side. "Just do it."

"What . . . what even is all this stuff?" I stepped closer and found that one shelf contained many, many hobnail milk glass ice cream dishes—like twenty. Another held not one but three hand-crank apple peelers along with other assorted ancient uni-taskers. A salad spinner. A Ronco Veg-O-Matic Food Chopper. Something in a box labeled 'The SuperSnacker.' All of it looked long forgotten and smelled musty.

I couldn't imagine Mac owning any of these items. So all this stuff must belong to his parents? Had he never cleaned out their belongings?

Were they hoarders? Or . . . no, it couldn't be Mac. His room was clean to the point of being Spartan.

No lie, I felt queasy at the sight of it all.

"No. No way I'm going to move your parents' things." I shrugged them off and started closing cabinets, but the girls were quick and they had me again before I managed to complete the job.

"Wait! You've gotta help us, Drew!" Charlotte clung to me with a pleading yet beautiful expression that I imagined she used to sell upscale perfume brands. "This is our one chance to dig out the old Christmas decorations and finally have a real Christmas. And while we're at it we can throw some stuff away."

"No way." I shook them off. "If I touch ANY of this stuff somebody is going to be pissed. And where would I put it once I took it off the shelf?"

"I mean, the garbage is right there," Charlotte indicated the trash can with a graceful motion of her perfectly manicured hand.

"Please Drew, please help us throw some of this stuff away," Abby said. "Nothing is going to happen to you."

"Then why aren't you doing it without me?" I felt this was a valid question.

"Because it's not our stuff," Abby said.

"It's not mine either," I said. I wanted nothing to do with any of this—I'd just been actually asked to help Mac investigate a murder. What if this somehow eroded his trust? Crossed a boundary? He'd never ask me to help him again.

"And therein lies the problem." Charlotte strode to the cupboards gesturing grandly like she was showing off the puzzle on *Wheel of Fortune*. "This stuff does not belong to anybody."

"Technically, the owner is Mac," I put in.

"But they're not his possessions," Charlotte said. "They're our parents' and our grandparents' and our great-grandparents' things. They're not his."

Charlotte's rejoinder surprised me both in the coldness of its logic and the sadness with which she spoke.

"Honestly, that's an argument in favor of keeping them where they are," I pointed out.

"Come on Drew," Charlotte drew herself up into what can only be described as a Power Pose, hands on hips, like Wonder Woman. "This is the kitchen. It should be your domain. Take up some space in this house."

I'll admit, that argument did hold some appeal. At the same time, I didn't want to become the tool that all the brothers and sisters used to work around Mac's decisions and choices. For all their warm welcome they also regarded me as a resource for dealing with their brother. Besides, Mac had already let me have a room for my office when

I'd moved in just so that I'd have my own territory in the house.

"If you help me clean this stuff out so that I can find the rustic angel tree-topper that our mom and dad brought back from their trip to Mexico," Charlotte said, "I'll show you the stupid pictures of Mac I took in high school."

I'm not made of stone.

But I'm also not an idiot. I'd accept the offer, plus I realized this gave me a chance to sound out the sisters on the subject of their uncle. "Even if Mac doesn't want them what about your Uncle Scott? You said some of these belonged to your grandparents, right?"

"Aunt Jenny doesn't want anything from this house." Charlotte flipped her hair back over her shoulder in a way that was both artistic and dismissive at once. "And Uncle Scott just does what's convenient."

Abby added, "He really doesn't like making waves."

My former employee, Dorian, had mentioned numerous times that Sheriff Mackenzie operated on a sliding scale when it came to investigating crime in Orca's Slough. Vagrancy would be swiftly dealt with whereas infractions like embezzlement or discreet drug dealing could go unsolved in perpetuity as long as no one made a fuss.

I said, "Okay what about this? You two look for the ornaments. I'll pack whatever you take out of these cabinets into boxes and ask Mac if he wants me to donate it. But you have to be the ones to choose what stays and what goes. I got no dog in this fight."

The girls' agreement was immediate and enthusiastic. As they disgorged the multi-generational kitchen hoard they talked and showed me this or that item. And at least it provided a source of conversation. Some of the articles produced were even intriguing, in the way that going through someone else's cupboards always is. Some owner of this kitchen had, at some point in history, collected items with a chicken motif. Another had seemed to enjoy tiki glasses. The cabinets held as many dishes as a small thrift store. None of them seemed to be Mac's style and many were covered in dust so thick and old that it had become a sticky grime.

Charlotte and Abby indulged themselves in rearranging and editing the contents of the rest of the cupboards while pretending to search for the fabled Christmas ornaments.

Eventually I retreated, found some eggs and flour and set about making some pasta.

By the time I finished dinner the sisters had emptied, examined, cleaned and rearranged about two thirds of the cabinets. Several boxes of rejects and detritus were stacked in the hall, taking up most of it. Just as I began to wonder if the ornaments existed at all Charlotte and Abby unearthed the mother lode: five cardboard boxes simply marked "Christmas," in neat cursive handwriting.

"Oh my God this feels so good." Abby washed her hands and flopped down in front of her plate of ravioli. "I've been wanting to do that my whole life! Let's do the closet in your office after dinner."

"We don't have any more boxes to fill up," I said. "Let's wait till later to tackle my office."

"No, we have to get it done before Mac gets back or he'll tell us to stop," Abby protested.

"Why?" I asked.

"He doesn't know what to do with our parents' things," Charlotte said. "We ended up just putting them all into that one closet and these cupboards then . . . none of us could finish the job somehow."

"I could finish the job but they won't let me," Abby muttered.

Charlotte gave her a glare. "It's because Mac doesn't trust you to be respectful."

"I am respectful of their memories," Abby countered. "Just not their old clothes and expired can of shaving cream."

"How about we see how Mac reacts to this first round before we risk the second?" I kept my suggestion as gentle as I could because I could tell Abby wanted to argue—and not just about a few sets of old dishes. "Charlotte still owes me some old pictures of Mac."

"Right!" Charlotte jumped up from the table, still holding her fork in her hand. "Be right back."

Abby's expression was sullen. "We just think it's not fair that you have to live with all this stuff that no one wants and isn't yours. They're just remnants."

I recognized that she wasn't really talking about me—just explaining how she'd probably felt all this time. "Just so you know—I'm permanently moving out in January."

"Really?" I hadn't heard this but it didn't surprise me.

"I'm getting a place off campus with a couple of my friends." Abby's tone was casual but her lack of eye contact told me she was practicing this speech on me. If she'd been Remy, I would have thought she was trying to get me to relay the information to Mac so she didn't have to but Abby was the most straightforward of the clan. I'd heard from Mac that his father had a tendency to get dramatic when receiving bad news so it made sense that all the children raised by him should be hesitant when acting as the messenger whereas Abby, who'd been mostly raised by the insuperably calm Mac, had no such aversion and could be direct to the point of bluntness.

I didn't ask Abby which friends or anything else about her arrangements. If Mac wanted to interrogate her that could be his job.

"Sounds fun," I said.

"So I'm going to take all my stuff back with me after Christmas break." She finally looked up, expression pensive. Then she popped a ravioli into her mouth. "My room will be empty and you can use that one for your office. That's better than one that's already full of dead people's furniture."

"What if I want them both?" I asked.

Abby's face froze mid-chew. "What do you mean?"

"I'm just saying that maybe it's time for Mac to stop living in the little room behind the bathroom and level up to the master bedroom with me," I said.

Abby snickered, then just muttered, " . . . *master* bedroom. . ."

"You're so childish." Charlotte plonked a shoebox down on the table. Then to me, "Please feel free."

The box was stuffed with paper envelopes from photo developers. The majority of them were clearly Charlotte's experiments with modeling poses, but here and there I'd come across a shot of bean pole teenage Mac wearing an Orca's Slough track team hoodie. But later pictures showed him already wearing his uniform and staring at the camera with little or no expression. The only photos that betrayed any of the warm character that I knew were those where he stood with his arm around Abby. She always appeared to beam up at him with devotion as she grew taller and more poised.

"You said you had dumb pictures of him," I said.

Charlotte glanced over. "He looks pretty spaced out there."

"It's not the same." I didn't go on to suggest that his expression was more like that of a severely depressed person than a space case. It didn't seem the time or correct audience.

"Oh, there's one here. Give them to me." She leafed through the photos herself, until she found one of a much younger and quite pretty Mac with a full face of makeup. "He lost a bet and had to let me put makeup on him."

"You went all in on the mascara." I took out my phone and took a picture of the photo for my own personal archive.

"You're cute," Charlotte said. "I can't believe Mac got a guy as cute as you. He's so awkward and your last boyfriend was, like, a TV star."

"Exactly like one, yeah. A professional." I zoomed in on teenage Mac's nose. It hadn't been broken by a random drunkard yet and was as aquiline as Charlotte's.

"Don't you ever, you know, regret breaking up with your ex?" Charlotte asked. Abby gave her a side-eye so icy that it would have frozen me right in place like a popsicle but Charlotte didn't notice. "Like you think about the good times and what a fantastic guy he is?"

"No," I said. "Not at all."

"And then suddenly you're looking at his feed in the middle of the night and regretting your decision and you almost text him but then you don't." Charlotte scooched her ravioli around her plate as if she was looking for a way to hide them underneath each other.

"I've never done that with anyone, but especially not Michael." I glanced to Abby, who only rolled her eyes and stood up.

"I'm going to make some tea. Anybody want some tea?" Abby pulled open one of the newly rearranged cabinets, retrieved a teakettle, and went to the sink to fill it with water.

"No thanks." Charlotte waved the offer aside. "But the thing with exes is that you know that the relationship is going to end because they always do so you might as well just be the one to break it off even though you're hurting yourself. At least you'll be in control of the timing."

It would be a lie to say I didn't understand her point of view but I'd also come to a place where I could no longer cosign on that strategy of avoiding heartbreak.

"Is that really a way to live though?" I asked.

"Right?" Charlotte leaned forward. Her long ponytail draped across the photographs strewn across the table. "But you can't turn back time."

I had no answer for Charlotte but her ruminations reminded me a little of Sam, when she was felling regretful, which was often. Then I wondered: had Sam been seeing anyone at the time of her death? Her coworkers would have definitely known that. I made a mental note to ask about that the next morning.

"God, Charlotte, why do you have to make your own life so difficult?" Abby spoke without turning around, staring straight out the kitchen window.

"I'm not—"

The end of Charlotte's retort was subsumed beneath Abby's piercing scream. She crouched down behind "Oh my God there's someone out there!"

"Out where?" Out of reflex I crouched down too.

"In the yard, looking in the windows," Abby whispered.

"Is it a peeper?" Charlotte had joined us in our huddle on the linoleum. "Gross. Did you recognize him?"

Abby shook her head. "All I saw was his blue and gray coat."

"I'll go check." I straightened up and walked toward the back door. "I'll be right back."

Chapter Four

The night sky glowed pink and the ground glittered with deep, powdery snow that evened out all the rough edges of the world, softening and unifying the jumble of shapes into one gently rolling mass of white. Absolute silence filled every crevice of the cold night. As quietly as I could I inched toward the corner of the building and peered around. There, in the freshly fallen snow, were footprints. They clearly showed the path our peeper had taken around the house to the window where Abby had seen him. But the man had gone. I stepped back inside and shoved my feet into my boots.

"Was there really a person?" Charlotte asked.

"Yeah. I'm going to take some pictures of the footprints." I shrugged into my hoodie.

"Don't go out there alone!" Abby protested.

"Whoever he was, he's gone now," I replied.

"What if he's just hanging around in the bushes?" she demanded.

"Then I will see his footprints leading into the bushes, which would be great because then I'd be able to follow them to him and find out who the creeper is right now." I zipped up my hoodie. "Back in a sec."

"I thought Mac was exaggerating when he said you had no sense of self-preservation," Charlotte remarked. Then she pulled on her own coat.

"Where are you going?"

"Out on the porch to be there in case you get attacked." She held up her phone. "I can film it."

And this was how Mac found us when he came home from work. Charlotte in her PJs filming me while I carefully documented the footprints in the snow as best I could by the light of my phone flashlight.

"This guy's feet are almost the same size as mine," I remarked.

"Yeah." Mac looked down at me from the porch then asked Charlotte. "Have you checked the surveillance cam footage?"

I stared up at him, his burly figure silhouetted by the pink winter night and said, "We have a surveillance cam?"

"Oh, right," Charlotte mumbled. "We do have a surveillance cam. And no, I didn't. I never downloaded the app since I don't live here."

"Too bad, you could have used it to look outside instead of . . ." Mac turned his attention to me. "Am I right in assuming you came out here to challenge him or something?"

I gave a kind of half-nod half-shrug that pretty much summed up my sense of guilty pride. Mac pulled out his phone and tapped through some applications, then he glanced up into the eaves.

"Looks like the lens is buried right now. He briefly disappeared into the kitchen then returned carrying a broom, which he used to brush the snow away from the around the camera. He trudged around the house to repeat this action. I followed behind, stepping in his footprints, wrapping my arms around myself to ward off the cold. Somehow when I'd been engrossed in the footprints, I hadn't felt it but now the cold stung.

"Does this happen a lot?" I asked.

"Peeping? No. Not since Abby went to college anyway. Before then sometimes guys would sneak around trying to talk to her at night and whatnot. You know, teenage stuff." Mac knocked the snow off the mailbox and porch light. "I mostly have the cameras in case of vandalism. I don't think this is dangerous though."

"Why not?"

"Somebody who's preparing to commit a felony would notice beforehand that it was snowing since they would know they're thinking of committing a crime. This is probably just some friend of Abby's trying to see if I'm home to avoid me before knocking on the door." Mac prodded the snow away from the eaves of the building to reveal the front camera. The dislodged snow fell in a glittering mass landing right on my bare neck.

I jumped. "Jesus that's cold!"

Mac laughed. "You couldn't even grab a real coat on the way out to confront some weirdo?"

"I didn't want to miss him." I looked with envy at his heavy coat, then decided that I would make it mine. I unzipped the front and stuck my arms in, wrapping them all the way around his warm back. He didn't hesitate to pull his heavy coat closed around me.

"I noticed you all cleaned out the kitchen cabinets. Pretty stressful evening at home?" he asked.

I considered denying it but what would be the point?

"That wasn't me, but yeah." I spoke into his shoulder.

"So when the guy came looking in the window you automatically went on the offensive." I felt his hand on the back of my neck. It was quite warm.

"More like took the opportunity to escape." I also took the opportunity to keep holding on to him for a few seconds, breathing in his scent. "I've had a long day."

"Me too." Mac rubbed his hands down my back. "Are you all right?"

"Yes but—is what you're doing really okay?" I whispered. "What if your uncle finds out you suspect he's involved somehow?"

"I don't know."

"This seems dangerous." I felt like I had to say it. If only one time. I knew nothing would dissuade Mac from the course he'd decided to take, but I wanted to say it out loud.

"It could be, or it could not be." Mac drew back to look me in the eye. "At this time the outcome is uncertain. I'm sorry. I know you like to have all the answers."

"It's okay. It's not your fault. But hey, the good news is I saved you some ravioli," I said. "So at least you'll have dinner."

"Let's go eat that then."

Chapter Five

Since snowfall on the Pacific coastal islands was both rare and fleeting, the town of Orca's Slough didn't own a single snowplow. Rather, it relied on a loose association of intrepid volunteers to clear the roads, so, though splendid and delightful, even a couple inches of snow brought the whole place to a dead standstill. That didn't stop people with inadequate vehicles from attempting to drive anyway, which meant Mac and the rest of the sheriff's department had their hands full the next day with various distress calls as well as complying with requests for welfare checks on the elderly.

According to the weather forecast, rain would wash away the blanket of white in a mere five days' time. Therefore, most residents opted to take the opportunity to cancel plans, call into work, and generally get an unexpected staycation.

I, however, am not most people. The Eelgrass had been booked entirely for a private event the same day the rain was expected to clear the roads, so I needed to go in to start prepping, even if I only got six or seven customers for the whole day. Plus, I needed a private office from which to conduct my interviews with Sam's coworkers at our sister restaurant in LA. I'd even snagged one of the small notepads the servers used for orders so that I could jot down notes like an actual detective.

My second-in-command, Lionel, was not thrilled by the news that the restaurant would be open.

"I'm snowed in chief," he said happily.

"Abby offered to drive out and give you a ride in Mac's truck," I replied. "She'll drive you back too. I need you to help prep, please."

Though sullen, Lionel agreed to come in, which left me a few minutes to make good on my promise to Mac. 'Consuelo' was the restaurant where Sam had been employed at the time of her death. When I called, Raven, the hostess who answered the phone, sounded about twelve years old but knew who I was when I said my name and asked for the GM.

"Oh, you're from the murder restaurant in Seattle," she remarked.

I decided not to challenge either of her statements. "Yeah, is Jamie in?"

"Yes, but she's talking to Chef Michael," Raven said. "Is it really true about Sam?"

"Yes, I'm afraid it is.

"That's so sad," Raven's voice grew soft.

"Did she say anything to anybody about why she was coming up here?"

"She said she had to take care of some stuff," Raven said. "This was the last shift I was supposed to be covering for her. She wanted to be back here for Christmas."

"That's rough." I tapped my pen on the empty note pad—then I realized Raven had actually given me some information—Sam had scheduled a return flight only a couple of days after arrival. She hadn't intended to stay on the island very long at all. "Was there anything specific she said she was going to do here?"

"I don't know."

"Is there anybody there that does know?" I tried to keep my voice very calm and not authoritative or bossy, which was hard because that's my natural state.

"Maybe Rico. Do you want to talk to him?"

"Please."

Raven set the phone down. I could hear the clinking of dishes, the low rumble of conversation. Consuelo served breakfast and I was calling right in the middle of service. I hoped Rico wasn't the lead line cook.

The dream was too much to hope for.

"Raven said you want to talk to me?" Rico's voice was a fine, lightly accented tenor.

"Yeah, I'm Drew from the Eelgrass," I began.

"What the fuck do you want?" Rico's tone turned entirely cold. "I have a full fucking rail of tickets."

"I know, I'm sorry," I said, going for the complete dissemble. "I'm so sorry but Raven said you might know why Sam came up here."

"Why the fuck do you care? She said you hated her," Rico growled. The noise of the dining room receded then I heard the sound of a lighter flicking then heard him inhale deeply. He'd left the building to smoke.

"We fought but I never hated her. I want to know what she was doing so that maybe I can help figure out who killed her," I said.

"Oh right—she did say you thought you were Sherlock Fucking Holmes or some shit."

So it had come to this—a pissing contest. Well, whatever it took.

"More like Drew—Nancy Drew. Anyway, look shithead, I get that you're pissed off about having to relinquish total dominion over the omelette station or whatever the fuck you were doing when I called but don't you even care about the fact that Sam is dead? Someone beat her to death like a dog." I waited for Rico's reply, wondering if I'd flexed too hard or not hard enough.

". . . that's so fucked up." I heard Rico's breathing grow slightly ragged. I wondered if she'd been sleeping with him.

"So please tell me if you know anything. Like anything she said would help. We can't even find her phone or wallet. The only reason her body was identified is that this is her hometown and the cop who was the first responder here recognized her." I dialed back my anger completely. "Do you remember if she told you why she was coming back to Orca's Slough?"

"She said she needed to go find something in her storage unit," Rico replied. "She wasn't happy about it and had to keep psyching herself up for the trip."

"But she didn't say what she needed to get?" I dug through my pants pocket to find my keys, checking to see if I still had the spare that Sam had given me when we'd rented that unit years before. Sure enough, it was there. And I was willing to bet she'd never changed the padlock.

"No," I heard him exhale. "Is it true that you're good at figuring out who did shit?"

"I don't suck at it." It was as far as I was willing to commit.

"Then I think I can solve one of your problems. Hang on."

I waited a couple of minutes then felt a text come through on my phone. There was an image of a map showing the section of Top Hat Butte Road that had the scenic ocean view turnout.

"Hello Rico?" Had the guy disconnected? "What's this?"

"Sam and I went to Coachella together, so we had that friend-finding app turned on. According to the app that's where her phone is right now." Again, Rico inhaled sharply on something—a cigarette—a joint—it was hard to say.

"Thank you so mu—"

"Don't fucking call me anymore." Rico hung up.

◆◆◆

One hour later I was standing by the side of the road on Top Hat Butte with Abby and Lionel, knee deep in snow staring down at the screen of a metal detector.

"Do you really know what you're doing?" Abby asked. Her cheeks and nose were reddened from the wind and snow. The morning sky above was almost the same color as the land, white and eerily flat.

"Oh yeah, my auntie lives for this thing. I've been using it since I was a kid." Lionel waved the wand slowly over the surface of the snow. "She liked to take me treasure hunting on the beach."

After Rico had hung up on me, I'd done some quick research on finding phones in the snow. It turned out to be a fairly common problem easily solved by a metal detection expert, and those were even easier to find—whole online directories of them searchable by region. What I had not expected to see, was Lionel's auntie listed as the resident metal detection specialist on Camas Island.

Lionel had kindly offered to sacrifice himself (and take the day off work) to help me try and locate the missing phone.

We'd needed Abby to drive Mac's truck, as neither my nor Lionel's car had chains, or even snow tires.

When we'd first arrived, I'd tried just calling Sam's phone but either notifications had been silenced or her battery had finally gone dead. This section of the winding road hugged the edge of the butte and had a scenic overlook pull-out that was a popular summertime stargazing/make-out spot for locals. The pull-out could fit five or six vehicles but apart from Mac's truck, was empty.

Few people came up here in the dead of winter. And apart from the ones we left, no footprints marked the snow. I walked to the railing and gazed out over the calm surface of the slate gray sea. The waves shone dully under the wan winter light, a vast, undulating sheet of dull aluminum foil.

Could this be where Sam's body had gone into the sea?

If she had been there, standing next to me, she would have been urging me to talk to her ghost and ask it for assistance. It was so typical of the magical thinking that had ruled her life, I couldn't help but actually do it. With my voice barely a whisper I said, "Sam, if you can hear me, help me find out what happened to you."

In the distance a seagull called but otherwise no spectral voice whispered any answer in my ear.

That's the problem with appealing to some imaginary force—it lets you get your hopes up, which inevitably leads to disappointment when it turns out to not exist.

Better to put your hope in something solid.

Mac hadn't answered my text explaining that I was going to go look for Sam's phone. Probably he was busy with welfare checks and other weather-related problems. I was just about to call him when I saw his cruiser rolling up and pulling to a halt behind the truck.

I slogged through the snow, got in the passenger's seat and gave him my biggest smile. "Guess you got my text. Aren't I great?"

"And humble too," Mac said. "I see you've roped Abby and Lionel into your shenanigans as well."

"One of my best qualities as a leader is my ability to delegate." I put my hand on his thigh. "I'm also good at rousing the morale of the troops."

"Is that what you're calling it?" His expression remained stern.

"Don't pretend your spirits don't get lifted by me." I gave a nervous laugh. "Aren't you going to tell me off for not conducting the search properly?"

"I'm off the clock now. Also, this is more or less what we needed to do given that we'd like to find this device before the snow melts and ruins it." Mac laced his fingers through mine. "I checked out Rico. Divorced. Two kids. He's got a non-violent felony charge from about a decade ago. He's been at work every day that Sam's been gone so even if he was the current boyfriend, it's unlikely he's the perp."

"Good to know," I said.

Mac nodded. "Do you know anything about the storage unit he mentioned?"

"I do." I broke into an even bigger smile. "Do you know how?"

"How?" Mac glanced at me sidelong.

"Because if it's the place I'm thinking about—I have a key." I reached into my pocket, pulled out my keychain, and dangled it in front of his face.

"Should I ask how you got that or not?"

"Please go ahead."

"Where did you get it?"

"I've had it for years," I replied. "Sam gave me the spare key in case she lost hers. For a while we had some stuff for the Eelgrass in there, but we moved it all out when she had to make room for Charlie's stuff. I never gave her the key back."

"Why not?"

I ran my finger along the edge of the key's rough teeth. "The storage unit was the first thing we got when we started the restaurant. It's my memento I guess. I don't want to forget about the good parts just because it all went wrong."

Mac rubbed his thumb across mine. "You're low-key super forgiving, aren't you?"

"No, I'm petty as fuck, I just never held a grudge against Sam for some reason." I took a deep breath as I struggled to put my feelings into words. "Getting mad at her for being unreliable and disruptive would have been like getting mad at a cat for meowing. It was just in her nature. Like a reflex. Even her deciding to come back here for some reason then getting murdered just before my first Christmas with your family is really just so damn on-brand for her." As I spoke, I felt my throat tightening and eyes stinging with unexpected tears as the previous day's shock finally wore off. "Crazy bitch."

Mac wrapped his arm around me and pulled me against his shoulder. The rough embroidery of his deputy's patch scratched against my neck. I glanced across and saw my reflection in the rearview mirror. Blond bedhead and tear streaks. Shitty black t-shirt from a metal band that I only liked ironically. I looked like a big gay disaster masquerading as a responsible adult.

Outside a sudden gust of wind blew across the powdery snow sending it sliding through the air like veils of glittering smoke. Then came the sound of sudden whooping.

I got off Mac's shoulder and lurched out of the car. On the other end of the pull-out I saw Lionel and Abby hugging each other.

I turned back to Mac. "I think they found the phone."

◆◆◆

At first it was impossible to tell whether the phone was damaged or just had a dead battery. Mac brought out an evidence marker and photographed it in situ before carefully picking it up and placing it in an evidence bag. The phone was sitting on the ground with no snow beneath it which meant that it had to have been here before the weather turned the previous afternoon. Otherwise, the ground was undisturbed.

That meant that Sam had most likely died on the day that she'd arrived.

Abby volunteered to take Lionel home and for a moment Mac sat in the car staring out at the winter ocean, tapping his fingers slowly on the steering wheel.

"Is something wrong?" I asked.

"I'm wondering if I can enter and search Sam's storage unit without a warrant."

"Maybe you can't but I can." I jingled the keys at him.

"You still having a key doesn't make it not trespassing," Mac said with a laugh.

"What if my name is on the rental agreement?"

"Is it?" Mac looked hopeful.

"Indeed it is," I replied.

Chapter Six

After stopping at the gas station to dine on a couple of lackluster hoagies, Mac and I rode to the public storage out at the industrial end of the marina.

I'd never especially liked coming out here. It seemed like every person present was perpetually involved in shady goings-on. The owners of the storage unit apparently felt this way as well and had equipped the place with numerous surveillance cameras.

I shrugged and pushed open the car door. A flurry of fat snowflakes blew into the car. "Coming?"

Mac switched off the ignition and followed. We crunched through the deep and drifting snow to the relative warmth of the storage facility. As we stood, stomping the snow off our feet, another car drove up, saw Mac's cruiser and then Mac himself, then reversed and left the parking lot immediately.

"You know him?" I asked.

"I've had the occasion to meet him a couple of times. He has at least one outstanding warrant." Mac gave me a smile. "But it's his lucky day because I've got a date with you. Lead on."

The halls of the storage facility were concrete and echoingly empty. Motion-controlled lights flicked on with loud clacks as we progressed through the maze of identical garage-style doors. It smelled like bleach.

A wave of nostalgia and sadness rose up as fragmentary memories of my times with Sam washed over me.

She'd been a hot mess.

A disaster-person who met a disastrous end.

She'd also been my friend. Tears blurred my vision again as I punched in the code to silence the alarm, then stooped to unlock the padlock.

Of course it was the same code and lock—Sam never thought about things like changing her passwords or having a lock re-keyed. Once you were in her confidence you were in her confidence forever.

Mac crouched down next to me, hand on my knee.

"We can always wait," he said.

"Maybe you can, but not me." I pulled myself together and heaved the door up. "I'm the kind of guy who reads the end of the novel first."

"What's the point of reading the book then?"

"To find out how it all went down. The journey is still just as good when you know where you're going as when you don't." I managed a smile. "So before we start sifting through this massive pile of crap will you allow me to propose a strategy to you?"

"Proceed." Mac reached into his pocket and pulled out two pairs of black nitrile gloves and handed me one.

"We don't need to go through this whole thing. Sam was not an organized person so . . . I'm guessing that she thought she'd find what she was looking for in these boxes right here that are in the front and also open." I nudged the stack of file boxes nearest the door with my toe. "I think we should start here."

"Wait a minute though, before you start—how do you suggest we look for an item that has already been removed if we don't know the original contents?"

My heart sank a little. "I guess . . . yes. That's not going to work, is it?"

"No. But we can still look in the boxes to see what kind of thing Sam might have been looking for, I suppose." Mac crouched down and removed the lid from the storage box and shone his flashlight into it. Inside were bundled letters still in their envelopes. "You said that most of the stuff in here is from Sam's cousin Charlie, right?"

"Yeah." I picked up one stack of letters. "How old school." Then I glanced at the address. "These aren't Charlie's."

Mac shone his flashlight deep inside the box. "They're Charlie's dad's. He was a doctor. He moved away from the island a long time ago."

This dimly rang a bell. During the murder investigation for my ill-fated first bartender, Dorian, I'd seen a photograph of Charlie's dad sitting in a boat on some lake with Mac's dad.

"Did Charlie's dad happen to leave the island around the time your dad died?" I couldn't help but ask. We already knew Charlie had killed two people. Why couldn't he have been involved in a third murder?

"No, he left later. After he retired." Mac cycled through the letters. "My dad was almost fifteen years older than

Uncle Scott—he was the surprise baby. That's how Uncle Scott and the twins, Charlie and Troy, became friends. They were in school together."

I nodded. During the investigation of Dorian's murder it had been revealed that Sam's cousin Charlie had killed his twin brother Troy and then assumed Troy's identity. I knew that Troy (or rather Charlie) had been close with Sheriff Mackenzie. But once the investigation was over, I was so relieved I never really thought about it again. Considering that now though, I had so many questions.

"But wait—if your uncle and Sam's cousins were friends for that long of a time then why couldn't Uncle Scott tell that Charlie was impersonating his brother Troy?" I asked.

"No one could tell," Mac said. "Except Sam, apparently."

"But is that really plausible? I've known several sets of twins and I've never had any trouble telling them apart," I insisted. "How did only one person in this whole town notice the switch?"

"You might have known a lot of sets of twins but were any of them trying to actively deceive you? Also, if any of them had been and it worked, you wouldn't know you'd been deceived," Mac countered. "And even if Uncle Scott did wonder—how would a person even ask that question? What would he say? Hey dude—quick question, are you actually your brother?"

"Point taken," I muttered. "So in the end I have this key that we need, which seems like fate but turns out coming here was a waste of time?"

"How are you jumping to that conclusion? It's neither fate nor a waste of time. If nothing else, we can use the security footage to help establish the timeline—which we'll do on the way out."

"Why didn't you ask about that first?"

"Because I don't want the owners to know I'm here in an official capacity yet." Mac laid a gentle hand on my shoulder. "You know, if you ever had to investigate crime like a real cop you would go out of your mind with boredom and frustration." Mac flicked the bundle of letters with his middle finger. "Each of these stacks of letters seem to be put together by date so if we look down here, we see all these loose ones are from the same year. So we can conclude that if Sam was looking for a letter, that it was in a bundle with the rest of these which she broke open." Mac crouched down and gathered them up.

"And that means . . ."

"I don't know, but it might be an alternate explanation for why Samantha was found with a rubber band around her wrist," Mac said. "She takes it off this stack of letters, puts it around her wrist for safekeeping, then forgets to put it back on."

"Wow. Very good," I said. "What I'm wondering is why would she be looking for her cousin's father's old letters all of the sudden."

"It's hard to say. This family has a lot of property everywhere on the island and, apart from Charlie, Sam was the sole surviving heir. Maybe she was looking for some paperwork." Mac cycled through the letters again. "A lot of these look like official legal docs. See, this one is a property tax statement for the building next to the Eelgrass that their family owns. This other one is dividends from mutual funds. And here . . . we have the title to a Toyota Corolla."

"This is a very weird way to store your important documents," I remarked.

Mac shrugged. "I've seen weirder. At least these are organized chronologically. Anyway, we've got a good working theory now that Sam was after some family paperwork from fifteen years ago. Let's hit up the front desk for the surveillance footage and I'll take you back home."

"Right." I dug out my phone to check to see if Lionel had made it back to his place all right and discovered instead a message from Evelyn. "Wait, scratch that. I need to go to the Beehive. I guess nobody has shoveled the walk there, so they can't walk out to the box to get the mail. She's asking me if I know a kid she can hire to do it for them . . . like kids do that stuff anymore."

Mac gave a short laugh. "It's sweet how she asks you for help, without asking, isn't it? Let's go render assistance then."

◆◆◆

The Beehive Assisted Living facility was only two blocks from the Eelgrass Café but with the sidewalks and roads blanketed in that dangerous slip-and-fall hazard known as "snow" the distance might as well have been as far as the surface of the moon. Only one set of footprints marked the knee-deep powder. I guessed these had been left by Katie the cook when she came to make the old ladies breakfast.

As we drove up, I saw Evelyn outside leaning on a snow shovel and glowering at the ground. She wore an olive-green parka that seemed like it had been purchased when she'd been taller and more burly. A pair of chunky snow boots I guessed Julie would not approve of, completed her ensemble.

During the past three years I'd come to know Evelyn very well—well enough to know that she'd absolutely attempted to shovel the walk herself but was making slow progress due to being more than eighty years old. Still, she'd managed to clear the front steps, which must have been exhausting but at least allowed her to hand over the shovel to me with a certain amount of dignity.

"I think I can find another one for you," she said to Mac.

"Okey dokey," Mac replied. Then, when she disappeared into the building, he just took mine and started putting his back into it.

I watched the snow fly for a couple seconds, wondering if I should have fought him for it then decided that I'd let him have the opportunity to make points with Evelyn and

Julie. Evelyn returned soon enough with another shovel for me anyway and when she did, Julie came hot on her heels.

"*Dieu merci*, the cavalry has arrived!" Julie wore red, as per standard, this time in the form of a pantsuit that probably had its origins in the seventies, but she'd added an elaborate, three-dimensional enamel lapel pin in the shape of holly leaves for some holiday flair. "Drew, is it true about Samantha? That her death is being investigated as a homicide? Oh, how are you, dear?"

Evelyn scowled. "There's been a murder. How do you think he is?"

"Well, I don't know darling, that's why I'm asking him." Julie patted Evelyn on the arm.

I nodded. "I'm okay, actually. We don't know anything else yet but . . . yeah."

"So . . . when you say 'we' you mean you and that man don't know anything?" Julie pointed to Mac, who continued shoveling snow like a human plow. "Or have you given up the culinary arts and joined the police force officially?"

"Me and Mac."

"It's so adorable that you're officially a *we* now. We heard from Katie that it's the talk of the town these days," Julie went on. "Her uncle owns the hardware store, you know."

"Oh my God." I couldn't keep myself from face-palming.

"If you're going to come outside then put on a hat and coat and close the door," Evelyn told Julie. "You don't need to heat the great outdoors standing there with it open."

"See how cruel she is to me," Julie said. Then, to Mac. "Hello, deputy."

Mac straightened up and jogged over as if he'd been waiting to be summoned all this time. He had on his professional smile—a clear indicator of unease.

"Hey there, I'm glad to see you both. I was wanting to make sure I invited you to our house for Christmas."

"The Mackenzie house?" Julie asked.

"We don't cele—" Evelyn began, only to be immediately cut off.

"Yes! That would be wonderful. I'll go pack my bag. It won't be a moment." Then, to Evelyn. "I'll get yours as well. Oh, I'm so happy. You have no idea how dismal it is here during the holidays. *Tres sombre.*"

Julie whirled and disappeared back into the assisted living facility leaving the three of us staring at one another. Then Evelyn broke into a smirk.

"Guess we'll be at your house for the next little while. I hope you like the Canadian TV channel that's in French," she said. "Cause you're gonna be hearing it from today all the way till New Years."

"We don't have cable at all," I murmured.

"I'm sure we can work everything out." Mac's smile seemed more genuine and relaxed this time, which I found alarming, given that he'd just accidentally acquired a couple of elderly house guests while issuing a simple dinner invitation.

Where were we going to put them? Did we even have enough blankets for two additional people?

"I guess I'll go help pack then." Evelyn turned on her heel and left us to clear the path in peace. Once he reached the actual sidewalk, though, Mac stopped and dug around in his jacket pocket until he found his phone. Then he called someone, introduced himself and asked if a certain phone number was on the call log for Charlie Lindgren. He let the snow shovel rest against his leg and started to text someone else while on hold with the first number.

"Do you think Charlie might be able to tell you what Sam was looking for?" I asked.

"That is correct." Mac didn't look up from his phone.

"Because you theorize that she called to ask him where to find it in his father's things?" I stepped past Mac to continue where he'd left off. The snow was fine and powdery and kept sticking to my jeans.

"Negative," Mac replied. "I *theorize* that he called her to ask her to bring him something."

"Didn't he say that he didn't know anything about the crime when you did the death notification?"

"Yes, but he's also a multiple murderer who assumed his dead twin brother's identity for more than a decade, which also makes him a lying asshole." Mac flashed me a smile.

"Touché."

Mac kept watching his phone. I kept shoveling. I was started to sweat from the exertion. I straightened up and stretched.

"What are you looking at?"

"The footage of Sam arriving at the storage unit and then leaving," he said, without looking up. "She isn't carrying anything when she leaves except her purse so it's looking like a document might have been what she wanted after all." He paused, expanded the screen and took a screenshot.

"So did you suddenly think of that scenario while shoveling just now?" I asked. I'd also been shoveling but it hadn't led to any epiphanies.

"No, I was thinking about all those deeds and titles and tax documents we saw. It's a fair bet that nobody owns that old car anymore. So why would a person keep the title? The answer is that nobody went through those boxes for a long time, which means that Sam probably didn't know what was in them. So why would she be searching them? The only person who would know is the person they belong to: Charlie. Therefore, Charlie must have sent Sam to retrieve something for him."

"I guess you could just ask him what it was," I offered. "Except for the problem of him being a liar."

"It will be easier to just listen to his call. They're all recorded," Mac said.

"So, is that as far as you're going with that thought?" I asked.

"I think so for now." Mac slid his phone back into his pocket. "The camera was able to get the license plate of the car she was driving. I sent it to Remy. He'll run the registration and we can find out who owns it."

"Then do you think you could get back on the task at hand? This snow isn't going to shovel itself." As soon as the words were out of my mouth, I could hear the prick tone of every single chef I'd ever trained under ringing through them.

Mac blinked in surprise then gave me a smirk. He said, "Yes, chef!" Then after a couple minutes, "Lionel's life must be hard."

"Just don't you worry about Lionel," I grumbled. But I could feel my cheeks turning red though my pride wouldn't let me back down. "Not unless you want to have a hard life too."

Mac's only reply was a silent laugh.

Chapter Seven

Julie asked us to stop by the grocery store on the way back home. At her own insistence she went inside alone, leaving Mac, Evelyn, and me sitting in the running vehicle.

Twenty minutes passed. Evelyn read the *Seattle Post-Intelligencer*, paper edition. Mac phoned the penitentiary and reentered the dark, hold-message-intensive labyrinth of interdepartmental phone transfers, searching for a person who could provide Charlie's call log.

I stared out the window at the drifting snowflakes, thinking about Sam. Following Mac's theory, Charlie had sent Sam to procure some kind of document that had belonged not to Charlie but to Charlie's father. We could be pretty sure that Sam had done what he'd asked given what we'd seen in the storage facility. So presumably Sam had read the document, understood the contents and then decided to take some action, which had led to her death, potentially at Top Hat Butte.

But there was no evidence of blood there, just the phone. So could she have been killed elsewhere and just dumped at Top Hat? It would have seemed like a good place to dispose of the body because there the base of the bluff was only approachable by boat. Unfortunately the way the tides work, the body had been carried back to the marina the very next day.

The killer must be a local resident then—to know the exact right spot to release Sam into the sea. But the lack of knowledge about the tides meant that the perpetrator—or whoever dumped the body—was not a sailor.

I heaved a sigh of frustration. Why the hell did Orca's Slough have so many loose murderers anyway? Whoever killed Sam could be in that grocery store right now sizing up Julie as their next victim—because why not? Julie probably had half a dozen hidden enemies in this town where murder appeared to be the go-to method of conflict resolution. What had Julie said before? That resentment wells up like magma before finally going kablooey? What if someone had seen her in the wine aisle and taken the opportunity to kablooey her with a bottle of chardonnay? The image of this was so vivid and inescapable that it spurred me to action.

"Do you think I should go and look for Julie?"

Evelyn did not look up from her reading. "It wouldn't hurt to nudge her along. She gets distracted easily."

To Mac I said, "Be right back." He replied with a light nod.

Inside, the store was busier than I expected given the mostly empty parking lot. The citizens of Orca's Slough had all apparently decided to spend their snow day walking to the grocery store in order to stock up for a white Christmas. I found Julie in the baking aisle standing behind a cart laden with Christmas paraphernalia.

Tubes of golden wrapping paper thrust up from the end of the cart like gun turrets on a red and green candy-cane festooned battleship. Inside the basket lay a strange assortment of items that could loosely be described as 'hostess gifts.' Candy, wine, shelf-stable cheese-and-charcuterie gift packs. Cookie tins. Also several packets of colored construction paper as well as scissors and glue. At least six poinsettias crowded together on the cart's lower level.

When she saw me she ducked down guiltily as though expecting some kind of rebuke.

"Well, I can't come empty-handed, can I?" she began.

"No, I get it." I lifted up a packet of the construction paper. "Mostly."

"Do you have any decorations up at your house?" Julie asked archly.

I shook my head. "We're just two guys. We don't even have a tree."

Julie stuck a manicured hand on her hip. "You see? What kind of joyeux Noël is it going to be?"

"I thought you and Evelyn didn't celebrate Christmas."

"We haven't, but that doesn't mean we can't," Julie declared. "We are not incapable of making Christmas, Drew darling, we just never had any children to make it for."

At that second, I realized that Julie was manifesting a long-held dream that had heretofore been blocked—probably by Evelyn—for decades. And I also understood that I needed to pick a side—would I stand with Evelyn and shut this down or become Julie's accomplice?

Not that hard of a choice. I was born to accomplice. In a hot minute I was down to make the Best Christmas Ever.

"Okay, what else do you need?"

Julie's eyes lit up. "The ingredients for bouche noel?"

"What are those?" I knew it was a chocolate cake in the shape of a yule log but beyond that I had no specifics. "The ingredients, I mean?"

"How should I know? Chocolate? Some sort of wheat?" She waived her hand airily at the bags of flour and then looked past me. Her brow furrowed. "Don't turn around but do you have any other exes in town? Apart from the TV chef?"

"He's in LA now, but no, why?"

"There is a man staring at you. Thirty-something. Chestnut hair. Beard. Unflattering oversized pewter and teal color-bloc anorak—"

. . . pewter and teal? I spun around.

There he was, not ten feet away from me, standing in front of a display of holiday themed beer cans that both towered over and enshrined him: he could only be the Peeper.

He smiled at me and gave a little wave. "Hi . . . Drew, right?"

Without thinking I charged forward and had him by the coat before I even took another breath.

"Who the fuck do you think you are?"

The Peeper cringed back—raising his phone as though it could explain everything. "I'm Josh. Josh—you know?"

"No. I do not know." The volume of my voice started to attract attention as the passing shoppers stopped to stare at us. I was dismayed to see Evelyn's crappy cousin Joyce among them. She took one look at us and disappeared down the canned food aisle. I was almost certain she was phoning the police.

"Charlotte's boyfriend?" he said weakly. "I have your picture on my phone."

The revelation that he was Charlotte's boyfriend did nothing to make peeping less suspicious. "Why were you creeping around outside my house?"

"I was trying to see if she was there." Josh winced.

"Is there something wrong here?" To my shock, Sheriff Mackenzie emerged from the mouth of the canned fruits and vegetables aisle because that was the way this simple shopping trip was going. He wore street clothes and was accompanied by his wife, Jenny. She was a tall, trim, fifty-something woman with dark, short hair and wide-set blue eyes. She wore a full-length purple puffer coat and gripped her bountiful shopping cart as if preparing to broadside me with it. Joyce stood right next to her. By now most of the people in the grocery store were gawking, giving the whole situation the juvenile air of a confrontation in a high school lunchroom.

Maybe that's the reason I automatically reverted to 'teen boys getting caught by the principal' rules. I let go of Josh's jacket and made a point of smoothing it.

"No," I said. I glanced at Josh—he didn't appear to know the sheriff either personally or professionally. "We just had a misunderstanding."

Josh smiled at me, or rather past me. I turned to see Mac entering the building. He caught sight of us all and then simply stopped walking, taking in the scene. Finally, he said, "This is Charlotte's boyfriend. His name is Josh. He's an orthodontist in New York City."

He stepped a little closer.

"Josh, this is my boyfriend, Drew." Mac inclined his head in my direction then indicated the sheriff and his wife. "And this is my Aunt Jenny and Uncle Scott."

Uncle Scott nodded. A silence settled over all of us and lingered so long that Aunt Jenny decided it was time to make a move.

"It's nice to meet you." She shook his hand. "Charlotte has mentioned you a lot. I'd love to see you at our party. It's the day after tomorrow. Mac has all the details."

While Josh spluttered out his thanks for the invitation, Julie wheeled her cart up between me and Mac. She gave Aunt Jenny the once-over, her face showing her open dislike for the other woman's shoes, which were, to be fair, extremely ugly.

Aunt Jenny looked right past Julie as if she and her parade float of a shopping cart were invisible and started engaging with Joyce in a conversation about party dips while Sheriff Mackenzie, Mac, and Josh negotiated a brief exchange of uninformative pleasantries. The crowd that had assembled to watch me fight a random tourist began to dissipate. I looked sidelong at Julie.

"We can come back for whatever else you need," I said. "Let's just get out of here now."

"Agreed."

"What the hell is taking everyone so long?" Evelyn's voice cut through the murmur of small talk like a fire alarm ripping through the school library. Her eyes fell on the shopping cart. "What is all that?"

"It's Drew's." Julie hot-potatoed the whole thing over to me. "I just came in for these." She snatched up a bottle of wine and a charcuterie board and scampered over to Evelyn. "Drew just went mad, darling. I tried to tell him it was too much but I think he's really excited to have a fabulous holiday celebration."

"Yes," Evelyn said blandly. "He looks it."

I was fairly certain that I did not look it, but Evelyn seemed to have reached the conclusion that it was best to pretend to believe her wife and just go about paying for those two items and returning to the car. Mac disengaged himself from his uncle and drifted over toward me.

"I can get that if you want," he said, indicating the hoard of Christmas bounty.

"It's okay, I've got it." I started to unload everything onto the conveyor belt. "What about Josh?"

"He's going back to his rental to shower but I invited him over later." Mac knelt down to pass me one of the poinsettias for the cashier to scan.

"Why would you invite your sister's stalker ex, who I found creeping around outside the house yesterday, to our house?"

"Josh isn't a stalker." Mac kept his voice to a near-whisper. "And Charlotte obviously wants him back. She's been crying every night because she got scared that he might break up with her, so she broke up with him first. She's just too embarrassed to tell him so. And he—I mean look at the guy. He flew all this way just to try and talk to her."

"It's weird that you would wingman your sister's boyfriend instead of your sister." I started unloading wine bottles—ten in all, plus two bottles of prosecco—from the cart.

"You only think that because you don't know my sister well. She's a pathological boyfriend dumper. I think it's because she saw how Mom just withered away after Dad disappeared. Anyway, you should be glad he's here. If he hadn't come, we'd be in danger of Charlotte moving in with us." Mac smiled at the cashier. "How are you today?"

"I'm well, thank you." The cashier looked familiar to me—one of Lionel's friends, maybe? She smiled as she met my eyes as though she couldn't wait to share the story of what just went down. Most likely in less than an hour there would be a social media thread dedicated to my almost fighting a guy at the holiday six-pack endcap. My distraction, sinking mood, and unease must have showed on my face because Mac suddenly squeezed my shoulder, then, very deftly stepped past me to get his debit card in the reader and pay for everything before I even realized what was happening.

"Damn it, Mac."

I looked to the cashier for support but she only shrugged and said, "Transaction's already complete, sorry."

◆◆◆

By five we'd installed Evelyn and Julie in the guest room—AKA my office—and I was starting to get hungry. Abby was still gone and Charlotte had just woken up from a nap, so I made that all-American classic "breakfast for dinner." Eggs, French toast, and bacon, which attracted everyone to the kitchen. Mac appeared last, but rather than sitting down he beckoned me to join him in the living room.

"What's up?" I asked.

"Remy sent back the info on the plate. It's a rental. Sam picked it up at SeaTac Airport Tuesday morning. They sent the GPS coordinates. He's heading out to try and locate it now."

"Then that means she flew into Seattle, picked up a car, took the ferry and basically drove straight to the storage unit." I gazed out the window at the already dark street trying to picture the scene. "And then she goes to Top Hat Butte—"

"We don't know that she was ever there, only that her phone was," Mac corrected.

"True. Okay then, after the storage unit she vanishes for about twenty-four hours until her body is found in the marina." I looked at Mac. "Then where was she in the intervening time?"

"That's the million-dollar question, isn't it?"

"I guess you probably already looked on her social media?" I asked.

"It was the first thing I did, yeah, given that she was a frequent poster. She shared a couple of inspirational seasonal images the previous day—the average thing—'finding joy' etc. No photos or locations though." Mac rubbed the back of his neck.

I automatically reached out and took over massaging his neck and shoulders for him, musing aloud as I did. "If I flew from LA to Seattle, then drove here, took a ferry and then went through a storage locker, what would I do next?"

"If it were you? You'd be really hungry because you wouldn't have eaten anything from the airport or on the ferry, so you'd eat lunch." Mac leaned back into my hands.

"That's right, she'd be hungry."

"She didn't go into the Prospector," Mac said. "I checked. Not the fish and chips place either."

My hands stilled. "Has anybody talked to Danielle yet?"

"Danielle Tomkins? I don't think so. You think that Sam would have reached out to her? I thought they had fallen out." Mac nudged his head back into my hands and I resumed the massage.

"My gut instinct is yes." I slid my hands down to knead the thick muscle of Mac's shoulders.

"Then why do you think Danielle hasn't come forward with that information?" Mac asked.

"Probably because she's been asleep. She's a bartender. She's most likely only been awake for an hour or so. I think I still have her number." I scrolled through the contacts on my phone until I found Danielle's information. "Go ahead and call from my phone. She's more likely to pick up if it's not you."

"Devious as always."

I shrugged. "I just know my own industry."

◆◆◆

Mac and I each bolted our breakfast-for-dinner while standing at the kitchen counter, then we headed out to meet Danielle, who had decided to bring along her brother Alfred to the interview.

The last time I'd seen Alfred he'd just started his freshman year of college. Only a year and a half had passed but he'd aged at least a decade. When I'd first seen him, he'd been fit and tan with hair bleached blond by the sun and a laid-back, hang loose attitude. Now he was thin and severe, his long hair cut very short. Danielle, too, seemed to have leveled up a whole generation in the course of only eighteen months. Extensive makeup couldn't hide the dark circles under her eyes. They'd agreed to meet Mac and me at the Eelgrass, which neither one of them had stepped foot into since the night that the Eelgrass's first bartender, Dorian, had been murdered.

The four of us sat at the table closest to the kitchen, where the staff usually ate their lunches. The restaurant's empty dining room and dark kitchen emphasized the feeling of sudden loss and I took a breath to steady myself.

"Coffee?" I offered. "Cola?"

"Water is fine. I don't drink caffeine anymore," Alfred said. He kept his snowboarding jacket zipped all the way up and had his hands stuck deep in the pockets.

"He doesn't do anything anymore. I'll take some caffeine though," Danielle said. She pulled off the hat she wore to reveal completely disheveled pink hair.

I got three coffees and a water and settled down opposite the two of them. Even dressed in his street clothes, Mac retained his usual, friendly neighborhood cop aura.

"Thank you both for agreeing to talk to me," he said.

"I don't know anything," Alfred said. "I'm telling the truth this time. I didn't even see Sam. Dani did. I'm just saving you the effort of coming to find me to ask me where I was."

"Okay," Mac folded his hands and turned to Danielle. "So why don't you take me through your meeting with Sam? When did you two make the arrangements?"

"Sam texted me when she landed in Seattle on Tuesday morning. She said she was coming back to town for a couple of days and asked if I wanted to get coffee," Danielle said. "We haven't really kept in touch for the last year or so because . . ." She gestured to her brother.

"I totally ghosted Sam," Alfred said.

"It made it awkward for us to talk," Danielle explained.

"But then suddenly she asked to see you?" Mac addressed his question to Danielle.

"Yeah, she swung by my place around two and we had a cup of coffee. I asked her where she was staying and she said she wasn't going to stay in town at all. She had reservations on the seven o'clock ferry to go back to the mainland."

Mac made a note of this. "Did she tell you what she was doing here?"

"She said she had some shitty family business to put right but, her only family is Charlie, so what does that mean?" Danielle shook her head. "She mainly talked about the different celebrities she'd seen at her new job in LA. She left about four."

"And she didn't say anywhere she was going, or mention anyone she was meeting?" I asked. Everyone at the table turned to stare at me as though I were some interloper rather than the actual facilitator of the conversation.

"No." Danielle took a sip of her coffee then glanced between me and Mac. "Why aren't you wearing your uniform?"

"I didn't have a clean one," Mac replied smoothly. "And I wanted this to be more casual."

"So casual that you let this guy ask the questions?" Danielle jerked her thumb at me.

"Would you rather go down to the police station?" I asked. "Cause that's where I had to go to answer these same questions and it was so not enjoyable."

"Well neither is being interrogated by your unqualified ass," she said.

"Can you think of anything else that might have been unusual?" Mac cut in.

"She mentioned this guy she'd met on the ferry ride over. She said that at first she wanted to talk to him because he was good looking and seemed like he had a lot of money. Turns out he was a dentist from back east. They talked about good places to eat on the island and good places to take pictures. She told him about Top Hat Butte and Oyster Beach. The usual spots. That's really it."

Mac and I locked eyes and I could tell we were both wondering how many East Coast dental practitioners could possibly have been on the ferry. Could the person Sam had spoken to be Josh? Did that make him a suspect? But what could his possible motive be?

Unless Josh was some kind of serial killer who killed strangers he picked up on the ferry all the time.

Mac shook his head at me slightly as if he understood and basically disagreed with my train of thought.

He asked both Danielle and Alfred about their whereabouts on the day of the homicide. Danielle had been at work and Alfred had been on the mainland. After dutifully jotting both these down Mac said, "I'd like to speak with Alfred privately for just a minute, please."

Danielle stood up and looked at me as if waiting for me to join her. I, in turn, glanced askance at Mac.

"You stay here," he said. "Please."

Danielle narrowed her eyes in a weird mix of aggression and fear, then retreated to a table at the front of the restaurant where she slumped into a chair, arms folded across her chest, half-glaring, half-pleading, but never taking her eyes off us. I had to admire her. She wasn't going to just leave her baby brother alone with us.

"I wanted to bring up a subject off the record." Mac turned his attention to Alfred. "From my previous investigation, I know that you and Sam took possession of a carryall that might have contained some questionable materials. Do you think that the bag's original owner or someone associated with him might have something to do with this?"

I blinked, not following Mac for a moment, then remembered that yes, Alfred and Sam really had stolen a lot of drugs from an East European gangster. That I could forget something like that spoke volumes about the rest of what had been going on in my life at the time, I supposed.

Alfred's eyes widened and he gulped. "I don't know what you're talking about."

I leaned forward. "Look Alfred, nobody cares about that—at least we don't anyway. We're only trying to rule people out so . . . whatever happened with that huge bag-o-drugs you stole? To your knowledge, did anyone find out it was you? Apart from me and Mac, I mean?"

I simply could not help this flex. It had been the first actual crime I'd ever solved and something of a triumph for me.

"Nobody ever came after me," he whispered. "And I haven't talked to Sam since the day after. Once I was sober I couldn't believe I'd agreed to do something so crazy as heist a bunch of drugs."

"What did you do with the . . . contents," I asked.

"They're someplace in the bottom of Puget Sound, bro. I dropped the whole thing over the railing of the ferry that day on the way back to Seattle," Alfred said. "But you don't have to worry about it poisoning the orcas or anything. All that stuff was wrapped in really thick plastic. Plastic is forever."

No doubt about it. Alfred remained a bulb of lesser brightness, but at least he cared about the wildlife—I guess?

Mac's brow furrowed slightly, as if he was thinking that Alfred was an even dumber criminal than he'd previously imagined.

After the two of them left, Mac and I sat staring at each other.

He said, "I know what you're thinking about Josh but I don't think it's the correct avenue of investigation."

"It does seem pretty unlikely that he killed Sam for kicks or whatever." I resisted the urge to declare the entire interview pointless since we had actually learned a couple of things.

"Now we know Sam was still alive at two p.m." I sloshed my now-cold coffee around in the bottom of my cup. "And that it definitely had to do with Charlie and probably nothing to do with stealing the carryall back then—great job remembering that, by the way."

"Thank you, but don't compliment me too much. Reviewing previous cases is all part of the service when you're a professional." Mac demurred, but his smug expression exposed the pride he felt at my compliment. He checked his watch. "We should be getting back though. Josh is going to be at our place at seven thirty and I want to be there to let him in."

"I can't believe you're doing this," I said.

"It's not a Mackenzie family holiday unless Charlotte's love life is on fire so . . . might as well let the drama play out quickly so we can all move on."

Chapter Eight

Charlotte's reaction to seeing the man she recently dumped standing in the living room was swift and immediate. She legged it up the stairs and locked herself in the building's sole bathroom. Josh watched her go with the resignation of a man who has sat outside many a bathroom door. Evelyn and Julie, who had been cuddled up on the couch under a blanket streaming *White Christmas* on my game system, watched all this with matching expressions that I can only describe as cheerful interest at the unfolding drama.

Josh gave them a weak smile and had just started to trudge up the stairs when Mac laid a hand on his shoulder.

"Let Drew talk to her," he said.

"Me?" I couldn't tell if I was more astonished or enraged at being pulled into this. "I've got no dog in this fight."

"Exactly. You're the perfect person to get her out of there. If I go up there, she'll just start swearing and break the doorknob off. We'll all have to walk down to the gas station to take a leak for the next week. I believe in you." Mac turned his attention to Josh. "Do you want a beer, man?"

"Sure?" Josh didn't seem to know what to do next. He allowed Mac to direct him toward an armchair.

"You all owe me," I muttered, then headed up the old creaky staircase to knock on the ancient and scuffed five-panel bathroom door.

"It's Drew," I said, then, before she even answered, "please, can I use the bathroom?"

I thought it was worth a shot. Sure, I'd accepted the mission but that didn't mean I had to work hard to accomplish it.

"I'll open the door when Josh leaves," she said.

"Okay then I'll tell him to leave," I started back down the stairs only to hear the door creak open when I hit the landing.

"Wait," she said.

I turned and stared up at Charlotte through the turned-wood balusters. Her hair had been combed and she seemed to be in the middle of brushing her teeth.

"What?"

"Are you really kicking him out?"

"Yeah." I took a step down.

"Just like that?" Charlotte seemed stunned.

"I just want to use the bathroom," I said. "I'm complying with your directive."

"Okay, wait though. I'm not ready. Come back up here fast." She beckoned me up.

Just then I did understand why Mac had nominated me to take back control of the bathroom. It was because I was the one person in the building who wouldn't attempt to persuade Charlotte of anything. Mac clearly had an interest in keeping Josh around. Evelyn and Julie would be full of opinions and bad ideas respectively. Only I had the capacity to ignore the curling brambles of Charlotte's self-contradictory thought process and just focus on liberating the toilet from hostile occupation.

I slid inside the door and Charlotte closed it behind me, then went back to brushing her teeth.

"Are you seriously going to stay in here while I pee?"

"Don't worry about it," she said. "I'm totally immune to every kind of nudity after being in so many dressing rooms."

"Yeah, but I'm not," I said.

"Well, I'm not going back out there so. . ." Charlotte gave a shrug.

"Can you at least stand behind the shower curtain?"

"So sensitive," Charlotte said but she stood in the shower anyway and pulled the curtain. "Okay, go."

"I can't just go cause you told me to." I had no idea whether I'd be able to force myself to pee and worried about that for a second. Then I realized that I could turn this to my advantage since she'd try and kick me out the second I was finished. "Just take a minute to meditate in there or something."

"I don't want to meditate. I don't want to think at all. How could Mac let him into the house?"

"I do think it's strange that he's on that guy's side," I said.

"Right? Shouldn't he be backing me up. I always backed him up. I sent money and cosigned everybody's loans. I bought everybody phones and still pay everybody's bill—shouldn't I get some respect?" Grievance sounded through her tone. "But no—Mac just wants me off his hands. He thinks because he found you everybody should be all coupled up now. What if I don't want that? What if I don't need anybody to take care of me?"

It took me a minute to catch up with her sudden segue but when I did it was quite the revelation.

"Is that what Josh said he wants to do?" I asked.

"Don't talk about Josh. He's terrifying."

"Does he hurt you?"

"What? No—he wants me to go to school for photography. I told him I'm too old. I'm too old to be a model anymore and I'm definitely too old to go to school." The frustration in her voice echoed off the tile surround.

"You're not even thirty though," I said.

"Way, way too old," she said.

"So where did you meet Josh?" I put down the toilet lid and sat. I thought I might be here for a few minutes.

"In the Met, in the photography room," Charlotte said. "We both really like Diane Arbus."

"Is he into photography as well?"

"Diane Arbus is a woman," Charlotte said.

"I mean Josh." I allowed a sour note to creep into my tone.

"Yes. It's his hobby. He has an orthodontic practice in Brooklyn. He's a good guy. But I don't want to be with anybody." This last sentiment contained unnecessary force which undermined her honesty.

"Fair enough," I replied. I leaned against the sink. "But if that's the case then why did you stop me when I was going to tell him to leave?"

"Because I don't want him to go," Charlotte said. "I didn't expect to see him again but when I did, I was just overwhelmed with this feeling."

"Of anger?" I guessed. That's how I usually felt when unexpectedly confronted with the presence of my exes.

"No! I was really happy."

"So you came to hide in the bathroom?"

"I didn't want him to know I missed him," she said. "He'll just ask me to marry him again. And then he'll tell me he believes in my art and that he'll support me."

Yeah honey, having a supportive boyfriend does sound like a fate worse than death—is what I decided not to say aloud at that time.

After congratulating myself on my restraint, I pulled the shower curtain slightly open. Charlotte was sitting, hugging her knees in the empty tub, pathetic as a stray cat. I wondered if she was like the kitchen cabinets—a person arrested at the point where her life fell apart, still hanging in the stasis of the unresolved crisis of their collapsed childhood.

It seemed so.

If that were true, then Mac's decision to allow Josh into the house could be—if not strictly correct, at least a better choice than I initially thought. It was the counterpoint to

Charlotte's wanting to clean out the cabinets. They wanted to help each other move on, but neither one of them was very good at accepting assistance.

So why not go back to the source of the problem—and untie the knot at the center of all the tension in this family?

"Is this because you spent a lot of time thinking your father abandoned your family?" I asked.

"What?" Charlotte shot me a glare so murderous that I felt it like a physical slap.

I held her gaze, noticing for the first time how similar her eyes were to Mac's.

"I'm not comfortable talking about this," she said.

"Okay." I held up my hands in surrender.

"And get out. You're not trying to pee. You don't even have your belt undone," she said.

"It's 'cause I can't do it while you're here." I folded my hands. "Also you technically can't kick me out of this room since I live here too but I'm going to ignore that."

Charlotte again fixed me with one of the most purely hostile stares I've ever received.

"Remy said you seemed chill but deep down you were kind of an arrogant prick," she said. "I get it now."

"Did Remy and Mac tell you that they found out Dirk Van Weezendonk lied about seeing your father leave town?" I asked.

"Yes," she said. "But even if he lied that doesn't make any difference."

"So, then you believe . . . what? That your father abandoned you all and is still alive somewhere?" I pressed on. She already knew what I was really like, so there was no longer any point in hiding it.

"Yes. I do." Charlotte stood up. "Men are really selfish and cruel and Dad wasn't the exception. Mac just needs to think he was different to keep living. Abby thinks all guys are like Mac, which is so dumb but she'll find out."

While I didn't necessarily disagree with her proclamation about the integrity of the average guy, I also sensed in her a sliver of doubt—a desire to believe in love. I decided to go for the coup de grace.

"Do you actually love Josh, but you're afraid he'll leave you so you're breaking up with him first?" I asked. "Because that is just the worst reason to break up with someone."

"Oh my God, you really do think you're some kind of detective don't you? Interrogating everybody. Thinking you know everything. Making assumptions. You and Mac are perfect for each other."

"At least we're not cowards," I said.

Breathtaking silence, like a gust from a blast chiller, descended over the room. I could not read Charlotte's expression at all. For a second it seemed like she attempted to pull out the Mackenzie smile but failed. I'd gone too far, but overreaching was the only tool available to me. I didn't have the subtlety or the time to carefully nudge the situation to an amicable conclusion.

"Mac shouldn't have brought Josh here without asking you," I said. "He owes you an apology for that."

"Yes, he does." Charlotte stepped out of the bathtub, rinsed out her mouth and put her toothbrush away in a small travel case.

"And I owe you one for being a prick about the fact that I live here now."

"That's also correct." Charlotte relaxed a little.

"I am very sorry. At the same time, can you agree that your actions are not really that mature?" I asked. "There is only one bathroom. You could have chosen to go to your bedroom and locked that door, but you chose the one room where we'd have to beg you to come out eventually. It's a mixed message, if what you really want is to be left alone. Just saying . . ."

Charlotte let out a heavy sigh. "OMG I'm the toxic one now, aren't I?"

"I mean . . ." I trailed off, at a loss.

"You gotta zig or zag!" Evelyn's voice came from the other side of the door. "And also come out of there. I'm old. I can't be standing out here holding it all day."

Charlotte and I exchanged a look and silently exited the facilities. Evelyn filed in, *Wall Street Journal* in her hand, closing the door behind her. Charlotte and I stood in the dim upper hallway.

"I'll head down then," I said.

"Don't you need the bathroom?"

"It was just a ruse." I gave a shrug and started toward the stairs but she caught me by the elbow.

"Listen," she whispered. "I'm really happy you're on Mac's side. And I know that he and Abby and even Remy all have their hopes up because that Van Weasel Guy—"

"Dirk Van Weezendonk?" I supplied.

"Yeah, him." Charlotte agreed. "He admitted to lying about seeing Dad board the ferry. But that doesn't mean Dad didn't leave us."

I frowned at Charlotte. Was it possible that she wanted to think they'd been abandoned? Did no one explain to her that Van Weezendonk had made a deal with an unknown party to make his claim?

"Look," Charlotte muttered. "I have a good reason to think our dad left on his own and isn't dead."

"What's that?"

"Every few years he sends me money," she said. "By Western Union."

"What!?" I involuntarily cranked the volume of my voice up as far as the knob would go.

Charlotte flinched at my raised voice and actually shushed me with a finger to her lips. And I was so shocked by her disclosure that I actually did shush.

"Did he ever call you or anything?" I whispered.

"No. But you have to have your ID to send money with that service so—that's how I know he didn't die. I never told

Mac because I thought it would hurt his feelings to know." Charlotte twisted the ring she wore on her index finger—it was clearly her tell. She leaned very close so that she was whispering directly in my ear. "And also, Dad told me that he was going to leave."

To say I was shocked would be an understatement. "What do you mean?"

Charlotte glanced around the hallway then pushed me into the front bedroom—the one she'd shared with Abby since they were little. She closed the door behind us and then went the extra step of drawing me all the way into the room so that we were close to the window. Outside was darkness, except for the circles of white cast by the streetlights. "The day before he left, he told me that things might be getting weird soon, but that he'd make it up to me."

"Weird, how?"

"He didn't say." Charlotte leaned her head against the window. "Dad and I got really close during Mom's first fight with cancer. Mac had to help take care of everyone else, but I took care of Mom and that meant talking to Dad a lot too. Right before Dad left, Mom said there was something wrong with him and that he had too many responsibilities. Then one day he was just gone. Mom didn't even blame him for leaving. But I did. The money he sends does not make it up to me."

"Is that the money you sent back to Mac?" I asked.

"No. Dad only sends money every few years and it's not really ever that much. A couple hundred dollars." Charlotte reached out and put a hand on my arm. "Remy said that you tell Mac everything, so I know you're going to tell him what I just said."

There was no point in denying this, so I just said, "I mean . . . yeah. Honesty is important."

"Could you wait until I'm gone to tell him? I don't think I can stand to see him . . . what that's going to do to him—

to know he's been wrong all this time." No trace of a smile could be found on Charlotte's face.

"Until you're gone? Aren't you moving back here?"

"No, I'm going back to New York after New Year's."

"What about Josh?"

"If you tell him to come up, I'll talk to him." Charlotte sat down on the bed to the right. "I can't believe he actually followed me here. He's literally scared of all nature. One time when we were upstate there was a deer standing near our car and I thought he'd pass out."

On some level I was irritated to have gotten tapped to play telephone to Mac again but on another I could understand why everyone lacked courage in this area. I descended the staircase, informed Josh he'd been summoned, and sat down next to Mac.

"Where's my beer?" I asked.

Mac reached down to the six-pack on the floor and retrieved a bottle which he opened then handed to me.

"Abby phoned," he said. "She staying at Lionel's because of the roads."

"Probably smart." I relaxed back into the cushions. Evelyn came back downstairs and, after one silent shake of her head, rejoined Julie underneath the blanket.

I leaned closer to Mac. "I'm worried that having everyone together isn't that great of an idea."

"It's gotta be better than keeping everyone apart." Mac shot me a smile. "Don't you think?"

Chapter Nine

The next morning Abby dropped Lionel off at the Eelgrass exactly ten minutes before his shift. He spent some time standing up to his shins in the snow, leaning into the car window, smiling a smile which I had never witnessed on his face before: the smile of a man crushing on his crush.

Being the dedicated mentor that I am, I began to tease him about it as soon as he clocked in.

"Had a good time last night?" I asked.

"Very, very good." His reply came with such calm confidence that I was thrown off. I then noted several details about him simultaneously. First, his hair was artfully arranged. Second, someone had painted his nails black with fine white patterns—a different one for each nail.

Technically, cooks are not allowed to wear nail polish as per health department directive, but I decided to let it slide since Lionel would be wearing latex gloves all day anyway. Besides, it had most likely taken a long time to get that manicure and it looked great on him.

If there was one thing I knew about Lionel, it was that he felt perfectly comfortable playing the makeover card when flirting with women.

"Wait," I leaned down to look him directly in the eye. "Did you actually get somewhere with Abby?"

"If I did I wouldn't be telling you." He shrugged and attached his phone to the kitchen speaker.

"Did you read a book aloud to her?" I teased.

"I did—*A Christmas Carol*." He tied his apron on.

"Wow. You keep a copy of that at home?" It was the only thing I could think of to say.

Lionel waggled his phone at me. "It's free online, chief."

I returned to my cutting board and resumed peeling carrots. "I thought you were suspicious of the Mackenzie family."

"I'm suspicious of the cop ones, not Abby. She's always been cool." Lionel walked over to the prep list and started reading down the tasks, most likely ranking them from most to least odious.

His actions were ordinary and regular, but he seemed somehow different. Maybe his shoulders were broader. Maybe his jaw was heavier. He seemed to have become an adult since the last time I took the time to observe him. It made sense—that is the direction time flows—but somehow I hadn't imagined that adult Lionel would have this much chill.

It was a good time to broach a subject I'd always wondered about.

"So, are you suspicious of the cop Mackenzies on principle or do you have some kind of intel that you've just never shared?"

Lionel glanced up at me in surprise. "What do you mean?"

"Has one of the cops ever done anything to you?" I asked.

"No, but my mom is an ER nurse, so she sees law enforcement people all the time and lets me know which ones to avoid." Lionel turned back to the prep list, running his finger down the messy, handwritten column of tasks that needed to be accomplished today.

"Don't you just avoid them all?" I would have, if I hadn't been dating one.

"Yeah, but she told me to especially avoid the Mackenzies. She says they put family first, but in a bad way," Lionel said.

"Did she give any examples?"

"Nah. It was something to do with a car wreck, I think but she wouldn't say anything more about it." Lionel at last put a checkmark beside an item on the list then disappeared into the walk-in, only to re-emerge with a case of whole chickens. He started to set up his cutting board to start breaking them down into quarters. "Why? Did Mac do something to you?"

"Like what?"

Lionel kept his eyes on his cutting board. "I don't know—choke you or something?"

"No, he's not like that."

"Abby says he has issues," Lionel remarked.

"I think they all might have some issues but Mac's are more of a 'stare silently into the uncaring horizon while carrying the weight of the world on his shoulders' kind."

"So emo." Lionel snickered. "Abby said he's cheered up a lot since he's been seeing you."

"Did you two really just do your nails and talk about me and Mac all night?"

"Nope." Lionel finally cracked a shit-eating grin then instantly pulled it back. "She wanted to know if I thought you were a player. I told her you won't even spend more than five dollars for a t-shirt."

"So what's that got to do with whether I'm a player or not? I'm just sensibly frugal."

"Yeah. Not a player." Lionel turned his attention to his chopping board and for a few minutes the only sounds in the restaurant were the staccato of knives hitting plastic and rapid-fire Korean rap. Lionel finished processing the chickens, switched to a clean cutting board and knives, and brought out a case of napa cabbage.

"You know . . ." Lionel paused in the midst of transforming the crystal-white cabbage into slivers of vegetable confetti. "I remember my mom saying something about a car wreck. Like one of the Mackenzies got caught drunk driving or something and the other ones just let him go? I don't really remember. She didn't think it was fair."

"That makes sense, I guess," I remarked. I wondered if it was Remy letting Mac off or the other way around. Uncle Scott maybe? Mac had a large scar on his arm that he said he'd gotten years back when someone swerved into his car and then fled the scene. Knowing him the way I did now, I felt certain that he wouldn't have been the Mackenzie who let a relative get away with a crime. Plus, he would have been too young at the time.

"Seriously though, why are you asking?" Lionel said. "Are you worried about turning over Sam's phone to Mac?"

"No, not at all," I shook my head. "I just want to get a better feel for the rest of the family. I'd rather not get blindsided by anything while we're trying to have our first family holiday."

"I hear you there." Lionel nodded.

We both returned to our work. Then in a lull between songs, Lionel asked "Did you two find anything else out about Sam?"

"Not really." I started feeding the carrots into the food processor and we both paused while the ungodly noise of it made conversation impossible.

"I didn't know her very well, but she was always nice to me, and I liked her," Lionel said once silence descended again. "She was useless, but I liked her."

My vision blurred as a flood of sadness rose up in me, crested, then receded without breaking over the embankment of my eyelashes. "Me too."

"Chief, can I just ask you a favor?" Lionel put down his knife and stared right at me.

"Sure thing."

"Can we be closed till the event on the twenty-sixth?"

"What? No. Why would we do that?" The suggestion itself felt like heresy and yet there Lionel was suggesting it.

"Because—because this makes no sense. You're acting just like my mom. Everyone is snowed in. Sam just got killed. We don't really need to be doing this, except it's like the way you avoid problems is to work more. But no one is going to come to eat here today so it's just futile to spend our time here right now. Can you just take a break and let me take a break too? Please?"

I stood stunned, absorbing that long string of truth, understanding how hard it must have been for him to deliver it.

"You just want to have more time to hang out with Abby before she goes back to Seattle," I muttered.

"That is also true," Lionel's expression remained amicable but stern. "And what's wrong with that? It's not like if you leave here you'll have to spend the holiday alone like last year when Big Mac was on duty. Abby said even Granny Evelyn and Julie are staying at your house now."

"What does that have to do with anything?"

"Aish!" Lionel suddenly grabbed his head as though the pain of listening to me speak was too much to bear. "Go be with them! Be a normal human, chief, I'm begging you. Just put a sign on the door saying we'll re-open on the twenty-sixth. You won't lose anything and no one will blame you. If you really can't stand not doing something, then try to figure out who killed Sam but don't stay here making carrot soup that nobody is going to eat."

My phone rang and I fished it out of my pocket. It was Lupe phoning to say she might be late.

"Don't worry about it," I said, eyes still locked with Lionel. "We're closing till the twenty-sixth. Have a happy holiday." I ended the call. Then, to Lionel. "Do you want to come over and help me and Evelyn make bouche de noel?"

"Will Abby be there?"

"I can't give you any guarantees but it's where she lives so the chances are good."

Lionel checked his hair in the mirror above the sink. "I'm down. Let's go."

◆◆◆

When I returned with Lionel in tow and announced that we'd closed the restaurant in favor of doing some holiday baking, Mac seemed both surprised and suspicious but kept all commentary to himself, remarking only that it must be nice to be able to give yourself the day off.

"I still have Sam's phone in rice. I don't want to risk turning it on for another twenty-four hours," he added. "I was planning to go run a few errands. Remy will be coming by later this afternoon. We usually all go to Aunt Jenny's Christmas party together."

"Don't worry about me. Go do what you have to do." I zipped his coat up the rest of the way. "I'll be here."

Inside the kitchen Evelyn had laid out all the gear she'd need to create the bouche de noel—famous French chocolate roll cake that's traditionally decorated to look like a log.

Not just any log—a highly decorated log, complete with meringue mushrooms and holly leaves made from modeling chocolate. Apparently, though, eating the decorations was Julie's favorite part of the cake so Evelyn always went overboard, making at least a couple dozen more mushrooms than necessary. She crafted little snails and tiny flowers from marzipan and chocolate—basically a miniature woodland to delight her wife.

"So, what should I—" I began.

"Prep the chocolate for the holly leaves and berries," Evelyn told me. "Where did Lionel go?"

"To talk to Abby, I think," I said.

"Huh. Probably best not to wait for him to start," Evelyn grumbled.

I got to work tempering the dark chocolate and warming the white.

"Whatever happened with that Van Weezendonk thing?" Evelyn didn't look up from piping mushroom cap after mushroom cap.

"What do you mean?" I watched the white chocolate slowly melting.

"I heard you mention his name when you were talking to Charlotte yesterday. Did you ever get anywhere with finding out what he knew about Mac's dad?" Evelyn kept her eyes on the cake as she spoke, lifting this or that decoration up to look at them like a person trying to accessorize an outfit might.

"No. Mac hired a computer guy to scour all Van Weezendonk's devices for anything but there wasn't even a crumb of information. Whatever he knew, he took to the grave with him." I prodded the candy melts with the tines of a fork, testing their solidity.

"That must be frustrating for Mac," Evelyn remarked.

"Yeah, it was terrible to watch. He really suffered then. It made me wish I could force everyone on this island to tell the truth or—just for one day—to find out what happened."

The white chocolate had gained full liquidity so I added green food coloring and started to pour it into a fresh piping bag. "Someone knows what happened or many people know part of what happened. It's only a matter of finding the right question to ask, but I just don't know who that is. Just like the situation with Sam, I guess."

Evelyn gave a dry chuckle. "Getting people on this island to tell the full truth about anything is like pulling hen's teeth." Evelyn put down a meringue mushroom and accepted the white chocolate that I offered. "Do you want to try?"

I shook my head. "I'd rather watch. I don't know anything about pastry and I don't know how to draw." Then after watching her work for a few minutes I fell into a reverie. Since I wasn't a girl, I had never been part of holiday baking in my own family. I suddenly felt lucky to be here, taking part in somebody's tradition, wondering if it would one day also be mine. Could I adopt it? Would that be all right? Would it make them happy, or seem presumptuous? I felt such admiration for both Evelyn and Julie and I wanted them to like me. At the same time, that desire itself made me shy. They were like people from some foreign film—way, way cooler than I would ever be. Yet, here we were together. How strange . . .

How strange was life that me and Evelyn would ever even meet though in this place and time?

Considering that, a question came to mind. "Can I ask you something?"

"Sure. I might not answer though," Evelyn replied.

"Why did you come back to this island?"

"To take care of my uncle—he was the other gay in the family—when he was getting old and frail. Julie and I had both retired at that point. She'd never been to the US and Seattle was really a happening place—this would have been in the early Nineties—so she agreed to move. Then we inherited the property from him and had a cheap base of operations."

"Was it hard to live here then?"

"Yes and no. I'm a local so I could always come back. Julie had a harder time fitting in here. That's why, until she broke her hip, we traveled most of the time." Evelyn didn't look up from her piping. Her hands moved slowly and intelligently with a decisive quality that was born out of decades of practice.

"Why do you still live at the Beehive?"

"'Cause neither of us wants to cook or clean or do laundry anymore and it's cheaper than a hotel," Evelyn said with a smirk. She handed me a bowl that contained a block of white modeling chocolate and red food coloring. "Knead this in for me. I want it bright."

I put on a glove and started to work the color in. "Is that seriously why?"

"Yep." Evelyn put down the piping bag and turned her attention to the unfrosted roll cake. It sat on an oblong red platter that I'd seen Charlotte and Abby take out of the cupboard the day before. "And Julie is really social, so the dormitory lifestyle suits her."

"Except at Christmastime," I added. "*Tres dismal.*"

"Yesiree, there's nothing that scares her more than melancholia." Evelyn finally finished and came over to inspect the vivid red modeling chocolate. "Under normal circumstances she high-tails it right out of the common room at the first sign of tearful reminiscence, but during the holidays she goes into total avoidance mode. I think it's because it's the only time she misses her family."

"Oh darling, that's not it. I'm not that sentimental." Julie swept through the kitchen trailing a cloud of expensive perfume.

"What is it then?" Evelyn looked directly at Julie, which I wouldn't have normally noticed, except that Evelyn rarely gave anyone her complete attention. This seemed to be reserved for Julie only. When talking to me or Lionel she was always looking at a paper or a sauté pan or her phone. Not so Julie.

"It's the only time I miss the world as it was when I was a child—*nostalgie*, not *mal du pays*." Julie draped herself across the counter next to Evelyn and gazed up at her. "I can never experience homesickness while you're still alive."

"Sweet-talker," Evelyn murmured.

"Are you going to make extra little champignon? I love those the most." Julie stood back up, laid a hand on Evelyn's back and leaned over to inspect the chocolate twigs and leaves that had already been finished. "Et escargot chocolat?"

"No, this is the year I've finally decided to disappoint you completely by forgetting everything about you," Evelyn said. "Also I just asked Drew—nothing ever came of the Van Weezendonk thing."

"Ah, too bad. Just the day before yesterday I was talking to Dirk's mother about her son. She admitted she'd known all along that he was the one who had robbed the bank but she'd never known who his accomplice was." Julie turned to face me, leaning back on the countertop as she did. Even as old as she was, you could see the remnants of the sexy grace that must have made her a bombshell back in the day.

"How did she know her son robbed the bank?" I asked.

"She'd seen the money while visiting his apartment and worked out where it must have come from. But she never said a word to anyone," Julie whispered. "You see? That's a mother's love. Oh, it's such a shame we never had a baby. I would have been a superb mother."

"No, you wouldn't," Evelyn's rejoinder was easy and without malice, as though this was a conversation they'd had many times. "You'd return a crying, puking, shitting baby to the stork in one day."

"True." Julie gave an acquiescent nod.

"You could always be my mom if you want," I offered.

"Don't you already have one?" Evelyn asked.

"Yeah, but we're not that close and I have to share her with five other people," I said. "Whaddaya say? Want to be my mom? For the holidays at least?"

"Will I be allowed to dress you in better clothes?" Julie indicated my ensemble with a wave of her manicured had.

"Oh, absolutely."

"I. Am. So. Happy." Julie stood still for exactly one second then rushed from the room.

Evelyn and I locked eyes. "You have no idea what you just signed up for."

The next few hours passed calmly while the elaborate decorations slowly got created. Josh arrived and Charlotte came downstairs. Lionel and Abby started haunting the kitchen, looking for snacks, so we opened up several of the charcuterie packets that Julie had brought with her for a simple meal. Mac and Remy appeared shortly thereafter, both looking tense but not angry.

The large kitchen reached maximum capacity. When Remy got caught eating one of the little meringue mushrooms, Evelyn had finally had enough.

"Why don't you all go outside and build snowmen?" Evelyn suggested.

"Nah, how about we build snow-thems?" Lionel said this to Abby who gave him a nod.

"Oh, can I judge them?" Julie balled her hands up in little excited fists.

"Since when do you need anyone's permission to do that?" Evelyn shot her a smile. "Anyway, scram all of you. You too, Drew. Skedaddle. You're bothering me."

Growing up in Wyoming, I'd had numerous opportunities to build snowmen in my life and therefore I understood that any snowman construction has three distinct phases. First there is the delight and wonder at playing with this remarkable substance called "snow." During this phase all snowman builders are usually helpful and supportive of each other's efforts. Then comes the second phase: competition. If there are enough snow-citizens being erected at once—i.e. at least two—competition and trash talking will ensue and at least one snowball will be thrown.

This leads to phase three: all-out snowball melee.

Abby started it. She took a pot-shot at Remy, who had been dissing Lionel's attempt at creating hair for their snow-them. Remy cringed and backed away and half-heartedly made an effort to return fire, but Abby dodged without much effort.

Emboldened by her first victory, she launched a missile straight at Mac. It caught him in the shoulder, spattering his face with icy shrapnel. He made no attempt to retaliate except brushing the snow off in her direction. Apparently, confident in her inviolability, Abby sent fistful after fistful, forcing her siblings to dodge the relentless fusillade.

Abby had clearly been the baby of the family, but she was no baby anymore.

"That's it," I told Mac. "I'm gonna get her."

"Good luck. She's a maniac when she gets worked up like this," Mac said.

"Watch and learn," I told him, then, to Abby. "I'm coming for you!"

"Bring it, Old Man!" she lobbed another snow grenade in my direction.

When in the middle of a frigid firefight such as this one, there is no underestimating the element of surprise and knowing the habits of one's enemy.

The rookie, or casual snowball fighter will bend down, scoop snow, form it into a ball with both hands and then draw their arm back to chuck it at another combatant. What many Wyoming winters had taught me, though, was that there's a way to eliminate a step: you simply wait until your opponent is just about to attack you—i.e. when she has a snowball in hand and is pulling back her arm in full anticipation of epically owning you. Then you dart forward and while her body is completely open and face unprotected, you launch an upper-cut assault, flinging the snowball up directly from the ground.

There is no defending against this attack and the snow is zinged directly into the shocked face of the person who a mere split second before was planning to gloat.

Sure, you might get hit in the back with that snowball, but your opponent will be scraping icicles out of their eyebrows.

And that's exactly what I did. I gracefully bent and in one fluid motion scooped a handful of snow directly from the ground into Abby's stunned and wide-open mouth.

So startled was she that she staggered backward into a deep snowdrift, failing even to nail me in the back on her way down.

I may have, at that moment, raised both of my fists to the sky like some victorious yeti bellowing out my triumph, which lasted exactly two seconds because unfortunately, I had a protégé who was on the enemy side.

The problem with teaching a person to copy what you do is that they get used to doing it, so the second Lionel saw me initiate this maneuver (after snickering with laughter) he turned the action back on me. Then I was the one with a face full of snow, spitting out curses and a couple random pine needles.

We finished the snow people quickly after that and Julie judged our efforts with an unstinting eye and arched eyebrows only to finally proclaim all three of them adorable.

When we went inside, Evelyn made hot cocoa and exiled us all to the living room.

The afternoon was starting to darken and the Mackenzies were starting to watch the clock. Soon they'd all be changing into their festive best to attend Aunt Jenny's

Christmas party. A ritual that none of them apparently enjoyed, but everyone did anyway. I suddenly felt guilty abandoning them.

"I think I'll tag along," I said.

"Not a good idea," Mac said.

"But together we could sound your uncle out—at least mention Sam's name when he's not expecting it to see if he has any reaction at all," I reasoned. "And you know all his close friends will be there. It could be that he's covering up for one of them."

"I'm not that good of an actor. I can barely look my uncle in the eye when we're at work and there are other people around," Mac said. "And who would be inappropriate enough to casually mention a homicide at a Christmas party anyway?"

"I mean . . . fear of being inappropriate rarely stops me," I said. "Besides, I can be grief-stricken and just blurt it out if necessary. So long as we go early and leave early it should be fine."

Mac reluctantly agreed. The plan hit a brief hiccup when I attempted to leave the house in an outfit of my choosing before being restyled by Julie.

"What are you thinking wearing something so drab?" was her comment on my nicest jeans and button-up shirt combo.

"For real," Charlotte said. Then, to Julie, "He could borrow my moto jacket at least. He's not that much taller than me."

"You have clothes here?" Julie asked.

"And then some," Mac remarked.

"My apartment in the city is really small so I ship all my freebies and samples back here. Would you like to see them? Some are so weird, but others are nice."

Julie and I followed Charlotte upstairs to the room she'd shared with Abby. The clothes inside were hung so tightly that Julie could barely push them apart to leaf through. She agreed on Charlotte's choice of distressed denim jacket and at first chose a cable knit sweater with shoulder cutouts, which I respectfully declined to wear. She then selected a gray and black printed t-shirt to go with it. It looked and felt extremely expensive. Charlotte attacked my hair with a waxy substance that made it look filthy yet somehow good and made my head smell amazing.

Julie stood back to survey their work. "It's a little haphazard but the pieces I bought for you haven't arrived yet."

I stood, momentarily stunned by the revelation that Julie hadn't even waited a day before choosing clothes for me. Did I feel some fear for my future at that point? Yes, I did. But Mac seemed appreciative when I descended the stairs, so it wasn't all bad.

◆◆◆

Scott and Jenny Mackenzie owned a large, modern house with a garage so expansive that it could have doubled as a second home. The entry and great room, complete with polished marble floors and decorative columns, seemed more like the lobby of a mid-range hotel than anywhere people actually lived. The effect was only heightened by the well-dressed crowd of mostly middle-aged guests milling between the bar, fireplace, and a truly monumental Christmas tree. Its branches had been flocked and were festooned with so many ornaments and swags of tinsel that the flickering lights could hardly be seen. The oversized gift boxes, complete with gold wrapping paper and massive red ribbons, looked more like set dressing than presents.

"Aunt Jenny's nursery sells Christmas trees and decorations during the winter off-season," Mac informed me when he noticed me staring at the tree.

"Is a guy in a nutcracker costume going to bust out of one of those boxes and begin dance fighting the Rat King at midnight?" I asked under my breath.

Mac suppressed his laugh.

"Jenny always goes all in on Christmas," someone commented.

Mac smiled. I nodded. Together, we drifted into the crowd.

I shook hands and exchanged greetings with Mayor Sheila, and briefly talked shop with Eugene Wang from Copper Kettle Confitures. He'd noticed the superior flavors of Evelyn's prize-winning jams and wondered if she'd be willing to consult on his new line of homestyle favorites.

"You'll have to ask her yourself, but I feel like she'd be open to the idea," I spoke with certainty, aware that nothing could please Evelyn more than being paid to criticize a kitchen noob.

I excused myself and ambled back toward the bar to scope out the bartender. Since the Eelgrass had been so busy recently, I was considering a new hire and the woman working this party seemed to have some flair. Mac trailed along behind me.

"You okay?" He asked quietly.

"Me?" Shouldn't I have been the one asking him that question? "I'm fine. You?"

Mac shrugged. It wasn't as if this was the time or place to talk about it. So instead I quickly squeezed his hand in my own.

"If you want to leave, you can blame me," I suggested. "Or claim we have an emergency with our houseguests."

"We just got here." Mac pulled me along with him. "There's a couple people I want you to meet."

I resigned myself and followed him.

You might think, being extroverted as I am, that I enjoy attending big quasi-formal parties, but the fact is I find them very stressful. I think it's because after making so many events happen, I no longer have the ability to let go and be a guest. No matter where I go, I keep monitoring everything—the level of the ice, whether or not the garbage needs to be taken out. The rate at which fresh appetizers appear and, of course, any signs of a crisis in the kitchen itself. Everything.

Currently I couldn't help noting that the drinks were being served fast and strong but with hardly a canapé in sight to help absorb all the alcohol. I squashed my urge to sidle back into the kitchen and assess the holdup. I wasn't Jenny Mackenzie's caterer and I didn't want to be either, I reminded myself.

It was just that working behind the scenes suits me best at gatherings like these—or at least acting as an anonymous drifter who haunts the drinks table for a couple of minutes then flees like a background character in a video game. Yet here at Aunt Jenny's party I couldn't pretend to be one of those non-player characters. Walking around with Mac in the most expensive jacket in the room, I became a main character—or at least the romantic lead. Of the hundred and fifty or so people present we appeared to be the only obvious gay couple and, even at thirty, among the youngest who weren't actual children.

Mac seemed intent on introducing me to people and his obvious pride in doing so made me feel glad that I'd gone in for Julie's glow-up. Particularly when he wrapped his arm around my shoulder and introduced me to the stocky pair standing near the fireplace.

Roy and Darla, the father daughter duo who owned Mac's beloved hardware store, appeared suitably impressed with me and delighted for Mac. Darla even gave Mac a not-so-discreet thumbs-up, which inspired a hilarious flush in his neck and ears.

Before I could fish out my phone and capture his bright red earlobes, Mac reached for his own phone. The happiness drained from his face as he read the screen. Then he stepped back from us to listen to the caller. A moment later he disconnected and leaned in to me.

"That was Remy. Something's come up and he wants me there."

"He probably doesn't know what to get me for Christmas," I commented for Roy and Darla's sakes.

"You're not wrong about that," Mac replied. He paused and I realized that he wasn't sure of what to do about me. Remy clearly wanted him there ASAP but Mac didn't want to just leave me, surrounded by strangers with no ride home.

"Just introduce me to your aunt and then go," I said. We pushed through the crowd till we got to the large and lavish kitchen. I wasn't surprised to see the vast expanse of marble countertops largely occupied by colorful glass jars filled with an assortment of legumes, which I felt certain had never been opened and were as old as the house itself.

Aunt Jenny wore a gold sweater dress that accentuated her height and brought out the shine of her short dark hair. She stood beside a shining chrome refrigerator with a box of mini frozen pizza rolls in one hand. She was not alone.

A pudgy fortysomething man stood farther back, next to a trashcan gazing into its contents with a vacant expression. He was one of those nondescript guys that I might not have taken much note of except that he was dressed so oddly. Instead of wearing the casual clothes of a guest or the standard black and white of catering crew he sported overalls and an apron with the logo of Jenny's nursery emblazoned across it. His nametag read: Trent.

Much closer to me was Joyce—Evelyn's cousin and unofficial evil twin. She sported a beige pantsuit, too many gold accessories of every kind, and blonde hair sprayed into a lacquer helmet. Joyce's granddaughter, Stacey, stood at the kitchen island, chopping a pineapple like it was the key to getting out of an escape room. She was around thirty, short and fine-boned. She wore a black chef's jacket over her catering uniform and her brown hair hung in a single braid down her back. I tried not to dislike her just by association with Joyce.

She seemed to be trying to make nice appetizers but kept getting derailed by her client, Aunt Jenny's, constant interference. Just as she finished cutting the pineapple, Aunt Jenny stepped closer to her and frowned.

"On second thought maybe we shouldn't serve them with the pizza rolls after all," Aunt Jenny decided. "A lot of people don't like that. Maybe it could be a pineapple filling of some kind?"

For an instant I thought Stacey might actually stab Aunt Jenny. As there was no walk-in freezer for Stacey to escape into, I stepped forward.

"Anything I could do to help?" I asked. "Mac got called away."

"Oh, Drew, good to see you. And just in time too. Here you go." Aunt Jenny handed me the box of frozen pizza rolls. "Stacey is a little behind so could you just pop these in the oven for us?"

I stared at the box, astonished, while Stacey kept her head down and began doing her best to throw together a fruit platter.

"Chaz would have been in here to help me, but something came up at work," Aunt Jenny said. "Those Mackenzie men . . . so unreliable. You'll find out, Drew."

I noticed that at the mention of Chaz's name, Stacey glanced up from her work with a slightly hopeful expression. Then she picked up a pomegranate and set to breaking it open.

Joyce and Aunt Jenny chuckled. Trent smiled and collected Stacey's discarded pineapple peelings as well as the vividly stained detritus of the pomegranate.

"Half the time I suspect that they come up with crimes just to get out of doing work around the house." Aunt Jenny looked to me. "I bet if it wasn't for having you as a roommate, Mac would probably starve to death."

"As is he'll probably have to watch his weight," Joyce commented. "Restaurant cooking is so fattening, you know."

I eyed the frozen pizza rolls and resisted the urge to frisbee one of the pale little chunks into Joyce's bleach blonde hair. As enjoyable as it might be, I knew that in the long run throwing food wouldn't help me endure this kitchen's terrible environment. So I defaulted into dish dog mode.

Every single cooking professional has this secret mode in their back pocket—the ability to shut up, put your head down, and just work. It's generally developed during the period of time when a restaurant employee is moving from the dishwashing position to the very bottom of the cooking hierarchy—prep cook. The dish dog is assigned any manner of shitty jobs that the older or more experienced cooks don't want to do. Need a hundred pounds of French fries cut? Prawns deveined? Tomatoes sliced in a hurry? Call the dish dog.

During this crucial stage of development, the aspirational dish dog keeps their eyes down and their ears open and tries to absorb as much raw knowledge from the atmosphere as possible in order to eventually be useful enough to get liberated from the smelly, greasy, hot wet hell of the dish pit.

So, I moved over near Stacey, washed my hands and started placing frozen little nuggets on Aunt Jenny's expensive, yet functionally crappy luxury-brand sheet pans.

"Do you think Scotty and the boys will have some free time come New Year? We were thinking of heading up to the lodge again," Joyce said to Aunt Jenny.

"I hope so." Aunt Jenny began distributing some other frozen item—were they a version of pigs in a blanket?—onto a different set of sheet pans. "This time of year Chaz usually helps me at the nursery. He's a wonder at maintaining the citrus trees through the cold."

Again I noticed Stacey's gaze lift at the mention of Chaz. Could it be that she had a crush on him? My own view of Chaz was largely informed by his sleepy arrival to the scene of Dorian's murder. He'd struck me as a softer sluggish variation on the tall, dark Mackenzie theme. Not to my taste but maybe he suited Stacey's.

I noticed that she'd begun chopping up a banana to throw into the already piecemeal arrangement of her fruit platter.

"But, wouldn't you know it," Aunt Jenny went on. "Someone has to go and get herself killed and I end up having to drive all over the island on my own. And half my lemon saplings have root rot."

I wondered if Jenny's callous dismissal of Sam's death was the result of personal dislike or just impersonal familiarity with law-breaking. I decided—for the sake of the holiday and getting along with family—that I would believe it was the latter.

After all, as the wife of the sheriff, she'd probably spent her entire adult life being inconvenienced by crime.

Still, she had to know that the person who'd 'gotten herself killed' was my friend, didn't she? Then again, maybe not. I'd never seen Aunt Jenny in the Eelgrass so it was possible that she didn't understand my position there. Plus, every statement she made about me was only as being adjacent to Mac—therefore it was possible that as an individual I had no real presence or history—at least in her perception.

Maybe this was what Lionel's mom meant when she said the Mackenzies put family first in a bad way—not that they relied on nepotism (although that was also certainly true) but that they acknowledged no one else?

Aunt Jenny continued, "And then with the snow I didn't even know if any guests would show up but I suppose everybody looks forward to this party as much as I do."

"That's sure true," Joyce answered. "It just wouldn't be Christmas without your party. How many years is it now?"

"Since I started the business. At least twenty-five." Aunt Jenny slid her sheet pan into the oven. "Are you finished with yours, Drew?"

"Yes, ma'am." I handed her my sheet pans then retreated to Stacey's side. "Anything I can do for you?"

"If you could just help me get these onto platters." Stacey waved her hand at a stack of covered hotel pans behind her. Then, in a whisper, "Everything is ready, I just have to put it out. I don't know why she's making pizza rolls."

"Got it," I whispered back. I removed the lid from the first hotel pan, which turned out to contain a few dozen deviled eggs. As I did this, Aunt Jenny sidled up alongside me.

"You're a good worker," she said.

"Thanks, I try."

As I uncovered the next silver hotel pan Aunt Jenny scowled.

"Tomatoes?" Aunty Jenny looked back at Stacey.

"Stuffed tomatoes are Chaz's favorite. He requested them specially," Stacey replied as she pulled apart a cluster of grapes.

"When did he have time to do that?" Aunt Jenny's tone was only half joking.

"We bumped into each other at the botanical garden in Seattle last week," Stacey didn't lift her head as she replied. "He'd just seen his doc—"

"Well, I'm sure I don't need to know all the details of his private life," Aunt Jenny cut her off in a rush. Then immediately turned back to me. "Let me tell you, Drew, you're going to have your hands full with that Mackenzie house. It's pretty on the outside but just about falling down inside."

"Needs a paint job too," Joyce chimed in. "Everyone I talk to at the marina calls it the 'Haunted House.'"

Why, I wondered, did everyone think I had any say in the fate of that building?

Not that I hadn't thought of trying to convince Mac to go more Painted Lady with the Mackenzie House's current drab blue-gray exterior—but that was because I possessed a sense of style not a sense of ownership. Still, in the interest of keeping the conversation going I said, "You know, I think Julie is sketching up some design proposals for that. She's trying to convince Mac to go with creamsicle with tangerine and white accents, but I don't think she'll succeed."

Joyce curled her lip slightly.

"Oh yes, Julie," Aunt Jenny said vaguely. "She's . . . a character."

"She and Evelyn are staying with us for Christmas this year," I said.

"Evelyn is celebrating Christmas?" Joyce raised an eyebrow. "The lord works in mysterious ways, I suppose."

I took a breath to reply but Stacey shoved another hotel pan in my direction while making heavy eye contact. I got the signal.

Don't take the bait.

Even though I truly wanted to mangle that bait I forced myself to just keep my eyes locked on the hotel pan. Against all odds, Stacey seemed to be my ally, or at least be as uncomfortable as I was with the direction the conversation was flowing.

The hotel pan she gave me contained stuffed mushrooms, stuffed dates, and cherry tomatoes stuffed with shrimp. I wondered if Stacey solely expressed her culinary ambitions through the medium of cramming filling into concave receptacles or if this had been at her client's request.

Aunt Jenny went back to telling Joyce her troubles procuring various items for the event as members of the catering crew collected platters of canapés and ferried them out to the guests. Aunt Jenny's voice receded to a droning background noise. From the outside I started to hear the familiar sound of hungry guests joyfully greeting the arrival of food.

I wondered if I could arrange the abandoned fruit on the kitchen island into individual servings of a tropical salad without hurting Stacey's pride or if I should just let Trent quietly whisk it all away. Then Stacey gently nudged me.

I looked up to see Mac quietly treading into the kitchen. He wore his coat and his professional smile. Whatever he and Remy had discovered in the last hour, I knew that it hadn't made him happy.

"Oh Mac," Aunt Jenny called out. "You aren't here to steal Drew back already?"

"Sorry Aunt Jenny." Mac laid a hand on my shoulder. "There's a little emergency at home. One of our houseguests needs some assistance."

Joyce looked pleased at that but Aunt Jenny at least had the good grace to appear slightly concerned.

"Nothing serious, I hope?"

"No. It should all be fine soon enough." Mac responded.

"Well, you take good care then. But I expect you to bring Drew back for my New Year's Party," Aunt Jenny declared. "I still have to show him off to all my guests."

Did she mean this literally? Probably.

I followed Mac out of the party back to his cruiser. Neither of us spoke until the door was closed.

"Two things—first we put out a call for anyone who had been on Top Hat Butte Road on the day Sam was killed to contact us with any information and we got a hit. Remy and I just interviewed a stargazer who happened to see a vehicle leaving the scene as she was driving up. Unfortunately, she didn't get a look at the driver. She thought the occupants of the vehicle might have gone up for romantic purposes, so she stayed far away."

"And so?"

"The vehicle description matches my uncle's SUV," Mac said. An expression somewhere between anger and fear passed over Mac's face. "But there are also a lot of other white SUV's on the island. Still, we now know the make and model of the vehicle that was there. Also, I got someone to play me the recording of Charlie's conversation with Sam."

"And?"

"Charlie was telling Sam to find a bundle of his dad's medical correspondence. Apparently Charlie's dad kept copies of letters that he wrote in case he was ever sued for malpractice. Sam asked him why he wanted them and Charlie said that there was something in one of the letters that could potentially help him get a mistrial. So he asked her to get the letters, then overnight them to his lawyer. There's only one shipper that does overnight in this town so I went there to ask and no one matching Sam's description shipped a parcel that day. When I called the lawyer to double-check she said she didn't know if her office had received anything or not, since she's been snowed in at her house."

"Okay," I said. "So we know that Sam did go to the storage unit and that she probably got this bundle of letters. Then I guess she probably started reading them—that's what I would do anyway."

"That's because you're nosy as hell, but yeah that's probably a fair supposition. So she reads the letters, figures out how they could get Charlie out of jail and then what?" Mac looked over at me as if expecting me to know the answer.

"Well, we know what she didn't do—she didn't ship the letters even though she had plenty of time to before the store closed," I replied. "The question is—why not? Why did she fly here to do this errand for Charlie and then not do it?"

Mac's expression conveyed a smugness that also managed to be sad. "Rewind a little. Why were the letters valuable?"

"Because Charlie thought they could get him a mistrial," I answered. "Are you trying to lead me somewhere?"

"What causes a mistrial?" Mac continued his line of questioning, that small, annoying smile still tugging at the corner of his lips.

"How the hell would I know?" I was starting to get frustrated with his little smirk. "Have you solved this thing? If so, please tell me."

Mac squeezed my shoulder. "A mistrial is caused by misconduct during the trial or during the investigation."

"Was there misconduct during Charlie's trial? How would that information be reflected in his dead doctor dad's old letters?" It was hard for me to imagine the Camas County prosecutor's office needing to succumb to chicanery to convict Charlie when Charlie had been caught red-handed in his attempt to bury me and Sam alive.

"Sometimes if an entire police force is found to be corrupt, then every conviction they ever made can be challenged," Mac went on. "So if the whole sheriff's department was shown to be crooked then Charlie has a chance at being acquitted."

"Is this about the car wreck?" I wondered aloud.

"The car wreck?" Mac's supremely knowing expression fizzled into confusion.

"The one Lionel's mom is mad at your family about because one of you did something shady to help another one of you, or something like that?" I offered.

Mac frowned. "I don't know anything about a shady car wreck. Remy might have let a fender bender slide if neither party was hurt or wanted to report it to their insurance companies."

"No. Lionel's mom told him 'Mackenzies put family first, but in a bad way'. It had to do with a car wreck," I explained. "Could someone in the family have covered up another family member's involvement in a wreck?"

"I want to say no. But even if they did I don't know if just that would be enough for Charlie to hope for a mistrial, of his case," Mac said. "Though, letting something like that slide definitely wouldn't make any of us look good."

"How about blackmail?" I prompted.

"Sure, but who?" Mac said. "It wasn't me. I doubt it was Remy. There's still Uncle Scott and Chaz but Uncle Scott is really bulletproof in this town. Charlie would have to have something really, really big on him and . . . my gut instinct is Uncle Scott is just not ambitious enough to have committed a crime big enough that Charlie could leverage it to get out of the pen. I think you might be conflating the two events. The misconduct could have been on the part of the prosecutor or the judge as well. Those medical records could contain anything. For all we know it could boil down to some secret baby somewhere."

"That still happens?" I was stunned.

"More often than you'd think even in this modern age," Mac remarked.

"Okay, then let's leave the car wreck aside and go back to Sam," I said. "We know that Sam went, got some medical records, met Danielle, told her she was clearing up some shitty family business, and vanished around four or five in the afternoon."

When I glanced back to Mac he was shaking his head at me. "I don't want to leave the accident aside. I might not be able to go any further on Sam's case but I think we should talk to Lionel's mom—figure out if she's a real witness or just repeating malicious gossip."

"We? Like you and I? Together?"

"Yes." Mac put the car in gear and started to slowly turn around, maneuvering his vehicle through the arriving partygoers. "Given how Lionel's mom feels about my family, she might not talk to me if you're not there so, yes, we, together, are going to go visit the hospital."

Chapter Ten

Whoever had been put in charge of decorating the reception area of Camas County Medical Center had gone all out. Red and green tinsel swags festooned the walls and 3D gold foil stars hung from the white panels of the drop ceiling. I locked eyes with an Elf on the Shelf while Mac and I waited for Lionel's mom to be summoned from someplace deep within the building.

Eun-ji Fogle was a trim, compact Korean American woman in her mid-forties. She had straight eyebrows and the same full, pretty lips as Lionel. She wore fuchsia scrubs and a flat, serious expression that suddenly turned to alarm when she saw me and Mac together.

"Did something happen to Lionel?"

"No, no, he's fine," I quickly reassured her. "We're here to talk to you about something else. Lionel mentioned that—" I broke off, unable to find a way to ask the question. Fortunately, Mac had way more experience asking awful questions than I did.

"Your son indicated to Drew that you might have knowledge of someone in my family covering up a vehicular crime." Mac spoke in a calm, friendly tone. "Is that true?"

"I'm sorry, he said what now?" Eun-ji's expression turned to annoyance edged with fear. She knew exactly what we were asking about but was stalling for time. Her eyes remained fixed on the star emblem on Mac's chest.

I stepped forward. "Nobody else knows we're asking you about this and the only reason we are is that it might have to do with my friend Sam's murder." It was a fib but there was no reason to tell Eun-ji that.

"Oh yes. I'm sorry for your loss," Eun-ji said. "Sam was very kind to give my dumb, blabbermouth son a job." Eun-ji looked at Mac again. "Most people get angry hearing bad things about their family . . . I don't want to say this in front of you. It's just. . ."

"I understand. Why don't you just tell Drew then. He can fill me in if he thinks it's relevant to the murder investigation," Mac suggested. Eun-ji nodded then Mac said to me. "I'll be in the cruiser."

Eun-ji waited until Mac was fully out the door to pull me over into the farthest corner of the reception room.

She studied me with an uncertain expression for a few moments and then commented. "The fried duck dish you taught Lionel to cook is pretty good. He even managed to impress his grandmother and aunty with it."

"He picked it up really quick. He's a smart kid." I wasn't certain why we were discussing Lionel instead of the car crash but it seemed important to her to establish that we both cared for Lionel. Maybe that we both trusted him and his instinct to trust both of us in return.

But after that brief exchange she seemed to relax.

"Way back when I first came to this town when Lionel was around three or so, there was a hit-and-run involving a cyclist. She died a half-hour after arrival. Less than an hour later Jenny Mackenzie was brought in by her husband with a busted-up face. At first, I thought maybe her husband beat her up so I felt sorry for her and I was hanging around outside the curtain to see if I could catch him threatening her or anything like that. But instead, I heard her and her husband talking about taking their car to Seattle and selling it."

"And?"

"And it was a brand-new car. They'd just bought it to give to their son. Why did they need to sell it?" Eun-ji leaned closer. "Because it had damage from hitting a cyclist—that's why."

"Did you ever tell anyone about this? Apart from Lionel?"

"At the time I was new, and I was nervous about making an accusation. So I tried to sound out another of the nurses, but she only said that I shouldn't be eavesdropping on private conversations if I wanted to keep my job. And then the doctor on duty went out of his way to inform us all that Jenny Mackenzie's broken nose and lacerated cheek resulted from a tree pruning accident at her nursery."

"The doctor?" I asked but I felt like I already knew the answer.

"Bill Lindgren," Eun-ji supplied. "He was close friends with the Mackenzie brothers."

Eun-ji stopped and laid her hand on my arm. "I know it's not my place to tell you what to do but you seem like a nice guy so I just want to tell you something—I would not get close with that family. They're not good people. When they were growing up those kids were in here constantly with this or that injury."

"And you think that—what? They were abused?" I knew that Mac's dad was supposed to have had a temper but nothing Mac or his siblings did or said had made me think they were abused as kids.

"Not abused but definitely neglected," Eun-ji replied. "Needlessly deprived of support. Why? Because the sheriff convinced a judge to let an eighteen-year-old kid become the legal guardian of five other kids, the youngest of which was only four years old. And then he gave him a job as a law enforcement officer. Who in their right mind does something like that?"

Put that way, it did sound insane. I had to admit she had a point. "Why do you think the aunt and uncle allowed Mac to have custody of his brothers and sisters?"

"Nobody knows, but it certainly wasn't for Mac's benefit or for the good of his sisters and brothers," Eun-ji said. She glanced to the holiday decorations festooning the far wall and sighed. "I did wonder if maybe Scott Mackenzie, the uncle, resented them because of their father's involvement with Jenny Mackenzie in that hit-and-run."

"What do you mean?" I asked.

"The timing of it all seems suspicious to me, that's all," Eun-ji said. "Sean took off really soon after that cyclist was killed. And after that it was as if the hit-and-run had never happened at all. No one was ever charged."

"Sean—you mean Mac's dad?"

"Right. The father." Eun-ji gave me a quizzical look. "It was about a month after the cyclist was hit that he suddenly abandoned his family. After that I always wondered if it was him who was driving the car when it hit the cyclist and his sister-in-law was only the passenger."

I considered the possibility and frowned.

"Is there a reason you don't think Jenny was driving?" I asked.

"She'd had carpal tunnel release surgery seven months prior and was still having other people chauffeur her around," Eun-ji replied. "She humble-bragged about it so much that everyone in town knew. She seemed to like it best when she could get Sean to take her around. So, you know."

For just a moment I didn't but then I put two and two together.

Eun-ji suspected that Scott Mackenzie resented his brother—and his brother's kids by extension—not because Aunt Jenny had preferred him as a chauffeur but because Sean had involved Jenny in a hit and run. Then he'd bailed, leaving Scott and Jenny to face the fall out. Doing so, he saddled them with a critically-ill sister-in-law, six kids, and a vehicular homicide.

Yeah, I could see how resentment might come into play there. All this might also explain why Uncle Scott would lie about Mac's dad calling him. He knew that his brother had run away to evade a conviction.

Except . . . There hadn't been any investigation to run away from. Bill Lindgren and the Mackenzies had all seen to that. And also, where did Dirk Van Weezendonk come into all this?

Just thinking about it all felt like sinking into mental quicksand.

"I can see why you didn't want to say this to Mac's face," I murmured. "I don't even want to repeat it."

"Maybe you don't need to. I don't see how any of it could be connected to Samantha Eider's death." Her expression turned hopeful.

"I'm not certain that it is either." I stood, taking in the quiet waiting room, the few patients who waited either to be seen or for their loved ones to return from their various treatments. "Thank you very much for talking with me."

"Okay, no problem. When you see him tell my son to come home more often, please, okay?" She smoothed out her scrubs and straightened her nametag.

"Isn't he going home for Christmas?"

Eun-ji sighed. "Yes, he'll be there but I'll be here, like always."

◆◆◆

After I returned to the cruiser and told Mac what Eun-ji had said the snow started falling heavily again, coming down in thick sheets. The night was so dark and the silence so complete that the crackle of the police radio asking Chaz for his location shocked me like a thousand volts straight to my spine.

Mac frowned at the radio then turned to me and said, "So what do you think happened?"

"I think—" I paused, afraid to go on then finally wrangled my courage. "Could Eun-ji be right? Could your father have fled the island after knocking down that cyclist?" I couldn't get my voice to go louder than a whisper.

Mac's response was immediate. "I don't accept this."

"Which part?"

"That my dad might have been the driver that she suspects. He wouldn't flee the scene of a crime or fail to offer assistance." Mac's face suddenly contorted with total rage. "And he wouldn't cover one up either. No matter who the guilty party was."

I did the only sensible thing I could do—I cut the ignition, grabbed the keys and jumped out of the car. The engine spluttered to a halt but the roof lights still flashed. In an instant Mac was out of the vehicle too. We stared at each other over the cruiser's roof. Falling snow and blinding lights filled the space between us.

"Give me the keys," Mac growled.

"What are you going to do?"

"Bring my aunt in for questioning." He held out his hand, palm up.

"I don't think that's a good idea right now," I said.

Mac started around the front of the car but I circled to the rear, holding the keys up. "We don't have any evidence that your aunt has done anything, so on what grounds are you going to arrest her at her own Christmas party?"

"Since when did you care about evidence?" Mac exploded with fury.

"I just don't want you to make a mistake. Especially if she's really guilty of something." I kept my voice low and calm—or at least I imagined I did. Sweat trickled down the back of my neck. "You haven't even charged Sam's phone yet. When you do, there might be something on it, right? Something that will give you just cause to bring her, or your uncle in. It's not that long. Just wait till you've seen what's there."

"Are you really doing this to me? Are you really standing there telling me to WAIT?" Mac's voice boomed through the frigid air. "I've been waiting for fifteen years. And I KNEW that Uncle Scotty knew more than he was telling but I didn't think it was this."

"But this information changes nothing. We still don't know who was driving the car. Was it your dad? Your uncle?

Somebody else?" I continued. "That's why I'm saying that you should wait. We don't have any proof of Eun-ji's theory. We have nothing. And—and what if it is true? What if your aunt was driving and did knock down that cyclist and then she or your uncle or both of them did something to your dad to keep him from reporting her? Right now they think they're safe, don't they? They think you'll never figure it out. And what if both these things are connected? What if that's the information that Charlie needed? The means to blackmail your uncle into finding a way to overturn his conviction?"

"This is really reaching," Mac said. He began to visibly cool down as he started to talk his way through it all but his breaths still burst out into the night in huge white puffs of steam. "But okay, let's just go down this rabbit hole for a minute. Let's say Charlie really did have hard evidence that Uncle Scott had done something wrong. Either the hit-and-run or . . . something else."

"Which he sent Sam to retrieve for him," I continued. "But then it went wrong. How?"

"She mentioned it to the wrong person and word got back to my aunt and uncle?" Mac offered. He'd calmed down considerably and now trudged through the snow to join me.

"I don't think so. I think that Sam turned on Charlie. She doesn't like confrontation so she agreed to get the evidence for Charlie while he was pressuring her during their phone call, but she really didn't want Charlie to get out of prison, so she took that evidence, whatever it was, and took it directly to the person it threatened, to make sure Charlie's plan wouldn't work. Maybe she thought that way she'd be safe from her cousin."

Mac came alongside me and leaned against the driver's door.

"That's plausible and also very sad," Mac remarked. "Because if you're correct it also means that that evidence, whatever it was, has most likely been destroyed."

"But Charlie is still alive, him and his knowledge are both locked up all safe and sound," I said.

"Safe and sound," Mac echoed. He put his hands on my shoulders. "You're right, this is all hypothetical at this point."

"I'm sorry."

"It's okay." Mac's grip tightened on my shoulders then he suddenly spun me around, yanked open the back door of the cruiser, and shoved me inside. I lay, facedown on the back seat, disoriented and bewildered, feeling him push my legs into the car and slam the door shut. Instantly I scrambled upright.

He'd locked me in the back seat.

"What the hell, Mac?" I felt a small satisfaction realizing that I still had the car keys in my hand followed by the disappointing knowledge that it didn't matter because Mac could start the car anytime he wanted to now that the fob was inside the vehicle.

Well played, Deputy . . .

Mac opened up the driver's door and leaned inside.

"I need to take minute," he said.

Mac walked a few feet away from the cruiser and stood, hands on his hips, staring up into the sky. I leaned back in the seat grudgingly, though still resentfully, admitting that I probably did deserve to be put in cop time-out like this. If not specifically for stealing the keys to his official vehicle, then for every other annoying thing I'd ever done to him.

I hated seeing him out there all alone though, in the cold, facing the reality that his own family might be to blame for his dad's disappearance.

I wanted to hug him. I wanted to punch him in the face. I wanted to make him turn around and look at me but I could do none of those things. I could only wait and in that process I began to worry that we were on the wrong track.

Could Eun-ji be imagining or even fabricating the conversation she heard? It had been a long time since then.

What we needed was to access the information on Sam's phone but to do that we had to wait for it to dry out. Nothing could be done tonight except to go back to the Mackenzie house, pretend everything was fine, and have Christmas. Mac seemed to have come to some similar conclusion because he came back, opened up the door and said, "Sorry about that."

I scooched out of the back seat and, after briefly considering the punch, just settled for the hug, pulling his head down onto my shoulder and resting my chin against his cold, wet hair.

"You're right," he said. "We can't go over to the party and call her out."

"I know," I replied.

"How can a person who I've seen literally digging his own grave actually be right about what to do now?" Mac's voice rumbled against my shoulder.

"I've learned a lot since then. Mainly from you." I stroked the back of Mac's neck. "Now this one time I get to be right, and you get to be the one acting crazy. How does it feel?"

"Terrible," Mac said.

"Would it help to know that being right doesn't feel good on me either?"

"No." Mac straightened up and glanced at his watch. "Oh, and it got so intense there I forgot to tell you—Remy texted while you were talking to Lionel's mom. He found Sam's rental car parked at the grocery store in the back lot. There doesn't appear to be anything inside but there's always a chance of trace evidence, so it's been impounded."

"So what do you want to do now?" I asked.

I hoped he didn't want to press onward. As much as I wanted to tell Mac what Charlotte had told me sooner rather than later, the sad truth was that time wasn't of the essence. Sam would still be dead in the morning. Mac's dad would still be vanished.

"I suppose it's time to go home, chug beers in the shower, and go to bed," I suggested.

Mac said, "Or we could check into the Cascade Motor Inn and spend a couple hours away from my family."

Blood rushed to my groin with a level of enthusiasm I found frankly embarrassing. "Or . . . yeah. That. That one."

◆◆◆

According to Evelyn the Cascade Motor Inn was Camas Islands' go-to location for cheating husbands and wives of all kinds so there was something pleasing about checking in with my actual boyfriend. Bucking the transgression trend. Not that the clerk cared who we were. He was a portly man in his late fifties or so who wore gold aviator glasses and a red Santa hat. He made a point not to look up at us as he shifted over the key to room eleven.

No room in this motel had been updated since the turn of the millennium, and that included the bedspread, which featured a busy pattern of oversized flowers that probably hid stains well. I made a note to take if off the bed entirely before use.

I'd barely gotten the chain lock across the door before Mac pushed me against it, crowding close, pinning me with his arms pressed to the door on either side of my face. We touched from chest to groin, the barest hint of friction. He stared at me. My breathing hitched as I waited to see what would happen next.

Sometimes we did soft, sometimes we did playful. More often than not these days, we did I've-gotta-be-at-work-in-six-hours super lazy blowjobs.

But on nights like this, when Mac had a fire in him, I knew he wanted to be in control, and I *wanted* him to be in control. It pressed all sorts of buttons I never knew I had. He leaned down and licked my lips, softly, a gentle caress. And then he ground into me, mouth seeking mine, tongue pushing in and out of my mouth, foreplay to what he planned to do later.

I groaned, grateful for the opportunity to not have to stifle my normally uninhibited sex sounds. His cock shoved against mine, the friction fluttering between delicious and painful. I was desperate to get my hands on him, but when I grappled for his fly, he guided my hand away and reached behind me, scooping my ass in his large hands and lifting me up.

I let out a cry of surprise in his mouth. It was a good thing the room was small and the bed wasn't far from the door; I think even Mac was a little unprepared for how cumbersome it was to pick up a man my size. We bounced loudly on the flimsy mattress and it squeaked so loud we both started laughing.

I kicked the dubious duvet aside while yanking my clothes off. We repositioned ourselves to the center of the bed, the whole time Mac's eyes never straying from my own. He could be so focused when he wanted to be. It was flattering to be under such attention, but also a little unnerving. He paused for a moment to rip through his trousers and pull out his wallet. Two small packets of travel lube appeared.

"Planning this for a while, were we?" I asked.

"Always be prepared." Mac stalked up my body on all fours. His body was a work of art—lean muscle, big and powerful, dark hair trailing from a thatch between his pecs down to his large and already leaking cock. He crouched over me and flipped me onto my stomach, like I weighed nothing.

I laughed again, but my insides fluttered with the strange pleasure of giving up control to someone I trusted enough to give it to.

A warm palm caressed my ass cheek, followed by a kiss. I hadn't heard him open one of the packets the slick finger up my crease surprised me.

"I don't think I can go slow tonight," Mac said, and his voice sounded strained already.

"Then don't." I pressed my ass back.

Mac let out a pleased grunt. He crooked his fingers and nerves buzzed through me, so sharp and shocking it was almost painful in its pleasure.

Always that first moment of panic, the anticipation, immediately dwarfed by a pleasure so great my toes curled and I let out a long moan, whole body trembling. That line between pleasure and pain, it was so thin on nights like this. And I trusted Mac to walk it.

"Ready?" he asked through clenched teeth. He looked like an ancient fertility god, feral and wild, eyes shiny in the dark.

"Come . . . on . . . already . . ." I gritted out.

He reached one meaty hand down to grip me at the juncture of my neck and shoulder. And then he pushed. Mac fucked with an unrelenting rhythm, long deliberate strokes. My own voice grew louder, primal, nonsensical. He reached down and pumped my cock and I fell apart around him, the jolt so powerful I felt my orgasm from my toes to the roots of my hair. It lasted seconds that felt like minutes. I noticed Mac speed up from a hazy, pleasure-clouded distance. He cried as though he'd been shot and came, big body shuddering over me.

It took me several seconds to come down from that orgasmic high. Several more to realize I was going to be feeling this all through Christmas.

But, I mean, there are worse presents to receive.

"Are we going to sleep here?" I asked. "Cause now that I'm not so horny I'm sort of scared of getting cooties."

"Oh, God no." Mac chuckled against my shoulder.

We rested a few more minutes before getting dressed and checking out.

The desk clerk had fallen asleep in the interval, and lay slumped over the desk, Santa hat shifted forward to cover his eyes. Mac gently nudged the key under his hand, then we went home.

Chapter Eleven

The next morning, Remy came by again and after a brief conversation, we decided that we couldn't wait any longer for Sam's phone to dry. I put in Sam's code and went to her photos.

The last photo taken was a close-up of a snowflake Christmas ornament hanging in a lighted tree. At the center of the ornament was a gold star. It was exactly the kind of thing that Sam would have taken a picture of and set as the background of her phone for the duration of the holiday season. But since the background was still a picture of a pumpkin pie I guessed she'd taken the pic very shortly before her death.

"Please have your location services enabled," I murmured then I hit the Info button. The photograph had been taken at 4:58 on Tuesday at Our Place Nursery.

I glanced over to Remy and Mac. "I'm sorry."

"Don't be," Mac said. "We knew something was wrong."

"This still sucks," Remy said. "Big time."

Mac nodded. "The question is what to do now."

"What are you two up to?" Charlotte demanded. "What's going on?"

The warm, coffee-scented atmosphere in the kitchen grew frosty. I saw Evelyn, who had been descending the stairs, turn around and start to go back the way she came.

I wished I could do the same. I did not relish being in the midst of what might be a huge family blowout. Behind her I saw Josh freeze, unwilling to take another step in the current atmosphere.

"Which two of us do you mean? Me and Mac?" I attempted a deflection but Charlotte wasn't having any of it.

"Those two." She pointed at Remy and Mac. "And you too, I guess? What is this? No girls in the secret clubhouse?"

Josh moved closer to Charlotte. I had to hand it to him, he definitely understood the "I'm your boyfriend" assignment.

"It's nothing like that." Mac held up his hands in surrender. "It has to do with work."

Remy just shrugged and crossed his arms, giving them nothing. I had a vivid image of him as a sullen teen refusing to divulge anything to anyone, but especially not his older brother and sister.

Abby lurked in the living room, just barely peering in through the door.

"But you two don't work for the same department, so how could it be about just work? It's about a case," Charlotte glanced to Abby. "That's why they've included Drew but cut us out. So, is it your friend's case? Did you figure something out?" Charlotte addressed this last question to me.

"Well," I asked Mac. "Did we?"

Mac hung his head in exasperation, hands on his hips, studying the floor.

"Never mind," Charlotte said.

"We think that either Uncle Scott or Aunt Jenny is involved with Samantha Eider's death," he said.

"Murder," I corrected. "Sam was murdered."

Remy's jaw dropped, his mouth hanging open in confusion. "What the hell, Mac? Why would you tell them this?"

"Because of the other thing that Drew and I found out," Mac said.

Abby drew nearer, eyes narrowed in confused suspicion.

"What are you talking about Mac?" Remy asked. "What other thing did you and Drew find out?"

"See?" Charlotte cut in, jabbing her finger at Remy. "See how it feels to be cut out of the loop? Not very nice, huh?"

"That's not helping, Charlotte," Mac said.

Abby silently looked between her older siblings one after another as if she could not form words. Finally Mac made eye contact with her and crossed the kitchen to lay a hand on her shoulder.

"I'm sorry about this," he said. "I know you like Aunt Jenny."

Josh raised his hand as if waiting to be called on, or perhaps maybe excused from the conversation.

"What's up Josh?" I asked.

Josh folded his hands in front of him. "I know I'm the new guy and that can be annoying but can anybody bring me up to speed here? You say you had a friend who was murdered?"

I have to say that this impressed me. I'd thought for sure he was thinking of fleeing the scene just like me. Instead he was trying to be helpful and engaged like some kind of superhuman. I decided to do my best to help him.

"Okay, yes, my former business partner was killed on the same day that you arrived in town. Actually, for a hot minute you were a suspect because you spoke to her on the ferry ride over. Her name was Sam."

"That woman?" Josh's eyes popped wide open. "Oh, my God! She was so nice."

"She thought you were nice too," I said.

"I started talking to her because I saw her looking at the Eelgrass menu on her phone," Josh said. "I said I'd heard it was good. I knew you were the owner, and thought I'd try to drive some business your way. Oh, I can't believe she was killed."

I glanced at Mac. Simultaneously we realized that we had never asked Josh about his conversation with Sam, even though he'd been one of the last people to see her alive. We'd gone down the rabbit hole of Eun-ji's suspicions about Uncle Scott and Aunt Jenny to the extent that we'd overlooked Josh as a resource.

Mac picked this up immediately. "Did Sam happen to say anything about who she might have been meeting? Or what she was going to do?"

"No, I mean, we were just sitting near each other on the ferry and I didn't want her to think I was trying to pick her up," Josh said. "I'm sorry."

I shrugged. It wasn't his fault. I went on with the story.

"After you spoke to her, Sam went to a storage unit to retrieve something then met her friend Danielle for a late lunch. Danielle confirmed that Sam had gone to get some kind of paperwork that her cousin Charlie, who is serving a life sentence in the pen, thought could get him a mistrial if it were made public. Are you following me?"

"Yes, I'm getting it," Josh said. Abby also nodded. "Sam was assisting a wrongfully convicted felon to prove his innocence."

"No, he's not innocent at all. He tried to bury me and Sam alive one time," I said, aghast at Josh's epically wrong takeaway.

"Oh wow, that's terrible," Josh said.

"Yeah, it sucked. No, what was happening was that a rightfully convicted felon was trying to pressure Sam into helping him get out of prison on a technicality," I said.

"Ouch. That's entirely different," Josh said.

"So different," Charlotte agreed. "What was the technicality he was trying to use?"

Mac said, "I believe Charlie was trying to prove that there is significant enough corruption in the Camas County Sheriff's department to warrant reexamination of his case. I listened to the recordings of Charlie and Sam's phone conversations and discovered that what he'd sent her to get was a medical record from about fifteen years ago that was evidence of some kind. We don't know what's in the record but that's what she was supposed to get and send to Charlie's lawyer."

I saw the unasked question, "is the accusation true," ghost across Josh's face and then vanish as silently as it came. He really was very polite. Remy, on the other hand, radiated belligerence.

"Did Charlie confirm that?" he asked.

"Of course he didn't," Mac said. "He's not saying anything."

"But we can infer that Sam decided to deviate from this plan because she did not want Charlie to be released from prison." I paused, not sure how Mac wanted to go about informing everyone of the rest.

"So because the sheriff's department would be implicated you think that the person she went to see was Uncle Scott?" Abby asked.

"No, I think she went to see Aunt Jenny." Mac offered Abby his phone. The screen showed a photograph of the Christmas ornament. "We finally got Sam's phone dry enough to turn on. That photograph was the last one taken at 4:45 pm at Our Place Nursery."

"But just because she was at Aunt Jenny's business doesn't mean that she was there to see Aunt Jenny," Charlotte protested.

"Charlotte, it's the off-season. There are currently three people working at Our Place: Aunt Jenny, Trent, and that high-schooler who runs the cash register in the evening," Mac said.

"Well did you check out Trent? He's always seemed shady to me," Charlotte said.

"I'll look into him as well," Mac said.

"Why Aunt Jenny and not Uncle Scott?" Abby still didn't seem convinced. She toyed idly with the fraying cuff of her oversized teal cardigan.

"I don't know," Mac admitted. "But we have an eyewitness who saw a white SUV similar to Uncle Scott and Aunt Jenny's at Top Hat Butte later that same night."

"OMG, where me and Lionel found Sam's phone buried underneath the snow?" Abby gasped.

"You dragged in Lionel? Am I the only person who isn't involved in this investigation?" Charlotte muttered.

"I'm not," Josh whispered. She smiled at him.

Remy remained tense. "So what else did you find out?"

Mac seemed suddenly reluctant to talk so I informed everyone about what Eun-ji had said about suspecting Aunt Jenny and their father of being involved with the hit-and-run fifteen years ago.

"We checked back and the hit-and-run occurred about one month before your father vanished," I finished. "Which is not to say that they were related—"

"You obviously think that they're related," Remy commented, though he looked at Mac and not me.

"There's no evidence to support that," Mac said. "But it is strangely coincidental."

"Then what are you planning to do right now?" Abby asked.

"I want to go to Aunt Jenny's nursery and look for that ornament but . . . I'm not sure what excuse I can have," Mac said.

"Oh that's easy," Charlotte said. "We can just say we're there to get a tree. We need a tree anyway."

"I'm not sure how long Remy and I can front that we're looking for a tree, especially if we're nowhere near the trees," Mac replied.

"No," said Charlotte. "When I say we I mean all of us. Everybody, Evelyn and Julie too. If we all go Abby and I can distract Aunt Jenny for as long as it takes you to look."

Abby seemed skeptical, while Josh gazed at Charlotte with a kind of star-struck awe.

Mac gave Charlotte a long, appraising look. "Aren't you going to argue that we're wrong?"

Charlotte shook her head. "What's the point? If you find evidence and confront them and you're right and they did have to do something with either the murder of Drew's friend or covering up the murder of Drew's friend then it's your duty to arrest them. If you go to confront them and you're wrong, then that will probably destroy your relationship with Uncle Scott and Aunt Jenny forever but that just means that you'll get to finally quit the sheriff's department and live your own life. It's a win-win."

"That's true," Abby agreed. "I didn't think about that. You can follow your dreams."

"I don't have any dreams," Mac replied.

"Then you'll have time to find some," Charlotte snapped.

"I like that you found a way to think of sudden, involuntary unemployment as win-win," I remarked to Charlotte. When she started to argue I reiterated, "No, really. Way to reframe."

"Well," She crossed her arms over her chest, seemingly embarrassed. "You learn to bounce back fast when you're in this family."

◆◆◆

I didn't have to explain the conversation that had just transpired to Evelyn and Julie, because they'd both been eavesdropping at the top of the stairwell for the entire thing.

It took about an hour to round up the whole group to prepare to make the five-minute drive to Our Place. Most of the hour was taken up by everyone getting, at Julie's command, "festively attired for the subterfuge."

Which is how I ended up wearing a tight red sweater—this one belonged to Abby, as well as a belt and jeans and stud earrings from Charlotte's collection, plus a jingle bell charm bracelet improvised by Julie on the spot using the ornaments we'd dug out of the kitchen cupboard.

She also styled my hair in a way that looked disheveled and chic simultaneously.

Honestly, I don't think I'd ever looked better in my life.

"That's hot," Charlotte remarked.

"Very hot," Abby agreed. "We should take selfies." She handed Charlotte a headband topped with plushy reindeer antlers and put on her own headband, which featured blinking LED Christmas lights.

The girls crowded in on either side while Julie admired her work. "You see I told you Drew would make an excellent model. Not as natural as Lionel but still—"

Evelyn gave me the once-over and smirked from behind her paper. "If you say so. Can we go already?"

A cold blast of air pushed through the kitchen as Mac walked in.

"The car's ready," he announced, then stopped and caught sight of me. He stared for a long time—so long that I could almost feel the weight of his eyes moving over my body. "You look good."

"Right? Well it's my first public appearance with everybody so I didn't want to let our side down." I squeezed Charlotte and Abby in tighter. Josh appeared in the doorway, lingering there as if he didn't quite know whether he was invited or not. The scene was so cozy I almost forgot the entire thing was a pretense.

Evelyn stood, her chair legs scraping noisily against the black and white linoleum tiles. "Are we ready?"

"Ready," I said.

"Let's go." She placed a hand on Julie's waist and guided her toward the coatrack near the door. As she did she looked over her shoulder at Josh. "Don't just stand there, New Guy. Get your coat and boots."

Josh burst into a smile and I could see his ears starting to turn red. He waited for Evelyn and Julie to exit then crowded in with us in the mudroom. As we all got geared up to endure the winter temperatures Josh leaned over to Charlotte.

"Your grandmas are cute," he said.

"They're not our grandmas," she replied.

"They're related to Drew," Abby said.

"They're my faux moms," I explained, though Josh seemed even more confused by this statement which, I suppose he would be. He seemed conventional, detail-oriented, and meticulous in the way that you'd expect a person who had dedicated their life to straightening people's teeth would be. "Family of choice, you know?"

"Not really, but right on." Josh zipped up his coat.

Charlotte fixed a red and green scarf around Josh's neck before pulling a matching set of mittens over her own long fingers.

"The old ladies are like a couple of barn cats who finally came inside because they got too cold," Charlotte said. "Like the 'I Don't Own a Cat' meme came to life but as grandmas."

"I like them," Abby said. "They're fun."

"You're not so bad yourself," Evelyn responded. "Now let's get a move on while it's still daylight."

I headed for Mac's old pickup and climbed in only to be shoved toward the center of the bench seat by Abby who climbed in to ride shotgun. When Mac wordlessly stretched out his arm across the seatback to rest over my shoulders she gave a snorting little giggle and took another selfie of the three of us, then started playing "Jingle Bell Rock" via her phone.

Everyone else crammed into Remy's Subaru and made the short trip to Our Place. As Aunt Jenny had said at the party the previous day, the nursery was a vital part of the Orca's Slough Holiday Season. SUVs and four-wheel drive vehicles crowded the parking lot. There was even a set of snowmobiles parked near the entrance. White fairy lights strung along the fence led shoppers back toward both the cut and roots-on trees as well as the pole barn. But instead of a dance floor, the barn now sported a treasure trove of glittery merchandise as well as seasonal plants like poinsettia, amaryllis, and paperwhites. Wreaths and swags were stacked along the side.

At least seventy shoppers moved in and out of the area, many clustered around a table where Aunt Jenny herself, dressed as an elf, dispensed paper cups of mulled cider.

Charlotte and Abby went there immediately whereas Julie navigated toward the trees, with Evelyn hot on her heels. Josh, Remy, Mac and I hung back.

"Would you mind helping out Evelyn and Julie?" I asked Josh. "In case one of them slips."

"Sure thing." He stuffed his hands farther into his pockets and followed behind the oldsters.

"There have been hundreds of people here between last night and now," Mac remarked. Remy nodded.

"We should still look for the ornament," I said. "'Cause I'd be willing to bet that if Sam took a picture of it she touched it first. She was a very touchy person. When she worked with me at the Eelgrass sometimes she would come touch every single eggplant because she thought they were so pretty."

Both Mac and Remy regarded me with deep confusion but neither disagreed with my reasoning. We split up, each taking a section. All around us, other families debated the merits of various trees, while the stereo played the light classical songs through the overhead speakers. Finally I felt my phone vibrate. Evelyn wanted my help.

I pivoted in place scanning for the motion of her typical "flagging down a ship" beckoning gesture and found her signaling me from a far, practically unlit corner of the lot.

I made my way down the snow-packed path toward her. The trees along the way were intermittently decorated in the same fairy lights and white and gold ornaments. I drew to a sudden halt.

They were all the same design as the ornament Sam had taken a picture of. Dozens of them decorated the eight or so lighted trees that defined the border of the cut tree zone. I opened up the photograph again, comparing it to the ones in front of me on the tree. In Sam's photograph, the gold star was slightly askew, which lent it a wonky charm—probably the reason Sam had taken the picture in the first place. I didn't find it on the first tree and Evelyn was texting me again so I took a pic of the tree and sent it to Remy and Mac then headed back to find out what the old ladies needed.

For some reason Evelyn had left the regular sales area and was standing near the compost. Several tired, sad-looking trees lay heaped on their sides in a snow-covered mound. Evelyn stood, arms crossed, watching Julie fuss over a somewhat decrepit tree that was being held upright by Josh. The tree was about seven feet tall with a broken tip and several branches missing from one side.

So Julie was the kind of person who would rescue a pitiful Christmas tree. Figured.

Also kneeling alongside them was Aunt Jenny's employee, Trent. He had a curved, serrated pruning saw and was slowly sawing the root ball off the tree. I glanced at Josh, who gave a silent shrug.

"Oh, here you are," Evelyn said.

"What's going on here?" I gestured vaguely to Trent, who'd just about made it through the unattractive tree's skinny trunk.

"Cut trees are half as much as roots intact," Evelyn said. "Trent's doing the modification for us since they were going to throw this one out anyway."

"Can you believe it?" Julie chimed in. "Such a lovely tree cast aside because it doesn't match the dull aesthetic of the bourgeois middle class."

I guess if I'd given the matter any thought I could have predicted that, being the people we were, we'd have to go rescue a garbage tree for Christmas. That didn't make what we were doing any less absurd. Josh, in particular, was regarding the tree with an uncalled-for level of disgust. Whether it was because it had been dug out of the refuse pile or because it was indisputably feral and unsavory-looking all on its own, I couldn't say—I sensed the New Guy might be growing disenchanted with my extended found-family group.

Fortunately, I had a different mission to send him on. I pulled up the picture of the ornament on my phone and leaned close, whispering, "Okay, we found where the ornament is located, it's got to be on one of those trees. Can you go help Mac and Remy look for it?"

Josh's face lit up. "Yeah, I sure can!"

"Yes, but if you find it make sure you don't touch it. Just tell Mac." I handed him my phone.

Once he was gone I turned back to Evelyn and Julie effusively thanking Trent for his help. The man only shrugged and kept sawing.

I said, "Are you serious about this tree?"

"Yes, we have to get this one," Evelyn said. Julie nodded vigorously.

"It's not its fault that it's suffered an accident." Julie gestured to the missing branches. "Nature is red in tooth and claw, as they say. You don't think Mac would reject my tree, do you?"

"No, it's fine. We'll just buy it and get it in the back of the pickup before anybody sees how messed up it is." I glanced over to where Charlotte and Abby were keeping Aunt Jenny fully engaged in conversation then back to Trent, who'd finished sawing through the tree trunk and stood.

"I can take this to your car for you," he said to Julie.

"That would be wonderful," she said. "Drew, darling, just take the tag to the cashier will you?"

I grabbed the tag and beat it up the path, past Josh who was looking at every single ornament with the exact thoroughness I'd expected, and Remy and Mac, who were observing the trees more casually. I reached the check-out where I paid the sullen, confused teen cashier full price for this substandard item.

Across the parking lot I could see Evelyn and Julie both shifted and stamped their feet as Trent put the tree in the truck bed. It was colder now and though I wasn't feeling it, they must be. I reached for my phone to text Mac to ask for his keys to let Evelyn and Julie into his truck to sit down, only then remembering I'd given my phone to Josh. I jogged back down the path toward him.

"I've got it!" Josh's voice rang through the cold night air and I froze, irrationally afraid that Aunt Jenny would somehow hear him over the noise of the other customers and the light classical music. I stole a glance to her, but she just kept cheerfully distributing cider.

By the time I reached the tree where Josh, Mac, and Remy stood, Mac had already put on a set of nitrile gloves. Remy stood to block the view from the storefront while Mac carefully removed the ornament and placed it in a brown paper evidence bag.

Josh's happy expression faltered as he watched Mac place the paper bag in his inner coat pocket. I clapped a hand on his shoulder and said, "You okay buddy?"

"There was someone there looking at us," he gestured with his chin. Turning, I saw Trent again, observing us. I waved to him, with a warm, nothing-to-see-here sort of smile then turned to Mac and asked, "Would you mind driving Evelyn and Julie back to the house now, they're freezing? I'll ride back with Remy."

"Sure." To my surprise Mac leaned forward and kissed my cheek, which caused Remy to immediately raise a hand to cover his eyes.

"God, not right in front of me, bro," he murmured.

As I watched Mac walk away I thought my sense of trepidation would leave. We'd found the ornament in Sam's photograph. If I was right and it had Sam's fingerprints we had physical evidence that she'd been here at the nursery. Shouldn't I be feeling relief or even elation?

But I felt only more dread.

◆◆◆

It was only once we were back in the house, trying to situate the bedraggled tree in the living room that I noticed it was even more unpleasant than I thought. I'd reached out to grab it and Evelyn had stopped me.

"Don't grab it there—it's got something on it," she said.

I peered at it. Black glossy blood and . . . what looked like hair was caught in one of the branches. I looked back to Evelyn, who smiled broadly. "What do you think?"

"What the hell happened to this tree?" I drew back my hand. "What is that?"

"Blood. And human hair," Evelyn said.

Everyone drew closer to better inspect this new and hideous revelation, which, I guess, was a dead giveaway about the general nature of the family as a unit. Even New Guy Josh moved in, although more sheepishly, and kept behind Charlotte.

"Are you sure it's human?" Josh asked.

"I've pulled enough hair out of food over my lifetime to be one hundred percent accurate." Evelyn leaned down. "Also there's a hard line where the hair dye ends."

Julie leaned down, pursed her lips then gave a solemn nod. "Letting your roots show is so fashionable right now."

"So that's why you wanted this one specifically," I said. Admiration for her low-key evacuation of the tree from Aunt Jenny's nursery welled up inside me. Evelyn might be old but she still had the stealth moves covered.

Mac knelt down and took a closer look at the branches then said, "Don't touch it, I'll be right back."

A couple of minutes later he returned with a crescent shaped pruning saw to remove the affected branches, which was more than thirty percent of them, a process that left the tree even more misshapen than it already was, but at least no longer marred by gore.

"So are we free to decorate this now?" she asked when he was finished.

I guess I wasn't surprised that Julie still wanted to rescue the pathetic thing. Apart from the fact that we'd just removed human hair and blood from it, the already unattractive tree barely qualified as even conical anymore.

Mac gave her a long, deeply perplexed look then said. "Sure?"

Josh recoiled, "Is it really okay to decorate the murder tree?"

"I'll ask you—is it okay to blame a tree that's done nothing wrong for a murder? Should we take away it's hope for a Christmas miracle just because it witnessed a terrible crime? No, it deserves a glow-up." Julie swept her hand over the admittedly sparse tree. "We can just accessorize more here . . . and also everywhere."

Evelyn gave a slow nod and stood. "We'd better get it in the stand then."

Abby went to work sifting through the boxes of ornaments, decorations, and paraphernalia until they finally located an ancient red and green steel Christmas tree stand as well as a faded green tree skirt. Charlotte tapped Josh to go upstairs with her to wrap presents.

Mac and Remy quietly withdrew to the kitchen and I followed them, with the excuse of starting a pot of coffee brewing. Oblique winter sunlight filtered in through the kitchen windows giving the illusion of warmth but the clear skies outside meant it was bitterly cold with the roads frozen solid.

"I've got to do my shift now." Remy gestured to the branches that Mac had cut and bagged. "These should be processed right away, I think. But not by you or me."

"Agreed," Mac said. "Would you be willing to drive them to the highway patrol station other side of the island?"

"Sure . . . as long as you agree that you're not going to go confront Aunt Jenny or Uncle Scott by yourself."

"I'm not an idiot," Mac remarked.

"That's debatable. Especially in situations like this." Remy gave him a long, skeptical look.

To be fair, Mac did have a history of solo confrontations but I still bristled at Remy bucking the chain of command like this so I said, "We won't do anything. Nobody wants to mess this up."

After Remy left, Mac stood at the sink, drinking a cup of coffee and staring out at the bright winter day. I could see thoughts playing over his face. Every few seconds another worrying idea seemed to occur to him then be resolved only to be replaced by another. Was he concerned about what would happen with his work? With his family? With the still-unresolved matter of his father's disappearance? Sam's homicide?

He glanced over and saw me watching him. "Do I have something on my face?"

"No," I said.

"Then quit staring at me, Drew, you're making me uncomfortable."

"I was just wondering what you were thinking," I admitted.

"Just now?" Mac set his coffee cup down. "I was thinking that I haven't bought a single Christmas present. I think it's going to be another year of last-minute shopping at the hardware store. Do you think there's anything Julie would want from there?"

"Are you serious?"

"Right?" Mac shoved his hands in his pockets. "It's a tough question. Anyway, you want to come with me?"

Chapter Twelve

Camas Hardware Supply—or CHS, as it was known—was not just a retail venue—it was an island institution and its employees, in their red polo shirts and khaki slacks, were revered like great scholars of old. CHS sprawled through three connected storefronts taking up a full third of Main Street. Mostly it sold actual hardware but here and there one could find items of interest to the hardware aficionado, such as work boots, lawn ornaments, all-weather overalls, and the occasional novelty lighter.

The parking lot was surprisingly full for the road conditions and inside guys in heavy, washed-duck utility pants and snow boots contemplated spigots and flanges with tense, thoughtful expressions.

Because all restaurant equipment is always breaking down, I'd been in this store dozens of times, but never learned anybody's name. Not so for Mac. Every single employee knew him and had a few words for him as we passed by—even if it was only to wish him Merry Christmas.

Mac had often mentioned that this or that guy had helped him over the years when he was taking care of his brothers and sisters. The staff seemed to have collectively adopted him.

Under this light, Mac's sudden urge to go Christmas shopping on the precipice of a family crisis made some sense. This rabbit warren of a shop with its assortment of potbellied old guys who knew how to fix things, had at some point become Mac's comfort zone. With each new person we met he'd go through an introduction as well as some variation of, "You know Drew, right? We live together now."

This information wasn't news to anyone in town—Katie from the Beehive had made sure of that—but the fact that Mac went out of his way to point it out was sweet.

I gave silent thanks that the morning's styling by Julie was still intact even if I did catch a couple of the guys eyeing the homemade jingle bell bracelet with slight concern.

The employees there seemed to have expected Mac to arrive this way and had their own suggestions for last minute gifts, ranging from high-tech plungers to DIY earrings made from washers to actually good presents like fancy multi-tools, which is what we ended up choosing for Josh. Mac didn't seem to be seriously shopping though, so much as threading his way through the maze of aisles like some sort of meditation.

Finally he stopped in the rope section, seemingly lost in contemplation of the enormous spools of different length and weight of cord.

"Are you going to try and make a plant hanger?" I asked.

"No, I was thinking that even as strong as she is it's not possible for a person Jenny's age and height to lift a dead body over a wall so she must have had help," Mac said. "The question is—who was it? Uncle Scott? Chaz?"

"What about Trent?" I asked.

"Also a possibility. And if that's the case, could it have been Trent who committed the crime after all?"

"You won't know until you ask, I guess." I ran my hand along a section of rope.

Mac shook his head. "It won't be me asking. After Remy turns the evidence we collected over to his boss, I'll probably be put on leave. Maybe Remy too. I don't know if I'll ever be able to come back to the sheriff's department. And

I don't know what people in this town are going to think of me."

"Did you ever consider that maybe they'll think you're a man of integrity? I asked.

"Honestly, I don't know," Mac said. "And I can't find a single thing in this store that I think Julie would like."

"May I suggest the grocery store?" I asked. "I think she'd be pretty happy with a stack of glossy fashion magazines. It's just something to tear the wrapping paper off of, anyway."

We spent another hour picking out presents for the family. Since Abby was about to move in to her own place Mac decided to buy her what she'd need for a basic tool kit as well as the high-tech plunger. Remy, Mason, and Clayton all got gift certificates from CHS.

"I'll send Charlotte a card to somewhere nicer online," Mac concluded. "A coffee shop, maybe?"

After that we checked out and made our way to the already dark parking lot. Only a few cars remained as CHS was about to close. As we trudged through the snow a single white SUV approached, cutting us off before we got to the car. The window rolled down to reveal Aunt Jenny.

"I need to talk to you, Mac," she said, smiling. She killed the engine and got out of the car leaving her lights on and door open.

"Can't it wait?" Mac asked. "I really need to get home and wrap these."

"It's pretty important," she came closer, stepping up directly beside me. I tried to remain calm. Pretend that I didn't know she'd killed Sam, but my heart raced and sweat began to trickle down my back as I felt the unmistakable chill of a metal barrel pressing into my lower back.

"Mac, I don't want to alarm you but I think I can feel the business end of a gun in my back," I said.

Mac's attention snapped to his aunt. "Is he serious, Aunt Jenny?"

"Dead serious." She pressed her car keys into my hand but I didn't take them, letting them fall. They landed in the deep snow at my feet. "Pick up those keys and get into the driver's seat of my car and drive."

"Drive where?" Mac asked. "Where do you think you can take him?"

I didn't move.

"Wherever I tell him," she snapped.

"Why—why are you kidnapping Drew?" Mac's face was an absolute blank. Was he really going to play dumb? Would that work?

"Don't try to pull that stupid act on me Mac. You know damn well why I'm kidnapping your . . . whatever he is."

"Boyfriend," I supplied. I couldn't help it.

"You keep quiet." She pushed the gun harder into my back. "Just give me back the things you took from the garden center and I'll let him go and we'll pretend like none of this ever happened."

"Okay, Aunt Jenny, I get it. You're angry. But it's too late. I already handed the evidence over to Remy's boss. It's out of our hands now so . . . everything is going to run its course," Mac said. A flurry of bitterly cold wind whipped through the parking lot, sending stinging ice crystals over all of us.

"Like hell it is," she said.

"Please think about this," Mac said. "Anything you do from this point on will only make things worse for you. You have to know that."

She did not seem to know that—or rather she seemed unwilling to accept it.

"I am not going to allow you boys to humiliate me like this." She glowered at Mac and jabbed the gun barrel into me again. "How can you take the side of some loose drug addict like Samantha Eider against your own family? Don't you have any loyalty?"

"We're not taking her side—" Mac began only to have Jenny cut him off.

"The hell you aren't! Sneaking around my place of business, looking to implicate me."

"That's because we don't know your side of the story," I said. Could I keep her talking long enough for someone in the hardware store to finally notice what was happening? Maybe. I'd found over the course of the last couple of years that people who are threatening to kill you generally wanted to be heard and feel understood while doing it. "Mac was just telling me that there was probably a reasonable explanation."

I caught the slightly disbelieving glint in Mac's eye but then he seemed to recognize my intent. He nodded.

"We worked out that this all started with an accident fifteen years ago. But from what everyone has told us you weren't the one driving," Mac said.

"Of course I wasn't. My hand was still too weak from surgery." Jenny leaned forward so close that I could smell the coffee on her breath. "But who was driving doesn't matter. That cyclist woman was the one to blame. She came out of nowhere and nearly got us all killed."

"You were hurt enough that you had to be taken to the hospital," I tried to sound sympathetic though it was a challenge what with her keeping the muzzle of her gun jammed in against my spine.

"So it was all just an accident?" Mac edged ever so slightly closer to Jenny.

"Obviously." Jenny heaved a sigh of frustration. "But Sean just would not let it go."

At that Mac's gentle expression froze.

"Did you kill him?" Mac asked.

"She didn't." Sheriff Mackenzie's voice drifted to us as

he strode across the parking lot. Both Mac and I startled. We'd been so focused on Jenny that we hadn't even noticed him drive up and park across the street. Now he trudged through the snow towards us, with a deeply weary expression.

He glanced to his wife and offered her a sad but affectionate smile, as if holding me at gunpoint was a charming quirk of her character, which I naturally found outrageous. Not that I could do anything about it.

"There is a surveillance camera right over there." Sheriff Mackenzie pointed to the camera above the back entrance of CHS. "Darla and Roy called the station when they saw someone appear to jump Mac and his . . . roommate."

"Well, Scotty, you just tell them that we're playing a holiday prank," Jenny responded. "They can go on and close up and go on home to their families."

Holiday prank? Elf on the Shelf appearing suddenly in the refrigerator was a holiday prank. But who in their right mind thought ambushing your nephew and attempting to abduct his boyfriend at gunpoint would pass for seasonal mischief?

Despite the vulnerability of my position I couldn't help but roll my eyes.

Sheriff Mackenzie gave me a stern disapproving glance, as if I was being rude. Then he pointedly turned his attention to Mac.

"You know, you ought to have turned any and all evidence you discovered over to the sheriff's department," he told Mac.

"For what? So that you could cover up a homicide?" Mac asked.

"It was self-defense! That little witch was trying to blackmail me," Aunt Jenny broke in. "She threatened me!"

"Sam—who was so scared of confrontation that she left the state and sold her half of our business rather than facing me at work—threatened you? Really?" I couldn't help my disbelieving tone. "The last thing she would have ever done was to go out of her way to threaten someone."

"Shut up!" Jenny jabbed the gun into my back harder.

I should have played meek and harmless but I was getting exhausted of feeling scared and my very fashionably-dressed feet were really, really cold.

"If Sam approached you, it would have been because she was terrified that Charlie would get out of prison and come after her," I snapped. "She would've brought you the evidence she found, thinking that it would prove she was on your side. She'd want your help to keep him locked up."

As I spoke I recognized that this had to be the truth. Sam always latched onto a partner in any endeavor—whether that was a business with me, attending Coachella with Rico, or heisting Dorian's drugs with Danielle's barely-of-age brother, she never could face uncertainty alone. But she'd made a fatal error when she'd selected Jenny Mackenzie for a comrade.

Jenny's head bobbed in an involuntary nod of agreement with my words, but then she sneered at me.

"Well, you weren't there. So it doesn't matter what you think." Jenny said flatly. "I say that Sam wasn't any better than her cousin, Charlie. She was probably drugged-up when she busted into my business. She came at me and I fought her."

I locked eyes with Mac. The wounds were on the back of Sam's head, not the front or the side. Jenny had clearly attacked Sam from behind, most likely without warning.

"So then?" Mac asked his uncle, "You helped take her body up to Top Hat?"

Sheriff Mackenzie's gaze dropped from Mac's stare. His hand brushed over his gun belt but then fell to his side.

"No one helped me!" Jenny snapped." I used a sled to move her. I had one in the car because I'd heard it was going to snow."

"Jen," Sheriff Mackenzie's gaze toward his wife remained affectionate. The hint of a sardonic smile curved his lips. "The evidence isn't gonna support that claim."

"I got a drifter to help me move her," Jenny supplied without batting a lash. "He was back by the compost drinking all day. I gave him a few dollars from the till and he left on the ferry the next morning. You'll never track him down."

Because he never existed—was what I just stopped myself from saying. At the same time I was stunned by how quickly Jenny seized control of the conversation as well as her ability to concoct a bold-faced new lie on the spot.

"I don't know about that one, Jen." Sheriff Mackenzie responded as if he was assessing his wife's latest casserole recipe rather than her attempt to muddy a murder investigation.

"They canceled the ferry crossing due to the snow," Mac stated but his focus remained on his Uncle. "Jenny's already admitted that this started with her involvement in a hit-and-run and the fact that my dad wouldn't stop investigating it."

I heard Jenny take a breath in preparation to make some new protest but Sheriff Mackenzie held his hand up, gesturing for her to stop.

"What really happened to my dad?" Mac asked.

Sheriff Mackenzie's smile fell away, leaving a bleak, tired countenance.

"I just wanted him to stop before he did real damage to our family," Sheriff Mackenzie said softly. "The truth wasn't going to bring that woman back to life, it would only have ruined Chaz's future."

Chaz?

My shock was reflected in Mac's face but only for an instant. Of course Chaz would have been driving; his parents had bought the car for his sixteenth birthday. It was just that Chaz was such a drowsy, forgettable figure that it was difficult to imagine him harboring such a terrible secret. He certainly seemed to sleep well for someone who ought to be haunted by the part he played in a gross injustice.

"He doesn't know he was to blame," Sheriff Mackenzie went on. "It was the first time he had a really bad seizure—"

"That cyclist woman came out of nowhere and startled the life out of him," Jenny said. "That's what brought it on."

"Chaz has epilepsy?" I asked.

Mac appeared flummoxed by this revelation as well.

"That's nobody's business but ours!" Jenny glared at me like I'd brought up a shameful secret. Then it struck me that maybe to Jenny it was. Maybe that was why no one knew and Chaz never mentioned it.

"He's got it mostly under control now," Sheriff Mackenzie stated. "He sees a specialist in Seattle. He's doing just fine."

Except that he'd been brought up hiding a core fact of his life. He couldn't tell anyone in town about what he was going through or why he might be feeling unwell and exhausted. I couldn't help feeling a pang of sympathy toward him.

"So then the hit-and-run really was just a terrible accident?" I wondered. "Why cover it up? Why not just come forward—"

"And have our son be branded as a misfit and a murderer at sixteen? It would have ruined Chaz's future!" Jenny snarled. "How could he ever have joined the sheriff's office if people knew about his . . . condition? Who would have trusted him behind the wheel of a police vehicle or with a gun after that?"

Sheriff Mackenzie heaved another heavy sigh.

"I just needed Sean to understand," he said to Mac. "But back then your dad . . . he wasn't in a good state of mind. Your mother getting sick again, it made him mad at the whole world. He was spoiling for a fight and I gave him one. But neither of us really meant to . . ."

"It was self-defense," Jenny pronounced.

Sheriff Mackenzie bowed his head. "It escalated and he got hurt. It was an accident. I didn't realize how much stronger I was than him, you know?"

"But you didn't tell anyone," Mac ground out. "You let us—no, you made us—all believe he'd just abandoned us. You broke Mom's heart. Tore our family apart—"

"He did it for your own good!" Jenny put in. And if she hadn't had a gun on me I thought that I would have told her to shut up.

"For our good?" Mac's face flushed with anger. "How in the hell was that good for us?"

"If everything came out then Jenny and I could have faced prison sentences," Sheriff Mackenzie lifted his head to glower back at Mac. "And then who would have looked after all of you?"

"Everyone knew your mother wasn't long for this world," Jenny sounded almost proud. "You kids would have ended up in the foster system. Separated and handed out to who knows what kind of strangers. But Scotty and I made sure you kids got to stay together. He even sent money in your father's name to Charlotte while she was off cavorting in New York."

As she was saying this, I noticed a lanky figure edge from the side of the hardware store and duck behind one of the few remaining cars in the lot. I briefly met the man's gaze and recognized Remy. Then farther back behind him I spotted two other men in State Patrol uniforms. Alarmingly, both of them had drawn their guns.

Then it struck me that no one had contacted the sheriff's office since the people in the hardware store called in to report an armed assailant accosting Mac in their parking lot.

The protracted silence on our end would have been alarming the longer it stretched on. Someone in the sheriff's office must have contacted the State Patrol for support.

As I looked to Mac I noticed his gaze flicker over something—or someone—behind Jenny's SUV. He shifted his attention to me.

It hadn't been too long ago that we'd been in another situation like this, though this time there wasn't a burnt-out barn about to tumble down on us. I'd promised then that I'd get better at rescues. Playing the helpless hostage was hardly an improvement.

"Aunt Jenny can you please put the gun down?" Mac spoke calmly. "There really isn't anything I can do to stop the investigation now."

"You've tried nothing and you're all out of ideas? You Mackenzie men . . ." She shook her head. "You could call Remy. Tell him there's been a mistake and that he needs to bring the evidence back."

"What?" Mac sounded as confused as I felt.

"You can say that you planted that evidence to frame me, but now you're feeling guilty. Figure something out. Once you've handed it over to Scotty he'll call me and I'll release Drew." Jenny gave a tight smile. "See how easy that was to come up with? All you need to do is be a little bit creative."

"So you're suggesting I call Remy and tell him that I planted the evidence that we found together? " Mac asked.

"You put your mind to it Mac, and you will find a way to get that evidence back," Jenny stated coldly. "That or . . . I guess I could shoot Drew right here and now—"

"No!" Mac brought both his hands up in surrender. "I'll get it for you."

Before this moment, I thought that Charlie was the evilest person in Orca's Slough. Now I understood that Aunt Jenny surpassed him. And beyond her—who knew?

Was there something in the water that created sociopaths? Or was it the geographical location of the island itself? The ley lines? Aliens? What was wrong with this town?

Sheriff Mackenzie gave his wicked witch of a wife an impressed nod. Did he truly believe that they were going to get away with this?

He had successfully covered up a vehicular manslaughter and his own brother's murder, so maybe he did expect that he and Jenny would carry of another string of homicides. Because no matter what Jenny implied I think we all knew that she wouldn't risk me or Mac surviving longer than she felt she needed us. There was no point attempting to reason with her, or the sheriff. Instead we needed to let them think they'd won, get them to drop their guard and get away, so that Remy and the officer on the other side of Jenny's SUV could take action.

"All right, Aunt Jenny, I guess I'm going with you," I said. "Just give Mac a little time. It isn't going be easy to fix this."

Again, Mac and I held each other's gaze, and it was like we both understood that we needed to make our move now. I shifted my attention back to Jenny.

"I just need to bend down to pick up the car keys, okay? Then I'll go with you."

Aunt Jenny took a half-step back. For the first time I saw her gun. It was pink. I found that deeply annoying. She said, "Do it slowly."

"Sure thing," I said. "I just have to reach down here because the keys are really deep." I hooked my cold fingers around the heavy keys and then locked eyes with Mac, willing him to predict my next move. A faint smile twitched at the edge of his mouth.

"Aunt Jenny," he said.

The moment her eyes moved away from me I dove sideways and whipped the mass of snow and frozen keys directly into her face. At the same instant Mac elbowed Sheriff Mackenzie to the ground and pounced on Jenny.

A deafening gunshot cracked through the air and I froze, half buried in the snow, pain knifing through my left eardrum from the proximity of the gunshot. The metallic smell of gunpowder sizzled through the winter air.

Then I heard the sound of a middle-aged woman swearing.

Swearing a lot.

Swearing at the whole world, as well as Mac in particular.

I pushed myself upright and saw Mac forcibly restraining his aunt in the snow.

A few feet from him another man dressed in a deputy's uniform pinned the sheriff down, cuffing his hands behind his back. The deputy glanced up and I realized that it was Chaz. He must have been the officer crouching behind Jenny's SUV. His eyes were red-rimmed as he hauled his father to his feet.

Remy, the two highway patrol officers, and three guys from the hardware store all jogged out to join us. Remy pulled me onto my feet while the patrol officers took Jenny and Sheriff Mackenzie in hand, Chaz tersely informing them of their Miranda rights.

◆◆◆

"When Darla saw what was happening on the camera she couldn't believe it." Roy handed me a cup of coffee. I sat at a table in the small CHS break room, where the employees had taken me to warm up and dry off.

"Is there someone always watching the camera?"

"Oh no, Darla was deliberately trying to catch Mac doing something romantic and screen capture it to tease him with later." Roy gave me a grin. "She's like that. It's all in good fun. Don't mind her."

The State Troopers requested that Mac accompany them to their station so I after I took a minute to warm up

I started trudging through the parking lot to drive Mac's truck, laden with last-minute gifts, back to the Mackenzie house.

Then I noticed Chaz waiting beside the truck. My heart began to race.

He tried to smile but it only made him appear more desolate. "Hey, Drew. You mind if I talk with you for a few minutes?"

"Sure, but can we do it inside?" I asked. "I've had about as much of standing around in the snow as I can take."

"Right." He appeared at a loss then. "Do you think it would be okay if I . . . I mean I'm not sure if Mac or any of the rest of them will want to see my face."

Would they? It wasn't my place to speak for any of them but then I considered what I knew about Mac and his siblings. They weren't the kind of people who'd blame Chaz for what his parents had done. And if anyone could recognize the courage it must have taken for Chaz to arrest his own mother and father it would be Mac.

"Of course you'll be welcome. You just saved our lives," I told him.

"From my own parents," Chaz responded but he appeared relieved.

He followed me to Mac's truck and after we reached the rambling Mackenzie house he helped me carry in the battered bag of presents. Inside we were greeted by a veritable crowd.

"You are not going to believe what we found!" Abby announced then she glanced past Chaz. "Where's Mac?"

"Helping to file charges against my mom and dad for—" Chaz stalled for a moment. "For taking your dad away from you."

"Oh shit," Lionel muttered. "That's just what we discovered going through all those nasty cupboards."

"What?" I stared at them in stunned amazement.

"Come in and sit down, both of you." Evelyn beckoned us to the dining room table where hot coffee and fresh cookies waited along with an aged folder. We all settled down together. Between coffee and bites of cookies Abby, Charlotte, and Lionel excitedly informed Chaz and me of their discovery.

It turned out that while Mac and I had gone shopping, Abby and Charlotte had enlisted Julie, Evelyn, Josh, and Lionel to help them clear out the kitchen cabinets. Among the items discovered had been a folder containing a paper evidence bag full of fragments of a broken headlight housing, notes detailing the repairs done to a car belonging to Aunty Jenny, which matched the broken headlight, as well as a copy of Aunt Jenny's medical records from the day of the collision with the cyclist. Alongside that had been Sean Mackenzie's handwritten notes, detailing his suspicions and intention to confront his brother.

The evidence they'd needed to understand their father's disappearance, as it turned out, had been in the house all along.

"I guess Aunt Jenny was trying to protect you." Abby reached out to give Chaz's shoulder an awkward pat.

"Protect me?" Chaz looked genuinely confused. "Not me. Her own reputation. She didn't want to be the mom of some idiot who couldn't even drive right." Shame clouded his expression. "The truth is that I remembered a little bit of the accident but I was too scared of her to come forward. Time passed and I mostly forgot about it."

"Right." What more could a frightened sixteen-year-old kid do—especially if he knew that his parents were . . . less than totally ethical. He'd have been in their power.

Chaz offered the chocolate-chip cookie in his hand the most forlorn look I'd ever witnessed someone give a cookie. Finally, he said, "But then Dirk Van Weezendonk got killed and I knew I couldn't ignore what happened back then anymore. At first I was worried that Mac had killed Dirk. Mac had threatened to do that before, way back then. But then it turned out to have been Dirk's accomplice in the bank robbery and wasn't related to Uncle Sean's disappearance. Then Remy told me that Abby had been in contact with Dirk—catfishing him or whatever and that he'd actually come back to Orca's Slough to finally tell Mac the truth about what happened to Uncle Sean. So I got to thinking about that and I wondered how Dirk would know anything about that case, you know? And I realized that the property Dirk's mom owns abuts my mom's nursery in the back."

"I didn't know that." I began to feel uneasy but also excited. I saw my expression mirrored in every single face in the room. What more could Chaz tell us? Didn't we already know everything?

"Right around the time of my car accident, I heard my dad and Uncle Sean fighting. Really fighting—loud. I was sure Uncle Sean had found something that my dad or mom had tried to hide from him. He was good at investigating. He'd gone to these special courses."

"I didn't know that," I said.

Both Charlotte and Abby drew closer, crowding in on either side of me, all attention on their cousin.

"Yeah, Mac is like him that way. Good at picking things apart until he works it all out, you know." Chaz nodded. "Anyway, that night I even heard Uncle Sean mention my name but I wasn't sure why. Then everything was quiet and I never saw Uncle Sean again after that." Chaz rubbed his eyes hard. "Sorry, stress makes me sleepy."

"It's okay, just relax and tell your story," I said.

"Yes, yes," Julie spoke up. "Take your time to speak your truth."

Chaz smiled at her and then allowed himself to take a bite of the cookie.

"For years after that I was like you, Charlotte." Chaz glanced to her and Charlotte nodded. "I believed Uncle Sean ran off. But after Dirk was killed I started to wonder if maybe my dad or mom—or both of them—had . . . had killed him." Chaz took a deep breath. He seemed to be doing better—less pale and shaky. He took another bite of his cookie. "And after that I thought, 'well, one of the ways people get caught in homicides is that they can't adequately hide the body.' That's because it's actually really hard to get a grave deep enough that animals don't dig up the body by yourself unless you have a backhoe."

"Which your mom has at the garden center," I finished.

"Right. I wondered if Dirk had somehow seen my parents doing something to Uncle Sean or his . . . you know, remains. So I went through the old photographs of the nursery looking for anything that had really changed—for example a large planting that would have been visible from Mrs. Van Weezendonk's house that would indicate the ground had been disturbed, and I found six or seven new plantings from around that time then I saw one and I knew." Chaz pulled out his phone and handed it to me. "I got a picture of it when I was helping Mom get things for the party."

The picture on the screen showed a planting of dense, deep green trees that had grown into one another. Charlotte leaned closer, hand resting on one of my shoulders.

"What is it? A hedge?" Charlotte asked.

"Let me see," Abby requested and Chaz nodded his agreement. The phone was quickly passed around the table. Josh complimented Chaz's composition, but despite everyone studying it and zooming in on the image, no one seemed able to find what was special about it. At last the phone made it full circle back to Chaz.

"It's a yew hedge—the Tree of the Dead," Chaz explained. "Gardeners can't resist tapping in on the meaning of plants. It's a subconscious thing."

He put the phone away and looked to Charlotte and then Abby. Then he bowed his head.

"I don't know if I can face Mac—to tell him this. I can barely face you two, but that's where I think you'll find Uncle Sean."

Chaz briefly lifted his eyes to look at Charlotte and Abby whose expressions were, to me, only somewhat unreadable. Maybe Charlotte felt some anger, but she seemed to mostly be stunned. Abby's expression seemed to be leaning toward pity. Josh looked like he was solving a hard math problem. I knew what Lionel thought though. He thought this whole thing was beyond fucked up. Evelyn and Julie weren't watching us, rather they looked at each other, seeming to be having a silent conversation then Julie whispered, "Kablooey."

"I don't think you have to worry about Mac. You put handcuffs on your own father." I shot a glance to both Charlotte and Abby. I couldn't change how they might feel, but at least I wanted them to know how Chaz had stepped up. "You investigated this whole thing by yourself for half a year. You've done something really admirable."

"It's all just a supposition," Chaz said. "Someone will have to go out there with ground-penetrating radar to see if there's really a grave. Or else an investigator could just ask my father to confirm. Mom would never admit anything to anyone ever but I think Dad might tell the truth if somebody finally asked him."

"Thank you for telling us this," I said. It couldn't have been easy for him. "What are you going to do now?"

"Make my own confession about the hit-and-run." Chaz gave a mirthless laugh and gazed up at the ceiling. "Write my letter of resignation. I'm not sure what will happen after that."

"Well at least you know what's gonna happen tomorrow," Abby told him. "You're gonna have Christmas with us."

"I don't think—" Chaz began but Charlotte cut him off by suddenly lunging forward to pull him into a forceful and astonishing hug.

She said, "You must have been really scared for a long time. We're not going to let you be lonely now."

Chaz sat absolutely still for the space of a breath and then crumpled forward, sobbing into her embrace.

Late that night, when Mac returned, I was already in bed. I couldn't see his face and he said nothing but I could feel the sadness and fatigue radiating from him and could hear the almost imperceptible hitch in his breath. So I gave up feigning unconsciousness and whispered love and comfort under the secrecy of his old quilt until he fell asleep.

◆◆◆

When I got up the next morning, it was to the sound of the French Christmas carols drifting from Julie's iPhone as she, Evelyn, and Josh—who was still accustomed to Eastern Standard Time—crooned along with them.

Evelyn caught sight of me first.

"Coffee's already brewed," she informed me. "When do you think we should start breakfast?"

Months before I'd sworn that I would not rise early to labor in the kitchen on my day off. But now . . . Well, I just wanted to do what I could to make this day better for the people I cared about.

"No time like the present," I replied.

I sauntered into the kitchen, and she followed me. Together we set to work whipping up one hell of a Christmas breakfast. Eggs, sausage, bacon, mushrooms, toast, and black pudding. I also opted to add in a dish of stuffed cherry tomatoes, as I recalled Stacey saying Chaz loved them.

Fortunately we'd gone for generous portions because just as we were all about to sit down together, Mason and Clayton arrived at the door.

News travels fast around the island and learning that their father's disappearance—and demise—had at last been solved, they'd both rushed back to join the rest of the family. I'd only met each of them once when they'd come for the family meeting concerning Abby's investigations. From that encounter, I'd expected them to be just as calm and disinterested as they had been before. Instead, Clayton gave me a long, two-handed handshake with eye contact so intense I had to look away while Mason collapsed on me in a tearful hug, thanking me for helping to find their dad. I patted his back and listened to his snuffly sobs while Remy stood behind, pointing and silently impersonating his ugly-cry until Charlotte came and gave him a quick, but vicious pinch.

"Quit it," she said.

"It's not my fault he's like this," Remy said.

Her rejoinder was swift and deadly. "This is why your girlfriend left you."

"Ouch." Remy gave an exaggerated cringe then took Mason off my hands. "Come here you big crybaby."

Because his mom was at work, Lionel had opted to stay the night with Abby, and Chaz had never gone home, which brought the ranks waiting for breakfast to twelve. Evelyn ambled out of the kitchen and surveyed the additional guests.

"Holy hell," Evelyn muttered. "We need more cooks." Then, to Josh, "Get over here New Guy. I need you to butter some toast."

Mac sat apart from everyone as he usually did when they were all together, just observing.

At times like this it's important to know what to do to comfort someone. Unfortunately, I had no idea what Mac might or might not need after having been put through the wringer. So I just went and sat on his lap and asked him what he got me for Christmas.

"A sense of shame," he replied. "I saw that yours had worn out."

"Ha! Joke's on you. I never had one in the first place." I laced my fingers behind his neck. "Come on, get up and start passing out presents."

In his haste to wrap the presents after returning the previous evening, Mac had mislabeled a couple of them so Mason got the stack of glossy women's fashion magazines, while Julie received his set of wood chisels, which she met with a great effusion of thanks and many promises to use them in her plans to design distressed jeans. Mason, too, took the gifting error in stride, using the magazines to critique Clayton and Remy's current wardrobes and to quiz all of us according to articles revealing "What Your Style Really Exposes About Your Personality" and "Twenty Indulgent Foods You Didn't Know Were Good For You."

We drank Irish coffee and ate buttery dinner rolls and turkey with gravy and that dark chocolate cake adorned with a woodland of candy mushrooms. We listened to swinging French Christmas carols from the Sixties and we listened to "Jingle Bell Rock" and we listened to K-pop.

There were gifts and music, laughter and tears. Promises and apologies. The air itself felt lighter, as if the cold and lonely ghost of Mac's father had finally left the premises, clearing the way for everyone to start living without the angry ache of his absence. He'd been found and life could, at last, move forward.

So my first Christmas in the Mackenzie house passed like a waking dream. Each of us brought our own traditions, which somehow fit together in the same way that ornaments accrued in different places over the years still manage to look right when they're all hung on the same tree.

Finally on Boxing Day the rainclouds rolled in and the snow all melted in a day. Business resumed in Orca's Slough.

City Hall nominated Mac to fill in as acting sheriff until the next election and after only a little convincing he accepted. Mac oversaw his father being disinterred then reburied next to his mom at Bayview Cemetery outside of town.

Because he was not conscious during the car accident that killed the cyclist so many years before, Chaz was not charged with any crimes, but he left law enforcement for good, opting to take over running the family's nursery. Both Aunt Jenny and Uncle Scott were charged with two counts of homicide as well as a few other crimes such as attempted murder and kidnapping.

The residents of Orca's Slough were shocked by the volcanic eruption in the social fabric of their town, but not for as long as I might have imagined. Soon enough everyone had either recalled or fabricated some suspicion they'd had about the sheriff or his wife over the years and the magma cooled and solidified again, and everything went back to normal.

Or at least as normal as it ever was.

Upon hearing that the sheriff of Camas County had been arrested for the murder of his cousin, Charlie immediately demanded that his own conviction be reviewed, but because he'd originally been arrested by Mac rather than Uncle Scott, nothing came of it. Lionel and I attended Sam's cremation and spread her ashes in the scattering garden in the cemetery outside of town.

I went back to the restaurant and spent most of the following week with every seat in the dining room full at every service. Lionel worked alongside me every day and was quick to get off work every evening.

Abby didn't spend much time at the Mackenzie house that week.

No one mentioned it.

But on New Year's Eve as we were locking up, Lionel lingered on the sidewalk in front of me, chef's coat in his hand, looking like he had something to say.

"I've been thinking, chief, maybe I should go to culinary school," he said.

"Yeah?" I asked. "In Seattle?"

Lionel shook his head. "California. I wanna go big. ICE."

"Fancy." Of course he'd want to go to the best culinary school in America. Why would a kid like him shoot any lower? He had grades, looks, an interesting backstory, and a celebrity boss. Who knew—in ten years' time, me and Mac might be seeing him walk across the television screen as well. "Gonna take advantage of being in Michael's restaurant group?"

I could fault my ex for a lot of reasons but meanness wasn't one of them. His company offered tuition assistance for workers getting culinary degrees.

"I think so, yeah," Lionel said.

"I thought for sure you were following Abby to Seattle," I remarked.

Lionel shrugged. "We've only been hanging out for a week, chief. Besides, we'll keep talking . . . and how do you know she won't follow me to California in a few months?"

"So that's how it is." I shook my head. "Well, okay then, I'll call Michael and talk to him about transferring you."

"Thanks, chief."

"You're welcome, now get out of here."

Lionel grinned. "Happy New Year."

I smiled back. "Don't get too drunk tonight. We're going to be slammed tomorrow and I don't want you to cut your own hand off before you have a chance to go big."

Lionel rolled his eyes. "I love you too, chief."

◆◆◆

I got back to the Mackenzie house around eleven that night and found Mac sitting on the couch channel surfing. He wore jeans and a cashmere sweater that Julie had purchased for him. It was the color of wet sand and suited him well. I took a shower and changed into a pair of loose flannel pants and long-sleeved t-shirt.

"I thought of bringing a bottle of prosecco home with me, but I didn't think you'd want to drink it," I said. "So I brought beer."

"Good call." He leaned against me, and I put my arm around his shoulders. For a few minutes we watched replays of fireworks that had already exploded in different time zones while the clock ticked down. Finally he said, "What would you say if I told you I'm thinking of running for sheriff?"

The clock struck midnight and immediately the air filled with the sound of firecrackers and the smell of gunpowder. I leaned forward and planted a soft but lingering kiss on Mac's lips and said, "I think you'd be perfect."

Acknowledgments

Honestly, when I finished the first story in this volume, "Entrée to Murder," I thought it would be the last story I would ever write. Not because I no longer had anything to say, but because I'd lost the willingness to say it. In other words: I had stage fright. I didn't want to share my fiction with anyone—not even my partner. I'd come to some sort of impasse where I didn't want to enter into the state of vulnerability that one must assume when telling a story in public. It's only due to the extreme kindness of my friends that I've been able to work through my fear of the audience and start sharing my work again. So I have a bunch of them to thank. First, I have to thank Josh Lanyon for inviting me to be part of the *Footsteps in the Dark* anthology. I'm not sure that if I didn't have people asking me to follow up on Mac & Drew's story that I would have had the motivation to start to write fiction again.

Next, I must extend my gratitude to Dal Maclean and Astrid Amara for lending me their expertise with tough scenes and Ginn Hale for letting me talk to her about the elements of a cozy mystery for as long as I wanted to—which was hours and hours and hours.

Another big thank you goes to Zita Porter, my first editorial intern. You did a great job on this piece.

Finally, I want to extend my heartfelt gratitude to Marjorie Liu for her endless enthusiasm and support. Let's keep our mutual admiration society going forever.

About the Author

Nicole Kimberling is a novelist, professional cook and the editor of Blind Eye Books. Her first novel, *Turnskin*, won the Lambda Literary Award. Other works include the *Bellingham Mystery Series*, set in the Washington town where she resides with her wife of thirty years as well as an ongoing cooking column for *Lady Churchill's Rosebud Wristlet*. She is also the creator and writer of "Lauren Proves Magic is Real!" a serial fiction podcast, which explores the day-to-day case files of Special Agent Keith Curry, supernatural food inspector.

Printed in the USA
CPSIA information can be obtained
at www.ICGtesting.com
CBHW030842240923
1109CB00007B/3